A Numina Parable

A CHILD OF THE CHANGELING

MᶜKENZIE CATRON

Whimsical Publishing

Whimsical Publishing

For information address Whimsical Publishing, whimsicalpublishing.ca

ISBN: 978-1-998195-55-8

Edited by Micheline Ryckman & Deborah O'Carroll
Cover art by Hillary Bardin & design by Micheline Ryckman
Interior illustration by Hillary Bardin & Shane Ryckman

To my sisters
*Though our relationships have waxed and waned—and we haven't
always been the best of friends—I will always love you all dearly, to
the moon and back.*
...Even though you are a bunch of spoons.

Grim: Prologue

*O*nly three witches remain in the world... And they know we're coming for them.

A decade has passed since Rose and her sisters emerged from Wyrd Mountain as Death, Fate, and Fortune, and now, there's a rumbling in the dark. We can feel it. The Numina can sense a disturbance in the threads. The Sun and Moon say it echoes like the plucked chord of a harp. Even I can hear the low vibration running through the strings that connect humans and faeries to their luck and destiny.

Fearing extinction, one of the witches has cast this growing darkness, spreading an unnatural disease that's crept from the bogeyman's very shadows. A contagion—one that spreads like wildfire. Entire villages have been struck down with a moldy blackness that crawls through the streets, blooming through blood, and consuming the hosts' hearts.

With the help of her husband, and some of Sparrow and Rush's flock, Hazel has been searching for a cure. Though the practice of the Healers is once again alive and well, even the former Elder Mother has yet to heal the toxic gloom we now call the Stygian Brume.

The disease affects some faeries in radically different ways.

The Pooka, those that still run rampant, escaping our clutches, are changing. For the last five years, these unchained prophets have become contorted, sick monsters. No longer do they appear in the forms of animals and deliver cryptic messages. Instead, these corrupt monstrosities, which we now call Phouka, have become shifting beasts with too many limbs or too many eyes—masses of pure, contaminated chaos. And even though Rose and I have help from some of our nieces and nephews, the Phouka are trickier now, and it seems they've multiplied since the Brume arrived.

Worst of all, this sickness is affecting The Numina as well. The threads from Fortune's spinning wheel are corroded with darkness, the tapestry of life tinged with black. Even the watery visions of the future in Time's pools are now cloudy. Everything is being polluted by the Stygian epidemic in one way or another. Poppy and Posy are the only Numina who've been rendered physically ill and feverish. We don't understand how or when this infection slipped into their veins, but because of it, the sisters are blind to what's coming next. Years ago, Poppy foresaw some uncertain times, but those paths of chance were hazy and none of us thought anything of them. That is, until a wall of roiling witchcraft, carrying the Stygian Brume, flooded the world. It was sudden. We didn't have time to prepare, and now war is nigh. The witches must die.

Since bogeymen have no threads of luck or destiny tying them to the tapestry, The Sun and Moon must peer beneath the web, searching for crumbs of information. This is how we know that there's only three witches left to find. But crumbs are not enough, and all three bogeys' identities and locations remain a mystery.

As Rose's familiar and partner, I've been sent out in search of these malicious women. While we both listen to the shadows for whispers of the Phouka, most days I'm following any trace of the witches I can find. My Lady Death has entrusted me with discovering the poisonous source of the Stygian Brume while she continues to ferry the ailing folk, those who accept her welcoming hand, guiding them to eternal rest in the After.

Sometimes I'm so weary with exhaustion from my pursuit that I lose track of time, but Rose is my person, my Dark Angel, and I would follow her to Purgatory and back. I would do anything she asked of me. And I always come back to her, no matter how arduous the hunt. Even lost with dirty, red sap-stained hands, and bitter breath oozing from my tongue, I return to her. I always will.

"Come to me."

That soft, silken voice plagues my mind, so I follow it, like a length of white-flowered ribbon, deep into the forest.

Swan: Phouka Hunting

G rowing up, Mom and Dad always warned us changeling children not to run with sharp objects, but now, creeping through dead leaves with my siblings breathing down my neck, I nearly stab my own leg. Twice.

Kestrel is the first to knock into me while wading through the forest. The jostle causes the knife in my grip to almost graze my thigh. Robin bumps my elbow after I switch the small, salt-annealed blade to my other hand, and the flat metal hits my knee as the three of us find cover behind a craggy boulder.

"Sorry, Swan." Robin winces, whisper quieter than a breeze.

I hush my littlest sister with a numb finger to my lips and she rolls her shoulders inwards, folding in on herself as we listen. Guilt coats the back of my throat. Robin didn't mean any harm, and her voice hasn't endangered us. Hopefully... Tucking the sable waves that fall over the side of her face, I brush away her meekness with a quiet smile. Cautious confidence renewed, Robin straightens to look at Kestrel. He shifts to peer over the rock, crushing my foot with his heel as his silver gaze searches. My desensitized toes and I have become used to his blunders over the sixteen years he's been alive. So, I just tap my brother's calf until he moves. When he does, the bow and quiver of arrows strapped to him whack me in the back of the head. Robin, also familiar with Kestrel's clumsiness, shuffles to the side, giving me room to escape as we wait.

My fingers still wrapped around my throwing knife are buzzing, my skin hot as the nerves inside my hands burn. I stash the weapon amongst its twelve identical siblings at my hip before shaking out my damaged extremities, trying to ease the prickling fire ant pain. I'm gently blowing on my palms and the redness blooming over them, when Robin pokes my arm. A small translucent parchment bag sits in her hand. The misshapen clusters inside the package are aplenty, and I can already smell the candied sunflower seeds. They're laced with caramelized sugar and pickings from the golden flowers the gnomes collect in Robin's magic-grown garden.

"I made them for you this morning." Robin leans into me as she uses a hand signed language to communicate wordlessly. *"I was making sweets to keep Starling's sugars up and figured you'd want a dose of your own."*

While I may not have a disorder of the blood like our brother, I do have a disorder of the mind. Robin grows vibrant fruits and flowers with her gift, and she says that certain plants have properties that help people like me—people whose minds are more susceptible to unprovoked depression. But sunflowers have always been my favorite and the most effective. Plus, it keeps me out of the dissociative mental attic space I tend to slip into throughout the day for longer. Taking the homemade sweets from Robin and being careful not to let the parchment crinkle, I fish out two vanilla-speckled pieces. A sunflower cluster gets tucked in my cheek before I offer my sister the other. Robin's grin is rosy as she pops the candied seeds in her mouth.

I squirrel the bag away in my cloak, about to reground myself in the task at hand when I'm met with Kestrel's fake, affronted expression. My brother pouts further when I mimic his deepening dramatic frown. His eyes widen, and he thrusts his hand out as if to ask, *"Candy, please? Candy for the weary, needy boy?"* I don't relent. I'm the eldest child, which means messing with my brother, even for a few precious moments, is necessary. Kestrel's mouth quivers, brows about to curl into swoops when a high keening sound rumbles through the forest, making us all freeze.

Kestrel's eyes flash in the watery rays of sun bleeding through the sparse canopy of trees above us, searching for the source of the noise. This was what we were waiting in silence for. The three of us treat the haunting sound like a trail of breadcrumbs and work in practiced tandem to hunt down our target. I cue Robin west and Kestrel east. My sister breaks away first, heading farther into the autumn forest, the waning gold light glinting over her silver charm bracelet as she disappears.

Much like our grandparents, Kestrel hunches over and lumbers away in his heavy boots. The crunch of crisp crimson and copper leaves under his troll-like steps makes me want to hang my head. You would think two years of tracking down shadow beasts would mean he'd mastered the art of silence. But alas, Kestrel is all long, sturdy limbs and no grace. I love my brother; he's my best friend, but I swear to The Sun and Moon, his lack of coordination will be the death of us someday.

Advancing north alone allows me to be stealthy, focusing on making my leather-soled feet glide over the dying foliage. If only I were half-goblin like my dad. Concealing myself would certainly come in handy right now—my internal wish falls flat when a familiar trill rings out. It fills the air with a bird song that sends my heart thumping. Robin's projecting whistle shakes a few leaves from the towering tree above me, but I'm heading northeast before they hit the ground. Our godmother composed this call, a signal she implemented once us kids first left the glade and the haven of its perimeter. The tune is only whistled if we're separated, or there's danger nearby. Though we primarily use it when Robin joins Kestrel and me on these quiet jobs. Hazel's song ensures her Healer-in-training always stays safe. But right now, her someday Healer is a hunter, and she has found our prey.

With featherlight strides, I race through the forest, everything a blur of fiery color. I whip past trees and hurdle over logs, pumping my arms in rhythm with my heartbeat. A poem about sprouting wings takes flight in my mind, urging me faster as a recognizable pattern of footfalls comes up on my right. Kestrel and I share the barest nod, and we hear the whistle again. It's close but a bit more east. We adjust our course, barreling on until we discover a path of what looks like soot streaking the leaves ahead. And I know the corrosion coating them isn't ash. It's darkness and decay.

Slowing to a hushed crawl, my brother and I find cover behind a large elm tree. Robin is nowhere in sight. Hopefully she's scurried up a tree for higher ground, like I taught her. The Phouka, however, is here, and it's monstrous. A thing of pure pitch-black nightmares. This ebony faerie might've been a fox once, but now the lanky, infected creature is grotesque and tripled in size. Its legs are longer than they should be, crooked and spider-like, a broken shape that causes its head to hang between its shoulders like a loping wolf. But worse than the needle teeth protruding from its muzzle are its seven garnet eyes, all narrowed and seeking. Three smoky tails sweep from it to drag over the ground as it searches, and I now understand where the trail of rot came from.

"Oh, this one is hideous," Kestrel mouths, chest rapidly rising and falling as he catches his breath.

Scanning the branches above for Robin one last time, I nod as we watch the shadow beast from about a hundred feet away. Pookas were never evil-touched bogeymen. When Uncle Grim was a Pooka, he wasn't affected by the purifying sun, and no elder tree or ring of salt would've kept him out of the glade.

Although now salt *does* affect the witchcraft-infected Phouka, but sunlight does not. Uncle Grim's theory is that the old framework, of what the Pooka were, allows them to still wander in daylight. Like the one before us. It's rooting around in the magic hour-dappled leaves, foraging with its toothy snout.

Its choked snuffling will be a sound that haunts me tonight.

"It's your turn," I sign to Kestrel. *"Go get it."* He clings to the bark of the elm with a wrinkle in his upturned nose as I give his shoulder an encouraging pat.

Kestrel turns with a look that reminds me of summertime and pumpkin guts. Specifically, the day Mom told Dad it was his turn to scatter the musty compost in the garden to prepare the beds for gourd season. And yesterday, when we carved the pumpkins we'd grown and relieved them of their slimy guts in preparation for Hallowtide in two days.

"You go get it. You're older," Kestrel retorts with a revolted grimace chiseled deep into his face. Much like the will-o'-the-wisp lanterns sitting on our porch, waiting to be lit when night falls in a few hours.

"By a year. Anyway, you're bigger." The barest teasing hint tugs at my lips. *"Take out one of Auntie Rose's special arrows strapped to your back and trap it."* With a scooping hand, I gesture toward the curved elder bow clinging to his back, then toward the Phouka. We peek at the monster in time to hear a hiss of satisfaction before it pulls a squeaking rodent from the cover of brittle leaves. The Phouka whips the tiny animal into the air before it catches it...with its jaws. The crunch that comes afterward makes me wince.

Poor little mouse and its little mouse family, it will be missed.

Kestrel's mouth is agape as he signs an echoing fraction of my thoughts, *"Poor little mouse."*

Yeah, my brother and I definitely spend too much time together.

He rolls his eyes when I jostle his shoulder. *"Technically, Swan, this bow and these arrows are yours. I am but a mere walking arsenal."* He glances back at the Phouka enjoying its supper and shudders. Kestrel places a broad palm on his chest as he gawps at me, a suppressed smile making his face twitch as he signs again, *"Besides, you know I'm a pacifist."*

"You have literal magic perfect for hunting." My expression is deadpan as I tug at the shell of his slightly scalloped ear, recalling hours of Dad's lessons and years of frustrating target practice. Kestrel sat on a stump and just watched for months on end. He never needed any training because his changeling gift ensures he can never miss, no matter what he's armed with or what his target is. And while I've envied our dad's concealing ability, I've wished harder to have a gift like my siblings. Despite the troll-charmed elder twigs nestled in all six of our chests, just like our mother, I am the only one without a magic gift. Even Crow, at ten years old, the youngest of us all, has had his gift since he could crawl. The torturous thought of being the black-bird of the family makes me queasy. *"You could be blindfolded and still pin that thing."* Distracted by my brother and pitiful nausea, I relax the clench of my jaw and sign with the airy softness of a moth's wing, *"Use your gift, Kestrel; you're lucky to have one."*

His face drops, and the sharp, play-fighting expression melts away at my unspoken words.

Despite my giftlessness, I am skilled with weapons of the pointy variety. Auntie Rose and Uncle Grim have had me in the field hunting down Pooka and Phouka since I was twelve—with supervision, of course—Mom would've unleashed her trees and hunted *me* down in her elder wheelchair just to return me to the safety of the glade otherwise. It wasn't until my knack for capturing loose shadows was well established that she let me go alone, though well-equipped. It's been five years since then, and now I've acquired my own team in Robin and Kestrel. The latter has always had my back, whether he's protecting me from the things that go bump in the night or even my own hurt feelings. Unlike our brother Starling, who takes every opportunity to rub in the fact that I'm the sole giftless outcast of our powerful family. But now is not the time for Kestrel to be stubborn about the strange *"do no harm"* motto he mysteriously adopted in our childhood, not when a Phouka is skulking near the glade.

"For Timesake." I roll my eyes. *"You're lucky you're my best friend."*

"Darn right I am." My brother signs with a straight-toothed grin, knuckles thumping my leather-padded knee.

With a fond yet exasperated smile, I set the Phouka in my sights and reach toward the bow over Kestrel's shoulder. My hand stills. The spot where the monster was snacking is empty and nothing but a wet patch of blackened leaves remains.

"Where'd it go?" we gasp in unison.

Way too much time together.

A puff of cold, fetid air rolls in from behind us, sending loose curls from the bun atop my head forward into my mouth. Goosebumps ripple over me as the sick, metallic smell of decomposition and blood shoves its way down my nose. Kestrel meets my gaze for a split second before the Phouka descends, razor claws first.

The creature shrieks when we each dive and roll in different directions. And as I tuck my shoulder under me, my tongue is freed from its hairy confines, but my body is momentarily caught. A smoky paw lands a hit to my side, pressing into my rib cage. But my momentum keeps me going, and there's a sound like parchment tearing. My knees hit the forest floor, and I rock back on my heels. Was that the sound of my skin splitting open? My heart thunders and my torso is numb like my hands. Springing to my feet, I check for blood. All I care about is Kestrel on the other side of the beast with his weight centered and bow hanging in his grasp. I see the shaking of his right hand poised halfway between his side and the quiver of green-fletched arrows protruding from behind his head. His limb is still suspended, frozen in the pre-Hallowtide air when the Phouka's many glowing eyes focus on him.

A shrill, tuneless whistle pushes from my teeth. "Hey," I shout, waving my arms to pull the monster's attention away from my younger brother.

The bogey ignores me. A clicking noise bubbles from its throat as it slowly prowls closer toward Kestrel, decay leaching from its oversized paws.

Saving my knives for the right moment, I reach into my cloak and fish out a small handful of Robin's sunflower sweets. Then, I say a silent apology, hoping that she doesn't hear me curse or tell on me over dinner before lobbing them at the Phouka. "You mangy buggard! Over here!"

It doesn't even flinch. Instead, the infected former Pooka's shoulders roll forward as it takes another hunkering step, and I realize with great sadness, the medicinal candies ricocheting off its hide are wasted. Worst of all, its inky body is coiled back, flank muscles set and ready to spring.

"Kestrel, move!" My yell is like the snap of a whip, spurring the creature forward.

My brother and I stare at each other for the better half of a second. There isn't an ounce of fear milling about his silver eyes. Not even with the open maw of a giant mutated fox fixated on his shorn curly head. Kestrel, stupid, brave Kestrel, chooses to meet the abomination halfway. He sprints towards it before collapsing on the ground once the bogey becomes airborne. The bow leaves Kestrel's hand and skitters forward through the leaves ahead toward my feet as he slides beneath the Phouka. But the monster is quick. Much like an overgrown cat, it pivots before all four crooked, spindly legs connect with the earth. Then, it pounces again. And I have just enough time to pick up the solid bow inches from my toes, plant my boots, and *swing*.

The crack of elder wood meeting mutated bone reverberates around us, reminiscent of a clap of thunder. The weapon clenched in my pale-knuckled grip is surprisingly still intact. But the Phouka's head still swivels in our direction. Drool made of shadowy wisps, like candlewick smoke, drip from the Phouka's bared teeth. The behemoth is angry, red eyes aflame and lupine-esque body trembling as the misty hair on its knobby spine raises. It's ready for a pound of flesh, but so am I. Earlier, I made the mistake of getting distracted, which put Kestrel in danger, but now my hands are hot and ready. The ruined nerves beneath my skin feel like they're vibrating as I shove the bow at my brother, now standing beside me. When the faerie starts for us, I suck in a steadying breath, and a small smile comes with it.

It's funny how this monster thinks it's now hunting us when we've been hunting it.

The moment the Phouka's deformed front legs predictably leave the ground, I draw one of the twelve blades at my hip. My aim isn't at the creature's chest when I throw my knife, but at the second of its three tails. It cuts through the air, flying straight before piercing the fox's middle tail and sinking tip-first into the earth. The Phouka's jump is stopped short, slamming its dark, bony body into the ground. Wild keening cries spill from its chest when it realizes it's pinned. I'm sure it feels the sizzle of my salt-annealed blade, a process that Auntie Posy's brilliant mind invented. The purifying grains were melted into the metal by her sister's hands; Auntie Rose doctored the whole family's weapons to be traps. Everything from my knives to Kestrel's arrows. Even Starling's axes, the sharp tools in Lark and Robin's Healer kits, and Crow's slingshot pellets.

Kestrel stands at my side as we witness the salted blade do what it was crafted for. The Phouka is scrambling, clawing at the dirt as it shrinks into itself. It grows smaller and smaller as it's pulled towards the throwing knife jutting from the ground until the shadow monster's body looks less malformed and more like a formless mass. Nothing but a wriggling ball of smoke no bigger than my hand, constrained and harmless.

I whistle our family signal for Robin.

"Are you okay?" I ask, giving my brother a once-over and checking for bumps, bruises, or scrapes.

"Yeah, but Dad's going to cry," Kestrel remarks as he brushes dried leaves off my back, bow dangling from his other hand.

"What? Why?" I gape, checking Kestrel's face again while I blindly pat my body for damp patches of blood.

My brother stares down at my torso, and I follow his line of sight. Any pride I might've had in myself for capturing the Phouka dissipates with a groan. A tear the length of my forearm runs through the front flap of my cloak. Our dad spent months embroidering the midnight blue wool. He embellished the whole family's clothes, creating a custom pattern for each of us, designs detailing our namesake birds entwined with intricate florals or ivy weaving through fated red and fortuitous gold threads. The Phouka tore through a stitched elder tree and some variegated blooms of open and closed anemone flowers. It even split the painstaking visage of a swan right at its curved neck.

Wonderful.

My only hope of surviving death by shame is by brokering a deal with Kestrel: "I won't tell Mom you're the one who broke that shelf in the living room and everything on it. That weird statue she got years ago and Lark's new ceramic mortar and pestle are all past saving. But we can save each other if you don't tell Dad." My plea is sweetened with my pinkie held out, hopeful for a promise.

Kestrel snorts, throwing his hands up with cool, oak-toned palms facing me.

"I refuse to get in between Dad and his sewing. Besides." He shrugs. "Mom hated that lumpy 'Changeling Queen, Slayer of Witches' shrine thing; it was just a funny birthday gift from the aunties. And if Lark is going to start working with Hazel in the villages more, she'll need a more durable stone mortar and pestle." Kestrel grins. "So, if you think about it, I did them both a favor."

Knowing my brother won't save me this time makes my pinkie go limp and my stomach sink like a capsized ship. "Tell that to the fifteen-year-old who saved up her chore money all year for that handcrafted ceramic," I sigh, frowning down at my cloak.

"It's only two-ish months till Christmastide; I'll make it up to her. How you'll appease Dad, well..." Kestrel swirls his finger around my nose. "That's up to you to figure out."

"If you're not careful, you'll lose that finger one of these days. Whether by some freak accident, Starling's cold soul, or my teeth," I chuckle, unable to stoke any heat behind my words. Kestrel knows I'd never let anything or anyone harm him. "Guess you should've just made the pinkie promise." I bat my brother's taunting hand away from my face. "Now get out of here, you nib."

He dances away from my reach, laughing as I whistle for Robin again. With the danger subdued now, the reason for our song is to relocate each other. Sweeping the trees and squinting past their remaining yellowing leaves, I search for my youngest sister. Not only do I not hear her answering trill, but I see no telltale sign of her ivory skin or her rusty orange cloak. Her disappearance is strange but not unusual for the fourteen-year-old. If she saw us trap the Phouka from higher ground, she's most likely making her way home without us for dinner. It's happened before. Instead of worrying, I ask Kestrel to summon Auntie Rose.

Plucking the gold bowstring—made from Auntie Poppy's spinning wheel—three times in quick succession summons Death. It only takes moments before she appears with a lustrous burst of light and a flurry of scented air that reminds me of snowdrops, midnight, peat, and pine. It's no surprise when I see her pure white, opalescent hand looped over Uncle Grim's black-clad arm. The Numina and her partner make quite the pair. Her with her crown of gloom and uncovered stone eye, and him with his flame-like shadows and shining yellow gaze. It's rare to see one without the other.

"Hello, chickadees. What've you got for me today?" My aunt's smile is dazzling, though it's perpetually tinged with something a little wry and youthful. Perhaps it's because she hasn't aged a day since she became Death a decade ago. She'll always look seventeen, always be a little sarcastic, but behind her one real silver eye is a wizened twenty-seven-year-old woman.

"Another infected," I say, wiping the cooling sweat from beneath the curly bangs brushing my forehead. "Lark and Crow were behind the barn putting out a little imp fire and they saw it outside the perimeter of Mom's trees."

Uncle Grim studies our surroundings before his pallid, unaging face falls and he rubs his abnormally reddened palms over the sides of his thighs. "So close to the glade?"

"They're getting bolder straying that close. This darkness is spreading too fast for us to keep up." Detaching herself from the once-imprisoned-Pooka-turned-shadow-prince, Auntie Rose strides over to the writhing shadow pinned to my throwing knife. When she crouches to examine it closer, her dress fans out around her like poetry. I can't resist peeking my consciousness into that safe mental attic of mine to write on a slip of paper:

AMID THE FIERY *ground of an autumn eve*
   A pool of ink reflecting a starry sky not yet born
   Crowned by a pearl pale and sweet as the north wind
   A youth captured by a garnet wire

. . .

DEATH PULLS the shears from her hip.

Kestrel and I have seen this many times before, but watching our aunt work never ceases to make my blood bubble with effervescent excitement. Death grabs the wriggling smoke and pulls, stretching the creature until it's as thin as a cut of thread. Auntie Rose snips, freeing the Phouka from its trap. The diseased faerie thrashes, trying to escape her hold, but Death is in control here. It's effortless how she puts away her scissors and subdues the snake of smoke so desperate to flee. She wraps it around her wrist like a bracelet, and when her power flares to life, the beast sinks into her skin. It leaves behind another band of black, like a tattoo, and the edge of the shadow sprouting from her heels stretches and grows. The monster we caught is yet another in her collection until The Numina can figure out how to cure the bogeys.

"Auntie Rose," Kestrel starts, plucking my weapon from the dirt and offering it to me to return it to its rightful place. "Are you ever afraid that whatever's infecting the Phouka will affect you?"

Kestrel asked a good question, one I've never thought to voice. Though the world around us is quickly changing for the worse, I've always trusted my aunties, uncle, and the rest of The Numina to fix it. They've never steered me wrong. Well... besides the time Auntie Rose convinced me to put garden slugs in Starling's bed, saying it was justifiable retribution for him pushing me from the barn rafters, where I nearly broke my arm. Although, that was long before she became Death and had divine responsibilities to mature her.

"Me? Afraid? Never." Auntie Rose grins at Kestrel, crossing her arms over her ribcage-shaped corset in a way that displays the thin bands running up to her elbow. "I'm Death incarnate;

nothing can scare me. Trapping these creatures is tiring, and makes me a little grumpy—"

Uncle Grim snorts.

My aunt fondly rolls her eyes at him before continuing, "But the Phouka can't infect me. They're not the source of the Stygian Brume." The front of her brows wrinkle. "But Poppy and Po, we don't know how they caught some altered form of the sickness yet. They've barely left the temple since their visions of the future were blocked, and—"

Uncle Grim abruptly spins toward the horizon and stares off into the distance, silencing us. He cocks his head, listening. To what, I'm not sure. Nothing stirs the autumnal forest. The former Pooka bows his head and pinches the bridge of his nose with his red-stained fingers before his posture stiffens. "There's someone at the gates to The After," he rumbles. "I must go." Uncle Grim's words sound odd, almost disconnected from his mind and body. But before we can say anything, misty tendrils from his shadow envelop him, crafting a blanket of blackness as he disappears.

I blink at my uncle's quick exit. "Is he okay?"

"I'm not sure," she sighs. "I believe my Reaper is stressed. It's been almost impossible to track down these last few hags." Auntie Rose rubs the Phouka bands on her arm as she looks at where her companion last stood. "He's been coming home to Wyrd Mountain so discombobulated and dirty, like he's fallen down a rabbit hole each time. But the spread of this epidemic has gotten to all of us in one way or another. The Sun and Moon are overworking themselves alongside the Healers and now the days are shorter, and the nights longer than they should be for the season. I don't think they've been back to the Mountain in weeks. Poppy isn't as cheery, and recently, she took the spinning wheel into her room; I hardly see her. Posy just flat-out doesn't look good. She's running herself so ragged, trying to peer into the past with Time to figure out how this all started, that she's been lying down for days on end." Gravity claims Death's tightening features as she slips into her role as one of The Numina. Now, she's hardened, a grown woman with the world's weight on her shoulders. Perhaps even a portion of the world's fate on her shoulders, considering Auntie Posy's developing condition. "We still can't figure out what the big black wall blocking all of her and Poppy's visions is. Icarus's pools of time are murky, and even present events are near incomprehensible. Something bigger than just The Numina can handle is coming very, very soon. It may be here already."

A shift occurs as her voice peters out. Death recedes, and Auntie Rose comes to the forefront again, aware that who she's talking to isn't just anyone. We're her niece and nephew, and despite our gifts or skills, we're children scared for the world the bogeymen have tried relentlessly to destroy. A softness melts back into our aunt's eyes as she puts a reassuring hand on both our shoulders. "But you guys don't need to worry about that. We'll figure this all out, and everything will be okay. I promise."

I can see right through Auntie Rose's frail smile when her doubting gaze darts back to the space Uncle Grim had occupied. She's not doing well either, which makes my insides tangle into nervous knots.

"How's Grandma Aspen and Pop Pop doing?" Kestrel asks to alleviate the pressure from our heavy conversation, like the saint he is.

"They're doing well." Our aunt's smile eases into true peace. "They're neighbors now in The After, and my father is finally back to the man he was before Black Annis's cage."

"Tell them we love and miss them," I request as the sky fills my view and I realize from the position of the slow, sinking sun, how late it's gotten. It's time to go. "Kestrel, we've missed dinner. If we don't return soon, they'll send a search party for us."

"Yes, go," Auntie Rose urges us with a wave. "And tell Robin and Lark that Hazel is asking for them tomorrow. I was just in the villages ushering a patient of hers to the gates. She could use an extra hand at the Apothecary." Our aunt winces. "Things in the villages are getting dire. The Infirmary is packed."

Kestrel kisses Auntie Rose's cheek. "Will do." Then, he sticks his tongue out at me, like the mature sixteen-year-old he is, before jogging into the trees with a grin. He's setting us up for a race back home.

Death shakes her head as she watches him go. "He's looking more and more like Rush each day. He's even developing that same smug look my half-brother often gave me. Mostly when Aspen was scolding me for something he explicitly told me not to do." Auntie Rose smirks. "You'd better beat him home and bask in that win for me, chickadee."

I'm laughing when I press a chaste kiss to her left cheek beneath her magic stone tiger's eye. Laughing harder when I catch up to Kestrel. And all-out cackling when I sprint past him and closer to the protective ring of elder trees around the glade. Sometimes, the biggest joy of being a big sister is making your younger brother absolutely eat your leafy dust.

Swan: Gifts and Skill

*T*he cheers of my triumph spill into the glade.

Kestrel had tried cheating by grabbing my hood and pulling me back. In retaliation, I'd yanked on the recurve of the bow on his back. My brother had tripped, trying not to choke himself on the string crossing the base of his neck, which caused him to fall behind me. This helped me win; it was sort of fair and almost square. And I'm still coming down from a cloud bursting with victory and energy when we run into Starling. Kestrel and I are knocking shoulders as we stumble down the pathway, but the judgment in our brother's seafoam eyes sucks the giggles from our chests.

It seems Starling had been taking an evening stroll, reading under the remnants of autumn sun. But now, one hand is pocketing his journal in his olive trousers while the other supports his gilded book about poisonous flora. His fascination with deadly plants scares me at times, but he hasn't tried to kill me yet, which should count for something; still, I don't feel much better. Especially when he lowers his book with a raised brow, the pages closing over his thumb while he surveys us head to toe. A smirk slides across his sharp mouth when he sees the state of my cloak. Before he speaks, I know his words will be unkind, and my insides curdle with sour anticipation. It's a stark contrast to the fleeting bright spirits I was just reveling in.

"Well, look at what the Phouka dragged in. You two look like a pair of windblown, sloppy Buttery Sprites," Starling drawls. "You smell like them, too. The stink of spoiled food is so vile that I almost didn't recognize you." My brother's posture and grip on his book loosen as he sinks further into his slippery grin. "Maybe I'll get lucky, and Mom and Dad won't recognize you either, and they'll throw the both of you out into the compost bin."

Kestrel snorts at our brother's rudeness, dropping into an exaggerated bow and dramatically sweeping his arm through the air. "Ah, yes! Greetings, Your Highness. Please excuse our ruffled appearances and supposed stench; we were out in the forest battling a monster to protect your royal derrière."

A bleat of laughter escapes me before I can stop it.

Starling snaps his book closed and glares at me, gaze cold and foreboding. "What are you laughing at, *Duck*?"

One would think Duck is an endearing pet name. And perhaps it would be with better context, and said by a better person, but my brother is a bully. When he refers to me as Duck, he's singling me out as the family freak. It's an unfortunate coincidence that our parents named me Swan long before reading us *The Ugly Duckling*. Even more so when Starling latched on to the tale. Though he's never had the guts to use the nickname in front of our parents, he hasn't called me Swan in private a single day since.

Sometimes I can escape Starling's torment, if we either ignore each other, or if I succeed in avoiding him, but he usually gets in a few unwarranted digs a day. All the while, my well-mannered curses stay locked away inside my attic, no matter how badly I want to speak them. *May a colony of booklice find their way inside your journal and eat away at your favorite pages, you big bufflehead.*

"Please, can we not do this today? It's been one of my better brain days, and I'd like to keep it that way," I say to Starling, trying and failing to hide the plea in my voice.

Any lingering drops of happiness drain from me like a leaky bucket when Starling juts his bottom lip out. "Aw, you poor thing," Starling goads, tone radiating a sarcastic chill.

Kestrel stands a little straighter when he realizes Starling isn't getting bored yet and doesn't plan to roll his eyes and walk away. Not this time. So, Kestrel expands, pulling his spine up and his shoulders out as he shifts to put a foot between our brother and me. "Knock it off, Starling," he rumbles, quiet and calm. But there's a threat beneath those simple words, and the warning is palpable.

I step back and stay quiet; I've learned it's the best way to keep from adding fuel to the fire with Starling. Everything gets worse if I'm snarky back, and I've yet to defend myself and not regret it later. Instead, I watch my younger brother stick up for me again, pulse thrumming and mouth clamped tight. Starling looks between Kestrel's eyes, weighing the worth of picking a fight today. They're used to this back-and-forth, but Starling doesn't harp on Kestrel like he does me. Not when Kestrel has the physical strength and self-assurance to give him more than a fair fight. And while Starling might be Kestrel's senior by a year, he's a few inches shorter and not as broad. Even though he tries to make himself look taller by tilting his scarred chin up, we all know an argument over something as stupid as this exchange isn't worth it.

A warm, chirping voice solidifies that.

"There's my little hunting birds," Mom calls, rolling down the stone path toward us with Crow at her side. "How did it go? You were being careful, yes?"

The tension leaves my cramping muscles when I hear our mother's voice. Mom might not have physically birthed us, but we were made with pieces of her, the same twigs from the same trees. All six of us know who we are, and we know who we want to be, our parents' changeling offspring. The trolls designed our bodies to grow up looking like our parents, and now at thirty-eight and thirty-nine, Mom and Dad are winsome faerie people. Most of us are the perfect balance between the two—a combination of their skin tones, eye color, and features. Others, like Robin and Kestrel, take after one parent more than the other.

"Mom, you're just in time! I was just welcoming my brave siblings back home," Starling croons, dimples masking his ire as he turns on his heel.

I've never been one to tattletale. Peace between my siblings and I is important to me. But Robin—and on occasion Lark or Kestrel—rats everyone out for their misdeeds. Our parents know Starling often stokes the flames, and they do their best to put them out before they even spark, but the saccharine divots indenting his cheeks always try to convince them of his innocence. They're on full display now as Crow and Mom join our makeshift circle. She glances between Starling, Kestrel, and me. Her bottle-green eyes drop to the lip tucked between my teeth, and Kestrel's rigid posture as he glares at Starling. "Sure you were, honey," she says to him with a knowing tone. The half-smile she aims at me promises to make time, and a safe place, to sit together later tonight.

Seeing this exchange, Starling clears his throat as he crosses his arms over his chest, tome of poisons tucked flush against his sternum.

Mom pulls Crow to her side, where he can see our faces as we talk. "Did you end up catching that Phouka Lark and Crow saw?" she asks while her hands gracefully move, using our hand-based language for my youngest sibling to follow.

When Crow signs, his movements are quick and fluid as he bounces on his toes. *"Did you see Uncle Grim?"*

After a decade of communicating this way, the mechanics of

my reply are subconscious. "We did." I grin, knowing how much he favors the Shadow Prince. Crow would attach himself to the Reaper's hip if he could. "We caught the creature you saw with your clever eyes. Auntie Rose and Uncle Grim came to collect it, but Uncle Grim didn't stick around too long. I guess he had somewhere important to be."

"Did you trap the Phouka?" Crow signs to Kestrel, matching silver gaze aglow while he looks up at his big brother.

"Swan did." Kestrel reenacts our encounter with the monster with silly broad movements. He mimics me swinging the bow and throwing my knife, followed by playing the part of the wounded Phouka. Crow presses his cheek into Mom's shoulder and laughs.

Dad strolls down the conjoining mill path with Lark, smiling as he watches this show. Double chestnut braids leaping from her shoulders, my sister skips ahead until she reaches my side to hug me. It warms my twig heart when I embrace her in return, and she beams at me. Her roving turquoise eyes and the quick examination she does of Kestrel and me, doesn't go unnoticed. The astute little Healer-in-the-making is always worried when we go hunting.

"You smell nice," she mumbles, finishing her visual sweep over our brother. "Like the forest and warm sage." Her arms around my middle tighten, making the parchment of sweets in my pocket crinkle. "Burnt sugar and maple too."

"So, not spoiled food," I snort, thinking of Starling's comment and the leaves covered in Phouka decay that I could've rolled in when I escaped its claws.

My sister cranes her head up with a frown and curious eyes, but I shake my head with a wry smile and tune back into the conversation. Dad is standing behind Mom's wheelchair, chuckling at Kestrel's antics. His hand is absentminded, brushing a stray lock of Mom's hair behind her ear and tucking it into her low bun. She reaches with berry-stained fingers to entwine her black-banded pinkie with Dad's as he settles a palm over her shoulder. Mom is still youthful, but she reminds me more of Grandma Aspen the older she gets.

Moments after I observe this, Kestrel's theatrics end, and Crow recovers from his giggle fit to gesture toward me. *"Did you lose any of your knives? If you did, you could take me into the forest, and I could help you find it."*

My littlest brother is desperate to venture from the glade, to use his gift to find the things missing and forgotten. He tries to make excuses or create opportunities that would allow him to go on a search for lost items. Or to help us hunt the Pookas and Phoukas for Auntie Rose and Uncle Grim. But the world is a scary place, with the last of the witches scrambling to survive, and now one of them has poisoned it. We must be careful, which means protecting each other and hiding away the youngest and most innocent child of the family. Crow will have his adventures one day, but while the witches remain unknown, and the plague of darkness runs rampant, he must be patient.

"Sneaky little chick," I tut. "We collected the one I used on the Phouka." When Crow's face falls, and his hands move to hide inside his pockets, I jump to preserve his joy. "But I did lose a button off my favorite blouse today. Maybe you could find it for me later?"

Crow's answering grin is brighter than any sunflower growing in Robin's garden.

"Speaking of finding, have you seen your sister?" Dad asks as he glances around our circle, scratching a patch of silver hairs at the edge of his beard. When his gaze glazes over me, he pauses on my cloak. I cover the tear with my hand and give him a sheepish smile until he sighs and moves on.

Then I catch up with him and count the heads around me from oldest to youngest. Me, Starling, Kestrel, Lark, and Crow. But that's not right. There's supposed to be a kid between Lark and Crow... Mom's tiny twin is missing.

Catching this as well, Mom frowns, tapping Crow on his arm since Dad is out of his line of sight. Her hands shake as she signs. "Where's Robin?" The white scar running through her left brow and forehead tightens.

Dread pools up at my toes, rising like a tide, and my hand falls from my cloak. "She's not home?" I ask.

"Swan Jove. Don't tell me that you and your brother left your sister in that forest." Even though her hands tremble, Mom's voice remains even.

"I swear we didn't. We used Hazel's signal, but there was no answer, so we assumed Robin went home." My signs are a mess, my fingers tangling together as I fumble to keep up with the fear surging up around me. "She's done this before. You guys know she—"

When Kestrel saves me with his interruption, his speech and gestures are slow and seamless. "Robin could've gone straight to her garden. Maybe even the cellar for her preserves or something? I know she mentioned making Swan some sunflower jam biscuits earlier."

"I can go check if she's with Bramwell and the other trolls," Lark says, also coming to my rescue.

Extending a grateful hand, I squeeze my sister's shoulder in thanks. But Starling is in my peripheral, and I can't ignore the simper pasted across his mouth. He's hoping I get in trouble, no doubt about it. But there's a sharpness to him too, a certain kind of razor-edged tenseness to his body. Even his fingertips are pale where he grips his book. I guess it's good to know his soul isn't frozen solid. He's also concerned for Robin and her whereabouts.

"*She could be with Fern and his brothers,*" Crow suggests, his hopeful positivity leaking into his signing as he springs back up on his toes. If anyone could find our misplaced sibling, it would be him. "*They asked her to use her gift to whip up some strawberries now that they're out of season.*"

27

Dad murmurs to Mom, "It's okay, Sparrow. I'm sure she's around here somewhere." He kisses her crown, but it doesn't displace the deepening concern wrinkling her brow. Tapping Crow's shoulder, Dad jerks his chin back up the path before ensuring his lips and hands are in view. "Come on, son, use that gift of yours and help me find your sister."

As we all split up to look for the missing piece of our flock, I meet my mom's watery green eyes. At the sight of her distress, tears well up in mine. Her hands graze the wooden visage of the sparrow and elderflowers curled within her wheels before she grips the rims. Her knuckles go white.

I turn and start my search before she sees me drowning in self-reproach. I'm the eldest child; it's my job to be responsible. I help Dad keep the house tidy and assist Mom in caring for and protecting our land. When needed, I'm of service to The Numina by clearing our surrounding forest of infected monsters. Above all else, I keep my siblings safe and, preferably, in one piece...now I believe I might've just failed my most important task.

-

Robin was, in fact, not somewhere. She wasn't anywhere, at least not in the glade. We walked everywhere with Crow, twice as he used his gift, but he couldn't sense her within our safe haven. He was pulled toward the perimeter and we realized that Robin was still out there beyond it. And while his magic is useful, Crow is too young. It's too risky to take him into the forest, for the very first time, in the dead of night while we're all panicked and off-balance. Not to mention, the possible bogeys crawling about waiting for any opportunity. So, Dad, Kestrel, Starling, and I traverse into the dark. Mom had loaded our pockets with salt, and stayed behind with Crow and Lark to light the candles inside our carved pumpkins to act as beacons.

We're all hoping that Robin will turn up before morning, praying that she just got turned around and the lights will guide her home. My sister is clever, though; she could find her way even without the help of spooky-faced will-o'-the-wisp lanterns, a fact that drives my concern deeper.

The four of us are armed to the teeth as we sneak back through the forest, searching for any sign of Robin. What happened to keep her from home? Perhaps she stumbled across an injured animal, or she twisted an ankle?

"I'm sorry," I say to my father after my brothers split off together to cover more ground.

Dad's goblin ancestry causes his eyes to refract in the dark, much like the glowing flash of a wild animal's. His gaze switches from silver to yellow to red and back as he turns his head. "I know, sweetheart." He hefts the elder wood bow Mom made him for their eighteenth wedding anniversary higher on his shoulder.

"This is all my fault. I should've tried harder to find Robin, double- and triple-checked our surroundings before we left for home." Feeling bitter about the foreboding self-pity trying to creep into my veins, I glare at the waxing, gibbous moon as it casts the forest around us in a pale blue haze. "Maybe if I had a gift, I—"

I'm interrupted before I can even finish my thought. "While I agree that you and Kestrel could've been more responsible," Dad starts, "your and your brother's gifts have nothing to do with your sister's disappearance."

"You mean my lack of gift." I grumble my reply.

Dad sighs as he scans the foliage at our feet, looking for any disturbance, tracks, or trails…any blood. The only good thing about the forest floor revealing nothing is that the dead plant life isn't further decaying with sickly black rot.

"You might be going senile, Dad." I kick a thick pile of leaves, watching them flutter before scanning the uncovered dirt and moss. "Because you've managed to forget that I'm the only one in the family without a gift."

We forge on, muscles tense, and footsteps light. I can hear my brothers' voices off in the distance, and Robin's name being called floats through the chilled air. It would be wise to stay silent and lessen the chance of running into a wandering beast. I don't want to become a midnight snack, but being loud enough for Robin to hear is more important than whatever monster lusts after faerie meat.

"You're not alone, Swan," Dad says. "I don't have a gift either."

A disbelieving snort slips from my nose. "Technically, that's not true. You have your goblin sense of smell *and* ability to conceal yourself."

The fleeting look my father gives me is soft and worn, like an old, patched sweater. "So can every other goblin. But if we're getting technical, there's different kinds of gifts someone could have. Things like skill. And you and I both have a special set of skills." He taps the worrying fingers that I curl into a loose embroidery string hanging from my cloak.

"What skills?" I ask, sheepishly unwinding what used to be the head of a stitched swan from around my fawn-hued digit.

"Well, I know my way around a sewing needle for one. And two, I have a knack for traveling." Dad's color-shifting eyes crease. "I also have the most valuable skill of all, wooing your mother."

"Dad—" I begin when an arm is thrown into my gut, and a whoosh of air leaves my chest with an *oof*.

My father pulls me to a stop, dark brows furrowed as he puts a calloused finger to his lips. That's when I hear the rustling to our right. It sounds like the scuttling pace of something sprinting toward us. Dad has an arrow nocked and ready when a little figure darts from the trees. A surprised squeak, followed by a small burst of flame, has us sighing. After the lone imp scurries away into the night toward the glade, Dad eases the tension on his bow before stomping out the tiny fire that shot from between the petrified faerie's fangs.

"Uh, should we be worried that something might be chasing that imp?" I ask, wary. "A Phouka, perhaps?"

Dad shakes his head, causing a fall of his chest-length hair to hang over his shoulders. The beach glass beads braided onto some of the dense ropes with embroidery thread sing and twinkle with this forbearing movement. "No, I'd smell infection," he responds, followed by the intake of a deep and calming breath. "There's nothing out here but old traces of things that passed through, and the ghosts of you and your siblings from past hunts. There are even some wisps of Rose and billows of Grim, but no fresh Phouka."

Relieved, I nod, and we carry on our search. Something akin to uneasy doubt sends shaky sparks from my heart to the soles of my burning feet. Based on the whiffs our father caught with his enhanced half-goblin nose, Robin isn't out here, and she hasn't been in a while. It's wishful thinking, but I can only hope his keen nose is wrong.

"As I was saying—" Dad's head swivels, peering past the silhouetted trees, and the green shine beneath his dark umber skin catches in the moonlight. He looks like the faerie knight mom's recollected teenage adventures always colored him as. "You have a skill for being sensitive and kind, even when Starling is being Starling. You selflessly take care of your younger siblings, and always help your mother and I, even when you don't need to. You're observant, thoughtful, and quite the budding poet. But your best skill is your willingness to learn." Dad seems distracted as he lists these things. Like part of him is here with me, consoling his eldest daughter; the other part is somewhere else with his youngest, somewhere vulnerable and scared.

"When you were little," he starts again with a low, lulling

hum, signaling the beginnings of a story, "I taught myself to use a bow and arrow, knives, axes, and spears. Anything I could think of so I could help you be a brilliant markswoman. Then, I taught you what I already knew about hunting and holding your own. And at the same time, I got to bond with you and your brothers, on the occasions they joined in."

This new information feels like discovering that unicorns don't actually exist.

But hearing this also uncovers a distant memory tucked away in the attic of my mind. It's the safe space I retreat to when I write, but also when I feel too much, or nothing at all. I forgot about the tainted trunk in the shadowy corner. It feels like pushing away silken cobwebs and dusting off the lid when I remember the warmth of a blossom-scented springtime. There was a restless day when Mom told me and my siblings that Dad was out working in the barn and not to disturb him. Of course, that led to Kestrel grabbing me and Starling, and we snuck to the barn to peek through the holes in the slats. Rummaging inside my trunk, I recall Dad throwing knives at a bale of hay. He was huffing and puffing, groaning when the blades didn't stick. But soon, Kestrel was pointing out a rout of my favorite snails on the nearby path, and we were off, barn and hay bales already forgotten. When the trunk lid snaps closed on me I'm pulled from my mental attic instantly. And now, I realize that all those years ago, Dad was practicing something he never knew so he could teach me what I know so well today.

"I thought you already knew all those things." I gape, pushing away the long curls skimming my eyelashes to see my father's profile better.

"I could hunt small animals if needed on my travels, but I was clueless about weapons and precision," he admits with a halfhearted laugh. "I didn't even carry a pocket-sized knife when I went with your mom and godmother to track down Black Annis. But after my half-sisters joined The Numina, I saw your siblings' gifts set in, while yours stayed dormant." Dad's nose turns to the air and he frowns. He redirects our course northwest and I no longer hear Kestrel and Starling's voices. "Not knowing when your gift would wake, I wanted to be capable of teaching you a special skill, something to use when going out into the world and adventuring like Primrose and I did. And in mastering different acquisitions, I hoped you would feel like you had a changeling gift of your own."

I've always looked up to my father and wanted to be strong like him, but understanding how Dad has always seen me makes my appreciation for him grow tenfold.

Still, an insecurity-shaped woodlouse nibbles at the base of my skull, trying to find its feast at my attic door.

"So—" I draw out my vowels before trying to fish out the intruder with a jesting tone. "What I'm hearing is…you expected me not to develop a gift?"

"That's all you got out of that?" Dad chuckles this time, looking down at me with a fond exasperation. His mirth is short-lived, soon replaced with a wince that carves the shadowed parts of his face into something morose. This early morning, moonlit search for Robin doesn't call for laughter. My insides flip at Dad's secondhand guilt, somersaulting onto my own rueful stomachache. "Sweetie, I have full faith in you," he says. "Changelings didn't have special abilities until The Numina came back. We still don't know much about the magic you've all inherited from the elder trees." His face is soft and open. "Now who's the senile one, *hmm*? Don't you remember? Your siblings developed their gifts in a time of need."

Of course I remember.

Kestrel was the first to get his; I was there when he hurled one of the jacks we played with across the room. It stuck into the wall, spearing the black widow beneath it. The venomous spider was creeping dangerously close to a dozing Starling.

And Starling started summoning his birds with a whistle

MCKENZIE CATRON

when a bugbear tried and failed to bypass the glade's barrier by climbing along the limbs of a tree. The bogey left the perimeter screeching after the birds in Starling's control nipped at its behind.

Lark came into her gift one night when singing to an infant Crow. He'd contracted a horrible infection from the same fever that damaged my nerves. But Lark's magic songs instantly calmed Crow and eased his pain before the illness rendered him hard of hearing.

Robin developed her gift one frostbitten winter when food was scarce. She saved us, and all the faeries who share our land, from a treacherously hungry season with vines sprouting through the snow, carrying an abundance of summer melons.

And little Crow, who'd just learned to crawl, found Mom's wedding band. It had fallen after she took it off to knead spiced pears into cider bread dough the day prior. Crow's giggles and chubby hands incessantly slapping the ground eventually brought Dad to pry up the floorboard, uncovering Mom's ring.

Revisiting these memories, like pictures on a wall, makes me trip on the log Dad steps over. As always, he's there to catch me. It's not embarrassment or frustration that makes my throat tighten and eyes water. "But Dad, I'm in need *now*," I croak, half kneeling on the old fallen tree. "I need to find my sister."

Dad's steadying hands guide me up and over the lichen-strewn wood with more grace than I can manage right now. "You'll find yourself when the time is right." He hugs me, slotting the top of my head underneath his scruffy chin. I clutch onto the back of his cream cloak, numb fingers grazing the bow strapped across it. With a shuddering inhale, the soft wool that smells of rolled cinnamon quills and home is seasoned with my tears. My father's bobbing throat vibrates against my temple as he speaks of Robin. "We'll find the both of you when the time is right."

—

We cross the barrier of elder trees back into the glade at dawn, and its faerie occupants are still asleep. The darkened blue sky is dissolving into the shades of crisp griddle cakes smothered in honey and sweet, sweet marmalade. My body is shaking, and my stomach is cramping from the lack of food. Kestrel and I never had dinner, but he seems to be faring better than me. Starling looks ashen and ready to drop. No doubt his sugar is low from exertion and sleeplessness, though I do see a boiled sweet rounding out his cheek. My blood doesn't need sugar like his, but I'm close to crumpling into the grass like a doll made of soggy rags.

I'm tempted to fall anyway when I see the figures amassed before our family home. We're too far away to identify anyone, but I look for shorter silhouettes. One is Mom in her wheel-chair, another is Crow, and a slightly taller one should be Lark. But there are three others who are of varying heights. And one of these figures must be Robin.

My brothers and I break into exhausted jogs as Dad leads our flock home. Closer and closer we get. Higher and higher, the sun rises. The silhouettes start taking shape; one has deer-like antlers, and the other a flickering crown. But surely the shorter person between Auntie Poppy and Auntie Rose is Robin. Closer and closer, higher and higher. The figure between my aunts is stooped over, and as the four of us come to a gasping stop amongst our family, a golden cane falls to the ground.

Robin has still not shown up, but the triplets making up one-half of The Numina have. And something is horribly wrong.

Swan: Unexpected Visitors

*F*ate is slung between Death and Fortune. Their limbs are a clash of teal, opal white, and lavender, and their coal-black curls are strewn about, covering most of their faces. One of my aunts groans, but I can't tell who the pained sound bubbles from. I think it's Auntie Rose who grunts under the weight of the triplet that sinks to her knees after her cane.

"Posy," Dad shouts when Death's grip on her sister slips. He dives onto the grass after his half-sisters, catching Fortune by the arms when she topples like a felled tree with Auntie Posy's limp arm still hooked behind her neck. Auntie Rose strains under Posy's other arm until she crouches beside her.

My mom is perched at the edge of her seat as she lurched forward when Dad did, but she didn't quite make it to the ground like him. With her hands held out in surprise and grasping at the empty air, she looks as helpless as I feel. Lark puts a hand on her shoulder, and Crow runs to bury his face in my stomach when our eyes meet. My mom's expectant expression and the glimmer of a hopeful return for Robin breaking through the worry for her sisters-in-law, crushes me. It feels like a boot to the chest when I shake my head, and that glimmer goes out.

Lowering my chin, I stare at the neat rows of small twists along Crow's scalp, avoiding Lark's realization too. A selfish thought crosses my mind as I cup my littlest brother's head and let him stay squished against my abdomen. I, too, wish I could hide away, squeeze my eyes closed, and disappear into silence. It's horrible to think that it would be easier if I couldn't hear the outside world, or the terrifying things inside it. But I do, and it's a privilege even when it's a burden. So, I keep Crow tucked under my wings, fortified with Kestrel at my side and Starling beside him.

I listen to every single one of Auntie Posy's distressed whispers.

"It's here." She releases Poppy to reach for her fallen cane. "It's here. It's here. It's here." Her hushed mantra slips through the waterfall of coiled hair that hides her face. And when her palm slides over the leaves and meets the twisting cane of metallic sunlight, her trembling fingers fail to curl around the wood. So, despite needing the mobility aid to help her incurable pain, Auntie Posy tries to go without it and shifts her weary body as if to stand.

Fumbling, Auntie Poppy grabs at her, attempting to keep her seemingly delirious sister from climbing to her knees. She hushes Posy, bending her head to her sister's level to cancel out her whispers with soft reassurances of her own. The magic-grown foliage and spring flowers dangling from Poppy's antlers have begun to wilt. Dad must notice this too, because he puts a steadying hand on both Auntie Posy and Poppy.

But the murmuring doesn't stop.

Moving to assess further, he takes the bow and quiver from his back and discards them in the grass. Dad's forehead wrinkles as he peers at Death, the only sister still capable of responding. "Rose, what's happening? What's here?"

She's short of breath, and the shadows crowning her head mirror this by flickering with the rapid rise and fall of her chest. "After a few trips to the gates, I returned to the Mountain looking for Grim and stopped in Posy's room to check on her. I found them together like this." Auntie Rose sits back on her haunches, staring at her sisters with pinched brows. She uses a tired hand to gesture to them before it falls against her thigh. "I didn't know where else to go."

Curving his spine, Dad reaches through Auntie Posy's wild hair to cradle her face. He gasps when the skin of his palms meets her cheeks. "She's burning up."

Auntie Poppy leans closer to her sister, turning until her forehead presses against her drooping shoulder.

Dad is twice as gentle when he pulls Auntie Posy's head up, and extra soft when he tilts her chin to bare her face to the day's first light. When my aunt is revealed to us, she's fevered; her normally dark-toned lips are barely a shade of the lightest turquoise. And her citrine eyes are glassy, unfocused. Auntie Posy doesn't look like the mighty Fate I've come to know, not one bit. Yes, she's wearing an elaborate long-sleeved gown in her signature ruby, worthy of a storybook princess, but her mind has gone missing along with her haloed crown and train of fated red threads.

"You didn't want to take her to Hazel?" Mom's quivering voice asks Auntie Rose. When Lark leaves her to stand on my other side, Mom's enchanted chair pulls her onto the grass. Something in her deflates as she leans over Dad's shoulder to tuck Auntie Posy's coils behind her long, rippled goblin ear. Mom gravitates toward Dad for stability, and I'm sure his nearness is why her tone is stronger and more maternal, more Elder Mother-like when she speaks again. "It's clear to see she's unwell and in need of a Healer."

"The Infirmary is packed." My dark-clothed aunt shakes her head, vehement. "Besides, we can't have people knowing that something is wrong with one of The Numina." Auntie Rose does a double-take at Auntie Poppy, who's braced her hands on the ground and now hangs her head between her shoulders.

"With this strange witch-born disease spreading and all the Phouka popping up, it would create mass panic," Death continues. She glazes over the wall of bodies my siblings and I have created behind our parents, eyes searching before she lands on my sister. "Lark, will you go fetch Robin? We will need both of your minds and every medicinal thing Hazel and Time taught you two. This is what you girls have been training for."

"I—I don't—" Lark looks up at me like a lost doe.

Without thinking, my hands tighten on Crow, making him uncover his face to study my lips as I speak to our aunt. "She never made it home after the hunt yesterday. We've been in the forest all night looking for her." It doesn't even occur to me that Crow must think I was speaking to him until it's too late. He jumps from my arms to Lark's, and in doing so, I see the tears coloring his tawny face with a wet flush.

I am the absolute worst big sister to exist. Ever.

"What?" Auntie Rose gapes. "First Grim, and now her too?"

A small, wounded noise escapes from Mom, and an echoing "*Too?*" bursts from my brothers. But Auntie Posy's head rolling in Dad's hands with a pained groan halts us all. And though her lips don't move, her voice rings out loud and clear. "*It's here.*" It's a strange ability she gained when she became Fate, but her pinched face paired with her strong yet urgent out-of-body words…it's never shaken me more than it has now.

"Po, we don't understand." Dad readjusts his hold to gently pat her face as her eyelids flutter closed. "What's here?"

"The war," Auntie Poppy answers quietly and simply, head still turned down. Her shrunken presence faded away behind the dire condition Auntie Posy showed up in, coupled with the panicked grief over Robin's whereabouts. But now, realizing how profound her quietness has been doesn't bode well.

"How do you know? Are you able to have visions again?" Auntie Rose asks, voice verging on a croak.

"I can't see anything; that's how I know," Fortune says, tired but resolute. And then she finally lifts her head.

Black veins sprout from Auntie Poppy's temples like hairline fissures, fracturing her lavender skin and spiderwebbing into her eyes. Which should be the pink of spring berries. But they're not; her eyes are gray and cloudy, almost like the film on a days-old glass of milk. Her gaze flits back and forth, but her eyes don't settle on anyone or anything; they roam, lost. Auntie Poppy is blind. We knew she had been a little worse for the wear when the Brume spread, and she and Posy couldn't make out the future's chances and destinies. Time had even told us about its effect on his pools and the tapestry, but the problems The Numina were having before... wasn't this. And it seems Auntie Rose didn't know it was either.

"Son of a cyclops," she curses, grabbing Auntie Poppy's chin, fingers slipping over the sweat beading on her poisoned skin. "Poppy, why didn't you say anything! When did this—"

"Last night," Fortune interrupts. "I was sitting at my wheel when I felt the darkness rolling forward. As my sight narrowed, I ran to Po and found her fevered out of her mind. I only saw a glimpse before my vision was gone, but her skin—" Auntie Poppy reaches a clumsy hand forward, trying to find Auntie Posy. She fumbles until she locates her sister's arm and lightly tugs. "The prophecies on her skin were quicker than normal, so quick and frenzied it looked like they were trying to escape."

Lark pulls herself from Crow and gently ushers him back to me before she kneels beside Dad. This time, when my brother clings to me, his head is turned, and his ear is pressed to my ribs. He watches Death move Fate's head to lie in Fortune's lap. Then, Lark begins a Healer's examination, pushing the billowing sleeve of Fate's dress up her arm.

Just as Auntie Poppy said, the gold prophetic words on her

40

skin are frenzied. The cursive no longer shifts along Auntie Posy's body like leaves atop a teal spring. Instead, they race like raging rapids. Shards of prophecies swirl, crashing and drowning and surfacing again. The phrases *"Elder tree will be the heart of the glade"* and *"when friend became foe"* merge and then splinter off like splitting streams. The longer we stare at the words, the more I notice fewer fragments. The stray letters that might've once spelled *"storm"* or perhaps *"morts"* that drifted in and out of the crease of her elbow are all gone. So are the phrases *"blue flower"* and *"Alis propriis volat"*—that I recognize as Latin but don't know the meaning of—that I saw sink between her fingers. And the previous piece about the elder tree now swims laps around her wrist. The word *"bird"* disappears from her forearm.

Auntie Posy's closed eyes scrunch tight, and her teeth dig deep into her lip. *"It hurts,"* her suspended voice cries out.

Crow jolts against me, picking up his head to survey the glade. I know he didn't hear our aunt, though his neck swivels as if he did and he's looking for the source.

Seconds later, fated words rise from the depths of Fate's veins and float onto the surface of her skin. These words are anchored and unmoving, but not only that, they're all the same, and pitch black. Lark pushes the other sleeve up and moves the hem of our aunt's dress to her calves. She even tilts Auntie Posy's head to examine the same new words printed across her throat. What I would assume is a prophecy is frozen and repeating, and every paragraph is blacker than any night I've seen.

Kestrel bumps me when he leans forward. "Tell me that doesn't say—"

"Beware, flock," Uncle Grim affirms. "Heed the shadow that has been recast as you seek the flowered pome and her flesh."

Everyone but Crow jumps, and Auntie Rose's head snaps up at the sound of his sudden appearance. Relief seems to flood her as the tension in her drops at the sight of her Reaper stepping into the leaf-scattered grass from one of the nearby stone trails.

Grim continues, voice wavering with exhaustion as he cites the words inking Auntie Posy's skin. "Shield your divine from The Between."

The closer he gets, the easier it is to see the dirt streaking his near-colorless skin and the deepened red-orange stains on his hands. Something about my hunter's instinct makes my grasp tighten on Crow as he fidgets in my embrace. He's locked eyes on the strangely grubby Reaper.

"Follow the sister's web to recover your kin." Uncle Grim's heavy, slow-moving footsteps fill the air with an eerie dragging sound.

A foreign scent rolls off him in waves, like spiced bitter sap and sacchariferous flowers, not his usual peat and pine. The tendrils that leak from his ever-moving shadow squirm, reaching like smoky fingers splaying from his back.

"Prepare your soil and unbar your home beneath the full moon's eclipse, for a child of the changeling must join the dark for the light to prevail." The former Pooka stops about ten feet away. I'm not sure how he knows what my aunt's skin says; he hasn't been a prophetic messenger since he was still chained in animal form under the control of the former Fate, Nemain. Once Auntie Rose pulled his ghost back into existence and gave the faerie a human-esque body again, he lost that prophesying ability. He became a Ferrier for the new Death, bringing people from this world to the gates of The After. So, he shouldn't—no, *couldn't*—know this information. Which is why the confusion hanging in the air is palpable.

Auntie Rose rises to her feet. "I've been looking for you," she says, tone trailing up at the end in an unspoken question. *Where were you?*

This movement from her spurs Crow, and before I can react, he rips himself from me. He dashes behind Mom's chair, narrowly escaping her quick hand that grasps at the tail of his charcoal cloak. Crow closes the distance and wraps his arms around Uncle Grim's waist, making something silver fall from the Reaper with the force of the impact. But even with a tear-streaked face, Crow still beams up at our uncle, arguably his favorite person in our family. My brother releases Grim long enough for his speedy little hands to sign, *"Uncle Grim, I knew you were about to be here! You'll know what to do, you always do. You can help Auntie Poppy and Posy and help us find Robin and—"*

Uncle Grim doesn't hug Crow back, nor does he even acknowledge the ten-year-old. The uncharacteristic indifference sends pins and needles prickling down my neck, straight to my tingling toes. Uncle Grim loves my brother, adores him even. He'd been so curious about how the trolls created changeling bodies that they let him assist with Crow. This bonded the two in a unique, magical way. The Shadow Prince doted on Crow as a baby, even let his drool-smeared fingers pull on strands of his raven hair. Uncle Grim would sit Crow on his shoulders as a toddler, never wincing when Crow's heels kicked his chest out of excitement—he's always been patient with my littlest brother, always acted as a playmate, teacher, and caretaker. But now, Uncle Grim appears...empty. He just looks at Auntie Rose with a distressed, glassy stare.

The vibrant glow of his yellow eyes flickers like a dying fire in a cold, ominous breeze.

"Grim?" Auntie Rose takes a tentative step toward him.

He extends a hand to her, but his fingers are straight and palm flat, telling her to stop.

Dad stands with a deepening frown.

Mom twists in her chair with a hand on Lark's shoulder to keep her kneeling.

A blind Auntie Poppy strokes her ailing sister's face with furrowed brows, a rippled ear tilted toward the action as her gaze dances aimless.

Starling uncrosses his arms, and Kestrel clings to the bowstring strapped across his chest hard enough to gouge.

Everything in me screams danger, and my fingers twitch towards my knives. But this is my uncle. He wouldn't put Crow in danger, and he certainly would *never, ever* hurt my brother... Would he?

A traitorous second later, the remaining light in Uncle Grim's eyes gutters out and his empty gaze drops to Crow as one simple, numb word falls from his colorless mouth. "Run."

We all hesitate, stunned by this unexpected change and our sudden, collective mistrust. My little brother's brows knit together, probably second-guessing what he's just read on our uncle's lips. I would be unsure if I hadn't just heard him say it myself. At least my father recovers, realizing someone should've done something when Uncle Grim first motioned for Auntie Rose to stop coming toward him. "Crow!" Dad calls out, even though my brother can't hear it. Dad repeats it louder, striding toward his youngest son. Kestrel somehow trips over Starling's foot as the three of us move in tandem to scamper forward after him. Even Mom urges her wheelchair to maneuver around Lark and my aunts.

But we're all too late.

The shadows writhing from Uncle Grim's back rise above his head, becoming a whirl of smoke that furls and contorts. Then, snaking tendrils descend to settle over the upper portion of his face. A half mask of Stygian shadows claims him, leaving only almond-shaped holes to see through, and everything from his nose down bare. A flare of light bursts through the mask like an ember come to life, and a color richer than blood consumes Uncle Grim's irises. The Reaper appears part lindwyrm, a winged, fiery-breathed beast from Mom's storybooks.

Unfazed, Dad is running now, closing the short distance when misty black wings rupture from Uncle Grim with a strong gust of tainted air. Crow ducks as this squall knocks Dad flat on his back. The rest of us freeze in disbelief and fear as these wings blot out the watery dawnlight.

Auntie Posy's previous mantra starts again. *"It's here, it's here, it's here."*

Crow stands, head craning back, to stare at the gossamer appendages from up close. Earlier, I thought Lark looked like a doe; I take it back now; my brother is a fawn, frozen in fear. With a grunt, Dad rolls onto his elbows and pulls himself off the ground before muscle memory has him reaching over his shoulder for his weapon. But his bow and arrows aren't there. He removed them when his half-sisters arrived earlier. And his unmistakable movement to arm himself makes Uncle Grim's smoky wings flare higher.

"Rush, wait," Mom says, no doubt fearing any further movement might put Crow in increased peril. That's why my brothers and I are now rooted in place too. Uncle Grim is an unpredictable creature now.

Dad pauses, and in response, the lindwyrm-esque wings droop. We all hold our breath. This can't be happening, this is our beloved uncle, our aunt's person, her—

"Grim, I don't know what's happening here, but please knock it off." Auntie Rose chokes out a laugh, trying to neutralize the charged air with her token humor.

Crow takes the slightest step back, looking between our family and the thing our uncle has become. When our eyes connect, I shake my head. Crow stops. And though his feet ceased moving, his entire frame still trembles, ragged breaths sending white puffs into the dawn sky. My heart is racing when I give him a close-lipped smile. *"Everything will be okay. I promise,"* I sign.

Auntie Rose speaks again. "You're scaring the kids." She tries for another chuckle, but it falls flat. Her voice cracks when she opens her mouth once more. "You're scaring me."

This time, when Crow looks back at Uncle Grim, something

at his feet catches his eye. Tentative, to not spook the newly formed monster, the boy bends to ferret around the yellowed blades of grass. When he straightens, a metallic object glimmers in his hand. Crow's eyes widen and his head whips toward us. Panicked, he coils to run, but Uncle Grim grips his arm, stopping him in his tracks. Crow jolts beneath the touch, dropping whatever shiny thing he's found. Even from here, Uncle Grim's grasp is visibly firm, triggering every eldest sibling instinct I have.

"Let him go," I scream as I stride forward with a throwing knife pinched between my burning fingertips.

Auntie Rose darts forward with an arm flung out, frantic. "Stop," she yells, staring at her familiar. Though I know her plea to not because harm is directed at me.

This is when Crow lets out a yelp that pierces my heart. Desperate to run, he claws at our uncle's hand like trapped prey as he fights to get away and fails. And before my brother can try biting or kicking him, Uncle Grim's wings swoop down and the shadows around the two of them bend. My brother and uncle start to disappear. Crow cries out, using his rarely-used voice for the closest person: "Daddy!"

With little else to lose, our father scrambles to his feet while blackness further surrounds Crow and his small, outstretched hand. My brother is vanishing into the darkness Uncle Grim creates to travel through his network of shadows. We will never find them, wherever they resurface. I consider throwing a knife into the smoke, but the fear of hitting Crow stills my hand. This minuscule lapse in time is just enough for Dad to dive forward though, his hand enveloping Crow's. The darkness absorbs the three of them. A blink later, the shadows collapse on themselves, and the space they occupied in the glade is empty.

Crow, Dad, and Uncle Grim are gone.

Swan: The Prophecy

"*N*o, no! Bring them back." Mom's wheelchair carries her through the daybreak's mist, dark lacquered wheels stopping where Crow's boots had broken the leaves beneath them. Her jade eyes squint as she stares at the light slowly rising above the trees, her pale skin bathed in the sun's terracotta glaze.

A tearful Lark glances back down at a calm, near-unconscious Auntie Posy cushioned on Auntie Poppy's legs. Moisture has collected in Kestrel's lashes, while Starling looks waxen and ill as he strides toward Mom. Auntie Rose is so stock-still that she blocks me, and I push past her to meet Starling where he stands beside Mom's wheelchair. His elbows are in the air as his hands scrub over his shorn hair, lost. But I can't comfort them, not yet, because the ground demands my full attention. I'm close enough to smell the scent of honeyed elderberries and sticky buns that linger around my mother now, but I don't approach her either. Crow found something—something that got kicked when he tried to get away, something damning. I *need* to find it.

I comb the grass and leaves with my foot—

Starling's gruff voice steals my attention. "What are you doing."

He didn't ask a question. No, it was a statement, and quite rude, I might add. I ignore him, for a moment. Kestrel has moved on to check on our other aunts while Auntie Rose advances on unsteady feet.

"Crow found something before he disappeared," I finally reply to my brother. I can't deny what I saw, and I *will* find it.

"You mean before he was taken," Starling scoffs.

I pause in my search again. Auntie Rose's skin is so pale she's almost transparent, and for a second my heart stutters in sympathy. "Yes," I reply as gently as I can for our aunt's sake.

Starling scrapes his rough palms over his head, creating the bristly sound of friction between his skin and shaven hair. As he attacks his skull more, he throws furtive looks at Mom while she stews in her own thoughts. A boyish expression, one that reflects his anxiety for her and our family, fills his face. Starling sways toward our mother like my favorite flowers to the sun. He's trying not to show it, but he's shaken. Starling has a soft heart, even if it is jammed deep down most days. And just because he's often a bogey toward me, doesn't mean he's all bad. Perhaps the wood the trolls used for his heart stunted his emotional growth? A few hard alder twigs or driftwood chips could have mysteriously gotten into the mix, maybe it's not his fault he turned out the way he did?

Despite Starling's grating personality, I still want to protect my brother. And the need to comfort him, like I would any of our other siblings, spreads like wings from my ribs. But if I tried to pull him beneath said wings, I'd probably lose a few feathers in the process. *But* he was my best friend once, and pain *is* only temporary.

"Hey, if you keep doing that, you're gonna go bald." I tip my chin toward his worrying hands. Starling drops his arms and scowls at me. I sigh and carry on with my persistent search.

Only seconds pass before I begin thinking aloud. "This time, the magnetism was different; I saw it on Crow's face. I think he even sensed Uncle Grim coming beforehand. Crow always seems to know when he's around, or about to be, but this was different, almost like he heard Uncle Grim coming through the shadows." My theory isn't backed up by any facts besides the pair having a unique connection, potentially even a magic-related bond; I just don't know how to prove it...

The area by Mom's feet is empty. I move to the left of her, closer to Auntie Rose, where she shifts her weight from one foot to the other as her arms hug her abdomen. Sweeping in large arcs, I pull my foot out, the grass folding and fanning like crunchy book pages. I do this so quickly that I almost miss the silver glint just inches from my mother's chair. "Ha," I puff, "Crow found this!"

Mom snaps out of her fretful haze, like the hope of finding and holding something vital will lead her to her vanished children and husband. "What is it? One of his treasures?"

Bending, I scoop up the metal piece and hold it aloft like an early bird getting its worm. The long, thin chain even wriggles as it dangles from between my thumb and forefinger. But my small victory fades...it's not one of the shiny little bits and bobs of lost and forgotten things Crow finds with his gift and collects in his pockets. This item came from Uncle Grim, but it didn't belong to him. "Oh," I breathe, lowering the chain into Mom's now open hand.

The brightening sunlight glints off the trinkets attached to Robin's beloved charm bracelet. For a moment, my brain tries to deny that it's my little sister's jewelry, but my heart knows she *never* takes this bracelet off. I recognize every charm. The first one she got was a coin gifted by our aunts and stamped with a wonky-looking unicorn. After that, Robin collected charms from a kitschy village shop to represent each family member and person she loves. There's a spool of thread for Dad, a tree for Mom, a feather for Starling, an arrow for Kestrel, a musical note for Lark, and a strawberry for herself. For Crow and me, she made choices that aren't connected to our changeling gifts. A star represents Crow because he was born at midnight, which, according to The Numina, is a very special thing; for me, she chose a drop of water because despite my depression, I adore the rain and stormy days.

Even The Sun and Moon have their own self-explanatory charms, while Time has an hourglass, and our aunts their namesake flowers. There's a bluebird for Hazel, knitting needles for Grandma Aspen, and a hammer for Pop Pop to represent his old days as a builder around the glade. Bramwell left a custom-made changeling heart for the trolls, and a mushroom for Fern and the gnomes, in the shoes she left outside last Christmastide. But the charm that always makes me laugh is the one that depicts a cat for Uncle Grim, to symbolize the first form he appeared to my family as. So many good memories are tied to Robin's charms, but now they're tainted and sour.

Mom takes a long, shaky breath and presents the bracelet coiled in her palm to her sister-in-law. Auntie Rose's knees almost buckle and she clutches the armrest of my mother's wheelchair for support. "Primrose," Mom starts, her voice surprisingly calm. "Where has Grim taken my children and husband?"

"I don't know, Sparrow. I swear I don't." The undertone of a plea seeps into Auntie Rose's speech. "I don't even understand what just happened."

"Your niece and nephew were kidnapped alongside your half-brother. Grim has become a Phouka and spirited them to Sun knows where," Mom asserts, plain and simple, eyes sparking to life as they melt from a soft jade to a deep amethyst. "Actually, no, I doubt The Sun or The Moon know where they are because you Numina are blind to our present. And let's not forget, our future has been hidden by some unknown witch that even the oldest beings in existence can't find."

My mother's fingers curl around Robin's bracelet, and her purple irises burn.

"One of your sisters is quite literally blind, and the other has only a single repeated prophecy over her entire body. One that sounds like it puts the rest of my children in danger." Mom's wheelchair creaks and groans beneath her as the twisted midnight branches forming the handles behind her shoulders unravel.

Starling and I step back, our arms pressing together where we stand. We've only seen this reaction from Mom once, when the other faeries living in the glade were shouting that something foreign and monstrous was outside, running around the perimeter, trying to get inside. That was the day we all saw our first Phouka. But even though Auntie Rose has now seen Mom as the most faithful and protective embodiment of the Elder Mother, she doesn't step away. Instead, Death listens and lets my mom express her grief, her own face drenched in sadness and understanding.

"Not to mention the rest of our family." Mom resumes her agonizing rant. "Hazel is drowning in villagers infected with the Stygian Brume created by this Timeforsaken mystery witch." The enchanted chair responds to her unbridled emotion, unfurling limbs reaching for the powdery morning sky. As they stretch and straighten, they create the effect of a sharp crown haloing my mother's head.

The elder tree twigs nestled in my chest grow warm as they recognize her power. A hum reverberates through each woven piece, making it swell and race. It's an overwhelming sensation, making me hyperaware of the shape of my heart, every bend and curve and piece that forms the appearance of arteries and veins. Judging by the hand pressing against the wine-hued wool over Starling's chest, he can feel it, too. I'd imagine Kestrel and

Lark do as well. But every cobbled, magic piece of me keeps my attention on the power of the Elder Mother before me.

"And Time! Where is he right now?" Her composure doesn't break, and her voice doesn't rise, but this involuntary change in my mom shows the cracks threatening her hardened veneer. "Everything is falling apart like a house made of sand, and no one knows how to fix it. *I* don't know how to fix it." Mom's chest heaves as her fist strangles the bracelet wrapped inside it. "I don't know how to keep my family safe anymore."

She sags as she brings her white-knuckled hand to her brow. Crinkles spread from the corners of her scrunched lids when Rose envelops her. I can see the apology in how tight she hugs my mother, and the forgiveness in her when she squeezes my aunt back. The branches that grew from Mom's chair shrink with a series of snaps and grating sounds, sliding and twisting as they put themselves back where they were. And by the time the two women part, the purple fire in the Elder Mother's eyes has died into cool green embers and her wheelchair has taken its original shape.

Our family is broken, and this feeling is only perpetuated by a sense of desperation and confusion. How, or where do we begin the repairs? Where do we—

It almost feels like a blessing when the solemn silence is splintered by a burst of glorious light and the ruffle of melted feathers.

"Huh, speak of The Numina, and he shall appear," I mumble to myself.

Starling releases a huff-like snort through his nose, but he's already schooled his mouth into a heavier, forced frown as we turn around toward the sound of Time's arrival.

"I felt something happen. Is everyone okay?" Icarus stumbles where he appears behind us, tripping over his wings in his haste.

"Uh—" I say. There's no simple way to answer such a question, especially when said question feels like lemon on a cut.

"My pools of time went dark; I can no longer see anything but the distant past," my godfather reveals. "The last I saw of the present, something dark converged on the glade." The Numina is nearly panting with panic before he stops to look around him. That's when he surveys the quietness, copper eyes landing on Kestrel, Lark, and my other two aunts, all mostly on the ground farther away. Time's large, candle-wax wings droop.

Auntie Rose attempts an answer. "I think the witch responsible for all this illness finally made her big move. The battle we've been expecting is here, and somehow, she's turned Grim to her side."

Icarus shakes his head. "No, that's impossible. He would never turn on you, or any of us."

"He's been infected," Mom says, her spine straightening in her chair as she gathers herself.

Time's brows furrow as he looks between my ailing aunts and us once more. The way his eyes arc over each of our heads tells me that he's taking a total count.

"Uncle Grim took Dad and Crow...he took Robin yesterday," I say, folding my arms around my aching torso.

"He's a new breed of Phouka now," Starling adds.

"What?" Time turns to Auntie Rose, wings folding and sinking into his back, revealing the mixed metal, wing-shaped embroidery Dad did on his cloak. "I thought he wasn't a Pooka anymore; how could he become a Phouka?"

My aunt massages her forehead. "That's the thing, I don't think he is. He's been a little off for a while now, but there's been so much going on that I didn't want to add to the issue by bringing it up." She drops her hand with a sigh. "I thought he was stressed, trying to find a trail on any of these witches, but I suppose his lapse in time and foggy memory wasn't just exhaustion. One of the hags must have captured him and forcefully plied him full of witchcraft. This isn't him, it can't be."

Seeing Auntie Rose struggle with her own conviction must soften something in Starling. "He changed right before our eyes," he tells Time. "He did try to warn us before he left with Crow and my dad."

"He told Crow to run," I tack on, wincing at how my words make Mom flinch.

My godfather puts his hands on his hips, mulling over the information. His gaze flits over to my other two siblings and aunts with an anxious expression that says he wants to check on the group as severely as I do. "Can we be sure that he wasn't coerced?" he asks. And when my aunt opens her mouth to undoubtedly argue, Icarus continues, "I'm not saying his alliance shifted for the wrong reason. But could it be possible, for whatever reason, that Grim thinks he's doing something for the good of the family? For the world, perhaps?"

"Whatever he's doing is against his will, Icarus, I know it." Death plants her feet. "Maybe he found the hag who's turning the Pooka and created the Stygian Brume." She becomes hurried as she attempts to manifest any solid reasoning, anything that would pardon her Reaper from this betrayal. "Maybe she got her talons in him before he could return to Wyrd to tell us where she was."

"What about your sisters? They've been progressively ill for a while now." Mom speaks up. "You must see that they didn't pick up this infection like some common cold, Rose."

Silence befalls us.

Time glances at Death with something like regret smoothing over his lightly freckled features. "It's more than probable that he poisoned them. Who better to do it than someone close and trusted," he reasons. "It's a tale older than me."

My aunt turns her face like she's been struck. "But why?" Her voice is soft and pained.

"We're a strong family," Time answers. "It's comprised of Numina"—he gestures to himself and my aunts across the way, then to my mom—"the Elder Mother, whose best friend and my wife, is an immortal Healer." He looks out toward Kestrel and Lark still with Auntie Poppy and Auntie Posy before tilting his chin to Starling and me with a wry smile. "And all these magic little twigs."

"Not all of us," Starling snorts as he pops a pink-and-white-striped sweet from his pocket into his mouth.

"Starling Janus." Mom scolds him with nothing more than his name.

Our godfather gently cuffs him on the back of the head. At the same time, my boot surprises me by boldly stomping on my brother's toes. He coughs, eyes wide and scandalized as he peers up at Icarus, then cranes his neck toward me. Starling smacks his lips as he rolls the candy from his tongue into his cheek. "I could've choked on that!"

Yes. Now, may those sweets rot your teeth. And when they all fall out, leaving you looking like a gummy baby, may you eat nothing but cold, unflavored porridge for the rest of your days.

Time clears his throat. "My point is that together, this family could return the world to what it was before the first witch, Quince, killed Macha, and the unbalance of her death pulled and trapped us inside The Between."

Once, on a Christmastide Eve, my brothers and I stole our godmother's journal from where our parents poorly hid it. I remember seeing the name of Hazel's best friend from more than six hundred and twenty years ago, lovingly written in purple ink. More importantly, I remember reading about how her best friend murdered Fortune while actually trying to kill Morrigan, the Death before my Auntie Rose took the mantle. And how Hazel's husband, and the rest of The Numina, disappeared to The Between right before her eyes. The lock on my mental attic door clicks open.

"The Between," I gasp, making Death jump. "When Uncle Grim recited the prophecy, he said something about The Between!"

Time looks at my aunt. "What prophecy?"

Starling opens his mouth with a slurp of saliva, candy clicking on his teeth as he switches it to his other cheek. "It's written all over Auntie Posy."

This spurs Time into action. He stops only to squeeze my mother's hand before trudging onward, and like the saddest parade known to all human and faerie kind, we follow. Besides the slight tightness of discomfort around her closed eyes and lips, Auntie Posy seems peaceful in her fevered slumber. Kestrel fretfully stares at her as he nibbles on his fingernails while Lark leans over, her fingers pressed to the black words staining Fate's teal wrist. My sister taps her thigh with her free hand in a rhythmic pattern, tracking our aunt's heartbeats. None of us dare to interrupt the Healer-in-training as she counts. Auntie Rose quietly joins them on the ground, kneeling next to her blind sister with a supportive arm wrapping around her.

A handful of terse moments pass before Lark speaks, and when she does, she sounds just like Hazel. "She's stable. She has a fever but doesn't seem to be in too much pain." My sister sits back on her heels, staring down at Auntie Posy with mature, clinical eyes. My chest clenches. My little sister isn't so little anymore. That feeling squeezes twice as hard when I think that, despite Robin's heart being too soft and squeamish to Heal family members, she should be right beside Lark, making the same assessments while Crow flutters in his curious-natured way close by.

Lark gestures to Auntie Posy. "All I can give you are hypotheses based on what Hazel and Icarus have taught me, and what we've encountered in the Infirmary." She gazes up at our godfather for confirmation. When he nods in encouragement,

56

she continues speaking with an intelligence that far surpasses any fifteen-year-old I know. "Auntie Posy's poisoned by witchcraft, but I don't believe it's the Brume. Personally, I think all her fated prophecies, the ones that were supposed to be destined before, were burnt away with whatever dark magic flooded her system. As a result, making her sicker. And as for my other patient, she only has a slight fever and needs rest." She motions to Auntie Poppy, who strokes the side of her unconscious sister's sweat-dampened face with her sightless eyes roving over and around us. "These veins—" Lark traces the air around Auntie Poppy's eyes, following the dark tracks creeping along her temples. Our aunt doesn't flinch, doesn't even notice her fingers. "They're also the work of witchcraft. Her physical vision and divine sight are gone. So, Fortune is, well, fortuneless. And I could be wrong, but presumably, the opportunities for chance and luck are now slim." After she says this, Lark looks up to Icarus with a grim face, and again, he confirms her words with a nod.

The way we all stare down at Auntie Posy's prone body makes me squirm. The sad parade I imagined earlier morphs and becomes a funeral gathering. My aunt's sleepy appearance only adds to the effect. The black letters printed across her sallow teal skin shove the beginnings of a poetic eulogy into my mind as I reread it, again, and again.

BEWARE, flock, heed the shadow that has been recast as you seek the flowered pome and her flesh. Shield your divine from The Between. Follow the sister's web to recover your kin. Prepare your soil and unbar your home beneath the full moon's eclipse, for a child of the changeling must join the dark for the light to prevail.

"SHIELD YOUR DIVINE FROM THE BETWEEN," I blurt, making eye

contact with Auntie Rose. "Is it safe to say the witch that got to Uncle Grim is trying to kill you guys?"

She shrugs and turns to Time. "How would a hag even know about The Between?"

"I doubt she does. But if she's using Grim as a pawn to make us weaker, it will be by picking off the others so it's easier to kill one of us," Time comments with a distracted frown.

Lark gasps. "You don't think Uncle Grim's killed Rob—"

"No," Auntie Rose interrupts her, detangling herself from Auntie Poppy to place a reassuring hand on my sister's leg. "He wouldn't do that."

Kestrel stands. "But Uncle Grim is the shadow that's been recast, right?"

Becoming aware of just how flippant his previous words sounded, my godfather's mouth opens and closes, at a loss for words—or perhaps at a loss for sugarcoated words.

"If my children were gone, I'd feel it. If Rush were gone—" Mom shifts in her wheelchair. "They're alive, and that prophecy proves it," she maintains.

We all stare down at Auntie Posy again, as if the answers to all our problems are spelled out for us as clear as a polished piece of glass.

"Are we going to ignore that last line?" Starling asks.

Prepare your soil and unbar your home beneath the full moon's eclipse, for a child of the changeling must join the dark for the light to prevail.

"No, sweetheart," Mom breathes. "But if my experience with prophecies the last couple decades counts for anything, then we know that some of those lines don't always mean what they seem to." Starling stretches out his arm, clasping his hand over her fist, which still holds Robin's charm bracelet. She gives him a tired half-smile. "I wouldn't let anything happen to any of you, even if it means drawing my last breath."

"I know, Mom." I grab her other hand, folding her chilly

fingers between mine, hoping their burning might warm hers. "But *I* won't let anything happen to our family. So, we need to divide and conquer and figure out how to get everyone home."

My statement unfolds a short series of events which include Time lifting Fate into his arms and carrying her across one of the glade's empty fields toward home. Although it is a shortcut from the stone paths, it feels like an eternity. Eons follow when Grandma Aspen's old house comes into view, and we walk past it, streaming past the watermill where Dad built our house. Crossing the threshold takes twice as long. It's a super-eon before we gather around the scratched and scuffed kitchen table while Icarus lays Auntie Posy in my parents' bedroom with Auntie Poppy resting beside her.

Kestrel rubs his palms together. "Where do we start?"

"Now that we know Uncle Grim's"—Lark glances at Auntie Rose—"sick, we shield the divine."

"Mm-hmm, great idea." Kestrel nods enthusiastically, but clearly, he's clueless. "What does that mean?" he asks, confirming my very thoughts.

Starling rolls his eyes at our brother. "We protect The Numina."

Kestrel's hands rub faster, and his head nods harder. "Totally on the same page." Then, he pauses. "How?"

"We stay inside Wyrd Mountain," our godfather suggests upon his return.

Auntie Rose crosses her arms. "No way, I'm not hiding. I want to find Grim and—"

"Exactly, Rose." Time mirrors her, though his stance isn't near as defensive. "That's what this puppet master of a witch would want. She took Grim from your side and expects you to come after him. Which is why we must do the opposite: we need to retreat with the Sun and Moon to the Mountain where no one can get in unless we want them to."

Mom sighs. "Icarus is right, Rose. If the hag gets her hands on one of you"—she gestures to her open bedroom door across the kitchen where her other sisters-in-law sleep—"then it's all over. All six of you will get sent to The Between, and everything will be plunged into pure chaos. And the other two witches, wherever they may be, will get word one way or another, and take control. Evil will spread and eventually—with none of The Numina here to rebuild the future—more witches will be made until the world is overrun. Rebuilding an entire world is a cosmic feat that no being, other than The Numina, is capable of. You all must be here, healthy and whole, after the prophecy has run its course to ensure the continuation of life for every faerie and human."

"So, what?" Auntie Rose throws her arms up. "We're supposed to hide under a rock and let you guys fight this stupid war alone?"

"I've helped kill a witch...twice." My mother stares straight into the face of Death. The four thick, jagged scars from Black Annis cleaving her chest open and sending her temporarily to The Between have lightened to a pale pink over the years, but they're still evident where the neck of her sweater frames her collarbones. There is also the long scar sprouting down her hairline over her forehead and through her left brow where the water witch Jenny Greenteeth's old mark pulls her skin with each facial expression. These scars make my mother's past hard to forget.

My aunt's shoulders drop. "Sparrow—"

"My babies are missing, Primrose, and the other half of my soul with them." Mom's quiet use of her full name, one that Death only permits her Reaper to call her, seems to hammer home her point.

Although Auntie Rose softens, she doesn't verbally concede. Instead, she asks, "How will you find Rush and the kids?"

Lark leans into the kitchen table, the morning light streaming through the window, turning her cloak's soft, spring yellow hue into a bright summer shade. "Well, the prophecy said to seek the flowered pome and her flesh."

"And then to follow the sister's web to recover your kin." Starling nods at our sister, lightly bumping her with his hip like a tap of approval. Lark beams at him, and I swear I see a potential smile in Starling's seafoam eyes.

"Any idea who this lady could be?" Kestrel asks the room.

"Rose?" Poppy's wavering voice calls out from the doorway of my parents' bedroom.

Auntie Rose disapprovingly clicks her tongue at the sound. "Poppy, you're supposed to be resting."

Tentative, Auntie Poppy walks forward with her hands out, but Auntie Rose is quick to unroot from her spot. Taking one of her sister's peaked lavender hands in hers, she guides her to the table.

"That's a little hard to do when I can hear you talking about our family's future from the other room," Auntie Poppy says after being led into the seat at the head of the table where Dad usually sits. "The prophecy is a clue to our mystery witch's identity, but it also made me think of someone else." She grabs for her sister's arm and misses twice. Once she finds her though, she prudently pulls at Auntie Rose's elbow like unspooling thread. "Remember when I first became Fortune, when I kept having visions about the paths of chance that different humans and faeries might stumble down throughout their lives?"

Death hums. "If I recall, you got a headache so bad it made you puke."

Poppy ignores her. "There were paths that showed different bogeymen reforming, letting go of their malignant ways, allowing me to see a hint of their human threads again."

"Yeah, but the only time that came true was Nanny Rutt." Slowly but surely, a visible dawning awakens Auntie Rose's pearl-flecked face. "And she became a Healer."

Time, who has stood quiet and contemplative, lights up as he basks in the same revelation. "Hazel's at the Apothecary with her and The Sun and Moon right now."

"Do you think they might have some insight on this—this—" Kestrel waves his hand like he's trying to wrap the right words around it. "Fleshy pom-pom person, and someone's sister's spiderweb?"

"It said sister's web, genius. Not spiderweb," Starling snarks through his cringing teeth.

Kestrel curls his fingers and makes them dance in front of Starling's face like scurrying spider legs, antagonizing our brother and his phobia. "Ooh, are ya scared you might see a creepy-crawly in the sister's spiderweb?"

Starling slaps at Kestrel's hands, but the latter persists. While Lark giggles, Kestrel taps at our brother's arm with his fingertips and runs them up to the side of Starling's neck. When he fails to get out of Kestrel's reach, Starling takes a shot at Kestrel's gut with a closed fist.

"Boys, please," Mom says in her soft, even-keeled way.

My brothers separate in an instant.

I meet Kestrel's eye, and he gives me a cheeky grin, a silent signal that his antagonistic immaturity was retribution in my honor. I pay him in kind by sticking my tongue out before Mom follows his eyeline and turns to me. Rearranging my expression to something more proper, I attempt to prove that I am, in fact, her eldest and most mature child. She stares up at me, waiting to see if I'll crack. My eye twitches when I realize how much her face reminds me of Robin. I'm quick to sober up as my insides wilt with festering weeds of guilt.

The inherent double duty of being equal parts mother hen and older sister makes me speak up. "I'll go to the villages and consult Nanny Rutt. I shouldn't have let Robin out of my sight in the first place; it should have been me who was taken. So, I'll spearhead solving this prophecy and bring everyone home. It's my responsibility."

Loose pieces of hair fall from Mom's low bun as she shakes her head. "Honey—"

"I was out there too." Kestrel sticks his hand up as if volunteering for some sort of job. "If we're playing the blame game, I get half the title."

Starling snorts. "How valiant of you."

"Put your hand down, Kestrel." I glare at him, though there's no heat behind my minty eyes.

He smirks and holds his hand higher. "Make me."

My eyes narrow. Kestrel forgets that someone as stubborn as Auntie Rose had a hand in raising us. "I will crawl across this table and force it down."

"You won't." Kestrel's chest puffs up as he preens under what he believes is a victory.

That is until I put one foot onto the bench before me and both hands on the tabletop. Kestrel's smile falls as I prepare to climb onto the seat and over the wood slab. Starling cackles as Lark steps closer to a fatigued Auntie Poppy, and Mom's head finds its way into her hand. The toe of my other boot is the only thing still touching the kitchen floor when Death and Time grab my biceps and guide me back down.

"Look," Auntie Rose starts, forcing her half-smile to flatten. "We could all sit around this table and hold hands while we take turns blaming ourselves all day. I should've figured out what was wrong with Grim sooner, right? Or maybe we"—she hooks a thumb toward Icarus—"should have figured out what was wrong with Poppy and Posy sooner. But that's not how this works, is it? The darkness has been on its way for a while. Timesake, it's been on its way since the very same day it was crafted. Now, a prophecy has been given to us, and we're meant to figure it out, squash the witches like the pests they are, and finish this. This world deserves to have peace again." Death puts a gentle hand on her sister's shoulder, careful not to startle her. "We deserve to have peace again," she repeats. "The bogeymen need to go. No more salt rings and magic barriers. No more anxiety and fear."

We all nod in agreeance.

Resolute, Auntie Rose puts her hands on the lightly crumb-dusted kitchen table. Her fingers move, visually outlining her plan as she speaks. "To decipher more of this prophecy, we need to move quickly. Quicker than the witch we're looking for. So, like Swan suggested, we divide and conquer." My aunt peers up enough to wink her stone eye at me. "Time and I will take Swan, Starling, and Kestrel to the Apothecary. Once we pick up the trail they're supposed to be on, I'll take the kids as close as possible to where they need to be without endangering myself." Her blunt, dark, lacquered nails draw a line over the scratched wood. "At some point during this commotion, The Sun, Moon, and Time will bring Hazel back here so she can help Sparrow and Lark move the faeries safely from the glade along the salt paths to Hazel and Time's cottage. Meanwhile, us Numina will get my sisters back to the Mountain and after that, Sparrow can 'prepare the soil' or whatever."

"What do you think preparing the soil is supposed to mean?" Lark points to the end of Auntie Rose's imaginary line.

Fortune answers her. "It sounds like instead of being at her home with her captives, the witch will show her face at the glade's perimeter. I'd imagine the reason for unbarring your home beneath the full moon's eclipse—even though there isn't supposed to be an eclipse for another year—is because you'll be letting her inside, past your protected ring of trees on Hallowtide, which does happen to be the next full moon." My aunt's blank, black-veined eyes float in the direction she heard Lark's voice. "The Elder Mother is the only one who can open the barrier."

Mom's brows pinch together. "You're asking me to stay here while my children wander around who knows where looking for the witch's home? Where who knows what kind of traps await them," she deadpans. "How am I supposed to do that knowing the risks?" She points at the window. "And it's like Poppy said, there's not even an eclipse tomorrow. I can't trust anything telling me to stay here, separated from my kids, when that doesn't add up."

Time turns to look outside at the sky, as if he's searching for evidence of an oncoming eclipse in the daylight.

"That's a problem for The Sun and Moon, not you," Auntie Rose mumbles before shaking her head. "If Poppy is right, and the hag is coming here instead of hiding in her lair, we can't risk the glade being without its guardian. And if the witch tries to get inside before the eclipse, there's no saying what she'll do in her attempt."

A hint of purple sparkles in my mother's eyes. "I—I can't—"

"Hey," Kestrel gently calls out. "Mom, we can do this."

"I don't like this, not one bit." The muscle in her neck jumps, and I notice that she still holds Robin's bracelet like a lifeline.

Kestrel gives her an easy smile, one that can only be described as nothing short of happy-go-lucky. "You've just gotta believe in us."

"Let them go, Sparrow. They can make it," Auntie Rose encourages Mom one last time. "It's not them who need your protection right now, it's the faeries who call this land home; they'll need your protection to see them safely onto the path to the cottage. The hag will be here, lurking outside. Not waiting for your kids."

Mom pauses until she deflates, tension easing, and the color in her eyes fades in surrender as she looks at Kestrel. "I do believe in you. You're only two years younger than I was when your dad and I left to face Black Annis. And"—she points at Auntie Rose—"the triplets were Swan and Starling's age when they left on their journey." She then motions for her children to come around the table to her. "I wish you didn't have a childhood built on fearing the outside world...But I have to believe you'll have a hand in making it a better place."

Starling tilts his chin high and proud. "Kestrel and I can go. The two of us are stronger, and we have our gifts to rely on. We'll find Dad, Crow, and Robin quickly before Hallowtide."

Mom raises a brow. "Swan is going with you."

"But—" Starling begins.

"No buts. Your sister is in charge." She gives me a knowing look as I lower myself beside her wheelchair. "I never wanted any of you to fall into your father's and my footsteps. And I certainly never thought our children would have to shoulder the same dire task of saving a parent. But you three are more prepared than we ever were."

"I don't know about that," I chuckle, gingerly prying the jewelry from her grip. "We have awfully large shoes to fill, O great Changeling Queen, our Slayer of Witches."

Taking each end of the silver bracelet, I hold it out for my mother. The little charms twinkle, swinging on their short chains as I wait. Mom hesitates before offering her wrist.

"There's no need to fill our shoes, you've outgrown them by leaps and bounds. If you three can figure out how to get along and work together, you'll be unstoppable." Mom's voice is thick as I loop the metal clasp together so she can wear her youngest daughter's prized possession. There is something like gratitude and hope written upon every mild wrinkle in Mom's porcelain skin. My favorites are the tiny bird feet in the corners of her eyes as she palms my cheek with a smile. "I am so proud of you." She looks each of my siblings in the eye, jade connecting with mint, seafoam, and silver. "I'm so, so proud of all of you. Your father and I love you from here, through The Between to The After and back, my little birds." Mom takes a deep and shuddering breath, and when she releases it, she releases us. "It's time for you to leave this burning nest and fly."

Grim: Her

*T*he ribbon led me to a dark place. This barren forest is a paradise, cool and comforting, like a talon-tipped hand to a hot brow. No life flourishes here. Nothing disturbs the visage of the perfect, dead, webbed trees, nothing but her white flowers that I dutifully pick. And I picked every single one just for her for weeks because she asked me to. She deserves such a lovely bouquet, one whose red roots drip with the richest bloody sap. The same sap that bled into my eyes, staining my hands and my mind. It sunk into my skin and makes me dizzy with joy.

This isn't joy, you fool. This is pain.

And when I fall into that wonderful, masked confusion, I hear her trumpeted call. Her voice, oh her voice, has played through my head like a glorious lullaby. Lulling. Loving. Controlling.

This is not a dream. This is a nightmare.

I hate that voice, the one that sounds like me.

He claws at the farthest reaches of my mind, in that prison that she skillfully designed. Scratches. Shakes. Pleads. He wants out, and he wants someone else. Someone that's not her, the one whose very bitter scent burns my nose so beautifully and holds me perfectly tight. Comfortable.

You mean captive.

No. I listen to her and do what she asks; I've brought her a girl and presented the young bird as a gift. And then she wrapped her up just so.

He screamed at me the entire time. I screamed at myself.

Wake up!

"Come to me."

Don't do it.

Shut up.

Her voice pulls me back through my shadows. I feel her touch in the wings ripping through my back and in the stifling darkness she placed so artfully around my eyes. Her marvelous, painful touch brings me to the forest. Drags me here where I crawl through the dirt to do her bidding. Here, I bring her gifts down with me. Screaming. Kicking. Crying.

We're hurting our family.

I've done as she asked again. I've gone above and beyond and when she asked me for a boy, I brought her two. Better yet, I brought her a man twice the size of the boy to add to her web, and she is proud. Her long carob claws running through my hair and grazing my scalp is a reward. She calls me trinket, and I welcome her touch as I kneel at her bare, divinely rotten lime-hued feet.

We hate this, we hate her very existence, and we certainly hate her touch. She's not Rose.

She's proud and happy as she puts them to sleep.

Stop!

Oh, but her voice is so wickedly persuasive when she puts a white flower on my tongue.

We're stronger than this.

"Stay."

Fight back!

Enough.

I hate him and his voice, she told me that I hate him. So, I drag the voice that sounds like me deeper under her bloody floral haze where he'll stay quiet for a time. And I obey her when she tells me to watch while she works on adding the youngest bird to her web. And I do, gladly.

Swan: Nanny Rutt

Traveling via Numina magic comes in handy when your entire world is crumbling around you. Death and Time whisk me, my brothers, and our bags away from home and into the villages quicker than I can blink. With just a brilliant burst of light, and rush of swaddling warmth, we are many hours away from home, in a quiet, disease-fraught town.

In the past, this village would've been alive with people bundled in brightly colored cloaks and scarves, busy with pre-Hallowtide preparations. The smell of fresh carrot maple cakes, and flour-dusted sour breads would have burst from the bakeries' open doors. And the window ledges would've been decorated with acorn-strung garlands and vanilla-scented candles lit inside warty gourds. The cobblestones would be littered with leaves that look like fiery gems against the paving, while vendors sold buckets and barrels of sweet, speckled apples and ears of multicolored corn still covered by their hairy husks. Tent shops would be selling full ceramic jugs of wines laden with mulling spices, and piping hot milken teas steeped with cardamom or clove.

But this southern village has none of those things.

The cobblestones are moist, and dingy. The white-spotted

leaves strewn over the streets float in murky puddles, are broken and full of worm-sized holes. The air smells of wet, forgotten food, and not one Hallowtide decoration embellishes a single cold, vacant window. Even a blackness hangs in the clouds above. It's almost as dark as the mold that creeps below us, reaching up from the paving, clinging to the sides of the surrounding buildings in bracken fern-like patterns. There are no tents or vendors selling their wares, instead coughing spills from the few shops with open doors. Only a couple of sluggish, red-nosed, and hollow-eyed souls cross our paths as the five of us descend the street. They either come or go from the market shop with black-tinged fingernails, clutching onto jars of preserved food. Or they pull roughly cut fabrics as blankets around their fragile frames as they mope from the haber-dashery.

One goblin man has lesions along his green ears that resemble strange sunburns festering with what reminds me of white tufted mildew. He hacks into the crease of his elbow as the stained-glass door we're heading for opens for him. He nods at us with watery eyes and a wince of an apology for the sounds that spew from his blood-flecked mouth. Then, he crosses beneath the swinging wooden, pastel lazuline shop sign that's embellished with gold calligraphy and intricate celestial carvings. I've long memorized this sign and know that its long-winded title reads: *"Hazel's Herbal Apothecary & Infir-mary—Home of the Healers—Makers of Tonics, Tinctures, and Salves."*

Hazel herself leans her hip against the door with her hand on the gold feather-shaped handle. She looks after the goblin man's retreating form with pinched, rose-petal lips. Her tired sigh is audible even over Kestrel's clumsy footsteps as he trips over a gap in the cobblestones. Starling's snort, on the other hand, catches her attention, and her blue and brown gaze brightens as soon as she lays eyes on her husband. But when she surveys the rest of our group, and notes our morale, the light dims, and she straightens.

Icarus swoops forward to kiss Hazel's temple in greeting.

Absently, she leans into him, but my godmother glances between me and Starling when she says, "Something's happened." And she stares at Kestrel when she asks, "Who's hurt?"

The latter of us three throws his hands up. "Why do you automatically assume whatever's happened is because of me?" Hazel raises her tawny brow and barely opens her mouth to answer before Kestrel shakes his head. "You know what, don't answer that."

The Healer clicks her tongue. "With you three, it's always something." Her duo-toned eyes slip past me, over my shoulder, and a slight wrinkle mars the eternally youthful olive skin of her forehead as she looks at Auntie Rose. With a curve in her shoulders and waves of flickering gloom cascading from her crown and dripping down her face like a mourning shroud, the tiger's eye stone in Death's left eye socket shimmers. She peers beneath her veil-darkened lashes as Hazel says, "Primrose, you're missing your shadow." I know she isn't being literal, since Death's ever-growing shadow still roils behind her, the Phoukas trapped inside always pushing at the edges, clawing for a way out. My godmother is talking about Uncle Grim's absence. When Auntie Rose doesn't reply, Hazel cranes her head up at her husband. "I can't imagine you're all crowding my doorstep for a casual visit?"

"Unfortunately, no," he affirms before quickly capturing her lips with his own.

"I didn't think so," Hazel says once Time releases her, blinking away the love-drunk daze from her eyes. She shoos at her husband, forcing him inside the shop and beckoning the rest of us with a fluttering hand. "Come on, you're letting the cold air in." We follow our godfather like a gaggle of scolded children, shuffling into the Apothecary.

Hazel's shop and I are well acquainted. I know its warmth, the colorful patterns from the windows that shine on the floor-boards, and the gritty sound the wood makes if Icarus has recently been inside. The bundles of drying flora hanging from the rafters are like familiar constellations. Sometimes, the more delicate flowers' crisp petals rain down on the patrons like a meteor shower, especially if they walk across the floor too quickly, or shut the front door too hard. I even know that under the front counter, there are shadowed cubbies where herbs steep in bottles of oil for weeks to infuse. The wall to my right is studded with numerous mahogany shelves, and amongst them, in the tightly packed, cork-topped jars, are dried ingredients like plants, powders, and spices. While the shelves to my left are teeming with jars upon jars of liquid ingredients like butters, extracts, and gels. Each container lining the shop is meticulously hand-labeled with cream parchment and purple ink.

The Apothecary's welcoming scent of lavender incense and infused salts fills my head with memories, both good and bad. I let it seep into my attic and fill the space with hope. Healers help people; they create herbal medicines that fix the wounds and ailments of those who come to them. Perhaps before Icarus brings them to Wyrd, Hazel can find something to ease Auntie Poppy's and Auntie Posy's symptoms. And Nanny Rutt can help my brothers and me find the missing pieces of our family... hopefully.

As if she heard my thoughts, the former witch emerges from the door behind the counter that separates the Apothecary from the Infirmary. "I thought I heard familiar voices," Nanny Rutt croons with a sharp-toothed smile.

It's been nine years since the woman reformed, turning from her bogeyman ways. Nanny said, in the beginning, when The Sun and Moon followed the lingering crumbs of her old human existence to track her down, she'd only agreed to reform to save her skin. But Hazel, who had just restarted her Healing practice, assisted the witch in ridding herself of the self-induced poison infecting her heart, the one that had changed her both body and mind. Only then did Nanny Rutt see clarity for the first time in centuries. As a bogey, she'd crossbred different wolfsbane flower species to concoct the *"perfect"* fuchsia-hued poison, which she'd consumed and used on her victims. But Hazel helped her turn her back on the malignancy she'd first cultivated out of spite and bitterness, and she'd shown Nanny Rutt how to use her knowledge of plants for good. The few traces left of who, or what, the woman used to be, can be found in her oddly sharp teeth, and the hint of color leftover from her wolfsbane creations dotting her skin.

The flecks of pinkish purple look like shiny freckles as she steps farther into the Apothecary. The Healer sweeps her way to the right side of the store, straight toward the flower shelf in the dry section. Her slinky movements have become natural to me over the years, though even now, she still carries a dangerous air about her. Almost like a domesticated wolf. There is some trust and respect at the root of the mutually beneficial companionship between Nanny and Hazel, perhaps even some purposeful care that requires making an active choice. But at the end of the day, a wolf is a lone, secretive, wild animal and if you cross it, you would be mistaken not to heed its teeth.

With an empty tea sachet in hand, Nanny flits over to the long shelf where Starling leans. She pops off the cork from the peppermint jar, adding two crispy leaves to the sachet. "Starling, will you be a dear and pass me the lemon balm and ground ginger?" she asks. "And Kestrel, can you grab that jar of hibiscus petals?" She points to a grouping of three new jars sitting on a workbench that have yet to be labeled and shelved by Hazel.

Starling moves, turning to search for the prompted leaves and spice. And Kestrel, in comparison to our brother, moves unhurried and almost reluctant as he squints at the trio of glass containers. "Uh, which ones?" he asks, an indecisive hand hovering above them.

The first jar on the left looks to be full of pink, curved, thinly veined rose petals. In the middle are dainty yellow flowers I'm unfamiliar with, and on the right are the red hibiscus flowers the siren-voiced Healer is looking for.

"Next to the cowslip," Nanny replies. She glances back at Kestrel for only a moment, fluttering her fingers in his general direction as she clarifies, "The red ones."

Kestrel's hand twitches, stalling over the rose petals, then the hibiscus, and back again. "You're going to have to be a little more specific," he says.

Starling breezes by our fumbling brother, picks the jar from the far right, and places it in Nanny's awaiting hand.

"Yep." Kestrel snaps his fingers. "Totally knew that. That jar was definitely the one I was going to choose."

Nanny hums. "Now tell me, why the long faces?" Nanny inquires with a razor smile as she plucks the jar of dried chamomile from another shelf.

"That's what I've been wondering," Hazel muses.

I am responsible. I need to take charge.

In the most efficient way possible, I recount everything that happened in the last twenty-ish hours. Nanny Rutt continues her drink-making, though her movements become slow, and every now and then, she pauses, surprised. The frown Hazel wears as I speak deepens, and Icarus pulls her into his side as she listens, arms crossed and expression growing more concerned. Auntie Rose stares at the floor, rubbing her forehead beneath her shroud. Kestrel helps fill in holes when my throat becomes too thick to describe Crow's abduction and finding Robin's bracelet. I'm the one to finish with Uncle Grim delivering the prophecy; our group discussion inside the house is soon followed by our arrival at the Apothecary. Once I'm done, the room is so quiet that a dried petal drifting to the floor would sound harsh.

"Oh *no*." My godmother pales, one hand flying to her mouth as the other clutches onto the front of her flowy dress. "I think I'm going to be sick." Her palm muffles her words, but they're not hard to understand. Not when she squeezes her eyes closed and doubles over.

Her husband supports her while Kestrel flies behind the counter to grab her a stool to sit on. Tentative, she lowers herself onto the sturdy wooden seat and calms her stomach with measured breaths. Still, her skin stays a sick shade of porcelain green. I've never seen the former Elder Mother like this before. So shaken. So disturbed. Of course, Time appears perturbed by her state, crouching to move her heavy, knee-length braid to her back and smooth away the stray hairs sticking to her temples. Even Nanny Rutt, a woman who doesn't often show what she's thinking, chews her magenta lip while the sachet she's been working on crumples in her constricted grip.

Their reactions almost make me wonder…"Hazel, you're not infected, are you?"

"No." She gazes up at me with moist eyes. "Just, those poor babies. Your poor mother. That ridiculous, heroic goblin boy. And your—" The immortal Healer stares at my aunt and shakes her head. "I think I'm getting soft in my old age. Perhaps a little tired and overworked with how crowded we are in the back." She leans into her husband's touch when he caresses her cheek.

Nanny Rutt clears her throat. "Let's not get ahead of ourselves with worry, hmm?" Nanny smooths out her tea sachet before tying it closed and turning from the shelves. "Why don't you three ducklings follow me and allow our dear Hazel to collect herself?" She shepherds me and my brothers with wide arms, collecting us into a wonky line as she shuffles behind the Apothecary's counter. I only get in a quick backward glimpse, and the poem I see is the perfect representation of what I feel inside—broken and crumbly.

THE ANGEL *of Death and the Angel of Time loom.*
   Silent, their figures are carved from shadow and sand.
   Color from the stained-glass spills from the pane,
   Stretching over the floor and pouring over their shoulders,
   Cloaking them in fragments of sorrow and uncertainty.
   The divine beings merge with the sacred mosaic behind them,
   Dissolving into the grief that fills the room,
   Becoming seraphic silhouettes behind the Healer of the Dark as she
mourns in the stillness.

"FOLLOW ME." Nanny Rutt urges us through the thick-grained door to the Infirmary. "And do keep your hands to yourselves. We don't need any of you getting sick before your journey."

Once inside, we're swallowed by the rows of occupied cots lining the large rectangle-shaped room where a fire burns in the hearth on the farthest side. Each Healer wears a large leather belt like Hazel's around their waist. They're all stocked with rags, small vials containing potions, tinctures, shallow ceramic containers holding salves, and balms. Some Healers carry pails of cold, fresh water, and others sculpted mugs with boiling water. Stools are placed on either side of each cot where Healers-in-training mop patients' brows and dress their moldering wounds.

Even the first Numina are here, helping the Healers they Blessed to become their gifted medicine workers, and teaching those who are learning and working to earn their Blessing. The Sun—stooped over on a chair too small for his imposing frame —shows a young Healer-in-training how to make a poultice. While The Moon sits with a child patient around Crow's age, holding the little girl's hand as she sleeps fitfully. The Moon glances up at us with her three crystalline eyes as we pass, nodding in greeting before bowing her silver-haloed head to return her attention to the fevered child.

Continuing down the central Infirmary aisle, closer to the hearth, is where the worst patients lay. Black patches of decay bloom over people's skin like inkblots on water. They stretch over limbs and trunks, climbing up necks and over the sides of faces. The half-selkie woman Nanny brings us to is the worst of the ailing. My brothers and I stand at the foot of her cot, hands at our sides and away from any stray, infectious bodily liquids that we could accidentally carry from our hands to our mouths or eyes.

Witnessing the woman's violent shivering, I find myself fearing that her teeth might crack from how they clack together. As if she might be thinking the same, the former witch takes a pelt from the foot of the bed and layers it on top of the blankets already pulled up to the woman's chin. What little breath she can draw rattles her body, and despite the cold month, she's drenched in sweat and looks wholly scorched by the sun. Most of her is overtaken, netted by sores, efflorescing with decay, like that of a dying plant. She's blistering and molding, and it makes no sense how a witch caused this.

All I can do is helplessly stand back and watch the Healer work in practiced movements as she takes care of her patient and steeps her a mug of medicinal tea. Nanny wipes her patient's brow and dabs at the corners of her peeling lips with a wet rag after she coughs up black, syrupy blood into the crook of her elbow. When the tea is strong enough, Nanny Rutt helps the half-selkie take a sip from her mug to cut through it. All the while, the woman stares at me and my brothers with dull, near-lifeless eyes.

My heart weeps for her.

The emptiness written over her pained, yet lax, features say she's given up. She's lost all hope for a cure, and waits for a certain Numina to take her to The After. I can only imagine this woman has seen many other patients in this room, prior to our visit, be peacefully claimed by my Aunt's merciful hands.

"Lady Death's Shadow Prince, did he show any symptoms like the ones you see in this room?" Nanny asks, nodding toward the rest of the Infirmary's occupied cots.

Kestrel gives the room a once-over while Starling glances past the handle of one of his signature axes. They both wince. It's clear to see that the Infirmary is fraught with affliction, full of fevered pain, and weepy mold and mildew. But not a single soul has grown shadowy appendages, nor does a spot of color brighten any of their faces, much less vibrant ruby eyes.

"No, nothing like this," I choke out. "If anything, Uncle Grim's symptoms took after the Phouka."

"His eyes are red," Starling adds. "And his shadows morphed around him to make him look part beast."

"I think there was something up with his hands, though," Kestrels says, staring at his oak-toned palm. Almost as if looking for a trace of the strange red-orange hue that we'd noticed our uncle adopted as well.

I nod at Kestrel. "I saw that too. But if my memory serves me right, they've been stained for a while now."

"Stained with what?" Nanny Rutt's question is accentuated by the bottom of the mug she held coming down heavy on the nearby stool.

"I'm not sure." Crossing my arms, I try to scrounge up the memory of a more detailed look I might've taken of my uncle's hands in the past. Perhaps the shape of the stains, or maybe an unusual texture to his skin, but I come up with nothing. Crow would've known. "I assumed it was some kind of paint or ink."

"Or maybe berries?" Kestrel swivels to point at me. "Remember Grandma Aspen's fingers were stained with berry juice all year round. Even Mom's are from making currant jam for the soul cakes and elderberry wine for Hallowtide."

"The only possible witch and poison I know of is sugar plum hellebore, and those flowers aren't red." Nanny Rutt puts her hands on her hips as she thinks. "I suppose it's possible she went a step farther than I ever did and crossbred hellebore with a completely different poisonous plant to create the Phouka and gain control over Death's Reaper. But that's risky witchcraft to do alone, the kind that could leave a witch a walking, rotting skeleton. I find it hard to believe anyone would be stupid enough to attempt that."

Starling makes a curious *humph* before taking out his pocket journal from his trousers. He flips through the cream pages, skimming over his cramped writing. While he searches inside what Kestrel would call *"Starling's little book of poisons,"* Nanny Rutt waves over another Healer to stay with the dying hybrid before ushering us away from the cot. The ex-witch hums to herself and sweeps us toward the Apothecary again. "Come along."

She nods at The Sun and Moon as we pass, and the couple exchange a look like the passing of a note. They must know something is wrong by now, maybe feeling a disturbance like Time did. He was free to storm the glade, but this pair have always taken their duty here very seriously. And more often than not, that means protecting and caring for helpless humans and faeries instead of spearheading issues of the magic variety. Although judging by the hint of a frown that The Sun tries to keep from his ebony face, I have a feeling The Numina will join us in the Apothecary soon.

"What do you mean she has a sister!"

Hazel's yell urges me over the threshold after the others, making the door close behind me with a violent thud. The ageless Healer now stands in the middle of the shop, prodding her presumably still queasy stomach with firm fingers.

80

"Who are we talking about?" Starling asks, nose still buried in his book.

Hazel's fingers slide up to pinch the bridge of her nose. "Baba Yaga."

"Like Baba Yaga, Baba Yaga?" I gape, glancing at the Numina creating a gloomy, pooling umbra where she sulks in the farthest corner of the room. "The same witch that took Auntie Rose's eye?"

"Indeed," Nanny Rutt says, her elbows resting back on the edge of the front counter. "My territory neighbored her sister's, Baba Roga. Nasty little thing," she tuts. "Witches don't encroach on other witches' land. As you know, they're solitary creatures, and what minor bogeys or prey that do take up residency, we owned. We didn't hunt in each other's territories, or cross-contaminate our poisons, unless we wanted to see who could drag who to Purgatory first. So, where Baba Roga's West Woods started, my plains ended, and that was the line that was never crossed."

"And she's important because..." Time starts from the seat his wife once occupied, features becoming long-suffering. "She's one of the three still alive, isn't she?"

Nanny's head lolls to her shoulder as she answers him with a breezy tone. "The last I heard, before I gave up my wolfsbane, Baba Roga was alive and very angry about her sister being burnt to ashes by The Numina." The ex-witch's head flops to the other side as she muses, "Admittedly, she didn't seem like the right fit after the children told me about stains on the Reaper's hands in the Infirmary. And from what you've all told me, she still doesn't. But if the prophecy is saying otherwise, then I'd feel comfortable betting one of my own pretty gray eyes that the old sugary Nightmare Weaver's web is the one to follow."

"Any reason you failed to mention these little tidbits sooner?" Time exhales slowly.

Failed seems like a tame word, considering The Numina

have been hunting the last three witches for quite a while, once including the ex-witch herself. And Nanny Rutt just admitted to knowing the identity of one of them and where she lives. Knowing the reformed woman's propensity for still being somewhat mischievous and sly, I can't say I'm totally surprised. But I am somewhat surprised, since she works under Hazel, and the immortal is a woman to behold. Especially right now... Nanny is very lucky that looks cannot kill.

"You're a Healer for Timesake," Hazel scolds, words steeped in ice. Though she melts a little when she turns to her husband, whose name she took in vain. "Sorry, my love." When Icarus waves her off with a loving smile, she turns back to Nanny, hardened once more. "We're responsible for treating the illness she most likely created!"

Nanny cackles, then sobers after a withering look from the fuming Healer. "I can assure you the Stygian Brume is not Baba Roga and her hellebore's doing. Her witchcraft is not capable of something this deadly and widespread."

Hazel's glare deepens. I'm not even on trial here, and I want to lower my head in shame. Kestrel, who stands just beside her, shrinks into himself to avoid getting hit in the crossfire. Starling is still preoccupied while Auntie Rose remains obscured. Time, however, fawns over his wife with a proud, honey-eyed gaze.

"Look, I apologize." Nanny Rutt stands, straightening her Healer belt with pink-tinged hands. "Some habits die hard; I'm working on it."

My godmother's gaze is alight with shades of glacier and hickory fire. She takes a slippered step forward with a livid finger leveled at Nanny Rutt. I grimace when she opens her mouth, but nothing comes out. Hazel presses her lips into a firm line and balls her hand into a fist before lowering it to clench at her side. "Listen to me closely. *You* are a Healer now; you live by a code, and you abide by *my* rules." Hazel shakes her head in what looks like disappointment. "I don't need you here. I have enough Blessed hands to help. But I want you here because this family of mine believes in second—heck—even third, fourth, and fifth chances."

Hazel's spine straightens, and she points to the Infirmary door.

"So, I'm going to go back there and salt every square inch of that room, and when I'm finished, you will oversee the front and back." Nanny blinks in quick succession, though my godmother's voice prowls forward strong. "I'm certain The Sun and Moon will need to shift their focus to the prophecy, so I'm relying on you. Do you hear me?" Hazel tamps her toes into the floor, eyes flicking over me, my brothers, and back. "My godchildren are in dark hands, and if you know anything that can help them get their siblings back, you will tell them. Do you understand me? You will tell them how to get those babies and that stupid goblin boy back home." Hazel presses on. "We are going to finish this battle. And once every witch is gone, we are going to live happily ever after. You got it?" The Healer's light-blue dress sways around her feet, but she stays rooted until Nanny Rutt responds.

She gives the barest of bewildered nods. "Yes, ma'am."

"Good." My godmother takes this as her cue to unearth herself, giving a tired, albeit appreciative look to her quiet, starry-eyed husband. The loving exchange is brief before Hazel stares at the shadowy smudge in the corner with concern. She pauses for one moment, two, and then she's on the move. Despite his indignant squawk, Hazel tugs Kestrel's head down by a rippled ear and kisses his cheek goodbye. Starling is absentminded as he stoops down for her to press her lips to his cheek without being asked. And when she makes her way to me, my tear ducts sting.

"Such a gentle heart," Hazel murmurs as she cups my face and settles a kiss between my brows.

Before she disappears back into the Infirmary, there's a

multitude of promises to be careful, along with declarations of love and bestowed wishes of good luck. And when Hazel pauses with her hand on the doorknob, she closes her goodbyes by saying, "And Starling?"

"Yes?" he answers, continuing to fixate on locating whatever it is he's looking for inside his journal.

"Your sister is in charge."

Hazel's halfhearted laughter is swallowed by the Infirmary door clicking shut. From his seat on the stool, her husband chuckles at my brother's annoyed grumbles. Though seconds later, Starling makes a declaration of his own.

"Aha!" He holds his journal aloft with a smirk. "I've been keeping track of all the witches The Numina tracked down and what their pick of poison was. Whenever I heard whisperings of names or plants in the villages, or when new travelers passed through, I wrote them down. I've organized my charts perfectly and kept diligent notes while researching each plant's properties and effects." Starling laughs to himself, side-eyeing me with a cocky glint to his seafoam orbs. "I think Dad would be rather impressed—"

Kestrel groans—much louder than necessary—to cut our brother off. "All right, chatterbox. Spit it out."

Starling huffs. "I was going to say that I have an unassigned plant written down. Bloodroot. I overheard some folk mention it a handful of months ago." He wiggles his book in the air. "Auntie Posy took me to the Great Library at one point, and I did some reading. My notes state that red sap leaks from the flower's roots, and it can lead to heavy staining. It's toxic if your skin absorbs it or if you eat any part of the plant, and it can make you highly susceptible to your surroundings. Or I guess in Uncle Grim's case, suggestion and control."

"On the off chance that Baba Roga hasn't combined her hellebore and a bloodroot plant, do you know which hag could just be using bloodroot?" I ask.

My brother's head bobs side to side as he weighs his thoughts. "Well, I have multiple variables, and according to—"

"Starling, I love you so much." Auntie Rose speaks up for the first time since we entered the shop, and steps from her brooding cloud. "But please get to the point."

Judging by the complicated dance of his thick eyebrows, my brother fights the urge to say something mouthy. Opting to play it safe, Starling sighs and says, "There's a handful of names I never matched up. Like Madgy Figgy—"

"Nope, she's dead," Death replies.

Starling's pen scratches over his paper. "Uh, Churnmilk Peg."

"Also, no," Time points out.

"The Noon Witch."

Nanny Rutt jumps in and waves her hand. "Never heard of her, so I call fable."

"The Cornflower Wraith."

Kestrel laughs. "Think about what you just said before. Bloodroot? How would Cornflower make sense?"

Starling rolls his eyes for the hundredth time today. All the while, the name makes something buried beneath my mental attic scratch at its floorboards.

"What about the Rye Mother? Allison Gross? Mama Padurii?" my brother offers after crossing out the other names.

Time holds up three fingers. "I recognize the third one; you can cross her out."

"And the Rye Mother is just a bogeyman," Nanny snorts, shifting her attention to pick at her pointed nails. "Not a witch."

"I've never understood how that works," Kestrel mumbles to himself as he scans the bundles hanging from the rafters.

"A witch is always a bogeyman, but a bogeyman isn't always a witch," Starling quips. "It's simple, like squares and rectangles."

Kestrel double blinks at him.

"The Rye Mother." Auntie Rose's shroud parts, slipping back

into her crown to reveal her pearlescent face. "You said she *is* a bogeyman, not *was*."

Seeming to pick up on her train of thought, my godfather comments, "They're small pond guppies in comparison, but there should only be a handful of bogeys left excluding the witches. I'm assuming you know where she lives, too?" he asks the ex-witch.

Nanny glances up from her pinkish talons with a flippant laugh. "Well, of course I do, right down to the very patch of dirt. She lives directly on the border between what was my territory and Baba Roga's in the West Woods."

A collective sigh ricochets around the room. Talking to Nanny Rutt can be like trying to herd cats into a partially built, booby-trapped maze...but I suppose at least now we know where to start.

Swan: A Blessing of Destruction

"Can you draw them a map from where the Rye Mother lives to Baba Roga's house?" Auntie Rose asks the poison-scarred Healer.

"No can do," Nanny Rutt purrs. "I've obviously never set foot inside Baba Roga's territory, but stories of her home have circulated for hundreds of years." The woman's gray eyes turn to my siblings and I. "The safest place for Death to drop you off is my old haunt; anywhere else, and you're opening yourself up for a trap. There are too many unknowns by starting closer." The Healer shrugs and scrunches her nose, pink freckles shimmering. "However, from the border, it will take two days to travel to the West Woods."

"Two days?" Starling scoffs. "The full moon is on Hallowtide this year; that's tomorrow."

"Then you'd better be quick. And smart." The ex-witch shrugs again. "If your aunt brings you too close to Baba Roga's house, the fate of The Numina—thus the world—will be in great danger." Nanny swirls a pointed finger in my direction. "That being said, you'll encounter some obstacles on your journey that you must be wary of."

Kestrel and I share a look as he speaks with a hesitant tone. It's very reminiscent of a child asking for a scary story at bedtime, even though they know the thrill will only end in nightmares. "What kind of obstacles?"

Nanny Rutt winks at my brother and pulls herself up to sit atop the front counter. "The bogeyman kind."

"Wonderful," Auntie Rose and Icarus mumble in unison.

"Like I said, beasties could live on my plains and within Baba Roga's woods to create distance between me and her. Considering we all sustained ourselves on things like hate and jealousy, a minor bogeyman's mere existence made sure we witches would never cross where we weren't welcome. Not that we really cared to anyways." Nanny pulls up one of her legs and folds it beneath her. "As I mentioned, the first bogey you'll encounter is the Rye Mother. Her domain is a large crop, and the straightest route to reach the Woods."

"Well, that sounds easy enough," Starling says, nonchalant as he slides his journal and graphite across the wooden countertop. "If you can't draw a map, can you write down coordinates to the border?"

Without so much as a word, Nanny Rutt takes the small book and scratches something onto one of the available pages. Starling is handing it to Auntie Rose to read when the ex-witch continues, "Perhaps traversing through the crop will be easy, but that's only if you don't come in contact with the rye stalks. Should your skin touch the grain, you will experience painful hallucinations. The kind that will hinder you and allow the Rye Mother to track you down and—for a lack of better words— harvest you."

"I would prefer to avoid this." I raise a hand to shoulder height, an action that's purely Kestrel. It's more proof that I spend too much time with my brother; his mannerisms have integrated themselves into mine.

Nanny Rutt swings her leg. "Then don't let the rye touch

you. And should you not heed this simple warning, well…move fast before the wolves come."

"I'm sorry, there's wolves now?" Starling huffs. Our aunt reaches across Nanny to slide his journal back to him. Then, she drapes one hand over the shears at her hip. There's something absent about her as her other hand scratches at the numerous black rings marking her arms. Even Starling watches her with scrunched features while he stuffs his belongings back into his deep trouser pocket.

The Healer hums in confirmation, pulling my focus back to her. "The Rye Mother is somewhat of a shapeshifter, and the hallucinations the field can induce will make you see multiple forms. But only one of the many wolves you could encounter is truly her." Nanny's leg skips a beat as she finally seems to notice the weight of the dark Numina's emotions. Auntie Rose is shifting her weight from foot to foot now, casting looks toward the front door while Nanny Rutt resumes her instructions. "Again, I beseech you children not to let her touch you."

"Okay." Kestrel vigorously nods. "Do not touch, and do not be touched. Got it."

"Primrose," Time interrupts. "Why don't you join me and step outside for a minute? I believe I need to get some air. I think some of these flowers in the rafters are making my nose itch." My godfather makes a show of rubbing said nose before crossing the shop in a few long, sandy strides to open the stained-glass door. He holds it wide in a welcoming gesture for Death, one that says, *Here, now's your chance to escape. Flee.*

Undeterred by the apparent fib, Auntie Rose follows Icarus outside to stand beneath the Apothecary's awning.

Nanny Rutt clears her throat and tosses her hair over her shoulder. "Once you leave the field, continue west until you come to an orchard where the second beastie lives. The Gooseberry Wife is terribly simple; only a fool would run into her." The speckled Healer eyes me and my siblings to ensure we listen to her next instructions. "Avoiding her is similar to the Rye Mother: just keep your hands to yourself. Don't pick anything from her orchard, and you'll be fine."

Starling crosses his arms over his chest with a confident smirk. "Easy."

Entertained by this, Nanny takes up swinging her leg again. "From what I know, once you pass the orchard into the West Woods, you'll find a distinct trail to Baba Roga's home. Apparently, it's not hard to miss."

"Do we know what might make this trail so recognizable?" I ask. My mind immediately goes to Mom's storybooks with labyrinths and spools of yarn. And her own tales about wishing for charcoal sticks and drawn arrows in mazes illuminated by blue witchcraft. But soon my head is full of ideas of my own. Everything from bones laid like bricks, to simmering coals, and broken glass. It makes the soles of my feet burn twice as hot as they usually do.

"Well, I can't be certain." The ex-witch shrugs. "But I do know that the sisters were known to welcome two different crowds to their enchanted abodes. Baba Yaga was known to be a hoarder, one who enticed adult travelers looking to trade pieces for the right price. In contrast, Baba Roga is known to lure children who've wandered too far from home or run away from miserable conditions. The difference between the sisters is, Baba Yaga's visitors left her home about seventy-ish percent of the time, but once a child sets foot onto the trail to Baba Roga's house, they're never to be seen again." Nanny Rutt crosses her arms with a needle-toothed drawl. "Stories about her have spread like a sticky web, terrifying the towns nearest to the West Woods. Parents warn their children of her to ensure they don't get out of bed in the middle of the night, consequently leaving the little ones with horrid dreams. Thus, Baba Roga's moniker, The Nightmare Weaver, was born."

Kestrel gulps beside me. Scary story indeed.

I cough to prevent my throat from making the same sound as my brother's. "So, when we find this sister's mysterious house, we're just supposed to go inside?"

Nanny Rutt leans forward. "If you want your family back, absolutely. But remember, Baba Roga is old and dangerous; she's been silent and brewing for a while now, so you have no idea what tricks she left behind." The pink-freckled woman's words are grave. "I meant what I said before; I don't believe she's powerful enough to be responsible for the Brume. And I don't believe the Phouka are of the Brume, so I don't think Baba Roga poisoned your uncle. But chew on this, what if Baba Roga crafted the Phouka to look as sick as the Stygian illness?" Nanny looks between Kestrel and I. "Neither you nor Robin have ever gotten sick on any of your hunting trips. Death has been just fine absorbing the little beasties through her skin and into her shadow." The former witch taps her nails on the counter. My stomach grows heavier with each sharp click. Nanny might have a point. So, I continue to listen. "Phoukas may not be contagious, but they're still a dangerous, impressive trick. They take time to create, and require a form of magic that I don't understand. There is no doubt Baba Roga's home will be fortified, and her craft strong, so you'll have to proceed with caution and power."

At this point, the bravado has fled from Starling, and he sounds unnerved. "Meaning?"

"Meaning, you'll need more than a little salt." The end of her sentence is followed by the sound of approaching feet and the turn of a doorknob.

"Now that Hazel has fully informed us of the situation, we might be able to help," The Sun says. Trailed by The Moon, The Numina glide from the Infirmary into the Apothecary, their presence flooding the space with eloquence. In their presence, I can almost feel the word *eternity*. The word *everlasting* is a like a buzzing inside your ears that you can't quite hear. And the word *immortality* feels like the pressure of a phantom hand, despite there being a hairsbreadth of space separating your skin and its weightlessness. All impossible things, yet here these infinite beings are before me, glimmering gold and silver beneath their skin, flawless bodies of pure magic.

Their splendor is only heightened when The Sun births a resolution tucked between the lines of a short allegory. "Being stuck in The Between was trying. My wife and I were each split in half, flesh and spirit. Our physical forms remained in that liminal space, while our spirits were left to inhabit our numen in the sky. And to think—" The Sun trails off and gestures toward Kestrel. "May I?"

Brows lifting to the rafters, my younger brother lets out an articulate, "Uh?"

But his confusion doesn't last long. The graceful, evergreen being is in front of him, plucking an arrow from Kestrel's quiver before standing back beside his star-dusted partner. The feathered weapon looks minuscule, almost like a child-sized quill, in his perennially lucent hands.

The Sun picks up where he left off, now pinching either end of the horizontal arrow. "That needless, violent uncoupling was made possible because a voracious girl—christened by something as sweet as a fruit—committed malfeasance out of discontentment. She befouled herself to the point of no return to seize the magic from Death that she was refused, a power she deluded herself into believing could absolve her wickedness and capture her best friend's forgiveness if she wielded it herself." A slow hemorrhage of sunshine leaks from the Numina's nail beds, and when I meet the bottomless black galaxy of his iris, I latch on to the gold ring shining around his pupil and hang on to his every cryptic word. "The girl only magnified her destruction and plunged everything further into ruin when she sought to kill Death. But Fortune shielded her sister-in-arms. And in the end, with an act of synchronous murder on the first witch's part, and martyrdom on Hazel's, they were both delivered to The Between as well." The light pouring from The Sun's wide hands pulses with the emotions of his memories. They drip with every building syllable, sending shocks trickling throughout my skin. "The world is the way it is right now because of a singular arrow." He rolls his fingers, and the plain wooden shaft between them twists like a roasting spit.

The Sun passes the projectile to The Moon. The salt-infused iron reflects the silver glint beneath her skin; I follow the twinkling from where it dances up her lean, muscled arm to her sharp-featured face. Out of habit, I avert my eyes to stare at the edge of the formidable woman's hair, where it follows the line of her cheekbone. I don't escape The Moon's direct attention because she's a cold person; the empyrean being is quite the opposite, and the creation of the Healers is evidence. But her stoic face and mellow demeanor, coupled with her magnetizing beauty, are intimidating in a way that leaves me starstruck.

Then, The Moon speaks. "When our spirits were bound to the luminaries we each presided over, The Sun and I were forced to watch the land below us change. Witchcraft spread far and wide like dandelion seeds, and its birth grew to strangle everything good around it like milkweed. We witnessed the world darken as it was sewn with bogeymen and fear." Pausing, The Moon runs a nail down the arrow's emerald left-wing fletching. The barbs part under her reminiscent touch.

"Whilst these mutinous creatures ran rampant in the dark, I continued as I did before. I provided a clement, guiding light that influenced the purest things in nature, like the oceans and all the flora you see here." The Numina uses the arrow to point at the Apothecary shelves. "But over time, my moonlight became less of a guide for people to travel, or for animal migration, and more of a tool for seeking safety away from bogeymen. And that just was not enough. Not for The Numina, not our dwindling Healers, nor the humans and faeries we were sworn to serve." The curl of something wry tugs at The Moon's lips. "My numen couldn't provide a single one of them protection or warmth anymore."

The Sun places a hand on his wife's arm; his touch loving as it visibly radiates comfort. "Seeing this, I learned that I could harness the fiery energy found within sunlight, so that in the daytime, it could blaze through creatures of evil and purify the corruption in their veins. Darkness cannot exist in the light, because it cannot look upon its own ugliness and cruelty. In the sun, evil has nowhere to hide. With an abundance of heat, we learned that water begins to evaporate. With that, we discovered natural pure resources like—" The Sun looks deep into his wife's eyes before giving her a proud nod. "Like salt from The Moon's precious oceans that can cleanse the wicked and turn it all to ash."

"And from ash, there can be new life. But first, one must have the tools to slash-and-burn weed-ridden crops and swidden the fields once cultivated with nutriment." The Moon pivots until her body faces The Sun, who mirrors her position.

Then, he clamps his irradiating hands together. "A sacrificial fire, one might say." He pulls his fingers apart. In seconds, the interior of the shop is the sunniest day, making me squint.

My brothers are shading their eyes, but I don't think any of us miss the orb suspended in the air between The Sun's palms. We gape as he turns it, molding and shaping, drawing it out until the orb becomes a rod, a rod that stretches until it becomes a thread. It dances like a tongue of fire, and The Moon holds out the arrow. Soon, the thread of fire is reaching, writhing until it finally winds around the wooden shaft. The Sun lowers his hands and the thread sinks into the grain; the arrow glows like molten metal straight from the village forge.

A sudden plume of fire from the fletching makes me gasp; Kestrel trips backward, Starling jumps, and Nanny Rutt puts both legs up on the counter for safety. But the green feathers don't burn away. Instead, they smolder like embers. The Moon wraps her hand around the fletching, and I gasp once more, expecting her to cry out in pain. But the Numina isn't burnt. She releases her grasp, and what I see of her skin is perfectly normal, at least according to Numina standards, almost like the arrow she holds, which looks no less ordinary than when her husband pulled it from Kestrel's quiver. And it would be just as identical too, if it weren't for the previously green fletching now being a vibrant red. My tingling fingers want nothing more than to hold the arrow, to know if I can feel the infused magic. What would it be like to nock it? Would there be a perceptible enchantment zinging down to my bicep as I pulled back on the bowstring? *Oh, how I could make it fly.*

The Sun gently takes the Blessed weapon from his wife, and my heart leaps. What an honor it would be to receive such a gift after years of lessons and grueling practice. My burning toes curl in my boots as the ancient Numina approaches.

But it's not me he gives it to. It's Kestrel.

"Uh…" my brother states again, the arrow shaft now sitting in his splayed hands with his wrists awkwardly at his chest.

Like salt dousing a snail, I shrivel into myself, hurt but also embarrassed as my heart takes a very humbling plummet. I'm a fool. Of course The Numina would want Kestrel to use the Blessed arrow against Baba Roga. It was stupid to assume they'd bestow such trust on me. My brother is the one with a magic gift from the elder twigs constructing his changeling heart. *He's* the one with an ability fit for a supernatural hunter, perfect for this kind of divine responsibility. Not me. I'm capable of average errors, such as missing a target anywhere from a few millimeters to several feet. No matter how bad I want or need one, I don't possess an inherited gift. For all I know, the twigs in my chest are useless and without a drop of magic to be found.

Kestrel clears his throat and stutters, "I—I don't think I'm the right one to—"

With a small shake of my head, he stops. In a matter of seconds, we have a whole conversation with only our eyes and minute movements of our faces.

Now is not the time to argue, Kestrel.

It should be you.

No, it shouldn't. And you know it.

I don't like this, Swan. I don't want to do it.

It's fine, I'm okay.

But—

Now is not the time to argue. Put the arrow in your quiver.

But—

No buts.

Fine.

Sliding my gaze past Kestrel's shoulder as he does what he's told, I see Starling. To my great surprise, his face is not a mask of mirth like I would expect, having seen my small moment of humiliation. My brother almost appears indifferent. Almost. His calculating stare takes in the arrow, our brother, then me, and glazes over Nanny Rutt to The Numina and me again. I'm not too sure what he's thinking. We don't have silent conversations anymore, not since I started training with Dad. That was when he distanced himself from Kestrel and me.

The Sun's rumbling voice draws me back to the present, and just in time to hear his instructions based on the brief they said Hazel gave them in the Infirmary. "Once you reach The Nightmare Weaver's West Woods, locate her so-called web. When this arrow hits, it will deplete acres of land, destroying the witch, any of her enchantments, and everything she has infected: trees, roots, soil, and all."

"A bonfire." Kestrel rubs his hands together as if trying to warm them on a bitter, cold night. "Sounds cozy."

In tandem, Starling and I smack our younger brother's arms with the backs of our hands, and the ex-witch sitting cross-legged on the counter snorts.

The front door of the Apothecary opens, and Icarus slips inside. "Kids, don't hit your brother."

I think I see Kestrel sticking his tongue out at Starling in my peripheral, but I'm more focused on Auntie Rose still standing outside the shop. The way she crosses her arms to hold her elbows reminds me of sticks at the mouth of a dam. Sometimes, they can hold everything together, but if a strong enough current comes around, everything being held back will pour out. I don't know what that would look like for Death, and I'm almost afraid to find out.

"Time, we must discuss the eclipse and fulfill our end of the prophecy," The Moon says, pulling the sandy Numina into the conversation.

"Certainly, you must know that there is no eclipse on Hallowtide," he chuckles, though it peters off into something stilted. He is talking to one-half of the party that makes such a thing possible, after all.

The Moon has a razor-sharp brow arched as she administers a blunt explanation. "Which means we must make sure that there is one, yes?"

"This kind of magic could be crippling," Time says, tentative.

"Hence, you must join us in this task at Wyrd Mountain while we trust our Healers to protect this shop," The Sun retorts. "From what we know, the children's days of travel are numerous. Even if the prophecy did not mention an eclipse, the journey would still be impossible to complete in time. That is unless time itself can be slowed to the right moment."

"If the three of us devote all our energy and attention to this feat, we should be able to give the children those extra days," The Moon adds.

Icarus closes his copper eyes and rubs the bridge of his nose in a manner that I've seen from Hazel thousands of times. He stays this way for several heartbeats before conceding. "While you two grapple with the last phase, I can slow time, but I can't usurp the balance and stop it fully. Everything existing and living on this plane will continue moving, including the elements." He turns to my brothers and me, his focus jumping to each of us individually like a game of visual Leaptoad. "This strange kind of interference in nature could make the impossible possible. There will be bogeys out at all hours." Time sweeps a longing glance to the door behind the counter where his wife is lining the Infirmary with an extra barrier of salt to reinforce what was already built into the walls. "It's dangerous for all of us...but necessary."

"Indeed," The Sun agrees. "We can only hold this amount of magic for so long, and there will be a cost to slowing the luminaries cycle; we will be drained and of no other help to you afterward. You must fulfill the prophecy before the end of the eclipse."

The Moon cocks her head. "The sky itself will hang in a sustained interim between night and day; this could be less than ideal during your travels. Which is why I will present the three of you with this—"

The eye in the middle of the Moon's forehead illuminates first, throwing a ray of silver light past my head. When the other two orbs do the same, the Apothecary becomes a shower of fractured color. As the Numina bows her head to ignite her hands, the cast of hues race from the stained-glass window behind me to follow her. The halo around her head glimmers, like that of an angel. In this moment, the Moon is an ethereal effigy, as if she were a mythological goddess raining power and light from her depiction in the pane of a cathedral window. Ribbons of transparent rainbows dance within her moonlight, twisting and bending, flaring brighter and then dimming again and again as something takes shape in her grasp. She is beautiful and terrifying, and I want to retreat to my attic to write poetry about these windows. But I resist. I must.

I'm gasping, and the breath leaving my lungs is drifting,

yearning to be in her magnificent space as she works. The very air from my body tangles itself within the edges of the short pillar that appears. It intertwines with the white wick that grows from the swelling wax like a swath of silk. And it drips down to the chamberstick that now sits in her palms. Slowly, the light of The Moon's metallic eyes wanes, but the candle she's created stays lustrous. Making it so bright that I can only see the magic object's silhouette. That is until The Sun bends, snowy coils falling over his shoulder to hang at his waist. The divine, celestial being blows on the unlit wick as if snuffing out a flame.

The Blessed candle is revealed.

The round wax pan of the chamberstick stand is an elegant mix of silver and golden brass blooming with dreamy designs. And like a swan neck, a matching index-finger-sized handle curves from the edge. But the candle itself is the most captivating part. It's the width of a taper and the length of a pillar, and its glowing, star-like sigils twinkle over the otherworldly surface, highlighting the wax's strange phosphorescence. The candle appears both see-through and solid, not quite solstice blue or equinox purple, but somewhere in between. Though, it's clear that the slight cylinder is mighty. Without a lick of fire, it radiates outward, creating a perimeter of misty light nearly five feet from The Numina.

"This candle will light your way." Amused, The Moon beams at our awestruck wonder. "Although," she continues, looping her finger into the hole of the chamberstick to hold the candle with one hand. She closes the other into a loose fist that faces the rafters. "Like any magic, it has limits to maintain the balance. You may only light the wick once and may only light it with"—a glimmering light shines between her curled fingers, and when The Moon unfurls her fist, an open box containing three ornate silver matches sits inside her palm—"something born of magic. I would advise you to use these wisely." The triple-eyed woman gazes up at her glittering counterpart.

"Much like my husband's offering, the candle will burn with the same heat and purifying intensity as the sun itself. But to give you this constant weak light, the radius of this powerful fire will be much smaller. Perhaps only an arm's length away. So, only ignite it in the darkest time of need."

The Moon steps forward, ready to offer up the candle to the first taker. Since the arrow was forced upon him, Kestrel stays rooted in his spot. I'm surprised when Starling turns. And not towards the Numina's sharp features and outstretched hands, no. He turns towards one of the Apothecary's nearby shelves and scans it with what appears to be the guise of disinterest. My brother even plucks a corked bottle of Hazel's special clotting powder that almost instantly stops any wounds bleeding and shakes the muted sage mixture. I know from experience that one of its secret ingredients, besides a touch of Numina magic, is Woolly Lamb's Ear leaves and dried yarrow flowers. The ground petals stud the confectioners' sugar-like powder with specks of white, pink, orange, and yellow. Starling shucks a shoulder of his bag off and fiddles with the closure to slip the bottle inside.

Thus, I am left to accept The Moon's Blessed candle.

I can't help but cradle it in my palms, feeling the coolness of flat metal chamberstick against my burning skin. I'm afraid of breaking the pan. Or somehow achieving the impossible and lighting the wick just by looking at it for too long. My thoughts must be written across my face in bold ink because The Sun lets out a chuckle that sounds like summertime to my pointed ears.

"Here, for safekeeping." Before my eyes could process it, he'd handcrafted me a custom bag to safely carry the precious, invaluable guiding munition. It's a unique piece of art too; the embossed leather bag attaches to my waist like a belt and around my thighs with gilded buckles and stamped grommets. There's a compartment in the embroidered top flap for the box of matches to go. When I unhook the crescent-shaped closure, the walls fall open like origami pieces so I can remove the candle with haste. Then, upon layering them back in order, the candle slides in, and the leather walls hold it in a beautifully tailored, snug fit. The handle of the chamberstick pokes from a small opening in the side whenever I need to grab it. But even with this slight opening, not a drop of hazy light spills out.

Still, even after I secure this Blessed item to my body, I'm nervous—my hand hovers above the bag.

"I can assure you, our gifts are not fragile, Swan," he says, folding his perpetually glowing hands before him. "Neither my tailored arrow nor my wife's candle will suffer the breakable fates of their ordinary equivalents."

Starling snorts, smirking at Kestrel as he secures his strap back on his shoulder. "That's good news for a klutz like you."

Kestrel frowns and lightly kicks at our brother's ankle. "That's good news for an oaf like you."

The smirk drops from Starling's lips to mirror Kestrel's, and quicker than a viper, he lashes out and thumps Kestrel's forehead with the back of his pointer finger. Embarrassed, I ready myself to scold my brothers for their behavior in front of the ancient Numina. Especially before Kestrel does more than gasp at Starling with a yawning mouth and retaliates with some sort of sizable floppy movement that could end up breaking our godmother's shop. But a figure out the front window with a wispy crown is waving, trying to snag our attention and beckon us outside.

Bumping Kestrel with my elbow, I jerk my chin towards the door. "Auntie Rose is waiting for us." The two changeling boys put space between themselves, peering out the window to validate my findings.

"Best of fortunes to you, children." The Sun gives my brothers and me a deep nod, the gold band across his brow winking with the movement. "We will depart for Wyrd Mountain shortly to adhere to our promise."

The Moon's nod to us is shallow in depth, but there's a lightness to her when she gestures onward with an airy hand. "Consider this a head start."

As we take our leave, Nanny Rutt calls out, "Everyone and everything is counting on you. Raze that hag's land to the ground!" When I glance over my shoulder, the ex-witch is sitting back on her hands, legs dangling and lazy as they kick. "No pressure." Her tone sounds feline, which would make one think the woman is being insincere. But somehow, through her sharp teeth, I see the empathetic concern when she winks and mouths, *good luck*.

I only get three steps back into the moldy, damp street when Auntie Rose touches my elbow. "I need to talk to you for a moment, chickadee." She pulls me away as my brothers and godfather start the rumblings of what sounds like going over our half-baked plan again for good measure. My aunt guides me under the edge of the Apothecary's drippy awning, drawing us far enough away that any words we whisper won't be heard.

Death's expression as she chews at the thin skin of her lower lip appears pained, mentally and emotionally tortured. An opalescent hand hovers at her belt where her famed dagger-like shears are sheathed. Her fingers twitch above the charcoal-colored bows, but she doesn't put them inside the rings. It's clear that she's been debating something. "This is for you," she says, sliding the shears from her hip and flipping them to hold the end of the closed blades. She offers me the handle. "To use in an emergency during your trip."

"I'm not sure I understand." I gape. What use would I have for the tool the Numina uses to sever people's threads and clip them forevermore from this earth? "I don't think my parents would condone using this on Starling if you consider his mean streak an emergency," I chuckle, voice wavery. Despite my hesitant confusion, and ill-timed humor, I reach for the shears anyway. When they touch my skin, I snatch my hand away with a sharp intake of autumn air through my teeth.

The metal is cold, unnaturally so. Like it's been submerged in some mystical frosty water—scratch that—an icy river of loss. Auntie Rose doesn't appear surprised by my reaction, and she makes no effort to comment on the shears' strange temperature. Baffled, I do nothing but point where they still lie in her grasp and deadpan, "That is not normal."

"No, no, it's not," she confirms. "They became this way when I annealed them with salt. It essentially had the same effect as sharpening a blade on a whetstone, but that's beside the point, because, unlike your knives, my shears are meant for more than trapping a Phouka." Auntie Rose grabs my hand and presses the dull handle of the cutting instrument into my palm, forcing me to hold it and adjust to the cold. "If Grim comes after you or your brothers, and all other measures fail, use them as the very last resort."

She seals the shears-turned-weapon and my hand between hers. The hand covering my tingling fingers tightens, and I lift my head to meet my aunt's stare. The tiger's eye stone is glassy, but her silver one is steel. There is an air of sorrow around Death, but there is no fear in her gaze. She has bestowed this trust in me, armed me with something that could kill Uncle Grim with one single snip, yet she isn't afraid. Like me, she wants to protect our family, even if it comes down to cleaving her other half.

"I'm going to try my best to find a way to bring him back and fix him, even if it's the last thing I do. But if worst comes to worst, and Baba Roga makes Grim hunt down another one of you kids—" Auntie Rose stutters. "If someone must release Grim by putting him to rest, I want it to be me. I don't want that act weighing down on anyone else, and—and I think he'd want the last hand laid on him to be mine. And if that's not possible... well, I doubt you'll be able to see someone's thread the way I can with these, but intuition tells me if you aim the blades at his chest, you can't miss the cut." A fatigued, rueful smile slumps its way across her lips. "So, before you wield these," she says, releasing the shears into my grasp to bear the weight of magic, responsibility, and consequences forged inside them. "I need you to at least try to do whatever you can to avoid being taken without getting yourself or your brothers hurt in the process. Can you do that?" Auntie Rose asks.

This is a big ask for me; it would be a big ask for any teenager. Heck, anyone of any age. But my aunts were my age when they had to take on a world-ending, or saving, responsibility, and they accomplished what they set out to do. They came back as different beings in every way, shape, and form, but they struggled, survived, and saved us all. If they had to do that, then so can I. That's why, when standing eye to eye, I look into the face of Death, forever frozen in the body of a seventeen-year-old girl, and croak, "Yes."

Her shoulders droop with relief, though they gradually continue to lower with the lofty weight of guilt. "I'm sorry you didn't grow up in a better, safer world, chickadee. One where life-and-death journeys didn't exist," Auntie Rose sighs, laying a loving hand on my face, her thumb brushing my cheekbone. "Rush and I always wanted you to be a traveler, to write beautiful things about beautiful places. I know someday that will happen, and I can't wait to read all about them."

The embrace Death wraps me up in is like melting into the shade on a hot summer day. I capture her familiar gloaming floral scent and let its comfort infuse my mental attic with a sense of home before she steps away. As she does so, I collect her parting kiss on my cheek like a shell from a faraway beach, and I tuck it inside my music box with every song I've memorized. If only I could seal away these shears of hers as well. Maybe put them in a locked box stored beneath the floorboards to collect dust or in some secret nook to be forgotten. But I can't. Instead, I look for a place to stash them on my body, that doesn't already hold a dozen throwing knives, or a magic candle.

Tucking them behind the belt around my middle, snug and secure between the leather and my cloak suffices. Throwing them into my knapsack doesn't feel right, and this way, it's easy to access...just in case. Once I'm put together, my aunt and I reconvene with my brothers and Time. Icarus is quick to wrap each of us kids up in a hug that smells of sun-warmed sand, salty oceans, and bergamot-tinged beeswax.

"I promise to try to maintain my hold on the miracle that The Sun, Moon, and I are about to perform, but it will be difficult once the eclipse begins. Please know, that as long as you're all caught on an impromptu battlefield, I'll be hanging on to my part with all my might." Our godfather steps back, the sands of time that endlessly trail him crunching under his heel. "I have full faith in you three, and no doubt that I'll be seeing the whole family again soon." He squints as he bestows an encouraging parting grin. "Now, I think we all have somewhere important to be, don't we?" Icarus turns and ducks back into *"Hazel's Herbal Apothecary & Infirmary—Home of the Healers—Makers of Tonics, Tinctures, and Salves"* to bring Hazel to the glade before his quick journey back to Wyrd Mountain with my ailing aunts.

"Auntie Rose?" Kestrel says, shaking the jitters from his hands like drying them without a cloth. "You know where you're supposed to take us with those coordinates Starling showed you, right?"

Death grunts. "Unfortunately."

"I suppose it's time to go then." Starling rolls his shoulders before grabbing her hand and our brother's forearm.

"I suppose so," I echo, completing the physical connection between the four of us by latching on to Auntie Rose's and Kestrel's free hands.

An array of thoughts and emotions visibly flicker over my

family; it's hard to identify the overlapping swirl of them all. The prevalent thing that I can recognize is a sense of understanding. We know that when our feet disappear from these cobblestones, and reappear somewhere earthen and thousands of miles away, the race truly begins. And our lives will never be the same.

Grim: Nightmares

She is evil, and wicked, and all things wrong with the world, and that is glorious. I am her prisoner, but there is no place I would rather be than her bony arms, feeling how her talons make my skin crawl. My rightful place is at her feet watching her spin her web of nightmares through my lashes, the larger birdie I stole unconscious on the earth beside me.

You know him. It's Rush and he is your family.

Shut up. He is nothing and he will soon join his children.

"You did so well bringing us this much bait. You are my favorite little plaything I've made yet, trinket."

Her horrible, silky voice is inside my head again, praising me. It makes my insides turn with what must be pride. When she puts her sharp nail beneath my chin my insides scream. I get the privilege to look upon her unholy face and deep into her bloodroot eyes. I don't ever want to look away from her gaunt features.

Yes, you do.

No, I don't.

I try to ignore that sleepy voice inside my head, but my gaze trails to the gossamer webs of chaos and terror being woven around Rush. Around. And around. Around. And around. The squeal of the decrepit spinning wheel sounds like a choir singing to my ears. I am so full of joy that my eyes leak bloodied sap-like tears.

"Do not cry; the fun has only just begun." She laughs and the grating sound is perfect. She is perfect.

Rose is perfect, you idiot. This is a hag. OPEN YOUR EYES AND LET ME OUT OF HERE!

With her hand on the top of my head, she turns it and forces —no—she graciously allows me to look up. Together, we all watch Rush's prone body being hoisted up, up, up. There, he will stay amongst the others. The many, many others.

"Sleep tight," she cackles. "Do let the nightmares bite."

She was right; I did do a good job. I've gone off on my own without Death and found more Pooka, dragging the faeries here for them to do their work. Now the Pooka are Phouka and they have become the most beautifully hideous monsters. I helped do this and she is proud.

I'm sure Rose will be real proud, too.

I don't care what she thinks. It won't matter soon enough anyway.

You do care; we love her.

No, I don't.

Yes. Say her name.

No.

Do it.

No!

Say it! Say, Rose.

I said no!

Rose. Rose. "Rose."

Rose. Rose. Rose. Rose. Rose. Rose. Rose. Rose. Rose. Rose. Rose. Rose. Rose. Rose. Rose. Rose. Rose. Rose.

"What was that, trinket?" Her head turns in an impressive, unnatural way, gorgeous beady eyes narrowing. "Are you waking up in there?"

She puts the head of her wooden staff against my sore chest and pushes me, making me fall backwards from my knees onto my spine. Her filmy orbs glare as she tuts, "That just won't do."

Now look at what I've done; I've angered her. I would do anything for her, but now I've become her biggest disappointment. So even though the wretch inside my head does everything to fight back, I hardly struggle when she kneels beside me, pulling a healthy bloodroot plant from inside the wide, curled opening of the viridescent ram's horn hanging at her side by a thin gold chain. The white flower's roots drip over my face, its burning red-orange sap hitting my eyes and seeping into my system. My mouth waters only a little bit from nausea, and my legs barely thrash. Her talons hold my squinting eyelids open, and I silently thank her. I am so thankful to her for helping me and for letting me help her.

This is torture, not help. She's poisoning you.

And how wonderful it is, that swimming feeling that overtakes me. That makes me ready to conquer anything she puts me to. However, I'll admit it's unexpected when she removes her staff and grabs my face, forcing my lips open and placing a different, yet familiar, petal on my tongue. This one makes me oh so tired.

This is what happened the first time. We were trapped and forced a small dose of fresh sugar plum hellebore after following a lead we heard about Baba Roga's house from Nanny Rutt. We were put in a light enough sleep that we could be flooded with bloodroot so that when we awoke, we would listen unconditionally to the first thing we heard. It's happening agai—

"Now, when you wake up, do what I say." She grins down at me as my world shuts down and darkens.

Swan: The Plains

*a*untie Rose begrudgingly leaves me and my brothers atop a crest inside Nanny Rutt's old territory. From the hill we stand on, the pastures below look flat, and the flaxen sea of grass seems to go on forever. This is the kind of view where the eldest of poets and novelists would wax about the peace and tranquility of the boundless land. But I know better. My favorite pen would know better. Nonetheless, I still retreat to my attic desk to imagine metaphors, written in outdated freeform rows on cream parchment.

THITHER DREAD *in every dry blade of grass and trepidation in the soft breeze yond churns through the lowlands.*

A haunting history wast sewn into the soil whither seeds of loss and strife wait to claw from the ground cometh spring like bodies from the grave.

There is blood yond watered these fields and chaos that's grown whither bogeyman birthed their own luring plots of destruction.

We wilt carve through the plains waiting for us like sickles, farming the cursed weeds of duty and justice until we reacheth the other side.

. . .

OR SOMETHING along those dramatic lines.

But now isn't the time for flowery words about terrible things. We're on a schedule, and there's ground to cover. So much so that my already numb feet weep at the curves marking the wavy, mountainous hills on the horizon. Hills I know we'll have to climb once we get past the Rye Mother. This less-than-gentle reminder makes me heft my knapsack of food and salt before taking the first step down.

"So," Kestrel pipes up behind me, vowels long and drawn out as he follows my lead. "Are we going to talk about what you and Auntie Rose were whispering about, and why you have her scissors?"

A noise rumbles in my throat as I try not to tumble headfirst down the hill as the toes of my boots scuff along the deep decline. "Is that what you *really* want to talk about right now?"

"Nope," Kestrel says, lips smacking to pop the *p* in his oddly cheery statement. "But I figured, by the look on your face when she gave them to you, it was for an important reason."

A burning sensation blooms in my calves as I continue downward, the clinking of Starling's axes and the heavy fall of Kestrel's steps echoing mine. I'm slow to answer my brother; the pressure of Death's shears against my stomach is weighing me down. The crinkle of parchment as I dig a sunflower cluster out from my cloak covers the click of my dry tongue dropping from the roof of my mouth. "It's for Uncle Grim." I wince. The crunch of burnt sugar and seeds snapping between my molars fills the silence as Kestrel grasps the implication.

None of us speak as our momentum pulls us toward the bottom of the hill, forcing us to trot with clunky feet and aching knees. Kestrel's arms are pinwheeling in my periphery while Starling jogs the rest of the way down. The rough, brittle noise beneath our rubber treads fills the brisk air, before Starling punctures a hole straight through it all. "Do you think you have the guts to kill him?"

"What?" My spine pops as I gawp at my brother. "No way, it's not meant to kill him. Auntie Rose gave me her shears as a last resort; no one is killing Uncle Grim."

Not even our aunt. She was concerned about the impact his death would have on someone's conscience. But what about her? What if my aunt continued being one of The Numina for centuries? How is Auntie Rose supposed to exist without reliving the death of her familiar every single time she looks at her hands? I don't think she could. This is why our family is going to take down Baba Roga and hope that her death will free Uncle Grim. And if it doesn't...well, our family is smart enough to figure something out eventually.

Starling huffs. "Then she gave her shears to the wrong person, if you can't do what might need to be done."

"He's our family, Starling," I say, aghast.

"But what if our uncle killed our little brother and sister? What if he killed Dad?" He shakes his head. "They could already be gone, and he might be the one to blame."

"The witch who poisoned him is to blame." Kestrel widens his stride, matching with Starling to better see his pinched face. "When did you start to believe in an eye for an eye?"

A tense handful of seconds pass. Starling's jaw jumps with the force of how hard his teeth press together. "The moment I realized Robin was gone," he answers.

The emotion in his voice stuns me. My insides are off-kilter as I turn my face away from him to look at the sky. The Sun, Moon, and Time will start working their magic at any point now, and the strangeness of the world suddenly crawling at a snail's pace would be less foreign.

"She's not gone, none of them are." Kestrel's voice is firm, resolute. "They're just temporarily displaced."

I can almost hear Starling roll his eyes when he asks, "How can you be so sure?"

"Because we always find a way to survive, no matter what. That's what our family does." Kestrel grunts, and I'm pretty sure he trips before he continues, "Dying isn't an option."

"Fine. You're in charge, right, Duck?" Starling's expression is somehow both expectant and sarcastic. "So, what do we do? Find Baba Roga's lair and waltz right in? Maybe do a fun little dance around any traps and collect Dad, Robin, and Crow like they've been hanging around for teatime?" When I don't respond right away, he falls back a step. "You can't be that naive to think it'll be simple."

A long "*pshh*" pushes from Kestrel's teeth and out his lips. "Well, you're a featherhead, because Swan gets it." He laughs, making his toes clip the heel of his other boot. "Tell him, Swan."

I clear my throat. "I never said any of this would be simple. But The Sun gave us that arrow for a reason, and we'll find the right moment to use it after we discover the witch's home and covertly make our way inside. We even have The Moon's candle for a worst-case scenario. But no plan we make will be foolproof, because we don't know what we're walking into." Glancing at Starling, I can see he's not convinced, so I wrack my brain for an example. "Like when Mom and Dad and Hazel entered Black Annis's cave. They didn't expect a labyrinth, and they didn't expect to be separated inside it. So maybe we use their past experiences to our advantage," I suggest. Kestrel gives me an encouraging nod. "We go in open-minded and try our best to stick together while we locate Robin, Crow, and Dad. And perhaps if everything goes somewhat accordingly, we can sneak them out without triggering any defenses Baba Roga might've left behind. Then we light the house on fire once we're out and at a safe distance." Without even looking at him, I know by the smack from Starling's lips separating that he's about to tear my plan to shreds. The best I can do is develop a shaky

114

"plan B" that might cover whatever possibilities he's about to throw in my face. "Or," I interrupt, "things go sideways, and Uncle Grim is waiting there for us, and the smartest thing is running."

"Like cowards?" Starling bleats out with a laugh.

"No, like levelheaded people. It's not weak to run," I retort. Starling's trying to make me feel stupid, and it's getting on my nerves now. "We don't need to replicate Mom and Dad's plan of distraction and deception. We can run to safety while, presumably, Uncle Grim chases us like Baba Yaga chased him and our aunties in that swamp."

I've learned that not everything in life needs to be fought with tooth and nail. There is strength in knowing when to admit your weaknesses and instead finding strength in strategy. But, of course, you must be able to lower your pride to do so, and I'm not so sure Starling knows how to do that. At least, not anymore. Though in hopes of him understanding this somewhere deep down, I explain this in terms of a plan.

"If he does chase us, then, when we know we're free from harm, the six of us could take a moment of safety, measured by distance, to warn him about The Sun's arrow. This gives him a chance to escape into his shadows before we strike Baba Roga's home like one of The Moon's matches. Her house would be the tinder that burns her territory to ash, and with Uncle Grim gone, we're free to summon Auntie Rose to take us home." The word home rings out and hangs above us, making my ears buzz. My heart pounds just thinking about our triumphant return, and all I can do is hope this plan gets us there.

Apparently liking the sound of my plan, Kestrel turns to Starling with a wide grin. "You've gotta admit, that's not a bad idea."

Starling squints ahead. He chews on the inside of his cheek long enough for me to think he's ignoring our brother before he responds. "It has its holes."

"Aha!" Kestrel snaps and shoves his finger at him. "But holes can be filled. We just need to stay on our toes and work together."

"We each have our strengths, and where there are weaknesses, there's someone to back them up." Maybe it was Robin's sunflower cluster or perhaps Kestrel's sunny attitude; either way, a rare form of optimism warms some of the sadness in me. It even brings me a bit of a smile, which feels nice considering the duress that hounds us.

"Ah yes, one big, happy, gifted family." Starling ensures that he and I make direct eye contact when he tacks on a facetious, "Almost."

May Dad accidentally leave a needle in every article of clothing he sews for you, and may you always find this out the hard way.

Kestrel reaches to cuff Starling's head, but he dodges the blow and dances away. Starling launches ahead of us to walk backward so that his shiny smirk is in full view as he laughs. The warmth inside me dies. Why did I let my emotional defenses down? It's my fault Robin was taken, but there's no need for Starling to continue bashing me; I do enough of that myself. Against my better judgment, I say, "You know, Mom didn't have a gift when she left the glade."

Starling falters but quickly recovers and jogs back a few steps to make up for it. His smile has already melted when I continue, "She wasn't even armed. Besides Dad, all she had when she first went into the dangerous unknown was her old wheelchair, salt, rations, and a book. And she still became the infamous Changeling Queen, Slayer of Witches." Seeing Starling bite his tongue and stay silent bolsters my point. "Mom didn't let disability mean inability for her. So, while my lack of magic is not the same as her illness, my *'difference'* doesn't make me any less capable of being here than you."

With a proud tilt to his chin, Kestrel swings an arm around my neck as we walk. "Now that's gotta be memorialized somewhere important; we could make a painting from that somehow and hang it above the mantel. You're a true poet, Swan." My younger brother rises onto his toes to mash his lips into the top of my head with the exaggerated "*muah*" sound of a toddler-like kiss. "Just a word genius our sister is." Kestrel punctuates his tomfoolery by sticking his tongue out at Starling.

I shove him away and stumble from the momentum with laughter. "Knock it off, you kumquat."

"No, really, it could even be used as a mural in the villages." Kestrel's hand arcs through the air like a rainbow, and he gazes at his invisible trail with starry eyes. "I can already see it now."

"What I can see is Swan not being able to keep up." Starling scowls. "The last thing we need to worry about is her putting herself somewhere she shouldn't be and getting us hurt. Then, we'd have yet another problem on our hands and—"

Despite my brave words about Mom, Starling's jab pierces my biggest insecurity. Maybe he's right. I can hold my own when hunting, but what if there's ever an instance where my lack of a changeling gift becomes the sole reason one of my family members gets hurt...or even killed. My feet slow to a drag, and I follow my brothers in a pained daze. How could I live with such a failure?

Kestrel stops walking until I catch up to him. "You suck, you know that, Starling?" he bites out.

"I'm just being honest," our brother counters, putting his hands up as if they make him innocent.

Kestrel puts a gentle hand between my shoulder blades and guides me to a normal pace. "That's not honesty, man. You're being cruel and trying to get away with it by presenting that garbage under the guise of what you believe is the necessary truth." Kestrel shakes his head at Starling. "Sometimes I think you have a few redeeming qualities, but at the root, you're just a slimy little kelpie."

Starling rolls his eyes and turns to stalk forward. He throws a careless "Whatever," over his shoulder as he goes.

Silent, Kestrel and I climb the next hill side by side. I feel his eyes straying from the peak to poke at the side of my face. And after his tenth glance, I give in and raise my brow. "How can I help you?"

"You know you're better than him, right?" he murmurs.

Said *him* is lumbering ahead, scaling the steep incline. I've been staring at the back of his shorn head for a while now. I've even rememorized the pattern decorating the handles of the crossed axes that bump against the bag strapped beneath them. Starling is a force, not only mentally, but physically and magically as well. I might beat him when it comes to my compassion and empathy, but somehow, I don't think either of those things would help me in a battle against witchcraft.

"Kestrel—" I start.

"You beat him in every way that counts," he cuts in. "No doubt."

I know what my younger brother is trying to do, but under these conditions, all I can accomplish is a grimace parading as a smile.

"Don't let him get to you, he doesn't deserve to steal your sunshine."

A sudden, and divinely ironic moment strikes after Kestrel's compassion. All around us, the world darkens. It's almost like watching a flame about to extinguish. Whatever hint of color in the pre-Hallowtide sky drains away, and the light that slipped through the clouds before is smothered by at least a third. What's left reminds me of the winter airglow phenomenon. There have been many times as kids when Starling, Kestrel, and I would sneak outside and pad through the snow to climb the side of Grandma Aspen's old house after her passing. We'd sit on the roof and look at the white blanket covering the glade, except for the permanent bubble of spring around the flower-laden cemetery where she's buried. It could've been three in the morning, yet everything would be illuminated, like an overcast day but with a blurred, glowing atmosphere.

It seems that the eldest three Numina are at work, and our countdown to the eclipse has begun. What impeccable timing.

I give Kestrel a sarcastic, melodramatic look, glancing at the decelerated sky full of still-moving, moisture-heavy clouds and back. When he registers what he said and pairs it with the sun enchantedly hidden in the dim ether, Kestrel narrows his silver eyes with a deep, comedic frown. The near delirious, tired laughter that bubbles from my loosening chest lightens the crinkles at the corners of his eyes into lines of amusement. And it's moments like these when I know that even on the roughest, saddest, stormiest days, my personal sunshine will always be here with my best friend at my side.

I reward Kestrel's kindness by presenting him with a sunflower cluster. He gasps before snatching the treat from me and stuffing it into his cheek like a squirrel. His drooling smile is lopsided because of the spherical sweet stretching his face. It's so dopey and so wide that it reveals some of his back teeth. When spittle threatens to leak from the side of his lips, Kestrel quickly slurps the liquid back in his mouth and consequently, coughs with the force of it.

It's funny and absurd and frankly a little gross, but it's Kestrel. And it makes me laugh again. "Don't you dare choke on that! No one here will give you mouth-to-mouth if you die."

My brother attempts to stick his tongue out at me, but with the cluster still in his cheek, it doesn't quite work. Though I know what he meant to do either way, so I stick mine out in return before snatching another sweet from my pocket and placing it on my outstretched tongue.

"Will you two stop being idiots and move faster?" Starling grouches. "You're not only wasting my time, but The Numina's as well."

He's right. Though the small joys I share with Kestrel—and the fact that we'll most likely be seeing some rain soon—is enough to keep my bubble bright again. Starling hiking ahead, rude mumblings floating over his shoulder, doesn't bother me anymore. Not even when he periodically glares back at me and Kestrel, perhaps to see if he's brought a tear to my eye, or maybe to check if a wish for us to disappear came true.

The only thing that threatens to burst my improved mood is finally getting a closer look at the ocean of golden-brown grain ahead.

I didn't know until today that rye was longer and slenderer than wheat, and as tall as corn stalks. This rye must be more than six feet, judging by how it rises well above Kestrel's head. It even stretches as wide as it does long. And as we stand in front of the first line, staring down the path-like rows, the grain appears to go on for ages. It'll take well over an hour for us to walk safely through. If we're careful and stay in the middle of the rows, we should be able to pass through the rye without touching it, just like Nanny Rutt warned against. Kestrel and Starling might have a more challenging time due to the width of their shoulders, but it's doable. It has to be.

"This is not just a crop like Nanny Rutt said it was." Starling groans. "We're easily looking at thousands of acres."

Kestrel puts his hands on his hips, nodding. "And somewhere, there's a shapeshifting bogeyman living inside it."

Starling blinks long and slow at our brother. "Thanks for the reminder."

"You're welcome," Kestrel says with a full smile, ignoring the murderous look in Starling's eye.

Before Starling can move to either strangle Kestrel or kick him in the rear, I speak up. "Remember, don't touch the rye, and we should be fine."

Starling crosses his arms over his chest and takes several seconds to look left and right down the outside row. "You don't think we could try walking around the whole thing? Avoid the rye altogether?"

"Nanny said through was the quickest way." Kestrel takes one hand off his hip to wave it at the field.

Starling mimics him with a sour face. "She also used to be a witch."

"Don't be such a pixie." Kestrel waves him off. "You're always seeing the worst in people."

"I'm not a pixie," Starling barks, crossing his arms once more.

Kestrel huffs and copies our brother's defensive body language. "Oh, really? Then you wouldn't mind going in the field first."

Starling scoffs before glancing at the sea of hallucinatory grain. "Uh, of course not," he snickers. But to my ears, it sounds wavery and a little higher than his usual pitch.

A sly satisfaction lifts Kestrel's features as he gestures to our brother like a gentleman leading a lady through a doorway. "All right, then after you, Your Highness."

"I'm going," Starling snaps.

While trying to keep his grin contained, Kestrel points down at Starling's dirty boots. "Your feet aren't moving."

Putting his hands in his pockets, Starling follows our younger brother's finger. "Sure they are."

Kestrel's shoulders shake. "I'm pretty sure they haven't."

"You're obviously not looking hard enough," Starling mumps.

"Pix—"

"Moon almighty! Both of you—" With a huff, I scrub a hand over my face, muttering to myself, "May moths eat holes in every pair of socks you own for the rest of your lives."

Without a second thought, I march into the rye-shaded field and forge a trail. It surprises me that Starling is the one to follow me first, the measured pace of his feet quick behind me.

He's closely followed by Kestrel, launching himself after us with a heavy, uneven cadence. None of us want to be left behind, not here.

A scuffed, clumsy thump echoes my curse.

"Kestrel, for the love of Fate, watch where you're going," Starling rasps.

"Tuck your shoulders in," I instruct, ducking under a stray stalk that bends inward, arching over the pathway. "And don't touch the rye."

"Yeah, yeah." Starling sulks, his voice coming from a lower height as he complies with my directions. "I heard you the first time."

Kestrel squeaks when it's his time to follow suit. "Can we break out that fancy candle so we can see where we're going? I almost got a mouthful of rye."

The airglow sky, the charcoal clouds, untouched by The Numina's magic, continue to coast by. They do us few favors. Notwithstanding, taking the Blessed candle out from my bag would do us even fewer.

"We can't risk drawing any more attention to ourselves." I step over multiple downed stalks in my path. "Let's not forget, a bogeyman calls this place home, and we have no true sunlight to protect us."

Despite Kestrel's grumbling, we carry on in a silent single-file line for what feels like ages, but it's probably just over a half hour. My body is sore from tensing. I'm hyperaware of my limbs and the tingling burn of my nerve damaged fingers. And as I pull my cloak closer around me, it hurts how tightly I clutch at the hole the fox Phouka made. Avoiding the grain gives me terrible posture, but shrinking myself saves me when a slight rain-scented breeze shifts the field. But for all my efforts, my upper arm still grazes a bristly rye spike that suddenly droops toward me.

The three of us stop moving. I hold my breath...but nothing

happens. As if it would make me hear better, I brush my bangs from my eyes until the curls rest against my temples.

The hairy florets had only brushed wool and not my skin, so maybe we're safe?

My brothers and I walk slower after this, focusing on the task at hand, and dodging any handsy stems that lean our way as moisture thickens the noiseless air.

That concentration is how I hear the shift. We shuffle to a stop again.

It's a subtle change in the way the field sways against currents. The sound the rye makes when the stalks connect sounds less like a whisper and more like a hiss. It makes the skin covering the knobs of my spine prickle. The wall of grain ripples to my left.

"Swan?" Kestrel asks, hesitant.

I shush him as I listen to our surroundings. My ears strain until my brain creates a nonexistent buzz. It's a painful kind of false silence that sets my teeth on edge. Gingerly, I turn to face Starling, whose thick brows are drawn tighter than a bow. Kestrel's eyes, over the axes on Starling's shoulders, are a wide, darting silver. We stand like scarecrows, unwavering for a heartbeat, then two. The field engulfing us billows and I tell myself the new movement is just a harmless babbling brook. Though part of me knows it's more like a river that catches you unaware, one with a sudden drop into a raging waterfall that will swallow you whole. But I ignore that thought and breathe for one more withy heartbeat. Two. Then, three. And just when I'm ready to turn around to resume our crawling pace, the rows to my right rustle.

There's no denying it anymore...we are not alone.

Swan: The Rye Mother

"What in The Sun's sweet name is that?" Kestrel whispers, clutching onto Starling's shoulders.

Starling doesn't even care that he's wearing our large, younger brother like a second knapsack when he bends his knees to peer between the gaps in the rows of rye. With a hand pressed to my stomach over Auntie Rose's shears, I bend at the waist and look too. Because the stems of the stalks are thinner, and the sagging leaves fewer the closer to the ground they sprout, it's easy to search the least dense area of the field for the source of the movement. Which is how I end up looking straight into a pair of glowing white eyes.

At first, I'm paralyzed by the blood freezing into strings of ice throughout my extremities. But when a growl reverberates behind us, and the rye rattles reminiscent of a snake's tail, the air my half-filled lungs need is caught in my nose like a flue trap. I can't look away from the peeled-back muzzle full of fetid teeth, but I feel my brothers shift to glance at the beast behind me. For the first time in my short life, I know what it must be like to be hunted as prey, stunned and terrified. It's one thing to be taken by surprise by the things that want to eat you—the very things you thought you could avoid by following an ex-witch's explicit instructions—but it's another to know that these things will chase you no matter what you do.

Starling's russet hands move in front of my nose to break my trance and get my blood pumping again. The frantic forward arc of his index fingers as he repeatedly signs the word *"go"* registers with little thought, and the next thing I know, my feet are carrying me away. Kestrel and Starling's boots pound against the packed dirt close behind me, but they aren't as loud as the growling that now pursues us. With all the noise, it's hard to tell how many supernatural wolves are on our tail, but I don't care to find out. My bag bumps along my back as I duck beneath low-hanging rye and dodge the wavering strands that fall into the path like felled trees.

"I thought the wolves would only show up if we touched the rye!" Kestrel calls out. "What happened to those rules?"

"Not all bogeymen play by the rules," Starling yells back.

"Well, that's not very fair!" Kestrel pants.

"Nobody smart plays fair." In spite of his sharp words and tough act, Starling is only a teenager. He's my little brother, and we're nothing more than a trio of children thrown into a mysterious scary game.

Dad's teenage recountings about Black Annis's cheating ways, flash through my mind. According to my aunts, there was a musical bogey they met on their journey that adhered to the rules of his game, but the Rye Mother is obviously not like him. The snarling and snapping as—dare I say—a whole pack of unprovoked wolves barrel after us is a testament to this.

A rumble of thunder from the stormy clouds above us throws me off pace. I catch sight of the streak of fur and phosphorus-white eyes coming in diagonally from the shadowed rye. It launches itself at me. Throwing my body down, my knee bangs into the ground and a spray of dirt and dust puffs around my face. With grit in my teeth, I turn my chin and shout, "Starling, watch out!"

The way my brother comes to a sudden stop by rearing up on his toes and throwing his hips back makes the wolf pass between us. Through the haze of dusty earth, I still see the beast tumble back into the field and disappear. And at that moment, Kestrel—who'd been looking over his shoulder—slides to a stop also. It doesn't work though, and he rams into an unsuspecting Starling. I spring to my feet, trying to catch Starling as he stumbles forward, but I'm too late. His bare hands are the first bits of skin to connect with the rye, followed by his neck and the side of his face. Starling stands between our row and the next, the grain trampled underfoot. He screams and clutches his face. My fingers curl into the wine-colored wool covering his elbow and yank him back to safety, but the damage is done, and there's little time to waste. I pull him after me with a pale-faced Kestrel behind us. Two identical, skinny brown wolves with matted fur and snarling teeth are hot on our heels.

"It burns," Starling bellows. "My skin, it burns!"

His feet drag as I haul him forward. The end of this cursed field is nowhere in sight. "It's a hallucination, Starling," I gasp, trying, and failing, to find a way out. "It's not real; it's just a trick."

Starling's free hand curls into my hood, nearly choking me as he moans in pain. "It's bubbling! My skin is falling off; I can see it," he cries. "I can feel it!"

With wolves running on either side of us, the rye shifts like the tide. To avoid a wave, I must crouch sideways and pull Starling close to me. I have my hand on the back of his neck, forcing his head down to dodge the stalks curling in over us. Screaming, Starling tries to lower his body further and come to a crawling stop. Kestrel lurches, palming our brother's forehead, and shoving him upward. But even with the both of us now supporting most of his weight, Starling is heavy, and he's slowing us down.

"Pick up your feet!" Kestrel barks at him. "One of these

wolves is the Rye Mother and I really don't feel like finding out which one."

Our brother trips on, shaking his head and clutching his face, delirious. His eyes are fluttering like he's trying to keep them open. But the more he touches his cheek, the further it seems the hallucinations pull him under their spell.

With a grip on the back of his neck, I shake him, knocking his hand loose. "Starling, if you get us killed, I will refuse to go to The After. I'll become a ghost and appear to more than just Auntie Rose and Uncle Grim. I swear to The Sun and Moon I will haunt you so hard, and I promise you, I will be such an annoying ghost that you'll hate the rest of your existence." My brother moves to touch his face again, so I bat it away and harden my voice with a vow stronger than any red-threaded pinkie promise. "You don't want that, do you?"

"No," he groans, and the slightest bit of his sagging weight eases from my shoulders. The sharp sting from my palm, in contrast to the pain of his delusion, must wake him up a little. At least, I hope his lucidity is from me swatting at him, and not the motivation to avoid any mental torture he'd experience from being in my constant ghostly presence.

"Didn't think so. Now, run." I move fast, Kestrel helping me to drag him along. Although, now Starling is making more of an effort.

It's only a few breathless moments later that another wolf blocks our path. The beast looks exactly like the others, but the way its head lowers and its lips curl into a snarl to show its unnaturally sharp, yellowed teeth, is chilling. This Rye Mother's wolf is emaciated, and the foamy drool sliding from its maw proves that the bogeyman—whichever one she truly is—is more than hungry. The rolling bones in its shoulders look sharp enough to poke through its fur as it stalks toward us, ribs expanding with each breath. Copies of this wolf are also approaching behind us, and there's jaws snapping from my left too. Forward is no longer our way out.

All I need to do is make eye contact with Kestrel to know that he's reached the same conclusion. We'll have to throw Nanny Rutt's instructions to the wind.

"This is not going to be fun." I grimace.

Kestrel draws his hood up to cover as much skin as possible before taking the bow strapped across his chest in hand and darting to the right. He plows into the sea of rye like I expected, but what I didn't expect was him using his hands and bow to rip and swing at the grain, boots stomping and flattening as he blazes a trail. Guttural, agonized noises tear through him, but my little brother keeps going, using his much larger frame to attempt to make the field safer for me and Starling.

My stomach turns at Kestrel's suffering, I'm sick for him as we follow his path of destruction. But nothing holds a candle to the nausea I feel when the soft, wispy tendrils of a rye floret leaves a featherlight kiss on my cheek. The bile that scorches my throat is a pinprick in comparison to the fire searing through my face. It's a hundred times worse than the near-constant burning in my hands and feet. Worse than any mental, emotional, physical pain, or depression that has ever plagued me. This is Purgatory. Even Starling hisses anew, but that might just be from my nails digging into the thin skin of his wrist. The rye's fiery sting pushes me faster. I'm towing Starling along, his feet almost going out from under him as he tries to keep up. We even bypass Kestrel as everything in me screams to get out, get out, get out. The burning has consumed every inch of my flesh now.

It's not real, Swan.

All around me, the field blackens, withering and wilting like each stem has been dunked in poison. The leaves drip tar that smokes and sizzles, and the kernels making up the rye florets ooze a stench of charred hair and flesh. Paired with the magic airglow sky, swelling clouds, and pain fizzing inside my bones, my brain tells me I'm melting. I hold on to my face for fear my skin might slough off into the goop collecting beneath me. Something scratches at my brain and tears at the hinges of my attic door. Something that wants me so terrified that I'll stop right here and curl up upon the earth to wait for my death like a crop ready to be harvested.

This is the work of the bogeyman, Swan.

My poisoned instinct wins out and I seek out the wolves. They are rotting. Their skulls seem to smile as they chase us, patches of missing fur showing slabs of muscle and partial bones. These morbid beasts appear dead and decaying, yet still they run, aching for their pound of flesh. They are undead nightmares, full of horror, tears, and maggots.

I need to escape.

But I can't. I can't look away from these grotesque monsters, and it feels like I'm running in place. Or perhaps I've stopped running; I can't tell. Everything is numb, my mind, my skin, my insides. I just want to wake up.

"Duck!"

My terrible nickname peals from Starling's mouth, followed by a sharp clap of thunder that drops my hand from my face. Reality crashes back into focus—and the wolf that snaps at our heels spurs me back to life.

"Run!" I shout, shoving at Starling, urging him closer to Kestrel, who jogs backward, passing the back of a hand over his squinted eyes.

"I think it's wearing off," Starling gasps. "Kestrel, stop touching your face!"

"Short-lived magic, huh?" I wheeze, my body still drenched in a stinging pain.

My brother makes a noise that sounds suspiciously like a laugh as we close in on Kestrel. "The Rye Mother's victims probably never make it this far. No need for a long-lasting effect if your meal usually gives in."

The noise of countless beasts surrounds us, and a particular howl from behind boosts my aching legs. "We're still at risk of being dinner." A whole pack of wolves is wading through the grain behind us now. "We need to go," I urge.

A sharp, tinny sound of metal against metal makes my ears ring as Starling reaches over his head to pull his axes from their holster. "Kestrel, watch out!" he yells.

An unexpected wolf lunges out from the tall rye in front of us, straight at our brother's turned back. Starling is too late. Kestrel doesn't have the time to do anything more than tighten the hold on his bow and flinch before the fabricated beast is on him…and dissolving into smoke. My little brother's shoulders are up around his scalloped ears, and his eyelids screwed closed in anticipation. But when he's not knocked to the ground and disemboweled, he peeks one silver eye open to see the mist that used to be the wolf dissipate.

Kestrel turns. "Uh, what just happened?"

"Look!" I point. Now that Starling and I can see past Kestrel, there's a gap, and through it, hills framed by ominous rainclouds.

We've found the way out.

We book it to freedom. The Rye Mother's wolves are frenzied as they chase us, roaring and howling the closer we get to escaping. The cacophony of pure animalistic frustration makes me smile; we won the bogeyman's little game, and she knows it. I can't help laughing at the sight of the path's end. I'm even on the precipice of cheering. But I suppose there's something to be said about celebrating your victories too early, because presumption doesn't prepare you for the devastation of failure.

It's a terrible, desperate, gut-sinking horror when my brothers and I falter.

We were so close.

Maybe fifty feet ahead, three wolves creep through the golden-brown grain to block our exit. We stop and I turn in a slow, scrapping circle to find we're surrounded, swarmed by the entire pack of identical scrappy brown wolves. And one of these glowing-eyed beasts, licking its discolored chops, is the Rye Mother in disguise.

Taking a small step back to hide the movement, I discreetly brush my fingertips against a blade strapped to my leg. My brothers' backs are against my own. Starling's arms hang at his sides, an axe gripped in one hand while the other rests on the pouch of salt hooked to his belt. Kestrel still grasps his bow, but his other hand remains distinctly arrow free. I'm trying to postulate our chances of escaping, how to narrow down which wolf is the Rye Mother and how to stun or kill her, when the first beast jerks forward. It's aimed, claws first, at Kestrel's chest. A throwing knife is in and out of my hand, in addition to a shower of salt from Starling's fist as soon as its back feet leave the ground. Upon the salt and annealed weapon touching it, the wolf bursts apart like the first one that attacked Kestrel, however this time the mist that rises lingers.

Again, my brother didn't move a muscle to defend himself.

"Now I know what all Nanny Rutt's warnings meant. You never know which wolf is the real deal. She's toying with us," Starling mutters before more salt flies from his hand. Many wolves dance out of the way, muzzles wrinkled and lips frothing with anger. "Turn your back on the wrong one, and you're dead before you know it."

The creatures that meet the white mineral dematerialize, but they still hang around like a smoggy veil of dust. Sadly though, that vapor-like quality changes as the suspended mist gets thicker and clumps together. And the next thing we know, the clumps are funneling to the ground and separating. Where the first wolf my blade touched once stood, now stands three more. Where Starling's second salty attack ruptured four wolves, twelve fill their places. The horrible sight reminds me of an old myth in one of Mom's many books. It's sitting comfortingly on one of my attic shelves, but I can't remember too much about the story besides there being a giant water serpent with multiplying heads. If my panic-hazy memory serves me right, not even a sword could take the monster down. But this is not an ancient heroic epic; this is real life, and reality just keeps getting worse.

The augmented wolves create separate circles around us that prowl in different directions. They seem to weave around each other, creating an impossible snaking pattern that makes my eyes tired and my mind fuzzier. Not a single wolf looks different than the other. Every missing patch of hair is the same, as are the protruding bones, too-long claws, and fuming white eyes full of malice. There is no telltale sign of the true shapeshifting bogeyman, leaving us clueless, and very much in danger.

"All right, it's your time to shine, Kestrel," I gulp.

We could try a process of elimination, and let the wolves pass through us one at a time, but the risk is too great. Any one of them could be corporeal, and she could rip out my or my brothers' throats in a second. That said, the Rye Mother would also be making a huge, albeit calculated risk because once she reveals herself to us with violence, that gives two of the three of us time to fight back. We could try to pick her out faster by scattering all our salt until she's the only wolf standing. That is unless she's quicker and guts someone before we can take her down. Or she gets lucky and fells all three of us one after the other. It's a terrible gambling game of chance and wasted resources, and the odds are not in our favor.

And the Rye Mother's clones, eyes gleaming with wicked intelligence, seem to know this.

I swallow my spit, but it feels more like ingesting a rock.

"Come on. Now's a better time than any to use your gift," I say as I nudge Kestrel with a blind hand. "It's our only way out."

"There has to be another way," Kestrel bleats.

He shifts his feet as if uncomfortable with the mere thought of raising his bow and pointing an arrow at the bogey ready to eat us, a creature of pure evil and ill will. The grating noise of dirt and pebbles crunching beneath his boots peals like a dinner bell. The wolves take this as their cue to turn about and swap places. The two opposing rings gradually tighten, but the wolves are purposeful in their slowness. They want to make us sweat— the bogey wants to play with her food.

"If you don't take out an arrow, we're going to be harvested and gutted like Hallowtide pumpkins," Starling grouches, backing farther into us as the bogeys close in.

Kestrel's arm raises at this. He holds his bow slightly higher than his waist, but it's not high enough to shoot, nor is it aimed at the wolves. Not to mention, there's not even an arrow in his hand ready to be nocked. Kestrel's arm trembles with his choking grip and the wolves grow a foot closer. There's a buzzing in my ears again, growing louder with each advancing paw. Starling begins to shout at our younger brother but it's muffled, it sounds like I'm underwater, so much so that I think I'm calling Kestrel's name, but I can't be sure. The wolves' eyes are so bright, and their teeth so slick. Beads of fear-filled sweat trickle down between my shoulder blades.

I watch Kestrel's arm give out, and wish I would develop my changeling gift, right this moment. *Is this not a great time of need?* Especially when Kestrel lets the bow hang back down at his side? Because my little brother dooms us all.

Swan: Monsters

"I guess it's about time one of us grandkids visited Pop Pop and Grandma Aspen, huh?" Kestrel chuckles weakly, shaky voice piercing my ears just in time to hear an ominous rumble of thunder.

Something in my chest constricts at the sound, tightening, squeezing, panicking with every inch the wolves circle closer. The farther my shoulder blades press into my brothers, the more Starling's elbow jams into my side. The harder Kestrel's shoulder pushes into the back of my head, the harder I find it to breathe. We're prey. Captured like rabbits in a trap, lambs led to the slaughter, mice pinned beneath claws.

"Who knows," Starling scrapes out, anger changing to defeat as a branch of lightning races through the clouds and across the Numina-inhibited sky, "it might be nice this time of year in The After."

The fear dousing my brother's words and my sweat-damp skin must be normal when you come from a family that experiences tragedy after tragedy. Each member has faced some form of darkness, bending beneath the sadness and anxieties that come with every tempest turning our lives upside down. Though, I suppose we always find a way to crawl out from under it all. All of us have seen and experienced loss and battled it personally, some stepping in and out of The Between until eventually, one became Death. But I suppose not even a still heart can hold our family down; it didn't hold back Mom or Auntie Poppy, not even Hazel. And I won't let this bogey—whichever wolf she's masquerading as—take my little brothers from me to do the same.

It's time for this traumatic tragedy in our bloodline to end, and nothing can stop me from making it happen. Not those with evil intent, like the Rye Mother and Baba Roga. Not even those with the best intentions, like The Sun or Moon, could stop me. And they're the brightest, purest, and most powerful, their light is bright enough to cleanse this world. Like we already tried with salt. But The Sun and his fire...his fire is effulgent enough to raze the entire West Woods to the ground. And thinking about those flames, I'm almost positive the flawed hero from Mom's story I tried recalling earlier killed the water serpent and its multiplying heads with a torch. Admittedly, the rye field is not acres of trees, and we're not battling a serpent. Although, if we lit the slippery bogey that rules this place ablaze...well, it might purify the monster and set us free.

Sometimes the cost of freedom is high, and most don't have what it takes to pay it. Those who can't afford freedom must stoop low enough to steal it. I've certainly never been wealthy. But in this life-or-death moment, with Robin's, Crow's, and my father's faces flashing through my mind like the scorching bolts overhead, I'm learning I'm not above theft.

Eyes still glued to the shrinking circle of malnourished beasts, my chin turns toward Kestrel. "I'm sure they miss us terribly, but they're going to have to wait a while longer." Thunder booms above us as my fingers twitch, the tips seeking out glossy elder tree wood. "Which one is she?"

"Swan—" Kestrel begins to protest.

"I'm not asking you to shoot her," I assure him. "I just want you to use your gift to tell me which rotting fur suit the bogey is wearing."

Kestrel's silence is a second too long for Starling. "For Timesake! Duck's the eldest, right?" he growls. "Mom said she's in charge, so tell her where the hexing wheat woman is, or so help me, Kestrel! I know exactly how to poison you and get away with it."

The moment that Kestrel lets go of his hesitation is palpable. His long, emptying breath makes the tension leak from his body. The muscles in his arm uncoil until his hand hangs lower and the grip on his bow looser. Past the pins and needles prickling along the whorls of my fingerprints, I search out the curve of the bow's top limb. When my middle finger brushes the start of the gold enchanted string, the air around us changes. It's not a visible change, it's more of a sensation. Like the tingling creeping along your skin when you know someone across a room is looking at you. Dad has called this subtle change Kestrel's sixth sense, but his changeling gift is more than that. The magic running through the elder tree twigs in place of a flesh and blood heart makes the woven wood into a compass. When my brother calls on it, his gift knows what his heart is set on, and it focuses his desire until it becomes a target. Whether his true wish is to kill, maim, or slightly injure, Kestrel can't miss. Even if his weapon was a broken sword, a halfpence coin, or a dove's feather, his gift finds a way to carry out his intention.

Perhaps that's why his gift works even though he doesn't budge from his strange, unrelenting moral code.

Because his heart knew that when he pointed at the wolf slinking along in the second, farthest ring as it crossed in front of me toward Starling, an arrow would still find its way to it. It knew that as soon as Kestrel condemned the Rye Mother and her front paws crossing into the inner circle of her false copies, I would wrench the bow from his hand. Even if Kestrel didn't know it himself. His heart of twigs knew that when he found his target, I would be the weapon that doesn't miss.

When I position the bow in my right hand, the wolves recognize this shift, and the hair along the backs of all thirty rises. Reaching my left hand out to Kestrel, makes them growl in tandem, creating a dissonance louder than the rain crawling its way toward us. I don't dare look away from the angry beasts to pluck The Sun's arrow from Kestrel's quiver; doing so would be an immediate death sentence…but for whom, I'm not willing to find out.

"Kestrel, give me the Blessed arrow," I demand, empty hand still in front of him and waiting.

The sound of Starling's second axe sliding out of its holster stops halfway. "What?" he yells.

"Uh—" Kestrel hesitates.

The wolves close in, and Starling starts swiping at them with his axes to keep them away. I need to throw two warning knives with the hand I keep shoving at Kestrel, waiting for the Sun-touched projectile.

Starling grunts with each lunge and swing of his weapons. "We can't waste it! Are you insane?"

"We don't have time to fight about this right now!" I knock the side of my hand into my brother's chest before flailing my fingers, begging. "Kestrel, the arrow!"

"Okay, okay," he pants.

Kestrel bumps into me as he fumbles with the wide leather strap that crosses his ribs. From the corner of my eye, he twists his quiver around to paw through the fletching sticking from the tube's opening. The arrowheads rattle as they collide in the bottom of the quiver. Even though I stare down the wolf positioned in front of him, I can see the blip of red amongst all the green feathers, but Kestrel's clumsy fingers keep passing it.

"Come on, come on," I urge, swiping the bow at two

oncoming wolves, who dodge my blow and fall back into their rotation.

"I can't find it!"

To my surprise, Starling shouts at our younger brother. "The red one!"

"Oh Fate. I don't know, I don't know, I don't know!" Kestrel repeats this mantra as Starling's change of tune seems to make him more panicked.

"Kestrel!" I yelp, fingers frantically waving.

A war cry of frustration bellows from his chest. "Have you guys forgotten that I'm colorblind!"

"How have you managed to stay alive this long?" Starling snaps, and the next thing I know, there's an arrow in my hand and I'm turning the fletching toward me to nock it along the bowstring. The second the string is between my fingers, the real Rye Mother makes her move. All at once, the actively multiplying wolves burst into mist. I'm blinded by the murk, coughing and peering through slits, trying to lay eyes on the real bogey.

"To your left," Kestrel chokes out.

Pivoting, I follow his gifted direction and swing the bow to the left. My arrow is aimed just above Starling's shoulder when the Rye Mother launches herself through the vapor. She gets dangerously close to his face before The Sun's arrow flies, but not close enough. The deep *thunk* from the arrowhead pierces her abdomen, and the following *thud* of her fall to the dirt is a sigh of relief. Though this quickly becomes a gasp when the wolf attempting to stand transforms. The creature becomes a woman in a raggedy fur-trimmed dress with an arrow shaft protruding from her stomach. As the Rye Mother stumbles to her feet, dirty hair hanging over her face, the arrowhead inside her glows, and rays of light spill from the hole in her body. In an instant, the arrow shaft turns into gold, molten sunlight, and the garnet fletching ignites into flames. The sound of sizzling skin and bubbling blood is the first thing to spill from the bogeyman as she's purified from the inside out. The second is a shriek that would rival any banshee.

And as if this situation weren't gruesome enough, the Rye Mother looks up at us, hair parting to show her hollow face. She looks more wraith than woman with her white glowing eyes and sunken sockets. The fire that licks over the arrow catches her dress and turns the bogey into a living pyre. The smoldering light bounces off the sharp canine teeth protruding from her gums, making her appear twice as monstrous as she was in her wolf form. It's a horrific sight. Even more so when the stalks of rye behind her catch fire, the power of The Sun's magic spreading out from the Rye Mother as it chars her body. Within moments, the field is aflame, jumping row to row like a line of flammable dominoes.

Yet I can't seem to make myself look away.

I reach out and pat blindly at Starling's and Kestrel's arms. "We need to leave," I croak, smoke and unfortunately the dingy wolf mist caught in my lungs, making my voice scratchy.

Their boots scrape as they turn to jog the fifty feet to freedom, a span paid for with our Blessed weapon. I find myself walking backward, watching the wildfire as it spreads, the heat of it like sitting too close to a hearth. When Kestrel calls for me to hurry, the flames are threatening to trap us inside the field. The Rye Mother drops to her knees with her hands over her stomach before a wall of fire seals her away. I turn and run. Some of the frizzier curls in my bangs are singed by the time I catch up to my brothers. We run until the tilled earth turns to grass and the ground slopes upward. My gut is churning so fiercely that I stop and retch, heaving up nothing but remorse and disgust. And maybe a little bit of undigested sunflower seeds. Kestrel is close, doing the same, bending over to gag on his coughing fits. Starling shoves a waterskin in my face, so I can rinse my mouth of the devastating act I committed. To my relief, he doesn't say a word about weakness at this display. His complexion tends to favor the warm side of brown, though now appears cold and gray. His eyes are glossy, and his nose is running like mine. He doesn't say anything.

And then we keep moving.

We don't stop again until we stand far away, looking down at what used to be the Rye Mother's field from the top of a hill. The land is scorched and dusted with ash, remnants of smoke rising to meet the pewter clouds still heavy with lightning and dripping rain. Usually, the sight of a storm brings me joy. Not this time.

Kestrel is the first to puncture the dreary atmosphere with a snort. "Wheat woman?" He leans into Starling with a goading grin.

"Shut up, her name wasn't important in the moment." Starling shrugs him off with a grumble, making Kestrel hop to catch himself as he chuckles.

Thunder splits the sky and the rain pours in sheets in the distance. This sobers us. Even Kestrel quiets where he settles between Starling and I. The razed land blackens with ashen inky mud.

The Moon used analogies about beneficial fire and agriculture earlier. After the damage from something like a wildfire, the soil is supposed to soak up some nutrients. In time, the land should grow anew and become stronger than it was before. It's sort of a beautiful sentiment, life rebirthing itself from death, but somehow, as I stand here, I can't quite grasp that beauty. Not after what I've just done.

"I know she wasn't a witch and was never a person, human, faerie, or whatever," I muse, gaze fixated on the soggy remnants of the rye field. "But that bogey was the first thing with a real face that I've killed. It feels so much worse than the first animal I ever trapped."

"Hey." Kestrel's touch on my back makes me flinch. "It runs in the family. Murdering a bogey is kind of like a rite of passage at this point."

My brother's chipper tone is enough to make me dole out the kind of disapproving stare Mom would give him for cracking a joke at a time like this. Being his partner in crime, it's natural to find humor in his words. So, even when I shake my head, it's just for appearances. "That's not funny, Kestrel."

With a teasing lift to his brow, his index fingers dig into my side right below my ticklish ribs. "Come on, it's a little bit funny."

I press my lips together and try to keep my amusement at bay; I truly do. But my valiant attempt is easily broken by Kestrel's persistent poking. "Okay, it's sad, but it's a little bit funny," I admit, slapping at his hands until he folds them beneath his armpits with a pleased tilt to his lips. Giving him the satisfaction of my agreeance sedates him enough that I'm able to continue my honest thoughts. "But technically, we were just defending ourselves. And I suppose, morally, that makes this situation somewhat better, right?" My fingers search out the edges of the hole in my cloak, worrying at the fabric as my mind whirls. "That image. The way the flames climbed up her skirts—" I blow an upward breath that ruffles my bangs and lifts them off my skin. "It's going to eat at me, I think."

"I know," Kestrel says.

Now that the Rye Mother's face consumes my mind again, I can't stay still. So I pace past my brothers. Kestrel swivels to watch me, and Starling does what Starling does best, angrily brood.

"Gosh, the weight of something like this, the guilt and sorrow. It's too heavy." Chewing on my thumbnail while I burn my wavering energy only stops me long enough for the warning roll of thunder above us to make itself known. "I already have a hard enough time keeping my head above the water on a good day."

"I know that too. That's what I'm here for," Kestrel pipes up. The first sprinkling of rain drops on us as he continues and motions to his biceps. "I didn't get this big and strong for no reason," Kestrel remarks. Though I still hear his unsaid, *duh?*

Droplets hit the tip of my nose. "You're my little brother. It's not your job to carry my burdens and drown alongside me."

The nature of depression is quiet. It's not always tears and wracking sobs, nor is it always self-inflicted hurt or endless sleep. Yes, there are days that I've wished for that. When I've wanted to stay in my bed with my back to the door and lay there, day in and day out. There are times that I've wished to do nothing and speak to no one. But depression isn't just being sad and dissatisfied with life; its nature is often functional. The reality is there are chores to be done, work to be finished, siblings to look after, aspirations to accomplish, and sometimes a day of absolute numbness isn't an option. This is where its function fuels an anxiety inside me that makes me get out of bed every day and pour myself into my duties and passions. It makes me bundle this downcast mood and shove it down like a secret so that it doesn't affect those around me. I don't want to steal their joy too. My brother and our friendship are the joys that I tend to the most, and letting me share the heaviness that bogs me down puts his sunshiney attitude at stake. Kestrel must know this. He knows me well enough to know that—

His finger held up in front of my nose as he plants himself before me pulls me from my thoughts. "Correction," he dramatically coughs. "I'm your *big* little brother, and I would love to swim with you. Thank you very much."

Starling shifts to cross his arms as he continues to gaze down the hill. His ear is turned toward us, and his jaw shifts as he grinds his teeth. I know he's listening. On any other day, I would be too embarrassed to have this conversation in front of Starling. Maybe it's the effects of new trauma, or a flippant kind of tiredness, but I can't find it in me to care as I continue to stare at Kestrel, unconvinced.

Kestrel rolls his silver eyes before studying his own arms. "Sure, I'm a little more buoyant, but Dad showed me how to build muscle just by working in the barn lifting hay bales and stuff."

The way he curls his biceps to try to see his muscles through the thick wool insulating him is ridiculous. He flexes them hard enough that his fist shakes and his knuckles pale. Although, it's the tip of his tongue peeking out from the corner of his mouth that makes me laugh.

Starling groans, pulling the hood of his cloak up as the rate of the droplets quicken. "Your existence is giving me a headache." He turns from the scene we left far behind with a frown and pats his pockets. When his search comes up unsatisfactory, his frown increases tenfold.

Judging by the lack of color in his face, I'd say his headache is less from our brother's theatrics and more from the lack of sugar in his blood. I can't imagine he'd neglect packing hardboiled sweets for the journey, given that he's had this disorder for years. Not to mention, Robin just made him a whole new batch. He's lucky that I have a few sunflower clusters in my pocket to spare. I'm about to suggest we find cover from the storm so we can sit down to recoup and replenish ourselves, when Kestrel squints at Starling before pointing to his face.

"What's that on your cheek?" he asks.

With the kind of fear I've only seen from Starling after he took a spiderweb to the face while cleaning out an unused closet, he bats at his cheekbone. Frantic, he sweeps and swipes again and again, pulling his hand away to look at his fingers before trying again to remove whatever our brother saw.

"What? What is it?" he puffs with panicked eyes, scrubbing at his skin with the cuff of his cloak now.

"I don't know," Kestrel answers, a slow smile stretching across his features. "It looked like you were turning green for a second. Could that have been jealousy I saw? Are you jealous of my muscles?" He chuckles at the fury tightening Starling's dawning face. "I'm sure Dad could teach you—"

"Shut up! Just stop," he roars. "Stop talking about him—" The rest of Starling's yell is drowned out by another bout of thunder.

The rain is falling quicker now, fat drops darkening the shoulders of Kestrel's burgundy cloak. I make no movement to pull up my hood like he's now done. Our brother's outburst concerns me, and I approach him much like I would an injured animal. "Starling," I start, tentative, "Dad's okay. Robin and Crow, too. They're all going to be fine," I assure him. "We just need to—"

"You need to mind your business, Duck," he spits.

His advancing step toward me is aggressive enough to make Kestrel throw a hand between us. "Whoa," Kestrel interjects, tone stern and gaze just as hard. "That was completely uncalled for, man."

"It's her fault we're even here in the first place! She left Robin and let her get taken, and everything snowballed from there." Starling tosses a shaky hand in my direction as the clouds open up. "You know it's her fault. You won't admit it because you always take her side, never mine. Not anymore," he seethes.

"What in the world is wrong with you?" Kestrel gapes.

Starling points at me, rain dripping from his finger. "She used the one weapon that was going to help us bring our family home! The Sun gave us that Blessed arrow to specifically use on Baba Roga's land. And now look at us!" He gestures down the hill. "Besides The Moon's stupid candle, we are powerless."

"I didn't see another way," I almost whisper, soggy bangs plastering themselves to my forehead as I gently push away Kestrel's protective hand with a slow sweep of my arm. "You must've seen that too, because you handed me the arrow. Besides, I wasn't going to let you two get hurt. It's my responsibility to—"

The sardonic laugh that rips from Starling's throat could only be described as cruel. *"Responsibility.* I'm beginning to think your responsibility is to sabotage us."

My mouth drops, water trickling from my curls, pouring over my Cupid's bow. "Why would I do that?"

"The prophecy is unavoidable no matter what we do or what path we try to take. It said one of us was going to join the dark, right? Who better than the giftless runt of the family." Lightning flashes, illuminating the curve of Starling's weak smirk. "Helping the witches is the only way you can obtain magic, isn't it?" He steps closer, presence looming over me even though I'm only a couple inches shorter. "I bet, for a little bit of promised witchcraft, you sold us out while helping them kill Dad—"

Kestrel lets out a shocked hiss that can be heard even through the rain. "Are you even listening to yourself?" He steps up until he's toe to toe with Starling. "What could possibly be making you so bitter right now?"

Without budging, Starling glares down our brother, shoulders heaving with his rapid breaths.

"Huh?" Kestrel shouts, shoving at Starling's chest so hard that his own hood falls.

Starling stumbles back a step only to move forward and push back.

"Stop," I say, though it almost comes out as a whisper.

Kestrel steps forward into his space again until they're almost touching noses. "Maybe this little show is a seed of darkness." He shoves our brother before advancing again, but Starling does nothing to fight back this time. "Maybe it's you." Shove. Forward.

Starling's arms hang limp at his sides.

"Kestrel, stop," I call out.

"Maybe *you* sabotaged us by giving Swan the arrow." Shove. Forward.

Starling balls up his hands but doesn't raise them.

"Darkness is in your nature." Shove. Forward.

Starling's jaw clenches and unclenches.

"Kestrel, stop it," I warn.

"You've been nothing but a bully for years." Kestrel stops his violent dance, breathing hard as rain slicks down his skull. "The three of us used to be so close, inseparable even." He shakes his head, body practically vibrating. "What happened to you?"

Stalking forward the ten steps they've traveled, I pull back on Kestrel's elbow until Starling is well out of arm's reach. "That's enough," I snap, raising my voice at my younger brother for the first time in a long time.

It's clear to see on his face that Kestrel is surprised that I would defend Starling. As is Starling, but the novelty for the former doesn't last long. "No," Kestrel argues. "He can't keep getting away with treating you like this. We're family. It was supposed to be the three of us until we're all a bunch of senile old fogies wreaking havoc in the glade." Kestrel points a sharp, shaky finger at each of us. "You, me, and Starling. We pinkie promised each other—"

"Starling is kind of right," I shout over the torrent.

Starling shuffles forward, and Kestrel's eyebrows raise. "Come again?"

"The prophecy is unavoidable no matter what we do or what path we try to take. I don't know when Uncle Grim took Robin. But maybe, just maybe, Auntie Poppy could've been well enough, and I could've had a little luck on my side and prevented Robin from getting taken. Maybe we didn't separate from her, or I went looking for Robin when she didn't respond to the family signal." Wiping the rain from my eyes, I continue. "But it would've just delayed the inevitable. No matter what, someone in our family was going to be taken. Whether it was only Crow and Dad, or perhaps even Kestrel would've been taken first from the forest." A blinding flash of lightning illuminates the sky before the arc is followed by a clap of thunder that makes it feel like the ground is shaking. Or it might just be me as I try my best to calm the situation and the churning in my gut. "If things had played out differently, maybe I could've been the one snatched from the forest." I lock gazes with Starling and will everything in me to keep eye contact as he regards me with contempt. "Prophecies are unavoidable, and they're beyond tricky. And while you might not agree with me ninety percent of the time, you have to agree and realize that this—" I gesture at our drenched bodies and the world falling down around us. "—this is it. This is the catalyst, and there will be a battle back home on Hallowtide night no matter what. It's our family's fate to return this world to how it was before the first witch ruined it all."

Starling stares at me for several moments, jaw sawing back and forth. And when I think he's going to grind his teeth into nubs, he releases a quick breath from his nose. "You're right about agreeing on one thing," he says, pulling his wet cloak closer to himself. "It should've been you." Then, my brother marches off into the rain toward the trees and whatever lies beyond.

My posture deflates as the fight seeps out of me. Limp and dejected, I shiver before sparing a glance at Kestrel. His mouth is open, and words of comfort are on the tip of his tongue, but I'm not in the mood for comfort now. Starling thinks I'm some sort of monster in disguise. I just need to think.

I shake my head at Kestrel and pull my hood over my sopping hair as part of me retreats to the dissociative safety of my attic. All I can do as I separate my body and mind is hug myself for warmth before following Starling. The clock is ticking, and The Sun, Moon, and Time are hard at work, but changelings aren't eternal beings, and we need to find some form of shelter and safety. We need to rest and prepare for the next obstacles. And unluckily for Starling, it's going to be things much worse than me.

Grim: Claws

 y hands claw through the earth; there's dirt under my nails. As I drag myself up and away from the house, I notice something is wrong with the sky. There is a strong sense of magic in the atmosphere, and both the sun and moon have made an appearance. With what I know of the prophecy, I know this is the work of The Numina.

Good.

Be quiet.

I breathe the fresh, albeit strange, air. And I'm disappointed; it does not smell of her. Out here in the West Woods, there is no breeze to carry her floral, bitter spice scent to me. It does not have the mold and mildew that has infected her in these last desperate days of darkness, the things that have driven her to such lengths. The trees' choking, spidery limbs and shadows are good means of travel. Still, there is something about them I don't particularly like.

Perhaps they remind you of the poison in your body choking the free will from you?

The voice in my head that sounds like me is slurring. It's there but tame, floating on a bed of white-petaled flowers.

He is a prisoner inside my body, like I once was a prisoner

inside of Morrigan's shadow for hundreds of years. When I close my garnet eyes, I remember how cold it was inside the old Death's shadow. I can hear the voices of the other captured criminals who yelled and fought for their release. They would collide with my soul as they scrambled to claw at the edges of the Numina's shadow, looking for a way out.

In the darkest corners behind my lids, I can see the cold depths, the place where Morrigan placed my father's soul among the worst malefactors. Somewhere in the deepest recess, where they could not scratch and scramble with the rest of us. Or ever have the chance to become Fate's chained faerie messengers, the Pooka, who delivered the most important prophecies, the ones crucial to the tapestry of life. In this place my father couldn't get his nails in me, his killer. In a fit of rage, he took my mother from me—a gentle, soft-spoken woman who loved life more than anything. So, after I took my father apart, I took his life too, but only once he'd suffered as much as me. That is how I eventually arrived here, at this improved version of myself.

It's not too late to stop this. We're better than this; Rose made us so much better. The family would know that this isn't us. You could be forgiven.

My family is dead.

Your blood family is, but your—OUR—chosen family is not. Not yet, anyway. But they will be if you continue down this path and follow through with this plan.

I press my vermillion, bloodroot-scarred hands over my ears. I won't let this voice get in the way of my mission. I'll do what she asked of me, and I can't wait to see the murderous glee on her face when I return. And like a sign from above, I hear her call, that deep resonance from her horn that sings to the poison in my blood, drawing me to listen for her voice in my veins and obey.

"Find them."

Swan: Bloodroot

*T*he rain is only a drizzle by the time we stop in the forest. With no rocky overhangs, crevices, or caves to seek cover in, there was nothing to do but keep going until exhaustion stilled us. Now, surrounded by thick leaves and bark, Kestrel and Starling each empty a pouch of salt to create a circle around a thick tree. Well...with only a dim smudge of charmed airglow light seeping through the canopy of inter- twined branches to see by, it's less of a circle and more of a wonky, squiggle-edged oval. Either way, it will keep us safe and make the squelching ground a decent enough place to rest.

Taking the weight off our feet makes all three of us groan in relief. I don't even care that Auntie Rose's shears press into my stomach. Or that the trunk against my back is hard enough to bruise—at least I don't have to support my own body. Leaning my head back to close my eyes for a moment feels like paradise despite the cold water trickling onto my face. I could fall asleep like this, and I would have if Kestrel didn't nudge me to ask for my bag. To give him some light to see by, I unclasp the crescent hook of my side bag and pull out The Moon's Blessed candle, placing it on the ground inside the circle. The star-studded waxy flush only illuminates about five feet past the perimeter.

Although considering we couldn't see much but gray haze and tall shadows before, it's an improvement. The blue-lavender twinkling sigils remind me of fireflies as my focus drifts from the enchanted object to Kestrel sorting through our rations.

He unwraps a loaf of rustic bread from its cloth confines and my stomach rumbles. Under The Numina's influence, it's still the thirtieth day of the month, even though it should be early Hallowtide morning. We've probably traversed around fifty miles both walking and running, pushing ourselves through our fatigue into this dreary weather and closer to our destination. There's something about the kind of tiredness that comes from burning ourselves so fast that makes the simplest of foods taste divine. Any other time, I'd savor Mom's recipe, but my stomach is too empty, and the garlicky rosemary flavor too good to stop myself from stuffing the bread in my mouth. I don't even care that crumbs litter my chest, and flour from the crust coats the skin around my mouth. The water I wash it all down with is only from the glade's stream, but it tastes like nectar.

No one says a word as we feast in the fireless, phantom candlelight. Not even when Starling rummages through his knapsack and retrieves each of us a handful of roasted acorns spiced with nutmeg, and strips of molasses glazed hardtack peppered with cayenne and sage. It almost feels a lot like a Harvest Festival feast if I chew in the darkness behind my heavy eyelids. But the lightened rain hitting the crisp leaves, paired with the cold seeping through the wool covering me, and the soreness in my limbs, is a stark reminder that this isn't a peaceful family meal. In fact, my brothers and I are depleting our supplies. The contents of our bag are supposed to last us at least another day. Dusting off my hands, I cap what's left of my waterskin and stick it back into the knapsack resting between Kestrel's feet. This motion brings him and Starling back down from their food induced high, grounding them into our dreary reality again. There's not much left when they force themselves to return their food scraps to Starling's bag, but between the three of us, there's a decent amount of water to last as long as we're careful. If only this rain drenching my outsides, could absorb through my skin to quench my insides.

"My butt is wet." I press myself closer to Kestrel, who sits in the middle.

He sighs. "I'm pretty sure I'm sitting in a puddle."

The autumn's dropping temperature has caught up to me without movement to steal my attention. The sogginess of my clothes and the continuous drizzle makes it worse. It's honestly kind of miserable. "Surely all this moisture can't be healthy." I wriggle, my wet pants becoming more prevalent as I shift even closer to my brother for a semblance of warmth.

Starling snorts.

"Let's just be glad it's not winter," Kestrel yawns. "Then we'd really be in trouble."

Drawing my legs up, I mumble into my kneecaps, "I don't know, we might be susceptible to rot at this point. That is if a cluster of mushrooms don't claim us first."

There are worse matters at hand; who knows what state my siblings and father are in. But complaining about the weather makes this dismal quest, and the monumental fate our family has been sewn into, feel a little more normal. Makes me feel more like a seventeen-year-old girl whose only job is to be a teenager that leads a mundane, peaceful life. Like my destiny is to simply grow up and see where paths of chance can take me. Where maybe a thread could one day lead to permanent happiness, to joy that no longer relies on herbal treatments. Perhaps there's a red thread that allows me to be the glade's next caretaker, in a time when our home and the faeries don't need to be protected. Or another where I have a flowering wooden home of my own, across from the garden, constructed by the Elder Mother herself. I could spend my days in comfort, writing books of poetry, volumes that one of my siblings, on their way to an adventure, might carry into the villages to be published and sold on book carts.

It's all wistful thinking, but at least Starling doesn't drag me through the mud by calling me annoying and ungrateful for whining.

Instead, he leans forward past Kestrel to give me the driest look I've ever seen, especially in these conditions. "Well, if I knew we were going to waste precious tools we could've used The Sun's arrow to build us a nice toasty fire. Isn't that right, Duck?"

In response, Kestrel clotheslines Starling with an arm to the chest. There's a resounding *oof* when Starling's back meets the tree.

"Listen, I'm not saying that using the arrow was the right move, but I'm not saying it was wrong either. What matters is that Swan saved our soggy butts. Especially yours." Kestrel leans into Starling before his mouth gapes into yet another yawn. After he smacks his lips together and leans his head back with his eyes closed, he continues. "We'll figure something out; we always do. But let's focus on that after we're a little less sleep deprived."

Kestrel is right, and to my surprise, for the hundredth time today, Starling doesn't disagree with him either. So, the three of us huddle together, arms and hips sandwiched as close as possible for warmth. Being without sleep this long, paired with finally being still, takes my brothers to dreamland within minutes. I, however, slip in and out of rest, jerking awake every time my head tips sideways or nods forward. Resting my forehead on my crooked knees works for a little bit, but my legs sway, and their arch collapses again and again. Each time my leaden eyes open, and I try to find a new position against the tree, I look around to check the intact, albeit clumpy, salt ring. The scurrying of small critters and the flap of bat wings in the branches above us startles me time and time again, and every awakening makes this spotty rest period feel like an eternity. Kestrel's different snore patterns switch every fifteen minutes or so, and they become a marker of time to my subconscious. A repeat of the one that starts in the back of his throat makes me consider curling up in the wet dirt on my side. At this point, pressing my cheek to the earth to sleep amongst the striped snails emerging from the moisture would be more comfortable.

I'm about to do just that when a strange sound, like a shower of sand on a roof, sends me blinking. I don't know what I expected to find, perhaps nothing like the countless times I swept our surroundings, but the hulking thing sitting in front of me is not it. *What is tha*—a fist full of salt goes flying, grains hitting dense skin and hair before falling to the dead leaves below. The creature sits back on its massive haunches, just... looking at me. It's easily the size of a boulder, shoulders as wide and round. Beneath the heavy coating of green hair, or perhaps fur, its arms are as thick as my body, and its feet wider than my torso. The Blessed candle at my feet highlights the creature's form and deep, chartreuse eyes framed by spiky lashes brushing against the bottom of its caterpillar-like brows.

"Begone, bogey," Starling hisses from the safety of his spot on the other side of a deep-sleeping Kestrel before another volley of salt leaves his hand.

Again, the salt hits the big beast and bounces off its side. But its skin doesn't bubble and burn, nor does it flinch or try to get past our circle to wring our necks. It doesn't even move.

"Go away!" Starling's whisper is punctuated by more airborne salt. And when the creature still doesn't move, my brother resorts to throwing the whole pouch, leather and all. It just plops to the ground, limp and very empty. "Just leave, will you?" Starling groans. "Shoo. Away with you. Depart, foul beast."

When I hear him patting around, presumably searching his own body for more salt, I lean past Kestrel to see him. My suspicions are quickly confirmed. "It's not a bogey," I say in a hushed voice.

Even though I spoke in as soft of a tone as I could to still be heard, Starling reacts as if I yelled right in his ear. I'm surprised he doesn't scream as he tips backward, catching himself with one hand while the other clutches at his heart. "What is wrong with you?" he whisper-yells, righting himself and brushing off his palm. I could imagine seeing his cheeks flushed if the candle were brighter, but I still savor the mirth from his reaction.

"It's not a bogey," I repeat, gesturing to our new company. "The salt didn't hurt it at all."

"Yeah, I noticed that," he grumbles.

I can't stop my left brow from rising. Without a mirror, I know my expression reads, *"But did you?"* Starling can't even retaliate and use my exhaustion-induced sass against me. Not when I saw him almost wet his pants and waste an entire pouch of salt on something clearly unaffected.

Starling sniffs, casual as he straightens his cloak and readjusts his hood. "What is it then?"

The creature's head hangs between its hunched shoulders, making its neck disappear within its hairy fur collar. A bulbous nose protrudes from the center of its face, and beneath it is a very pronounced underbite with tusks over its top lip. Leaves and twigs cling to the green that sprouts from its arms and legs, and they don't come from the tall branch lying across its lap. The top of its feet sprout small out-of-season blooms that look like pearls and rubies. The flowers remind me of my aunts, specifically Auntie Posy.

I've learned a lot of things from her over the years; she's always been a walking library. When I started hunting outside the glade, she taught me that in certain regions, faeries act as guardians for others. Like the faun, sprites, or eloko. There are even faeries called bluecaps who look like trickster ignis fatuus, but will instead help you find your way home. While leshy or spriggan, who tend to be a little more malevolent, help you become lost, though only if you've disrespected their trees. This creature before me is none of those things. Considering its oversized stature, and the flora growing from it, perhaps it could be a woodwose, a faerie cousin to the trolls? Either way, there's no malice in its gaze, no other expression, or visible motive. I'm confident it's not a threat.

So, I can only face Starling again and shrug. "I'm not sure what it is. Did you try asking it politely?"

The look he gives me makes me glad that Kestrel sits between us, even if he is still unconscious. And why don't we wake him to alert him of the seemingly harmless thing looming over us? I'm not entirely sure. Maybe the mutual care we have for our younger brother? Or maybe strategy? Starling and I won't be getting any sleep now, and at least having one of the three of us replenished and rested ensures that someone will stay on their toes. Having Kestrel be the one who gets some sleep is the best choice anyway, considering his gift. If only we could get him to put aside his *do no harm* philosophy and use it against whatever bogeyman we might encounter next.

Still, it might do us all some good to determine if the woodwose intends to be a friend rather than a foe first.

Shifting away from Starling's steel gaze, I face the giant. My greeting is soft as I wave my awkward, buzzing fingers. "Uh, hello."

Large eyes blink back at me before it releases a breath like a small gale. It's strong enough that it pushes the curls around my face back and floods my senses with an earthy combination of cedar resin and oakmoss.

"You aren't going to hurt us, right?" After a moment without an answer, I pull my hood back. "Are *you* hurt?"

Only Kestrel's snoring bleeds into the night.

"I don't think this thing understands us." Starling leans forward in his cross-legged position, curious.

Perhaps not, but the massive creature is here for a reason because its unwavering stare glints with awareness. I try peppering it with questions like whether it needs help, or if it's hungry. The woodwose isn't startled when I test my luck and take a step closer to better see its candlelit face and ask where it came from or if it has a name. The only thing that stirs it, sending its massive frame to its feet with branch in hand, is when the forest quiets, followed by the cracking of a twig somewhere off in the dark. Not expecting the deafening silence, or the faerie's shockingly deft movement, I back away and just miss falling over Kestrel's legs. I steady myself with a palm against the rough tree trunk and note that even Starling is partway to standing now, hand close to the tail of my cloak. After what feels like several tense minutes, nothing else rustles in the distance, and the large creature settles back down, laying the crook-like branch back across its lap. Though this time, the woodwose has its back to us and its face trained forward. Almost...almost as if it's guarding us from what might lie beyond, lurking unseen in the shadows.

Like a wide-eyed owl, my head swivels to look down at my conscious brother. He does the same before our clueless wonder makes us glance back at the faerie. The thought of something out there, past the Blessed candle's small radius, is unsettling. Although, it seems like we now have a guardian watching over us and our misshapen salt circle.

I do one more sweep of our surroundings. The rain has stopped, and only droplets sluice off the near bare branches silhouetted against the heavens. Clouds cover and uncover the sliver of the moon at the end of its waxing gibbous phase on one side of the airglow sky and the dramatically weak sun on the other. They look strange existing together, especially in this semi-frozen atmosphere. Nature doesn't seem too confused, though. Crickets still chirp their songs along with the rest of what should be the nightlife symphony. It fills the air with the background noise you never realize is there until it stops. My hunting experience knows that the quiet that settled over everything before that twig broke was a warning. It was the same sort of foreboding silence that surrounds prey when a predator is nearby. But whatever crept close is gone now, and I'm satisfied enough to deem the forest temporarily safe.

Before I sit back down, Starling pulls out his little book of poisons and holds it at an angle to read in the phantom-colored candlelight. The way he flips through it with purpose is intriguing, so much so, that after a few seconds of hesitation, I round the tree to sit beside him instead of Kestrel still slumbering like a sack of potatoes.

Starling pauses.

Hugging my legs, I make myself as small as possible, hoping that he'll let me stay. When he continues his search without so much as a word, I swallow my sigh of relief and watch. Every so often, he stops to scan a page full of his cramped handwriting. The cream pages are full of notes, but they're also full of drawings. I haven't seen his sketches since we were kids scribbling on parchment beneath the kitchen table where we made our forts. They were childish renditions back then.

But the drawings in this book are now detailed and skillful. There are intricate diagrams of plants and items I recognize from Hazel's Apothecary. Some of his still-life drawings even depict corners of our house, or areas inside Wyrd Mountain. It's the portraits and their beautiful compositions that take my breath away, though. There are many people I don't recognize, some women with beautiful but harrowing, gaunt, witch-like attributes. I catch glimpses of Bramwell amongst the other trolls, Fern with his signature mushroom gnome cap, and an upside-down imp. Mom and Dad in the kitchen, The Numina, Hazel and Icarus, Lark, Robin, Crow, Kestrel, and Grandma Aspen and Pop Pop too before they passed away, which he must've drawn from memory.

There's even a portrait of me, one that looks recent since I started wearing my hair up a certain way while hunting, but Starling flips past it in his absentminded search before I get a good look. Now I know why Starling's so particular about his book. I can see passion in the spots of ink always somewhere on his hands, in the furrow between his brow. It's been a long time since I've seen my brother, truly seen him. Starling has grown so much. Of course, he's grown into his features; his cheeks have lost their baby fat, and his jaw and nose have sharpened, but his intelligence has sharpened as well. He's grown leaps and bounds, in so many ways, and I'm so proud that my throat tightens.

It's been years since we grew apart, and I don't really know why, but I still see my little brother in him. He was the one who comforted me after I scraped my knee on the stone path while we were racing once. The one who let our younger siblings win in said race. I see him sneaking into my room with a lantern where we would stay up to practice our letters so we could learn to read a storybook out loud together. We wanted to impress Mom and Dad, hear their clapping, and see their broad smiles. He's there in the glade dragging me around giving me little tests to try to discover and unlock my gift after a baby Crow got his. Even though he used to be afraid of thunder, he's sitting with me in the window with our noses squished against the glass when it started raining, knowing how much I loved it. He's the one tying a red length of yarn from Grandma Aspen's old stash around Kestrel's and my pinkies as we swear to be best friends forever. Starling is there in all the hijinks, and in every adventure, every promise and bout of laughter that hurt our bellies. And when he turns to look at me now saying something that I can't hear, I still see him in my heart. Even though I've had to bandage it up after he repeatedly tries to break it and escape.

"Hello? Did you even hear a single word I said?" Starling

waves a hand in my face, his expression fixed in something akin to a grimace. "Why are you crying?"

"What?" Blinking myself back to the present makes wetness fall onto my cheeks. "Oh, no. That was definitely rain on my face, probably just dripped from the tree." I scramble to scrub my tears away before clearing my throat. "What were you saying?" Even though I can feel Starling's gaze burning into me, I keep my eyes glued to the page of his open journal, hoping to avoid any judgment and ridicule. It's so quiet that it's almost awkward, but I wait my brother out long enough that he looks away.

"If you had paid attention," he starts, "I was saying that Big Toes over there reminded me of something." My brother jabs a finger at the extensive chart etched on the open pages. It looks like a list of names and corresponding poisonous flora. Some names are crossed out or have an *X* by them while others have an empty unchecked box. It's the list he talked about at the Apothecary.

"What's this faerie have to do with any of this?" I ask, poring over the organized chart of witches for any sign of a connection.

"The small white florets growing on that thing's feet got me thinking about flowers," he says, rooting around in his trouser pockets until he pulls out his graphite and he crosses out a name, Baba Roga, faintly written in the margin list before filling it into one of three open lines at the bottom of his chart. Then Starling prints *"sugar plum hellebore."* "I don't think Baba Roga is the one that poisoned Uncle Grim. The Phouka, maybe, though with everything Nanny Rutt said, I'm not completely sold on Baba Roga being fully capable of that either. But Grim," he mumbles. "I wholeheartedly believe it was some other hag."

My head jerks back as I stare at the side of Starling's face. "How? The prophecy pointed to Baba Roga's *'web'* being where we'll find Robin, Crow, and Dad. And it was very clearly Uncle Grim who took them there."

"Like I said at the Apothecary, hellebore isn't a plant capable of the kind of control Uncle Grim was under. And I think Nanny Rutt was probably right about her not being stupid enough to try harnessing two poisons," Starling continues. "Being one of the last three of your kind would have anyone making a big move, like infecting a whole race of faerie just to cause chaos. Though I don't think the level of witchcraft that's making the Pooka into these weird amalgamations of rot and behemoth, is something that can be done alone. And remember, the witches are desperate, not stupid. Baba Roga wouldn't crossbreed two plants and risk bringing her kind that much closer to extinction. But I do think she would stoop low enough to collaborate to ensure her own survival and the spread of darkness."

I blink my heavy lids, trying to comprehend my brother's hypothesis, but all I can do is spin in circles inside my attic. "Okay..." I trail off, more lost than a needleless compass.

"Hellebore causes many afflictions, but its main property is its hold on someone's heart. It slows it down to the point of putting its victim in a stupor and then into a deep and horrifying sleep. Enough of it induces a coma." My brother glances at me to make sure I'm following, though I don't think my nod is convincing. Tiredly, he rolls his eyes, as if all this information is common knowledge and not his extensive years of obsessive research. He then flips back a few pages in his journal to a page complete with a detailed sketch of a small-headed, daisy-like flower with tuber-esque roots. "As I said before, bloodroot is a flower with vermillion-hued staining sap that leaks from the roots. If your skin absorbs bloodroot sap, or you eat any part of the plant, you're in trouble. Kind of like Mom's story about Black Annis's belladonna kiss while she was in the labyrinth. Once poisoned, Mom was very susceptible to being under her verbal control." Starling taps the back of his graphite stick on the drawn petals of the bloodroot flower. "In some areas of the world, potion makers use bloodroot in recipes for love spells. The poison is potent enough to drag someone devoted like Uncle Grim away from Auntie Rose."I'm close to intruding on Starling's personal space when I lean in to turn back the journal's pages. "I don't see bloodroot attached to anyone on your chart." It doesn't occur to me that I touched his book without his permission until it's too late.

Thankfully, Starling is consumed by the snowball he's gotten rolling and just squints down at his dimly lit chart. "Not yet. But thanks to Auntie Rose, Icarus, and Nanny Rutt—" My brother trails off and finishes crossing out the names left as options in the margins:

~~Madgy Figgy~~
~~Churnmilk Peg~~
~~The Noon Witch~~
The Cornflower Wraith
~~The Rye Mother~~
Allison Gross
~~Mama Padurii~~

The rumored witches left from Starling's collection of whisperings and fables are The Cornflower Wraith and Allison Gross.

Whether or not it was on purpose, Nanny Rutt never commented on Allison Gross after Icarus confirmed that Mama Padurii was void. She just jumped right into talking about the Rye Mother being a bogeyman. I wouldn't be shocked if the ex-witch neglected Allison's name to meddle, but after Hazel's talking-to, I find it hard to believe. Either way, I think our answer is self-explanatory, it's between The Cornflower Wraith and Allison Gross being the witch working with Baba Roga.

A deep *humph* of confirmation escapes Starling. "Well. I guess we have our match." He then fills out the second to last empty space in his chart, jotting down Allison Gross next to bloodroot.

Presuming we're right, one would think uncovering the identity of the second witch The Numina have yet to find would be a relief. It should be something to cheer about and revel in, even if the location of the third witch and the cause of the Stygian Brume stays a mystery. But the implication of what the bloodroot sap staining the hands of Death's Reaper means is mind-boggling. "So, we're dealing with two witches now? They're supposed to be solitary power-hungry creatures," I groan. "Apparently, they'd kill each other if minor bogeys didn't separate them and uphold their territories. Baba Roga and Allison Gross can't be working together; it's impossible."

The thought of the wicked women working together is like imagining a pack of wolves having two alphas. It's a recipe for disaster. A situation that should've had the witches killing each other by now. Or at least fighting, then fleeing to their own territories to lick their wounds. It's been six hundred plus years —my brother is right—The Numina have whittled the witches down to desperation.

Starling snorts. "It's improbable, not impossible. At this point, two witches banding together is the only thing that could make them into a force strong enough to create the Phouka. If I had to make a bet, I'd say they're somehow capturing Pooka, and Baba Roga's hellebore puts them to sleep. At the same time, Allison Gross's bloodroot converts their inhibitions into mind-less aggression. The combination of opposing witchcraft in the Pooka's system is probably why they look so abhorrent as Phouka." My brother twirls the graphite between his fingers as he thinks. "But of course, that's just me guessing."

"I don't think you're far off," I murmur. "The Phouka have red eyes instead of yellow, and if that is an effect of bloodroot, then it makes sense for Allison Gross to be the one with a hold on Uncle Grim." I stare at Starling and the cool-toned cast of light illuminating the side of his wan face. "You don't think she's made him fall in love with her, do you?"

His silence is answer enough.

I drop my head with another groan. Imagining a bewitched version of Uncle Grim bringing my siblings and father to two conspiring hags makes me sick. "What are we going to do, Starling?" I whisper into my palms.

"The Sun's arrow would've been enough to take out both crones with one flaming stone. Without it?" he bites out, but it lacks heart and teeth. "I have no clue."

My burning fingertips press into my closed eyes, dropping me into a world of multicolor stars. When I pick up my head, the forest is in splotches until the dancing black spots disappear. The woodwose still sits with his back to us like a giant hairy knight, and Kestrel still sleeps, though somewhat quieter than before. Starling has put away his graphite only to continue staring at his chart. My eyes catch on his hand rubbing his wrist. I didn't know that I'd hurt him when I pulled him through the Rye Mother's field, but my fingernails had split his skin enough to leave marks.

"I'm sorry," I blurt. His answering look is empty until I nod at his subconscious soothing.

My brother clams up and goes sour in a second, face dropping and mouth screwing up. "It's whatever." He snaps his journal closed, features devoid of expression, signaling the end of whatever temporary truce we had. Then Starling crosses his arms and tips his bead back against the tree with closed eyes.

My chest aches, and my breathing grows shallow.

As quietly as I can, I reach inside my cloak and attempt to draw out the bag of sunflower clusters without waking Kestrel. I have it halfway out of the wool pocket when his breathing changes and sounds like it's come to a waking stop. I freeze until a new but familiar pattern starts up. With numb, nimble fingers, I retrieve the bag and put it in my lap, unrolling the crinkling paper with a wince. After some maneuvering and pausing, I finally fish out a cluster. The sugar and sunflower seeds taste like home and feel like sunshine. My breath settles. And when I reach inside the bag for a second cluster, it's more for the candy and homesickness and less for the medicine.

But my soul almost exits my body from multiple orifices when a hand reaches out in front of me, palm side up. My neck pops when I turn to look at Starling. His eyes are still closed with his head tipped back against the tree, and his other arm is still draped across his chest while he waits.

"My sugar is low," he mumbles. With jittery fingers, I place the sweet in his hand and watch him toss it into his mouth. "Thanks."

I contain my smile by retrieving another cluster and tucking it into my cheek. Starling would never admit it, not in a thousand years, but there's something about the way he showed his single-worded gratitude that tells me it was for more than sharing one of Robin's multipurpose delicacies. My belief in this is stronger when right before I start to nod off, I peek at my brother through my lashes. He's awake, looking over at our strange candlelit guardian while tracing the red crescent mark on his wrist from my pinkie nail with the tip of his opposite index finger. I fall asleep with two thoughts; the path paved for us is bumpy and dark. But even frayed threads can be mended.

Swan: A Helpful Gift

*K*nowing that the woodwose guards us, I sleep for a few safe hours. But when I wake again, in the still gloomy, airglow forest, the faerie is gone. The only evidence of its existence is the giant crook-like stick it left behind. Of course, when Kestrel rises brighter and more bushy-tailed than a squirrel, he's gleeful about the wood. His happy exclamation of *"stick!"* makes the sip of water I'd been taking spew from my nose. Starling and I tell him about our guardian, and after that, it's impossible to persuade Kestrel to leave the branch behind. The fact that it's almost twice the size of my six-foot-tall brother isn't even enough because his solution is to break the stick over his knee. Much to Starling's amusement, the task isn't without struggle.

As we leave our encampment behind, Kestrel gallivants ahead, poking around with his new walking stick. One might think the way the teenager dons my knapsack and leaves his bow and arrows for me to carry is an accident. You might even imagine his boyish brain is so overridden with new morning vigor, that it causes him to make a ruckus by jabbing the sharp end of the broken stick into the ground before tapping every tree trunk we pass. And I would agree with you. But Kestrel is smart enough to use all these things as an excuse to be rid of his weapon and the responsibility that comes with wielding his gift. And maybe even to rid himself of the physical reminder of not raising his bow in a crucial moment of life or death. I'm not sure if letting him get away with this makes me a good or a bad older sister, but I find comfort in the fact that Starling also says nothing about the matter.

We're only a couple minutes into our quiet walk when Kestrel hits another tree. He whacks the trunk hard enough with his walking stick that the branch bounces back in his loose grip, almost nailing him in the face. But it's not his harmless peril that catches my interest. A patch of leaves at the base of the tree stops me in my tracks.

"You're an idiot," Starling cackles as he walks ahead.

Kestrel rearms himself, bends his knees, and waddles toward Starling, wielding the stick against him like a fencing sword. The dull thud of wood against a warm body, and the scuffle that ensues is all background noise as I crouch to inspect the dead leaves. At first, they look rotted from the rain, wilted and wet, splattered with black and littered with holes. This decay isn't wholly natural though, and the tacky ichor that transfers onto my fingers when I drag them over the leaves confirms this. My blood is racing as I track the ashen trails dotting the foliage. The first rounds the opposite side of the tree and leads back the way we came in a concentrated line that shows a slow advance. The second trail seems to circle back and head the way we're going in a broader, more broken, fleeing line.

This was why the woodwose watched over us.

"Hey, guys," I start, wiping my sticky hand on the side of my trousers as I stand. "Looks like we had more than one visitor last night." My brothers freeze as I approach. Kestrel has dropped his stick in favor of putting our brother in a headlock. Starling has hooked a boot behind Kestrel's leg, ready to sweep his feet from under him. Leave it to them to be so lost in their wrestling that they were oblivious to the fact that I'd stopped walking in the first place.

Starling blinks first. Then he jabs a fist into Kestrel's lower back, making him breathe through gritted teeth. Kestrel quickly releases his hold and dances away with a hand pressing into the spot Starling's knuckles dug into.

"A kidney shot? That's just plain dirty, man," he groans.

Starling rubs at his neck before straightening his cloak. "Serves you right."

"In case anyone cares, there was a Phouka," I sigh. My brothers stop glaring at each other and focus. Even the forest is silent when I point to where I found evidence of the monster's presence. "Our guardian's appearance must have kept the Phouka at bay until it decided to run off. The trail it left behind is almost on its way to being dry." I motion for my brothers to follow me to the rot, readjusting the string of the elder wood bow where it crosses from my left shoulder to my right hip. "But it did go the same way we're heading, so we might as well keep an eye on it and see where it diverged."

We continue west, boots parallel to the decay. For a while, I keep my eyes trained on it as if it were a trail of black goopy breadcrumbs. But soon, my mind wanders back up into my attic, dusting off the shelves and tidying up papers scribbled with discarded quatrains and elegies. The crunching leaves beneath our three treads, coupled with the rhythmic beat of Kestrel's walking stick against the bark, sound like muffled music on the other side of my mental walls. At some point, Starling starts whistling to fill up space in the stagnant air.

It's different than the melodic one his gift uses when he summons his birds; there's no magic behind this song, which makes this tune pitchy. But despite it being off-key, it's a lovely melody. Something about it tickles my brain, and I go searching for a memory. It's inside the little music box on the lowest shelf of my gallery wall, and when I open the music box's porcelain top, I'm reminded of being tucked in as a child. If I couldn't fall asleep after Mom and Dad's bedtime stories, Mom would sing this soul-stirring, hushed song. A song she first started singing the day the trolls gave life to my crafted body. She stopped as I got older, but the night baby Crow and I got that fever, when I developed my nerve damage, Mom sang it to me for the first time in years. She called it a Swan Song, a melody slipped between the pages of one of her gilded books.

THE AMBER LEAVES FALL, *soft as sighs,*
    Beneath the stretch of autumn skies.
    The swan, now tired, with wings half-drawn,
    Prepares to leave the dying dawn.
    The winds grow cool, the days grow brief,
    A harvest moon glows through turning trees,
    She drifts in ripples, slow and wide,
    The season's change, the ebbing tide.
    The branches whisper of the cold,
    Nights long, and days bold—
    The earth will sleep in frost,
    And all the summer warmth is lost.
    Her feathers, kissed by fading sun,
    Glide through a world whose season is done.
    The waters speak in mournful tones,
    Of fleeting times and distant homes.
    With every stroke, the ripples part,
    Her song a tremor in the heart—
    A melody as soft as a dream,
    A story sweeter than it may seem.
    The leaves, like embers, burn and fall,
    While distant hills grow dark and tall.
    She rises, wings a whispering gold,
    Her swan song not yet sung, a tale untold.

And as she soars through autumn's haze,
The world stands still, a misty maze.
The chill is sharp, the twilight long—
And in the dusk, she sings her song.

I'D FORGOTTEN ALL about it, though it seems Starling hasn't. Listening to him whistle it now, in a soft, albeit imperfect pitch, makes me homesick and comfortable all at the same time. I let it lull me into a place of peace, losing all sense of time as I walk in a straight, subconscious line behind Kestrel. That's why, when the music box snaps closed and Starling's whistling stops, I'm sucked from my attic like I've woken from a nightmare.

My heart is thumping as I spin around. Starling's foamy eyes are downcast. "Why'd you stop?"

He points to the ground beside us, his other hand reaching back for an axe handle. "Because the trail stopped."

A chill floods my limbs, singeing my fingers and toes with a new burning sensation. My cold hands flutter around my torso, bypassing Auntie Rose's shears entirely. I can't decide if I should swing Kestrel's bow off my shoulder and nock an arrow, or pull a throwing knife from the side of my thigh. I'm caught off guard, waking from the fog of fatigue and childhood memories. I can only blame sleep deprivation. I should have been paying attention…I should've noticed the silence.

There's not a single unseen forest creature stirring. Not even a bug chirp or scuttle as I turn in a slow circle. An eeriness surrounds us. The crisp tapping of Kestrel's stupid stick against flaking bark chips ahead is the only thing I can hear over my breathing. But even that ends when Starling sharply whistles our family signal. This instantly alerts our oblivious brother of impending danger and pulls him to an abrupt halt ten feet before us. Slow and steady, Kestrel turns, rooted in place, wide silver eyes like gleaming alarm bells.

Inhale.

Exhale.

Past the noise of my lungs, I hear a faint burbling.

Inhale.

Exhale.

It could just be the blood rushing throughout my ears.

Inhale.

Exhale.

Something drips onto Kestrel's shoulder.

Inhale.

Exhale.

The branches far above him creak.

Inhale.

Exhale.

His head cranes up to the gauzy decelerated sky hanging between Hallowtide day and night.

Inhale.

The Phouka is perched in the branches. The old prophet was in the form of a raven before it was infected, but now it's twice the size any bird has business being. Where there should be one set of wings, there are two giant pairs, each with feathers of flickering smoke. And where there should be two black, river rock eyes, there are eight, each illuminated with a bright shade of oxblood. Its beak is split in half, creating four razor-edged prongs, and the tongue that forks from the middle to taste the air dribbles with grime.

My lungs quiver.

The Phouka's neck turns with a wet pop, flipping its head nearly upside down as it drinks us in. The beast's talons are the length of one of Lark's steel pestles, and they're *tap, tap, tapping* on the tree branch where it roosts, expectant. No. Excited.

My chest seizes.

Both pairs of mutated wings extend from its body and rise upwards in an arch. They shake and ruffle as it tilts its bony body forward, feathers expelling a strange hiss that sounds like harbinging whispers. With the deafening airless buzz in my brain, the Phouka's four-foot wings appear crowned with the simmering souls of the damned. I'm afraid that breathing will trigger the monster, especially as it tucks its wings tight to its sides. Even on the precipice of dizziness and a galaxy before my eyes, I keep my lungs full. And just when I think this standoff will end me, Kestrel takes a step back from the tree, and the breaking of leaves under his boot shatters the spell.

Exhale.

"Kestrel, move!" Starling thunders.

As the Phouka dives, falling headfirst like a shooting star, it aims directly at Kestrel with a screech. My brother stands his ground. Meaning, he faces the poisoned faerie with nothing more than a broken stick. Before Kestrel can raise the branch to defend himself, the Phouka unfolds its wings once more. Catching itself on the updraft of its own momentum, the mutated raven soars over his head, spewing tar alongside a grating cry. Its course change is quick, but I can see that the Phouka is Purgatory-bent on putting its talons in my face. With oxygen flowing through me, I can act with better instinct, twisting with my hips to face Starling and ducking as it swoops. The slice of its empty talons cutting through nothing but air sounds like the shears tucked against my midsection. But the guttural sound of the monster's frustration is just as chilling. Maybe even more so when the tip of its wing hangs a hard left, sending the monster hurtling at Starling's exposed back.

"Watch out," I shout.

Starling is ready for it. He plants his foot and pivots, his torso turning with him as he puts his weight behind his axe. With the head of the blade level with his ear, he swings down like Dad once taught him when chopping firewood. The Phouka banks away, a vengeful bellow gurgling from its throat before it tries again, attempting to catch him from the side. In turn, Starling compensates, using his position to pivot again, grounding the toe of his boot and crooking his elbow. This time his swing starts low as he slices diagonally up, catching the Phouka with the bottom horn of the blade. The moment Starling grunts and moves out of harm's way, I hear the sizzle of the salt-annealed axe connecting with one of the beast's lower wings.

The hit turns the Phouka's flight pattern erratic, and it soars upward and out of reach, wavering in the air, ear-piercing shrieks bellowing as spatters of what smells like liquid mold spill from the dark faerie. It's angry, but nowhere near done fighting. The creature careens back down, charging toward Kestrel, chomping beak first. Kestrel grabs either end of the woodwose's stick and shoves it skyward, meeting the Phouka in the middle. The wood is lodged in the rabid bird's mouth as it furiously beats its wings, causing Kestrel to turn his head to avoid its long reach.

"Uh, a little help here," he calls over the violent flapping of the monster's multiple wings. Stumbling, Kestrel's back hits a tree, pinning him with his arms above his head. Any second, he could lose an eye to a talon like Auntie Rose before he can raise a real weapon to the former messenger of Fate.

My fingers loop through the hole at the end of a throwing knife, spinning it into my grasp. Starling anticipates this. Only seconds before the short weapon leaves my hand, he's charging forward and heaving his axe again. Each of our blades hit a raven wing, one on either side, nailing the poisoned Phouka face-first to the tree above Kestrel's head. My younger brother drops to the ground to lie amongst the leaves, huffing and puffing. Above him, the Phouka squawks in outrage, its free wings flailing as the sick faerie shrinks. Strung between two salt-annealed blades, it grows smaller and smaller. Unlike the fox Phouka, the raven becomes a long, thin mass, like a snake of shadows rather than a ball. On the other hand, just like the fox, this wriggling Phouka is now constrained and harmless.

"Are you okay?" I pant, eyes roving over Kestrel, checking for any visible injuries.

"Yep. Good job, guys!" Kestrel is all smiles as he wipes his forehead with the back of his wrist. That is until he realizes he still holds either end of the branch, which is now in two separate pieces. "Aw, man. It broke my stick." He frowns at the faerie trapped above him.

"You're an idiot." Starling stares down at him with what might be a combination of disappointment and embarrassment. His face is flat as he shakes his head. "I can't believe I'm related to you."

Still, Starling offers Kestrel a hand, who grins at him in return. When he reaches up, holding the last piece of the wood-wose's handy gift, Starling slaps it away, making the wood tumble from Kestrel's grasp. The latter doesn't even get to dramatically gasp before Starling curls a fist around his thumb and hauls him to his feet. The moment Kestrel touches the back of our brother's hand, Starling winces. Kestrel pulls away like he has been scalded by a hot kettle. Instead of burns on his finger-tips, he's left with Starling's blood marring his skin. Kestrel's hand shakes as he stares down at the wet ruby coating, uneasy. Blood doesn't usually make him squeamish. But his startled reaction isn't my priority right now.

"Are *you* okay?" I ask Starling, but he doesn't respond. "Let me see," I demand, holding out a hand for Starling's. When he just stares blankly, I sigh, rolling my eyes, moving my legs as if I were walking away from him. And the second Starling looks away from me, I dart forward and grab his wrist. There's an actively bleeding gash streaking the back of his hand. The cut through his skin isn't deep enough to need stitches, but it's wide enough that it'll cause a scar. The Phouka must've caught Starling with a talon when he clipped its wing. That was probably

175

the grunt I heard from him. Guilt coats my throat like a spoonful of treacle.

I need to protect him better.

"It's fine." Starling tries to pull away. I hold on tight, and this sets him off. "Let go of me."

"If Robin were here, she'd say we need to clean and wrap this," I argue. "You put some of Hazel's clotting powder in your bag—"

"Well, Robin isn't here!" At the sound of our littlest sister's name, Starling is rough with his words, and rougher yet when he rips his arm from my grasp. "Don't baby me, Duck. I don't need your help."

Kestrel comes to his senses then and pokes Starling in the side with the fourth of the walking stick still in his possession. "Don't be difficult, not right now."

There's a brief exchange between brothers, a conversation held in just their eyes. Eventually, Starling sets his mouth to something that resembles a straight line, which must translate into concession because Kestrel heavily pats his shoulder. Then with a nod, he rounds Starling's back for his bag. Kestrel digs into the knapsack, collecting a waterskin, the cloth from last night's bread, and the vial from our godmother's Apothecary. He holds the last two items as I pour the fresh water over Starling's wound. His hand twitches in discomfort as he looks off into the distance, face showing no other sign of pain. It must hurt, though. The skin and veins around the Phouka's cut are reddened with irritation. And the edges of his skin are torn and ragged, weeping. Starling's only real reaction comes after I trade Kestrel the waterskin and uncork the glass vial, tapping at the amber bottle to dispense a line of clotting powder. Starling's head cranes back, boots gnashing into the ground as the sage-colored, petal-sprinkled substance bubbles. It foams inside the wound as it does its job of cleaning and drying the open skin before staunching the blood.

"Sorry, sorry," I mumble. "I'm almost done."

Listening to his teeth grind together makes me hold what Hazel, Lark, Robin, The Sun, Moon, Nanny Rutt, and the rest of the Healers do with much more respect. Helping someone is fulfilling, but having to hurt them in the process is difficult. I don't have the heart for it. My eyes prickle and my skin both flushes and freezes with empathy. How Healers can look upon the faces of their patients with such grace is beyond me. My only comfort in treating Starling is knowing that the clotting powder works. It's turning thick and growing pink, just as it should, and when I wrap Starling's hand and tie off the cloth inside his palm, I try to catch his eye, hoping to have a silent conversation with him like Kestrel. Like we used to be able to. I want to apologize again, but I also want to reassure and tell him that he did well. Maybe even show him that, despite being an ogre at times, I still love him. But he just fusses with the knot I tied, leaving me to jot those thoughts down on scrap paper in my attic for later.

"So, what are we supposed to do with this thing?" Starling asks, gesturing to the Phouka after I secure the leftover supplies into my bag on Kestrel's back.

"Usually, we'd summon Auntie Rose with my bow, and she'd come to collect it. But we shouldn't do that," Kestrel answers. After a short pause, he looks to me for confirmation. "Right?"

I shake my head. "We can't risk drawing her out, not for this. For all we know, this Phouka was sent as a trap for her, or a diversion to stall us."

"So we just leave it?" Starling raises a skeptical brow. "What about our weapons? We need everything we have if we're just going to waltz into Baba Roga's den."

"We leave the Phouka for now, yes. As far as weapons go, my knife will be enough to keep it contained until everything is said and done. I still have a good handful left, and we have plenty of arrows." When Starling continues to stare unconvinced, I rub my tired eyes with a sigh. "When time returns to its normal speed, and tomorrow rolls around, we'll have figured out and fulfilled the prophecy. Then the darkness will be vanquished, and Auntie Rose and Uncle Grim will be able to come back to collect this Phouka. After that they can figure out how to turn it back into a Pooka and give it a fair trial."

Wrapping my fist around the gold bowstring crossing my chest, I think about the Pookas Auntie Rose and Uncle Grim found and judged five years ago before discovering the first Phouka. Like The Sun and Moon did with the witches, Death gave all the ex-criminals-turned-messengers a choice to reform. Those who did not change over the centuries under the last Fate's rule were dispatched to Purgatory. And those that did had a choice: have their souls set free into The After, or turn their ghosts into a new version of their old bodies like Grim. Most have found peace in The After, and the unfortunate criminals who refused to change were sent to Purgatory. Most surprisingly though, out of the hundreds of Pooka they recovered, only one ever took the latter option and was released into the world to live again. I hope that after the final battle we've yet to fight, Death can extend that same forgiveness to her Reaper again. That is, if he can be freed from Allison Gross's poisonous influence. Imagining what might happen if Uncle Grim can't be cured makes the shears against my abdomen feel heavier, and the bowstring clenched in my hand burn.

As if Kestrel can hear my thoughts, he picks up the dangerous threads I'm dropping and reels them in. "Maybe when the witches are gone, all these illnesses will go with them? Just"—my brother balls his hand before throwing it open and waggling his fingers to mime an explosion—"*poof.*"

"Maybe," I echo, soaking in Kestrel's sunshine and optimism.

I want to believe everything can be fixed, and we can continue our old lives with newfound peace. But tonight holds so many unknowns and fears, and tomorrow we still have to deal with the Stygian Brume. Though I suppose we need to make it through today first, and we can't do that if we don't move. I yank Starling's axe from the tree.

Without being stretched between two weapons, the Phouka shifts from a writhing string to a squirming sphere pinned beneath the throwing knife embedded in the bark. "For now." I extend the axe handle-first to Starling. "We have some ground to cover."

Without so much as a thank you, my brother takes the weapon and holsters it on his back before walking west. Like it was his idea, Starling calls over his shoulder, "Let's go."

Kestrel laughs and shrugs. "You heard the man." And the next thing I know, he's bounding off after Starling, tapping every tree he passes with his twice-broken stick.

After a quick apologetic glance back at the Phouka, I amble on behind the boys. They're both in step now, and Starling is trying to get Kestrel to leave the foot-long splintered stick behind. Kestrel refuses, and a squabble ensues. At the very least, there's no shortage of entertainment with these brothers of mine.

-

As the forest thins, and we approach the stretch of land before the orchard Nanny Rutt mentioned, Kestrel drops the stick.

Well, in truth, Starling physically forces Kestrel to give up the woodwose's helpful gift, but it's the same difference. Their bickering continues and neither of them know that as I follow, I pick it up, putting the stupid piece of wood in my back trouser pocket where it sticks up under my cloak. Maybe I do it to secretly spite Starling? Who knows. But I marvel at how much my brothers, who appear as tall and wide as grown men at sixteen and seventeen, can act so much like kids. And as I've seen Mom and Dad do thousands of times, I distract them like the children they are with what's left of our food to end their fighting. Splitting the last piece of hardtack and dividing the remnants of spiced acorns between them is nowhere near enough food for stomachs like theirs, especially with Starling's disorder. But it's enough to keep them quiet, and an hour of walking in blissful harmony makes the dull pang of emptiness in my stomach well worth it. Hunger provides the clarity needed to develop a semblance of a plan, which includes ample inspiration from the Phouka's attack and the snails I spotted last night.

"Hey," I call out, jogging until I catch up to my brothers. "So I've been thinking—"

"*Great.*" Starling groans. "Hope you didn't hurt yourself because we don't have time to deal with that too."

My jaw snaps shut, and I lose pace, falling back a step. The sarcastic spirit Auntie Rose instilled in me wants to quip back with something like, "*It's nice to know that you care about my well-being, Starling.*" Or, "*I knew you had a soul in there somewhere, Starling.*" But no. My spirit is smothered with the same ease as blowing out a single wavering flame. Starling is already on edge, and what I'm about to say could worsen everything.

Tentative, I step back up to stride between the boys. "The Phouka kinda reminded me of something from when we were kids. It was after you all discovered your gifts and the three of us, um—grew apart," I stutter. "I think I had just turned twelve, but this was before Auntie Rose started taking me out to hunt. Starling was still eleven, and Kestrel, you were only ten; I'm not sure if you remember this. It had rained earlier in the morning, and little worms and slugs were crawling around. I was lying on the path in the garden on my stomach, watching a rout of ten or so lemon snails inching towards the sunflower patch. They were my favorite at that time. I loved how brightly colored and swirled their shells were; I could watch them for hours," I babble, getting lost in my old childhood interest.

Starling's expression flattens.

I jump forward in my storytelling to my least favorite part and rip off the bandage. "But uh, Starling, you came across me, and you—you used your gift."

"I remember this." Kestrel snaps his fingers as his memories ignite. It's a confusing contrast to the excitement of his redis-covery, but I glean something uneasy in his silver eyes, reminis-cent of what I saw earlier when the blood from the back of Starling's hand got on him. "Lark and I had been skipping stones in the stream when we heard you screaming."

Starling lets out a halfhearted scoff. "I don't remember this at all."

"Yeah…you summoned your birds." I swallow the discomfort at the base of my throat. "You had them dive from the sky to swoop down and pick the snails up one at a time. It was like a game the way your starlings whipped their heads back to toss the snails into the air before catching them in their beaks. Some birds flew off with the snails, and others played tug-of-war with their bodies and shells before they ate them right in front of me. I heard every one of them break; they sounded like cracking eggshells." My voice is almost a whisper when I finish.

Starling rolls his eyes. "No way, I didn't do that."

"You definitely did." Kestrel nods. "I saw your birds circling the garden, and I started throwing rocks before I saw you." He turns to me. "Lark had to use her gift to console you."

"She held my hand and sang to me for an hour." A weak, breathy laugh slips from my nose. "Mom ended up sitting on my bed and holding me; I absolutely soaked her tunic."

Kestrel's eyes widen, his footsteps picking up with the speed his brain must be going. "Oh man, Mom was so mad that all the elder trees shook and lost their leaves."

"...And Dad grounded me for a month," Starling finishes, a dawning expression rising on his face.

"Ah, so *now* you remember," Kestrel huffs.

Starling shakes his head. "I remember Dad flickering in and out of sight when he sat me down. He struggled to control that side of his goblin ancestry, but never once raised his voice. Not even when he said he was disappointed in me." Starling laughs, though it's lined with resentment. "He was going to take me into the villages that day, just me and him. But instead, I had to stay home to do the worst chores, starting with feeding and turning the compost. He even put me on imp duty for the entire month, and only a week in, they stole my journal. They burned a few pages playing fireball when one used the cover as a shield. I had to climb the rafters to get it while they tossed it back and forth."

"Ha," Kestrel blurts, pointing at our brother's scrunched nose and tripping over a small rock. "That's when you accidentally stuck your hand in that spider sac, and the babies hatched all over you!"

"Yeah, yeah, so funny. I was traumatized, and it was your fault." Starling jabs a finger at me.

Kestrel recovers quickly and lets out a scary, bitter laugh. "*You* were traumatized? Seriously, Starling? Did you not listen to a single thing Swan said?" He palms his forehead. "Oh, that's right, I forgot how much you love the sound of your own voice. You only care about yourself and never consider how you hurt others."

"You want to talk about hurt? 'Cause it's all coming back to me, and if I recall correctly, one of those rocks you threw that day caused this." Starling points at the inch-long scar on his chin.

Seeing the blood drain from Kestrel's face and his stride

slow is the last straw for me. "Okay, that's enough. The whole point of this story wasn't to dredge up the past."

"Then what was the point, Duck?" Starling turns to me with a sneer.

"The snails reminded me of your birds." I avert my eyes. "We can use them if you call on an entire murmuration. If Baba Roga and Allison Gross are working together, one of them may be holding down the fort. Or perhaps both witches are going to the glade, and Uncle Grim will be waiting for us if they plan on using him more like a guard dog rather than a bodyguard."

Starling clicks his tongue. "I don't think a cloud of songbirds could kill a hag or Death's personal Reaper."

"We're not killing anyone, least of all our uncle." I shake my head. "Your birds might serve as a distraction while we search for Robin, Crow, and Dad. Then, once they're free, we get far enough away to summon Auntie Rose with minimal risk."

I'm met with silence.

I know it's not the best plan, but realistically, we don't know what to expect. No one living has seen the surroundings or the inside of Baba Roga's dwelling. We don't know what the trail to it looks like, how big it is, whether we'll be trapped upon entry, or sent through a maze like Mom, Dad, and Hazel were twenty years ago. And assuming I'm right, and someone more powerful than us could be there too, that opens up a whole new set of doors leading to many new, equally terrible possibilities. The best thing we can do is have faith. We grew up hearing about our parents' and godmother's half-baked plan for trapping Black Annis in a ring of salt inside her own home. But in their story, things went awry. Mom and Dad had to deplete the salt they planned to use for Black Annis on vanquishing the water witch, Jenny Greenteeth, after she tried to drown Mom. And although their sole weapon and plan were gone, the trio still persevered, and they still accomplished what they sought to do. Sure, they encountered many trials and tribulations, but they ended Black Annis, saved everyone, and lived. If my brothers and I can have the same faith, and continue to follow in their footsteps, then fate should have a happy ending in store for us, too. Right?

"Before you argue, I want you to consider this." I hold up placating hands. "We've always been told that everything happens for a reason, right? Now that Auntie Poppy is temporarily blind, there are no chance encounters. And we saw all but one prophecy disappear from Auntie Posy's skin. My choice to use The Sun's Blessed arrow on the Rye Mother would always happen. No matter what, using that weapon on Baba Roga's territory would never have been an option. The woodwose would always leave that branch behind, and we would always face that Phouka. Which would lead me to this line of thinking and this very conversation in this exact spot." I gesture to the beginnings of an apple orchard around us. "So, whatever happens when we find Baba Roga's house, and however we get our family back, is how it's supposed to be. We're figuring it out." I start ticking things off on my fingers. "We've heeded Uncle Grim. We've found a way to keep The Numina safe. We're on our way to the sister's web. We'll make it home while The Sun, Moon, and Time still have a strong hold on night and day to make an eclipse. And Mom will open the barrier where we'll finish this as a family." I hold up five wagging fingers before folding all but my pinkie down. "It's our fate."

Kestrel smiles at this, wrapping his little finger around mine as we walk side by side, apple trees above our heads casting shadows onto our shoulders.

Starling reaches out and bats at our arms until Kestrel and I break apart. "You've neglected to consider an essential part of the prophecy. You know, the whole 'a child of the changeling must join the dark for the light to prevail' thing."

I stick my hands into my trouser pockets, concealing the

strange hurt I feel from Starling's reaction to the pinkie promise. "Mom said that prophecies don't always turn out to mean
what we think they do."

"It sounds pretty clear to me, Duck."

Kestrel rolls his eyes at our brother in a very Starling-like
manner. "You can't possibly still believe in your stupid sabotage
theory."

Starling shrugs. "I haven't ruled it out, but I've also considered what else it could mean if we analyzed the words differently. We could assume the definition of the word 'dark' in this
sense is literal, meaning shaded or the absence of sunlight. And
the word 'join,' as in arriving somewhere, or being in the presence of someone, or something." Starling kicks at a stray rotting
apple core in our path as he speaks. "We'd also still be assuming
that the changeling is Mom. But Robin and Crow getting taken
by Uncle Grim, a faerie made of shadow, or the lack of light,
could be a child of the changeling joining the dark."

I'm staring at the dead grass under our feet as we forge on,
processing Starling's musings, when a large shadow rises from
behind us, casting the shape of tall wings onto my outline. My
brothers don't seem to notice this anomaly since Kestrel is still
replying to Starling.

What sort of branches could make that shape?

Footsteps sound behind us. Before I even have a chance to
take another breath, the hood of my cloak yanks backward, and
I follow. The material at the base of my throat is taut and choking, but it's incomparable to the arm that wraps itself around
my neck. If my windpipe wasn't already being crushed, the air
would be knocked out of me as I'm anchored against an
unyielding body.

"My, *my*, nephew," Uncle Grim drawls in a cold, unfamiliar
monotonic cadence. "What an interesting hunch."

Kestrel stumbles.

Starling freezes.

Both whirl around to see the possessed man holding me hostage.

Our uncle drags me backward, and I step on his toes as I struggle to find some ground. I'm drenched in a cold and panicked sweat, but his next words are like plunging into a freezing ice bath. "Should we put your theory to the test?"

Swan: Tricks and Treats

"No," I choke out. "It was a very dumb idea, borderline ridiculous." Pushing myself up on my toes, I shove a hand between the crook of Uncle Grim's elbow and my throat. My brothers are standing there stock-still like the world's most useless garden statues. "Don't you think, Kestrel?"

He blinks upon hearing his name, shattering his stone mask of shock. "*So* dumb," Kestrel agrees, head vigorously nodding. Without tearing his gaze from mine, he reaches out with a clumsy arm and tries to pat Starling's. He misses several times, grasping at air before clamping on to our brother's bicep. "Isn't that right, Starling?"

Starling's lips part to reply before Uncle Grim clicks his tongue. "You ought to be nicer to your brother, children," he tuts. "Perhaps you need to be separated to think about how hurtful your words can be?"

"I don't know, maybe we would benefit more from family bonding time." Pulling on my uncle's arm, I stretch my neck up and to the side to further open my airway. His wings roil in the side of my vision, the shadows constructing them billowing out like the desperate hand of a drowning man. "It might do you some good to join us, Uncle Grim. I'm sure there's plenty for us to discuss," I cough.

The former Pooka's grip tightens at the word *uncle*, pressing my own knuckles into my throat. He leans to look at the side of my face, giving me an up-close glimpse of what he's become. The textured half mask of a lindwyrm's face obscures his own, dragon-esque scales almost glittering and wet with ebony ink; its sharp horns jut out like twisted stalagmites. I've grown so used to the Shadow Prince's calm, colorless skin and comforting sunflower eyes over the years. Which makes the stains of his blood running throughout the cracks and corners of his lips alongside the glow of his red eyes that much more terrifying.

"You've always been so good with your words. You just have a certain *spark* in that brain of yours." From what little air I can get, I smell the scent of something floral and metallic curling from his mouth. "What a shame it will be to see it snuffed out."

My calves give out at this, making me drop from my toes, almost hanging myself on his arm as my jaw slots into the crook of his elbow. My gut screams at me to fight. But something in my head, something on the other side of my attic door that reeks of guilt, and whatever was on my uncle's breath pounds at it. Its words leak in through the gap above the threshold. It tells me that I deserve to be taken. Because maybe then I could see my siblings and father one more time before I die. I'd know if, in a twist of fate, my negligence killed them, and I'd take the responsibility of paying for it. I'm sure Starling would be content with this. And maybe through this self-pitying, self-sacrificial act, he'll forgive me for whatever he thinks I've done. My eyes slip closed, and I wait in a metallic, flowery stupor as Uncle Grim continues to breathe into my face. Numbness from the slow deprivation of air rises from my loosening fingers to my heavy shoulders.

"So don't," I hear Kestrel say to Uncle Grim in his telltale, wavery, false confidence. "Let Swan go, and you won't have to see anything snuffed out, not even a wisp."

The poisoned Reaper pauses, bicep relaxing enough that I can breathe again. The numbness subsides to my wrists as oxygen flows back through my veins. Surprised at this sudden change, I peer through my lashes.

Kestrel smiles at me, tight, worried eyes flicking between my face and Uncle Grim's. My brother spreads his arms wide, a sign of hopeful negotiation. "Problem solved, huh?" Kestrel turns to Starling, elbowing him with an expectant raise to his brows. "Huh?"

Starling's silence is loud, but his glare and pale, pressed lips are louder. Hurt, or perhaps disappointed, that my brother wouldn't at least say one word to aid in my release feels like a punch. It stings enough for me to close my eyes and slip back into the darkness of my eyelids. Even darker thoughts wait for me to turn the knob of my attic door, now decorated with flowers nailed to the carved surface. *Where did those blooms come from?* The door shakes on its hinges as I feel my uncle laugh. The sound is more than disingenuous. It's empty, vacant of any feeling or thought, like the man's mind is far, far away.

Uncle Grim's head rests against mine as he chuckles, and his breath overwhelms my senses. "Did you really think that would work?" His arm tightens so my breathing turns shallow, making that strange bitter scent catch in my airways.

Kestrel's honest, absurd reply makes me want to laugh. "Uh, kind of, yeah."

My brother's silly answer allows something else to seep in from under the door. Something that tells me to open the window and let the sunlight hit my face, to feel my family and their love in its warmth. It reminds me of the faith Mom has in me, and the strength she instilled. Strength that would fight through the bloodroot my uncle is secondhandedly infecting me with. I need to continue to brave this mirrored journey. Taking

189

an imaginary deep breath, the petals are expelled from my door, and my attic smells like sunflowers as the walls echo with Kestrel's voice. I *will* see my siblings and father again. And it'll be on my own two feet with my brothers at my side and a weapon in my hand.

The orchard comes back into view as Uncle Grim's next words ignite my instinct to survive ablaze. "Well, playtime is over, kids."

Wings made of shadows sweep forward, invading my periphery before colliding and folding inward like a set of double doors, closing in my face. I can still see through their gloom. My brothers stand on the other side, a decent distance away, appearing torn. Kestrel is weaponless; his bow and the woodwose's broken crook are jabbing into my spine, and he knows what will happen if he tries to run and tackle us. And Starling's hand hovers over his shoulder, debating whether to take an axe from its holster and hurl it at Uncle Grim. The only issue is how the curved blade would presumably pass through smoky wings and hit me, considering our possessed uncle uses me as a faerie meat shield. Starling, smart enough to know this, searches the ground around him for something less lethal to use. That's when I know my brothers cannot save me.

But I can try to save myself. I must.

So, I buck like a wild horse, become dead weight, contort my body, and throw my weight forward. When that all fails, I kick back, jamming my heels in Uncle Grim's knees and shins. I claw at his elbow, nails digging into the fabric that covers his arm as I twist my hips to attempt to sweep his leg out like Starling almost did to Kestrel earlier. When that doesn't work either, I try biting him, all the while the former Pooka's shadows weave around us like a cocoon. The object tucked against my sternum, which I've tried so very hard to ignore, almost burns when Auntie Rose's words thrum in my pulsing ears.

"If Grim comes after you or your brothers, and all other measures fail, use them as the very last resort."

Being kidnapped by my uncle and brought to a witch's house is one thing, but my aunt giving me a weapon that could kill said uncle was another. But nothing is working. And my brothers are helpless to save me without risking my skin as well. Auntie Rose wanted to be the one to put him to rest, if he couldn't be saved, and she would do just that with the very blades she gave me. I'm not prepared for any of these options, least of all wielding Death's shears…at least not how she intended.

The arm trapped against my side can't reach any of my knives, but it can reach my belt.

My fingers wriggle until they touch the top curve of the bows.

If I could wound the Reaper enough to escape and not kill him, perhaps my brothers and I could lose him in the orchard.

One finger slips into a ring.

More specifically, I could stab him in the thigh to immobilize him while we run.

A second finger slips into the other ring.

Plotting where on his thigh to stab, and calculating how far we could run is pulled to a jolting stop with a single shout.

"Duck!"

It takes a few seconds for me to realize that Starling isn't calling out to me with his mean nickname.

Through layers of misty darkness, I see Starling reach up, ripping a hanging apple straight off the tree limb above him. I recognize his posture in a memory honed from years of playing catch with Dad's hand-sewn beanbags. And my head is leaning as far away from our uncle's as it can get when Starling draws his shoulder back. The apple shatters against Uncle Grim's skull, exploding into a spray of teeny, tiny, juicy pieces. Judging by the sound of the impact, there's no doubt that it hurt. My assessment is confirmed by the surprised hiss, followed by Uncle Grim's grip slipping and wings parting. It's the breech I needed, just wide enough for me to wrench myself free of his stifling grasp, sending the closed, dagger-like shears swinging forward into my palm.

I only make it two steps forward before the Shadow Prince recovers and latches on to my wrist. Yanking me back, he spins me into his gauzy shroud of black caught between the transition of dissipating to re-forming. Despite my preparedness for being snatched this time, I'm not quite ready for how his quick, reeling movement changes my intended target. My hand is slipping Death's cold shears into the meat of his shoulder, slicing through tendons and muscles before I can blink. And we stand there, staring at each other with ruby eyes meeting mint. My fist is still wrapped around the handles of Auntie Rose's ancient weapon, the metal freezing against my skin. The shears are so deep that the outside of my hand, along with my pinkie, are flush with my uncle's shoulder. I've shocked myself and the Reaper to the point I can almost hear his thoughts:

I can't believe this child just stabbed me.

And that makes two of us.

Dazed, I let go and stumble back. Despite the Shadow Prince's black clothing, I can still see the bright, garnet wetness seeping down his torso. Perhaps it's the trauma of what I've done, or a strange effect from The Numina altering time, but I swear I see something phantom-like wriggling from his body. It's so quick I almost miss it reaching out from his chest towards the shears. But when I blink, the golden thread braided with red, and something that reminds me of a tiger's eye stone, all dipped in black, disappears back into his sternum. Meeting Uncle Grim's gaze again, I swear I catch a flicker of yellow in his irises, like an old part of himself poured out with the spilling of his blood. As it glugs from his shoulder, it thickens like sap, reeking of bitter spice. When the mixture takes on a putrid green, witchcraft glow, I watch any trace of realness in his eyes die away.

Somewhere behind us, Kestrel's voice alerts me, my brothers are quickly approaching. The rough, bloodroot-stained grip that Uncle Grim has on my wrist tightens before he releases me and staggers away, taking the shears with him. His wings flare wide, though one droops, as does the corresponding arm, both as immobile as I'd hoped to make his leg. He disappears a millisecond later.

As quick as I can, I take the sunflower clusters from my pocket and pour the rest of the doses straight from the bag into my mouth. I need the salt to chase away the rest of this dark fog from the scent of the bloodroot. I'm about to bend over and catch my breath when Kestrel pulls me into a bungling hug. My nose zings with a crushing pain where the bridge smashes into his collarbone.

"You about gave me a heart attack! Your face was literally purple at one point," Kestrel babbles. The rumble of his voice feels like a hornet's nest in my head. "Are you okay?"

My reply comes out high and nasally, warped when I can't open my mouth all the way without consuming wool. "That's my line."

"Family bonding?" Kestrel pulls me back to look at my face. "Seriously, Swan?" he chides.

Even with my mind spinning from the last two days' odd and terrifying events, I want to laugh at his bewildered, albeit concerned, expression. His brows are so high they're almost receding into his shorn scalp. I want to tease him for being a mother hen, just to ease his frets, but instead I remove the quarter of the woodwose's crook I stashed away in my back pocket and present it to Kestrel. "Surprise?"

My younger brother's face lights up, like I had given him a puppy for Christmastide, and he gleefully releases one hand to take the broken wood. "Stick!" He gasps. "You saved it for me!"

Then, Kestrel's thick brows, along with the corners of his mouth, drop in a theatrical way. "No, wait, I'm supposed to be upset with you."

"You know I cope with inopportune humor sometimes, especially when I get stressed," I start. The dry rustling noise of a breeze stirring the autumn leaves snakes through the orchard, changing the tone of my deflection. "I think I was also sort of hoping that some of the sarcasm would ring an old bell and draw out Uncle Grim's old self. Maybe remind him of Auntie Rose a little bit."

Starling scoffs. "What you said to him was careless and stupid, and in the end, you lost Auntie Rose's shears. I swear, you're always begging to get yourself killed one way or another. And this time, it's like you were hoping to take us with you on the way out."

"Whoa. Come on." Kestrel lets me go to face Starling, sliding the broken wood in his hand into the knapsack over his shoulder. "That's uncalled for and way out of line, man. You can't just say that."

I had expected Starling to accuse me of being the dark link working for the witches again. Perhaps with a whole spiel about my supposed ulterior motives and more sabotage. And now I wish that were the case, because what comes next is *much* worse.

"We all have to tiptoe around you when you get in your mood," he says. Mentioning our family in his royal "*we*" makes me shrink back. "But maybe you're the one who needs to be more mindful. Because one of these days, when you decide things are a little too gloomy for you, you know who will have to reap those consequences? That's right. Us." With a tremoring hand, Starling gestures between him and Kestrel. The latter of which gapes at him, mortified. "Do you even know how mad Dad and Mom would be if we came back without you because you decided you were done? It would be our fault. Not yours."

Starling shoves a shaking finger at me. When he sees the movement in his hand, he crosses his arms and folds his hands
beneath his armpits. "That is just beyond selfish, and you have
no good reason to put that on us."

"Starling," Kestrel snaps again, a clear warning in his tone.

But our brother leans further into his tongue lashing,
throwing my own mental state in my face. "What is it that
makes you so screwed up, *huh?*" he asks, voice wavering like his
hands had. "We had a good childhood. We have a roof over our
heads back home, and we all get plenty of food in our stomachs
every day. We have the best parents. We have our entire family,
and you have plenty of their favoritism." Starling sniffs. "There's
nothing wrong with your life, Duck. Unless you're just acting
out because you don't have a changeling gift." He pauses when I
don't defend myself. I'm in shock though, not only from his
cruelty, but from the wild look akin to fear in his eye. "That's it,
isn't it?" He laughs, though it trembles along with his shoulders.
"Oh *boo-hoo*, get over yourself."

Kestrel's response to our brother is a thunderclap, much
fiercer than any that shook the sky yesterday. "Depression isn't
a choice, numskull. It can be biological, situational, or inherited." He glares at Starling with a mix of disgust and disappointment. "Hazel says that some people are missing a messenger in
their brain to communicate with their nerves. But you're obviously missing something even more important, especially if you
think your words are remotely okay. Maybe it's your heart." He
turns to me. "Don't listen to him, Swan. He's not worth it."

I want Kestrel to stop fueling him, and I want Starling to
stop looking at me like I've just dropped dead of my own volition. But I can't seem to find my tongue. I'm baffled. Starling
has never once targeted something as serious as the health of
my mind. Plus, the effect that the sheer amount of bloodroot
Uncle Grim had on his breath was not me; Allison Gross's
poison preyed on my illness. The confusing emptiness and too-

much-ness of depression can be heavy some days, but I do not want to die. I love my family, and I have so much that I still want to do, and write. Doesn't Starling know that? Not to mention, acknowledging the similar struggles our mom and aunts have had with anxiety, panic, sleep, delayed stress, and so on. But now, with how shaken he is, I think my brother is grasping at anything to find stability.

Starling looks between Kestrel and me, quivering before he sets his sights on me again. "You're so weak you can't even speak for yourself." He forces out a chuckle. "Tell me, Duck, are you going to have our little brother fight all your battles for the rest of your dull existence?"

I get it now.

Starling is looking for purchase, leverage to keep his own head above water. Usually, I would let him. But this is not a sink-or-swim situation; it's a battle of emotional wills and mental survival. I'll drag my brother to the surface with me, but not without a wake-up call. So, putting a hand on Kestrel before he lunges at Starling with bared teeth and balled fists, I take a deep breath.

"I don't think you see the real issue here. There shouldn't be fights in the first place," I say, calm and measured. Though I sound tired, even to my own ears. "Every day, I leave my bedroom filled with dread and fear, knowing that you'll verbally attack me any chance you get. Kestrel shouldn't have to protect me from you. I shouldn't have to speak up for myself like this, you and your words shouldn't be something I fear. You're my brother." A sad smile finds its way to my lips. "You're supposed to be my best friend, not the person who hurts me the most."

Starling blinks. His face is expressionless, but a flinch in his eyelids betrays him. He's being forced to digest my words like a horrible breakfast. Hope that this could be the beginning of a cornerstone for my brother and I blossoms, growing inside my heart like a garden of reconciliation. Maybe all this tyrannizing animosity could be put to rest upon a bed of yellow roses, once and for all?

The blooms wilt, withering as Starling's eyes droop. He begins a slow mocking clap. *"Wow.* That level of drama almost surpassed Kestrel's theatrics. That's impressive."

My insides sizzle, and I can do nothing to contain the explosion bubbling toward the surface. I can't handle it anymore, not now that I've mustered the dormant confidence from my attic junk drawer and tried to speak up. I was vulnerable and my brother tore me down and embarrassed me, again. I'm done with bottling everything up for the sake of family peace. We are no longer treading this water. I'm sending us flying out of this stupid ocean. My brother's fear about me almost getting taken by our uncle is masquerading as a means to guilt-trip and shame me. I won't have it, not anymore.

"Stop it," I bark. "You act like you're so high and mighty, but you're not impervious to basic emotions, Starling. I don't know why you pretend to hate me so much, but you have no right to treat me this way." My tone is that of a mother disciplining her child, but I couldn't care less. "So, unless you want to finally talk about why you're too emotionally constipated to communicate your own issues, and explain why you've made the last five years of my life a living Purgatory, you can save it."

Starling is seething and ready to retaliate.

That is until Kestrel interjects with a strange and sudden wobble to his voice, uncharacteristically glazing over Starling's incoming harassment. "Uh, so, completely off topic. Swan, can I have The Moon's candle?"

"No!" Starling and I say in unison, voices raised and angry, though not with our younger brother. We don't even break the connection between our scathing glares.

I'm heated, fists clenched, and toes scrunched in my boots. My hands and feet are on fire, and my veins feel like they're boiling with my nerve damage. I'm so mad that Starling continues to be so pointlessly bullheaded and mean that I'm vibrating.

"I think we could really use that candle right now." Kestrel holds up his index finger between us, flagging our attention before he rambles, "But, Starling, when we get home and this is all over, you're totally gonna get it." Kestrel points to me. "And Swan, super proud. But I think we should be running." He points outward, farther into the orchard.

Turns out the vibration isn't just me and my overflowing frustration. There isn't a breeze to rustle the leaves either; the orchard itself is shaking with a vibration that the rubber of my boots absorbs. The foliage on the ground quakes too. And, about five feet to my right, an apple sitting upright at the base of a tree topples over with the movement. This reminds me of the little shrapnel pieces of exploded fruit covering my clothing, and my stomach flips.

"The Gooseberry Wife," I gasp, widening eyes fixated on Starling. The image of him pulling the apple from the tree above him and hurling it at Uncle Grim repeats in my head.

At the sound of the bogeyman's name, my brothers and I bolt, though in different directions. I head west in a straight line, the opposite direction of the ruckus signaling the Gooseberry Wife's impending arrival. Starling hollers at Kestrel, who darted to the left toward the south, instead of north like him. I correct course as our younger brother careens around a tree, fingertips brushing against the earth to prevent a fall before he gets his feet back under him. Kestrel stands completely still, forcing Starling and I to stop as well. Confused, the three of us huff and puff as we take up positions in a triangle, each about fifty feet apart.

"Where are you guys going?" Kestrel shouts from his spot in the middle of an alley between tree plots.

"What do you mean where are we going?" Starling retorts. "You're running right to her, you idiot!"

Kestrel throws up his hands. "How am I the idiot when you're running towards all the noise?"

If they keep arguing over which wrong direction to run, we will have the great displeasure of meeting the Gooseberry Wife. I wave at my brothers, motioning them in my direction. "Seriously, you guys? Hurry up, come on!"

"Swan!" Kestrel points at Starling. "She's coming from— from..." The words die on his lips as he glances over his shoulder, listening. His arm falls and he faces me, so lost that Crow wouldn't be able to find him. "She was coming from there, but now..." Kestrel turns in a slow circle, glowering in each cardinal direction.

As the seconds tick by, the shaking ripples like earthquakes through the orchard. It sounds like hundreds of snake tails line the land, and everything atop the soil shifts. An apple falls from the branches above me, clipping my shoulder, encouraging me to close the distance between Kestrel and I. We're back-to-back now, but I fully intend to drag him with me. That is until I walk around Kestrel and see how unsure he is of his own ears. I listen more closely. Kestrel is right. The sound of the Gooseberry Wife's arrival is louder the opposite way. Our minds must be playing tricks on us, like the Rye Mother's hallucinations making us see our skin falling off and the field die around us. Or how mundane shapes, in a semi-dark room, can become terrifying, monstrous creatures. But when you turn on a lantern or light a candle, and the room is revealed to you, you'll find everything safe and ordinary. The form of a witch sitting at the end of your bed was only a stack of clothes waiting to be folded inside your wooden chest. A pack of rotting wolves, only mist.

That's the power of suggestion, fueled by existing fear.

"Remember when we were younger, and no matter how many times Mom and Dad warned us about playing by the stream, we never listened?" I ask Kestrel.

He shifts his feet, sparing our stubborn brother across the way a look before nodding.

The damp grass and salty, mud-scented nostalgia-tinted ghosts cross through my attic walls as I continue. "They had to take up the old and questionable ways of parenting, scaring us into being safe. That's why they started telling us not to get too close to the water or Nelly Longarms would grab us." With this theory in mind, I take the bow and quiver from my back and squat to sit on my heels. Kestrel and I both watch Starling's hesitant approach, his gaze sweeping north behind Kestrel before landing east behind me.

Starling shakes his head. "Get up."

"I think the warning of picking something from the Gooseberry Wife's orchard is the same, to keep people from stealing the harvest." I lay the gold-stringed weapon and green-fletched ammunition atop the jittering leaves. The bow and arrow rattle and shake upon contact, but I don't believe it for a moment.

"Get up," Starling shouts again as he picks up his pace, his tone harsher than necessary.

Considering he has no respect for me or my emotions, I hold Starling in the same regard by doing the opposite and proving my point. "This is all just a magic-based trick," I finish. With complete confidence in this orchard being nothing more than a visual and audible illusion, I place my palm on the ground.

To my dismay, it still shudders beneath my touch.

Time seems to slow even further. A combination of stupefaction and exhaustion sets everything into slow motion. Each of Starling's footsteps, as he sprints toward us, registers with every one of my unsteady heartbeats. As does the symphony of apples popping like soap bubbles beneath a great weight. A spray of juice hits my neck like a fine vapor. I cannot comprehend the glimpse I get over my shoulder of a monster with a woman's face before Starling rams into me.

My siblings have tackled me before, but we were smaller,

weaker, and more playful then. Never has any of them rushed me so violently, especially while trying to take two of us out in one go. The pain of the impact is delayed as events unfold. But I don't miss Starling's failed attempt at grabbing Kestrel's burgundy cloak to pull him out of harm's way, too. When I roll through the grass, Starling's limbs knock the wind out of me, and I catch upside-down snippets of Kestrel stumbling into the monster's rampaging path. Wheezing where I land, lying on my stomach, I pick up my chin just in time to see my brother topple right into the monster's arms. Before I can blink, she hoists him into the air. Then, the Gooseberry Wife unhinges her impossibly wide jaw and swallows Kestrel whole.

Grim: Oath

They are waiting for me when I get back, and I slither to my knees before her like a wounded animal. She looks furious but she strokes my face, her loving talons grazing my temples and cheekbones. My blood drips onto her dainty, rotten lime feet, but she doesn't mind. She just clicks her tongue at the shears jutting from my shoulder. "You poor, poor thing. How dare they damage my property?"

The way that she cares for me chills my blood in such a restoring way. Her words increase that intoxicating bitterness on my tongue. I can't imagine what she would've done had those invalid children taken me from her. I'm her favorite. She needs me.

Your family needs you.

Hush.

Don't you remember your and Rose's oath?

An involuntary, poison-hazed memory replaces the image of the ghastly, spellbinding woman before me. With it, the scent of snowdrops and midnight assaults my senses. I see Death where she stood across from me, a smile on her dark-lacquered lips, one that sparkled brighter than the rings and chains that hung from her rippled ears. We were somewhere secret inside Wyrd

Mountain, under the waterfall behind the old statue of Lady Time. There was an ornamental knot of red and black thread over where we pressed the pulse points of our wrists together. A corded length wrapped around our arms where we held each other's forearms.

"I am yours for an eternity, Reaper," Death had said before laughing. "You can't get rid of me now."

I shook my head at her with a fond chuckle. "As I am yours. You are my beginning and my end, Primrose. I promise that wherever you go, I will follow."

"Wherever you go, I will follow," she echoed.

We sealed our oath with only an embrace and then spent the night talking about things like literature, the stars, and our nieces and nephews, all over a shared tin of ginger men biscuits and elderberry wine.

I was...happy?

It doesn't matter now, though, because this fleeting and foolish reverie is shattered when she rips the shears from my shoulder and shrieks like a banshee. The blood-coated metal falls to the floor with a *thump* as she clutches her sizzling hand to her elegant, emaciated chest. My heart races for her. It's not excitement to see her in pain, absolutely not. My injury caused this. Stupid. Stupid, stupid, stupid.

Serves her right. Posy and Rose were geniuses for annealing everything in salt.

"I'm sorry, my lady," I grovel, bowing my horned head to her in supplication. "I should've done better. Please forgive me."

She clamps her steaming hand down on my wound, squeezing and pressing, and I do my best not to fold inward. I'm sure she's only trying to help. She is magnificent. Harder, she compresses my wound, staunching it with her striking strength.

Ah, yes. That's it. She's making sure I don't bleed out.

Don't be daft. She's punishing you.

Just when I think I might show signs of discomfort from her assistance, she lets go. Holding her hand up, turning it this way and that to see my blood glinting in the reddish light floating above our heads. Her tongue darts out and licks from the heel of her hand to the tip of her middle finger, cleaning it of my blood and the poisonous sap mixed inside it. I can hear the slight bubbling sizzle on her taste buds when she grins. "It's no matter, trinket. They'll get what's coming to them." She wipes the rest of my blood on her gown, but with its color, it blends right in. "Clean yourself up and pick up those scissors now. We must prepare to leave; there will be visitors soon."

"It's time."

Swan: The Gooseberry Wife

*K*estrel's name rips from me in a blood-curdling scream.

This is the first good look I get of the Gooseberry Wife, and it's as she guzzles my younger brother down into her long caterpillar-like body. She's a giant maroon-and-burnt-persimmon-hued creature with a ten-foot-long tail that turns into a midsection where it curves upward a few feet before blending into a human-ish waist. The upper portion of the Gooseberry Wife's body stands at least eight feet high, and from start to end, she's as thick and wide as one of her apple trees. It's almost like looking at a mermaid or siren, but much, *much* worse. She's all clacking insect legs, each sharp and spindly, and there are way too many shelled, hairy limbs to count. I was so wrong about the orchard. Yes, the ruckus and trembling were real, but it was still a magic-encrusted illusion. It was a distraction masterpiece, built so the massive bogeyman could attack without her prey knowing if they were running to or from her.

My mistake has gotten Kestrel killed. My sunshine is gone.

"*Kestrel!*" My arms shake as I push up onto my hands and knees, shrieking again for my brother. The sheer volume and desperation of my cries draws the Gooseberry Wife's attention. And when she sees the tears streaming down my face, she licks her lips with a blackened, pointy tongue.

I must get to Kestrel.

Starling grabs at my ankle as I try getting to my feet. I shake him off, though my brother persists, dragging me back, away from the bogeyman. She smiles at this, the corners of her mouth splitting her cheeks to reveal multiple rows of teeth, some of which are the size of arrowheads. I dig my fingers into the ground to fight forward, but Starling is stronger than me. Fistfuls of grass, leaves, and dirt come out in my hands as I claw at the earth, trying to reach the bow and arrows I'd so foolishly discarded.

"Stop it," I sob, kicking back at Starling. "Let me go!"

My boot connects with fabric-covered flesh, and my brother grunts. I don't care where I hit him. All I care about is sinking something sharp into the Gooseberry Wife. I will rend her limb from limb to get Kestrel back, and if Starling wants me to stop, he will either have to let the bogey kill me, or kill me himself. He's better off abandoning me, running straight to the West Woods since he's so quick to leave Kestrel anyway. Or what's left of him.

A grief-stricken fire is set ablaze in my gut, it's so hot, so all-consuming. But as Starling drags me back on my hands and knees, I reach for one of my eight remaining knives. The second before it leaves my hand, my brother tugs, and I collapse onto my elbow with only one hand supporting me. The pull destroys my aim, causing my throwing knife to land next to one of the Gooseberry Wife's many tarsal leg claws. The bogey's laughter sounds like a hiss echoed by a rhythmic clicking in the base of her throat. I'm aiming again though, right for that area, eyes focused on the bright orange along the expanse of her neck when her tail starts moving. It's the beginning of an inch, an action I've seen before from caterpillars on the glade's garden trellises, when the muscles starting at the end of the tail contract. The movement is like a ripple of water, but this looks much different, much ghastlier on a creature this big.

Following the wave of movement forward, the Gooseberry Wife advances with a wicked smile. I fight twice as hard against Starling, ready to meet the bogeyman in the middle. And I almost succeed in launching forward when Starling's grip seemingly slips. A wobbling knife flees from my touch and grazes the bogey's shoulder. She's not deterred—in fact, she doesn't even flinch. Anger rages through my limbs, and I use my newfound freedom to jump to my feet. Without so much as a backward glance at Starling, I propel myself with my dominant foot, pushing off the ground in a sprinting start. Only for my brother to use this against me, catching me around the waist the moment my weight is off my feet. Starling arches his back so my boots can't touch the grass, and hauls me away. All the while, the Gooseberry Wife watches on, amused and approaching at her leisure. She's feasting on my struggle, like a palate cleanser.

"You heartless coward," I screech, trying to pull my arms out from where Starling has trapped them at my sides. "We can't leave him!"

A noise of frustration and pain rumbles through him. "You'll die trying to get him back."

The way he says this, the implication that there is nothing left to do but tuck tail and run, grinds through my ears. It makes my molars zing. "I don't care, I have to try," I spit.

"Well, I care. I've lost enough," Starling says through gritted teeth.

Bucking back and forth, I ignore the pang of my brother's words and put myself into a one-trail mind. I need something longer than a throwing knife, something with more impact. If I can reach the bow, I can put an arrow right through the bogey's eye. "Let me down, I just need to get Kestrel's bow!"

"He's gone," Starling shouts, the tail end breaking as I wriggle hard enough to free my right hand.

To Purgatory with Starling.

To Purgatory with this Timeforsaken orchard.

To Purgatory with self-preservation.

The only thing that's ringing through my mind is Kestrel. My baby brother. Kestrel. Get to Kestrel.

Starling tightens his hold around my gut, trying to compensate for the lost space, but I'm on a mission. And when I reach over his bicep for a knife at my thigh, he jolts me to the opposite side. My toe brushes against the ground and I seize the opportunity to push off as hard as I can, attempting to throw Starling off. His grasp becomes crushing, but the movement does allow me to hook a finger in the eye of a knife and spin the handle into my hand. Cocking back my arm more than necessary, I elbow Starling in the face and release the blade. It flies handle over tip, completing two full rotations before it hits the Gooseberry Wife with a *thwack*.

With an agonized groan, Starling twists, heaving me over so I'm facing away from the bogeyman. In this position, he can lug me around more easily without my jerky movements while trying to walk backward. But I still caught the way the Gooseberry Wife stared down at the short blade lodged right below her navel in disbelief. Like she was surprised that I have the audacity to hit my mark, to attempt to kill her. I almost laugh until the bogey screeches.

Starling falters and turns, putting the furious bogey back into our view. The sight of her setting up, readying to charge, makes my brother's arms relax a touch. But a touch is enough for me to break the connection where Starling's hands lock onto his wrists. As the Gooseberry Wife storms the orchard alley, she crushes any apple in her path and flattens the grass. I need to get to Kestrel's bow before the bogey crushes that too. Facing Starling, I shove at his chest as hard as I can. Stunned, he falls back onto the grass, straight onto his tailbone, eyes wide and...misty? I don't register the emotion welling up along his lashes, I don't care, not right now when I need to make my move.

As I reach for another salted throwing knife, my forearm clips my leather side bag, and I'm reminded of The Moon's Blessed candle and matches. I could use them. The candle is the last magic item we have from The Numina. And when lit, it will burn with the heat and purifying intensity of the sun itself. I have three matches and one shot to light the candle, but I must be within arm's length of the Gooseberry Wife. It's risky. But this is the kind of situation The Moon gave me the weapon for, right?

I'm choosing the correct path...I think.

Propelling myself onward with reckless abandon, I rush the Gooseberry Wife. There's a slight tug at the tail end of my cloak where, presumably, Starling tries to lunge from the ground and grab the torn navy fabric. But I'm quicker and lighter than him. The muscles in my calves pull tight as I race forward, the airglow light bouncing off the curling lacquered bow. An echoing memory of Mom's laugh from the day an elder tree gave a branch for my brother's weapon passes between my ears, circling the patterned rug on my attic floor. It throws a hitch in my step. Kestrel would kick my butt right out of the After if I accidentally joined him there. Not only would the bow be a token of him, but we need it to summon Auntie Rose; she's our only way back home. My head spins as I start closing the distance, trying to weigh the possibility of snatching the bow and getting away. Although not too far away, because I need to light the enchanted candle close enough to kill the bogey without getting eaten in the process. The odds are slim. And our connection to the glade is more important than a short-lived spark of sunlight. Especially when I can still kill her with the bow and arrows.

I can smell the waves of fermented apples coming off the Gooseberry Wife when I dig my heels into the dirt to switch course. This decision makes me slip on a large leaf, sending me sprawling. The bogey is mere feet from trampling Kestrel's bow, to be quickly followed by my body, and I find myself frozen. I'm stuck in a response way less helpful than fight or flight; I'm paralyzed. All I can do is scrunch my eyes closed and turn my head, listening for the crunch of wood before the splintering of my bones.

But it never comes.

Cautious and confused, I relax an eyelid enough to peek at what should've been my impending doom.

The Gooseberry Wife stands as frozen as me, Kestrel's bow and quiver intact a half a foot away from her plentiful legs. She blinks down at me, a milky membrane flicking down over her solid brown eyes and back, much like a reptile. A frown splits the bogey's glossy, spit-slick mouth down to her chin. A shower of the Gooseberry Wife's brunette hair rests over her cheekbones as she looks down at my knife, still protruding from her lower stomach. I follow her lead as a peculiar protrusion wiggles its way down from her belly button toward the blade. If I didn't know any better, I'd think it was a massive baby's foot kicking from inside her womb. But it's not a foot that shoves my knife from the bogeyman's skin, making it drop to the grass below. No, it's the splintered end of a broken tree branch that sticks out of the puncture I made, making the skin stretch and widen. A small burble of thick toffee-colored blood leaks from her. Though it's quickly succeeded by a waterfall when the branch tears upward with a great force, splitting the Gooseberry Wife from the navel to the bottom of her bare sternum between the ribs. The slash is huge, at least six feet long, and the perfect-sized hole for a rather large teenage changeling boy. A hole that Kestrel falls from, gasping on his side and covered in goo, knapsack and all. The Gooseberry Wife falls over onto her side with him, making the ground and surrounding trees shudder. But unlike my brother, she fails to draw in another breath.

Kestrel, wielding the fourth of the woodwose's regifted, broken tree branch, gets to his feet. With his face tilted to the chilly sky, he fills his lungs with the magic Hallowtide air. My jaw is loose as he looks back at the bogeyman's corpse with disdain and halfheartedly kicks her caterpillar body. Kestrel weighs the stick in his hand before dropping it and sloughing the Gooseberry Wife's syrupy ichor off his face. He glowers down at his clothes as he causally walks past his bow, brushing off the goop atop the wool fibers covering his arms. I'm still frozen, almost outside my body. But it's not fear that keeps me rooted in place. I'm paralyzed by joy. The elation and relief drown me; my love for my little brother pouring from my heart, out through my eyes in torrents. He's alive.

My sunshine is alive.

And if Starling didn't just dart past me to pull Kestrel in by the neck and hug him, I might've turned into a weeping pillar of stone, and this orchard would've gained a fountain. Like me, Kestrel is stunned by our grumpy brother's touch, and his hands splay out as wide as his eyes. Starling's chuckle of tearful relief is muffled by Kestrel's slime-damp shoulder. The unfamiliar sound is entirely inaudible when Kestrel hugs him back. They pound each other's backs with heartfelt, albeit aggressive, pats as I creep closer. The brightest and most genuine smile is on Starling's face, something I haven't seen in years. And when he pulls Kestrel back by his upper arms to inspect him, my chest aches with how much I've missed Starling's dimpled grin. I'd forgotten that his right dimple is deeper. And how the left side of his lower lip pulls down more than the other side, revealing the start of his gums. He'd just lost his last baby tooth the last time I saw this kind of unabashed happiness. I didn't even know that when Starling smiles his crooked smile, and the flesh over his chin stretches, the scar marring it turns white against his burnished skin tone. It looks like a crescent moon, the much smaller half to the one lighting up his face.

"This might be controversial"—Kestrel looks at me with a smile that makes me cry tenfold—"but I think that went well," he chirps.

Through the tears blurring my vision, I see Starling put a hand on Kestrel's forehead and push him away. One might think this would ruin the tenderhearted moment between siblings, but Kestrel just laughs before folding me into a sour, apple-scented hug. Kestrel is tangible, and I can touch him. I can sense his heartbeat and feel his breath. I can even hear the growl of his bottomless, boyish stomach. This is real, and my brother is alive. But our reunion can only last so long because the wetness on my cheek, where it rests against Kestrel's cloak, is the Gooseberry Wife's insides.

"You scared me half to death. Are you okay?" I gag, mopping my face with my sleeve, cleaning it of tears and slime before punching Kestrel in the arm, not giving him time to answer. "You're not allowed to die on me, or else."

Kestrel raises his brows, amused by my empty threat. "Or else what?" he asks.

"Or else I'll tell Mom and Dad," I say. Kestrel sticks his tongue out at me, and I pay him in kind by curling my hand into a fist and sticking my littlest finger between us. "Pinkie promise me you won't do that again. I want to see how wrinkly your face gets when you're old, that way I can make fun of you and all your saggy glory."

My brother glows, laughing as he slings apple slop from his legs at me. Dancing away from the attack, I bump into a now stoic Starling. He's covertly running his knuckles beneath his eyes, wiping the moisture onto his wine cloak where not even a river of tears could stain it with wet speckles. Then, he glares at both of us. Something inside me, maybe a tiny sprout of hope in that vacant rose garden, shrinks, but it doesn't shrivel. I got to see *him* again, like under the woodwose's watch, I got to witness the best friend I grew up with. He was hugging our brother mere moments ago, that very boy. And that was him I saw, when he tried to keep me away from The Gooseberry Wife. When he tried to save me. The Starling that used to be thoughtful and sensitive is still there somewhere.

Though it seems that even seeing Kestrel eaten alive can't permanently sway whatever bitter, cold-resistant plant is living inside Starling.

"Hey." Kestrel nudges me, holding out his knobby pinkie as an offering.

Heart soaring, and head brimming with giggling memories and tales containing all kinds of red threads, I hook my little finger around his until our knuckles grind together. When we release each other, I allow myself a tentative glance at Starling where he stands with his arms crossed, wearing a mask of boredom. Despite this, I extend the same finger and promise I offered Kestrel, to Starling. My pinkie is an olive branch, an extension of an older sister waiting to pull her younger brother into the rafters as she teaches him to climb. I want him to climb out of this hole of contempt he's dug himself into, and my finger is the rope I'm pleading for him to hold on to.

"Grow up, Duck." Starling rolls his eyes and shoulders past me.

My hand droops as he walks away to retrieve the bow and quiver in front of the Gooseberry Wife's cooling body. His words are a knife. But he wields a self-sabotaging blade, one that keeps cutting the rope meant to help him, fraying the ends into broken and hurting strands. In the past, I thought it was about me, that I had done something wrong, but it's not, it's about him. And what Starling doesn't realize is that ropes can be mended and spliced back together in so many ways. When will he ever figure that out?

In the meantime, I lay a frustrated, well-mannered curse on him.

May the hole you hide in fill with spiders, peppermint sweets, a bushel of Robin's dirty blue worm-flavored peas, and all the other things you hate.

"Well, this all could've been worse." I usher Kestrel onward. We need to catch up with Starling so we can continue our way west. Quickly. "I mean, we thought you died, and you probably could've if The Gooseberry Wife had chewed on you first. Technically, we could all die tonight depending on how things go from here..." I trail off, clearing my throat instead of dragging Kestrel down into any dark uncertainty with me. "At least you smell like apple cider instead of intestines."

Kestrel chuckles. "Always looking on the bright side, aren't you?"

"You know me, cheeriest changeling in the glade." I laugh weakly.

The crisp click of my fingers signals our arrival, and Starling turns at the sound. He thrusts his arm toward me, the leather strap of the full quiver sandwiched between his hand and the bow grip. I don't have the opportunity to take them from his impatient grasp before Kestrel snatches them both. He slings the quiver over his head, wearing it diagonally along his back, and hooks the bow onto his shoulder like the strap of a knapsack. Kestrel thumbs the gold string where it meets the crease of his armpit, gazing in our intended direction and away from his prior prison of flesh and apples.

Starling wordlessly hands me two of the three of the knives I threw at the bogey. I didn't even see him retrieve the blades, and I don't get to thank him before he's crossing his arms again, this time with a smirk. "Look at you." He tilts his chin up at Kestrel.

"Finally feeling man enough to use your gift after escaping the belly of a beast?"

Kestrel stays silent, jaw twitching.

"Come on, don't tell me you feel bad about the bogey." Starling motions toward the Gooseberry Wife's massive body. "You gutted her like a fish, and with a stick of all things."

Kestrel's finger is digging into the bowstring, deep enough that it's indenting his skin and blanching the tip of his thumb. By his stiff posture, I can tell he isn't proud of what he's done, even though it was necessary. He's done everything in his power to not use his changeling gift, sticking to his semi-secretive *"do no harm"* motto, even in other perilous times of need. And that almost five-years-long practice was undone in only a matter of terrifying seconds.

"Drop it, Starling. He didn't have a choice," I say calmly, hoping that my contrasting frantic and pointed facial expression of raised brows, wide minty eyes, and pinched mouth conveys how bothered Kestrel is.

But Starling isn't paying attention to my visual plea. Starling's too focused on the side of Kestrel's tense face, searching for a way to tease a more significant reaction out of him to deflect his own emotions. "It's been a while since you used your gift. I bet it was itching at you to be used," Starling jabs. When this doesn't elicit anything, he pushes further. "Some part of you had to have wanted to hurt that thing, otherwise how would you be able to kill her with just a stick, right?" He uses sweeping gestures to try directing Kestrel's attention, motioning to the ground with broad strokes. "I mean, look at your big ol' target and your pitiful weapon of choice. Only *you* could've made it work."

Kestrel's thumb pushes further into the enchanted string. If it didn't come from Auntie Poppy's spinning wheel, I'd think it was on the verge of splitting under such pressure. Knowing Kestrel can't break it makes me more concerned, not for the bow, but for his skin. Imagining the golden thread wicked with Kestrel's blood makes me stand up for him once more. This time, carrying the same tone Mom used the first time she found the three of us climbing onto the roof of Grandma Aspen's old house before it was turned into the family library.

"Starling," I warn. "He obviously doesn't want to talk about this. Leave it alone, and let's go. *Now.*"

Of course, he ignores me to lean closer to Kestrel, narrowing his eyes with a sly, pale-lipped grin, like he's just sussed out some sort of secret. "Did you miss the power of your gift? Did it feel good to use the magic you were born with again?" Starling shoots me a purposeful and quick mocking look. "You can tell me, I won't judge—"

I swear I hear Kestrel's neck pop as he whips his head to face Starling, effectively shutting him up. His features are tight and angry. He raises an aggressive finger parallel to Starling's chin, ready to tell him off until Kestrel's stare drops to where he's pointing. His finger shakes, silver eyes flashing like flipping coins as he steps back from Starling. His voice isn't much louder than a whisper when he speaks. "Not another word."

Kestrel peels back to march his way west through the orchard. He only stops long enough to rip a shiny ruby apple from a low-hanging branch of a nearby tree. He spitefully bites into the fruit with forceful, bared teeth. I've never seen Kestrel in such a state. He's never been one to crumble so far beneath our brother's merciless taunting, and he's always the first to fight a Starling fire with nothing but his own mirthful waters.

I've only seen such avoidance and uncentered emotion in our parents and aunts as a response to specific triggers. While their bursts are never ones of anger, they're all caused by the ghosts of their pasts, traumas dusted in the remnants of blue- and orange-tinted witchcraft that stick to them like sand. Our family has been plagued by long-dead witches and loss alike, and every now and then, old feelings are stirred by hardship and harder days. But they did well in protecting us from experiencing what they have, up until now. Which is why I can't imagine what old wound Kestrel is currently reliving. All I know is that something haunts him, and I can only hope it won't possess him to the point of distraction. Because the sun and moon are getting closer to converging above us. And when the eclipse comes, our home will be crawling with shadows and wraiths, things more cursed than anything we've ever seen.

Swan: The West Woods

 e don't walk long before the apple laden trees become barren, and the organized orchard bursts into a dense wood. If I squint, only a thumb's width separates the sun and moon. With time slowed, and general magic cast over the ether, there's an absence of the orange golds and pinkish-red raspberries that should be highlighting strokes of plum on the horizon. Assuming I'm right, there would be a starting spark of the magic hour on any other typical evening, but not in this airglow sky. This Numina enchanted phase has stolen all the warmth from the atmosphere, casting morose shades of fog blue and flat grays from east to west. Both luminaries hang faded and ever so patient, waiting for the eclipse before illuminating the gloom and commencing Hallowtide. The beginning of the end.

The disquietude of this only heightens the sensation of offness around us. We're undoubtedly in the West Woods now, traversing Baba Roga's territory. I can almost feel the witch's presence. She's inside every root and shred of bark in these looming trees. She's in the spiderwebs looping through their branches, and the veins of the shriveled leaves caught in the sticky silk. The strands and finger-like twigs sprouting from the bare limbs cast shadows, running along the soil and over our skin, skimming us like sharpened fingertips. My brothers and I are the only signs of life in these woods, and our footsteps the only sound.

Well, Starling's and my footsteps and Kestrel's clunky, trollish tread.

He makes the most noise tripping over sticks and rocks as he cleans himself with water and a scrap cloth, mumbling all the while. I'm walking right beside him, and all I catch is the occasional *"stupid"* and *"Starling,"* but he's obviously still stuck in his own troubled head. I know better than anyone how isolating that can be.

"Are you okay?" I ask.

Kestrel's hand, scrubbing the scalloped shell of his ear, pauses. "Well, I'm cleaning the Gooseberry Wife off of me." He cringes before continuing his ministrations and switching to his other ear. "And it's either her blood or stomach contents, or both. Which makes me never want to see a green apple ever again."

I try to hold it in, I really do. But in the end, I cough to cover a laugh. "Red."

"What?" Kestrel takes his cloth-wrapped finger out of his ear.

"The apples," I say, schooling the twitching corners of my lips. "They were all red, not green."

My brother gapes. "You're messing with me."

"They were definitely red," Starling chimes in.

"Of course they were," Kestrel sighs, rubbing at his eyes with a clean corner of the cloth. "I'm starting to think we're all just cursed so that everything that happens, and everything we do, goes wrong. Either that or our family has an extreme case of bad luck." He glares suspiciously up at the sky. "And considering one of our aunties is the embodiment of luck and chance…that's a little cruel."

"We're not that unlucky," I laugh, openly this time.

"Really?" Kestrel raises his brows. "Then why does it seem like nothing goes to plan and we're always running?" He puts a hand up before I can answer. "No, better question: why are we all always being chased?"

My brother might have an arguable point, though I like to think our family is more fortunate. Even if that's a delusion, I feel somewhat better about our fates. "*All* and *always*, those words are a bit of a stretch, don't you think?" My question is more rhetorical. "Besides, the biggest mistakes we've made so far concerned Uncle Grim and the Gooseberry Wife, and that all panned out in the end."

Kestrel, being the living proof of this, halfheartedly chuckles as he stuffs the apple slop-stained rag into my knapsack.

"Oh, *I'm* sorry about *my* mistake," Starling scoffs. "Next time some diseased man tries to kidnap you and magically whisk you away to a hag's haunt, I'll just let him!"

"No one is trying to blame you for anything," I say.

"Right. Like you don't blame me for everything wrong with you." Starling rolls his eyes, although nowhere near as halfheartedly as I had earlier. "You've gotten everyone on your side by making me the bad guy. That's how you've wormed your way into being Dad's favorite, and turn Mom's disapproval onto me all the time."

My feet slow even though my mind is racing. Starling often flips emotional or lighthearted moments into attacks, or makes it about his hurt feelings without actually talking about them. This time is no different. But the topic of favoritism and disapproval is relatively new to his arsenal.

"Starling, what are you talking about?" I ask, genuinely mystified. "I've never done any of those things. And Mom and Dad love you!" I gesture to Kestrel, who is uncharacteristically silent. "They love all of us kids equally, and in many fair ways; we're all so different from one another."

"You can't tell me you're not the favorite." Starling juts out his paling lower lip. "Poor, sad little Duck and her clipped wings. She needs all the attention to make her feel special." He shakes his head with a mocking laugh. "Dad coddled you with all your stupid training. His time would've been better spent with—" Starling bites his tongue and snaps his mouth shut.

Everything clicks into place.

"With you," I finish. All those years that Starling separated himself so harshly from Kestrel and I are now crystalline clear.

"You do realize that Mom and Dad did their best, right?" I try to catch Starling's eye, to see if I can find any hint of understanding. But he keeps his face forward on the Woods as I speak. "They did everything they could to create experiences and memories together as a whole family, and spend quality time with each of us kids. They worked hard to foster personal relationships and cater to our individual needs at different life stages. Even our godparents and the entire group of The Numina, including our aunties and Uncle Grim, did the same."

"It's not the same though, is it?" Starling says, shoving his hands in his trouser pockets.

I can't believe I never knew why Starling was so mad when we were children, that even now, none of that time or effort mattered to him. Since the first time he started giving me the silent treatment, it's grown into years of bitterness, resentment, and bullying. My brother feels slighted that Dad made it a personal mission to prepare me for the world by gifting me with a skill through practice. Starling is jealous of how this bonded Dad and I so closely together. And he probably feels emotionally abandoned by the person he's always looked up to the most. He's jealous that he didn't get the same treatment. Jealous that Dad didn't spend hours on end teaching and passing on something to him. Nor did Dad dole out the same accumulative time my training took to each of my siblings during or after that period of our lives. Though that didn't seem to impact or matter to any of them the way it has Starling. Still, it's no less of a valid emotion for him. It crushed Starling, and I had no idea.

I gape at my brother, concealing my hands in my torn cloak. "This whole time…it was jealousy that drove you away? Star, why didn't you say anything?"

"I shouldn't have had to," he echoes, throwing a version of my own words back at me. "It's your fault no one noticed what was really going on. They were all too busy making sure your delicate little self wouldn't shatter at the slightest inconvenience."

I'm tempted to shut down, to let Starling win for the sake of saving us all from an argument. But that would only perpetuate the endless cycle. I can't keep hoping it will change, I need to embody the change, dredge up some junk drawer confidence and be the one to break it myself.

"Listen to me." My tone is soft, but steeped in strength. "It's not my fault any more than yours, or Mom and Dad's. We all failed to communicate, to resolve hurt feelings or misunderstandings. Something that should've been done at the beginning." I consider my brother's silence a good thing, especially when I glance at Kestrel, whose proud nod for me to go on is shortly followed by a small, hopeful grin. He's been waiting for a reunion with his best friend for a while, too. "We could do this all day, Starling. Saying that it was my fault for needing help when I didn't get my gift, or that I monopolized too many hours of Dad's time. My fault for first developing depression or nerve damage at such a young age. Or that it was your fault for being a kid who just wanted to feel a little bit more seen. Your fault for probably struggling to transition into learning how to use your gift. For not telling any of us why you were so upset." I shrug as a bunch of hypotheticals, that could've changed the course of our childhood, line up outside my attic door like imaginary guests waiting to knock. "Maybe Mom and Dad didn't push hard enough all those times they asked you what was wrong. Maybe they shouldn't have given up when you either said 'nothing' or refused to answer at all. You could even blame Kestrel if you wanted. You could be ridiculous and say that as a child—without even two digits to his age—he should've made the connection and come to you, as one of your best friends and brothers, to pry it out of you. Or—"

Starling gives me a look that cuts me off and reads, "*Really?*" But at least I know that he sees how improbable some of these scenarios are.

I lean forward, hoping to catch more of my brother's waning face, hoping to see what he might be thinking. "I understand, Starling, I do. Your feelings were, and still are, valid. But continuing to hate me while holding a grudge about something I had no control over is silly at this point." My heart sinks a little when he pushes his hands deeper into his pockets, his shoulders growing closer to his ears. "I'm sorry it took me so long to realize you've been hurting. You're my brother. I love you, and I've forgiven you a thousand times over for every mean thing you've said and done."

"I didn't ask for your forgiveness," Starling mutters.

It's clear that he's clamming up. My brother will either remove himself from this vulnerable conversation soon, or turn it on its head with something antagonistic. I'm losing him, and I at least want to say what's been on my mind for ages now. Because that way, I'll know I did my best to clear the air and reconcile.

"I miss you," I say. "I miss talking to you. I miss sharing all our secrets. Had I known the times we got in trouble together and spent all day playing outside were the last, I would've held on to you tighter. I'd give anything to listen to your horrible whistling of random snippets from village festivals," I admit with a raw laugh. "I want to hear about all the interesting things you've read that I don't understand. I'd even listen to you talk about cross-pollination for hours. Most of all, I want to know my brother again, I want to learn about who you've become and what you love or hate now. I just miss you, Starling." With a releasing sigh, a substantial weight lifts off my chest. I feel airy as I slip into a state of bittersweet reverie, no longer caring whether or not Starling has anything to say back, positive, negative, or nothing at all.

After several moments of only our three sets of footsteps filling the silence, Starling responds in a quiet, tired voice. "It's too late for that, Duck. We're not friends. You don't deserve to know me anymore."

My brother's words land, and an envelope slides beneath my attic door, gliding over the hardwood floor before coming to a gentle rest at my feet. I receive it and get a tiny paper cut on my pinkie while handling the worn paper. And I feel at peace when I open my mental desk drawer and stack it neatly inside.

Kestrel speaks up for the first time in a while. As expected, he sounds like his typical protective self. "Man, that's not true. You just said that to hurt Swan's feelings because you've been called out and feel exposed."

Feeling equally fractured and lighter, I ignore Kestrel and gaze over at Starling. "Is that how you truly feel?"

"Yes." Starling's eyes shift to the left as we pass a particular tree with spiderwebs that look questionably fluffy.

I nod, hands slipping out of my cloak to swing free at my sides. "Then that's fine. We don't have to like each other or be friends to be family; this doesn't change the fact that I still love you." Calm in nature and spirit, I take a profound, shivering breath and tilt my chin to a somewhat glittery path forming ahead. "Now, let's get going; I think I see a flash of red coming up." Without waiting for a reply, I walk ahead of my brothers and delve deeper into Baba Roga's territory.

—

I'm right.

A couple hundred feet away, a trail leads to an ornate mono-chromatic cottage with garnet accents. It's a small gothic struc-ture with black, steeply pitched gables lined with decorative tracery and fitted with rounded quatrefoil windows. The large piano-striped chimney protruding from the roof resembles a smoking tower decorated with crocketed pinnacles. And the red front door, surrounded by white trim and latticework, is in the palatial shape of a pointed arch. A florid structure like this, existing in the middle of these skeleton woods, would already be odd, but what makes it stranger still is the materials the cottage and the distinct trail are made of.

Lining the sparkling, sandy-sugar path is a steady line of gumdrops, each the size of my hand. They snake up to the home in alternating ebony, ivory, and ruby colors, reminding me of a sickly, sweet game of checkers. Even where my brothers and I peer from behind a wide tree, I can tell that the deep cinnamon-sprinkled walls of the cottage are made of biscuits. And the scal-loped roof tiles made of a dense, marbled pound cake. The alluring scent curling from the chimney and pumping through the forest smells like a perfect autumn morning: hot pancakes dusted in powdered brown sugar with poached ginger apples, and candied molasses nuts served with a sweating glass of milk.

From what I can tell, everything from the tracery to the trim, and the chessboard latticework, is piped with snowy icing and meringue kisses. The pillars holding up the porch are spiraled peppermint sticks, and the windowsills are edged in licorice strips. And the rounded hedges are giant dark chocolate truffles. Some are coated in cocoa powder while others are cherry fondant swirls or white nonpareils. I've watched Robin make hard-boiled sweets enough times to assume the windows are melted and poured sugar. At least judging by the frosted quality of the panes and the bubbles running throughout them. All this candy would be appealing to any child, but the tree poking from behind the welcoming cottage is a stark contrast.

The trunk not only grows taller than the rest of the West Woods, but it's broader as well. It's monstrous, with its soot limbs gnarled and twisted, chocolate curl branches choking neighboring branches draped with puffy webs like spidery tulle. Although, after studying the house made of sweets, I'm not sure the strands are spiderwebs; rather, they might be candy floss? The webs hanging above my head certainly appear to be the same texture. They look identical to the cotton-like sugar clouds I've eaten in the villages, the ones that are spun over broom handles and formed onto paper sticks during the summer festivals on the streets outside Hazel's Apothecary. But what sort of arachnids could be capable of making an entire stretch of these wicked woods into their sweet gossamer haven? And where could they all be hiding? I don't really want to know, but I have an inkling.

"I think it's safe to say we found it," Kestrel whispers, huddling beside me.

We're far enough from Baba Roga's home that we can knowingly dabble in the false sense of security without being too deluded by the severity of our situation. But we're still close enough to the elaborate candy cottage that my heart is racing, and we can clearly see the front door and darkened windows. I hate it. I hate how quiet it is here, how saccharine, yet melancholy...the opposing attributes make my skin prickle.

"This feels too easy," I murmur. "I'd bet a witch's life that the door itself is some sort of trap." Now that I've seen the trail to the house, it's no wonder that The Nightmare Weaver's young victims are never seen again once they set foot upon the sugar path. It's a sticky, enticing spiderweb, created for the smallest and most vulnerable hungry-eyed flies.

Kestrel nods. "I'll take you up on that bet. I'd bet the cottage is rigged with witchcraft, and the roots of that big tree behind it is going to send it on the move, à la Baba Yaga."

"Well, they were sisters," I mumble.

There's no light shining out through the windowpanes, yet smoke billows from the chimney. It's hard to tell if anyone besides our family is inside. Instinct tells me that at least Uncle Grim is. Perhaps he's waiting, wounded in the shadows? If that's the case, my follow-up question is: is Allison Gross in there with him?

Kestrel's fingers dig into the tree bark in front of us as he pulls his head back behind the safety of the trunk. "Then I'm doubling your bet."

"I raise you a third witch; The Nightmare Weaver's trap will be farther inside," Starling whispers with a wrinkled nose, gaze flicking up to the countless strings of candy floss. "Spiders wait for their prey to enter their web, not come near it."

Kestrel slowly lifts a hand and holds it by his owlish face. "I'd like to change my bet."

"No can do." I shake my head, scanning for any other sign of life, but from this vantage point, my search is fruitless.

"Fine, then how do you propose we get inside without setting anything off, or alerting anyone of our arrival? We're three kids with—" Starling stands beside our brother, his back against the tree as he points and takes inventory. "Two axes, a quiver of arrows, six throwing knives, a magic candle, and three matches." If his wan, wrinkled lip of dissatisfaction is anything to go by, I'd say he thinks this isn't the greatest odds. I'd agree with him. "We can't go in blind and expect to not get eaten."

Kestrel flips to mirror our brother's position against the rough, chocolate-barked trunk. "Yeah, I've been there and done that. I didn't care for it."

Starling's right. Even armed with what we have, sneaking into the cottage requires a bit more forethought. But looking up at the sun and moon growing closer in the half-lit sky, we don't have time to stand here and wait. We need to be proactive. At the same time, we can't just walk up the trail and press our faces to the windows either. If only there was some way to smoke out anything lying in wait. Sadly, actual smoke would potentially harm our family being held somewhere inside...

I'm about to propose the impossibility to my brothers anyway, when my eyes catch on the embroidery of Starling's wine cloak. The speckle-feathered creatures of his namesake birds dance amongst the red and gold threads. They intertwine with curls of ivy, soaring over bowing heads of lilies of the valley before coasting along the trumpeted curves of narcissi flowers.

Seeing the woven songbirds reminds me of my old plan.

"Don't you know, boys?" Grinning, I spin in a slow circle with my head tilted back to survey the tangle of thick branches surrounding us and Baba Roga's tooth-rotting home. "Birds eat spiders."

—

We climb a nearby tree. It's tall and sturdy, and easily holds the three of us in its branches, but it's close enough to the house that it's no longer safe to speak. From where we sit above, facing the burgundy door—that appears to be a giant slab of wafer biscuit—we're by no means completely hidden. Without obscuring our view, we're concealed just the right amount so that it would take a purposeful and thorough search through the tangled trees to locate us. Which we hopefully won't have to worry about. At least not with the "lie in wait" strategy I have in mind. The one thing I know that hags like Baba Roga and Allison Gross are very familiar with. Considering bogeymen have stalked civilization for over six centuries now, they're used to loitering outside salt perimeters, waiting for their prey to slip up and fall into their reach.

Assuming Uncle Grim is inside the cottage, and possibly Allison Gross, my brothers and I are an uneven match. But more importantly, we lack the seedy power of witchcraft. From my perspective, the only way to gain the upper hand is to use what little magic and resources we have. And hopefully we can surprise the poisoned pair. Hence the reason we've scaled this sticky tree like the children we used to be, hiding amongst the limbs washed in the pearly, semi-gray Numina-born shadows. Digging up that years-old garden memory earlier today, the one containing the brutal regaling of lemon snails and Starling's gift, was a spark of morbid nostalgic inspiration for my current plan. Luckily, my brothers didn't need convincing to breathe life into it; Starling summoned his birds before I even finished whispering my ideas.

Now we wait.

I've taken up the outside end of the branch by straddling it and locking my ankles together. My torso faces Kestrel, who sits casually, hands braced on either side of his hips with his feet silently swinging. Starling crouches beside him, his shoulder jammed against the trunk of the dark, chocolate tree. His lips are pinched as he switches from watching the sky to searching the unnatural webs partially concealing us.

Kestrel taps on Starling's shoulder, garnering his attention before he signs, *"Are you sure they're coming?"*

Starling nods.

"Are you?" Kestrel asks.

Starling nods again.

"Like, how sure?" Kestrel presses.

Starling barely lifts his fingers to create *V* shapes with his index and middle fingers before connecting his fingertips and pulling them apart. With the lack of facial expression or emphasis in his movements, Starling's sign for the word *"very"* isn't too convincing.

Kestrel's swinging legs come to a stop. *"So, on a scale of one to ten—"*

Before he can finish, Starling's hands interrupt him with a sharp rhythm. *"I will push you straight out of this tree."*

Kestrel produces a satirical pout, and I can physically see his mind turning as he side-eyes me with squinty features. When he looks back at Starling, a corner of his mouth twitches before he points to our brother's wine cloak and signs with a flurry of hastened gesticulation. *"Is that a spider?"*

Starling nearly falls out of the tree, wiping at his front with his injured hand, frantic as he scrambles to remove the nonexistent arachnid from his person. It was hard enough for him to climb up here, examining every inch of cocoa bark before he put a hand anywhere. He's scouted the webs above our heads countless times out of pure paranoia. But outwardly, the West Woods are dead, and if Starling falls out of this tree and breaks his neck, he will be too. So, I lean forward and snap my fingers twice to get his attention before reaching out to thump the center of Kestrel's forehead once he faces me. Realizing that our younger brother was only antagonizing him, Starling slumps back into the tree with an icy scowl.

Scandalized, Kestrel gapes. *"You've betrayed me."*

"Serves you right," Starling signs in reply, watching Kestrel massage the small circle of irritation blooming on his oak skin.

I should've expected Kestrel to retaliate; nonetheless, it somehow still surprises me when he aims to flick Starling's forehead in the same spot. The grump anticipated it though, knocking Kestrel off course with an audible slap to the back of his hand. There are three steady measures of absolute stillness while Kestrel gawps at Starling. Then, the two idiots start jabbing each other again, searching for soft spots and unprotected ribs with fingers ridged enough to bruise. They each try to curve their spines sideways to escape the attacks without throwing themselves off-balance. But all they manage to do is shake the tree loose of any leaves not caught up in the candy-floss spiderwebs, along with my patience. There is a time and a place to act like kids, but this high up in the air, outside a witch's home, where three of our family members are being held against their will is not it. Snapping twice more, I get my brothers to meet my deadpan stare. Each boy holds on to their undoubtedly sore sides with a protective hand while the other clutches onto the tree branch or trunk for dear life.

"I will push the both of you out of this tree and happily blame whoever is inside that house if you don't keep your hands to your-selves." I sign this with a stern set to my mouth, almost making me feel like Hazel for some authoritative reason.

Unfortunately, how my brothers glower at each other only promises more tomfoolery.

With the inside of my wrist facing me, I raise my curled fist to head height and flip my index finger up. Considering I can feel the annoyance on my face, raising my eyebrows is the sole thing that changes my sign for *"understand"* to a question rather than a demand. Either way, my warning does what I intended it to. Kestrel mouths the word *"fine"* with a roll of his silver eyes, and Starling nods. This is quickly followed by him flicking Kestrel's ear in a small act of defiance before he genuinely yields by crossing his arms and hunkering further into the trunk. Kestrel, of course, quietly flails, gesturing to Starling to ensure I saw what atrocity he committed. A silent expression that screams, *"Did you see him? He touched me!"* paints Kestrel's tattle-tale face in pitiful strokes of disbelief. A tiny part of me wishes to follow up on my empty threat and push the boys out of the tree—of course, only as long as they weren't hurt on the way down—but there's nothing I can do to retribute Starling's slight, and we all know it.

Besides, the petty act no longer matters because Kestrel's indignant flapping, and Starling's badly suppressed smirk, are eclipsed by fluttering wings. Many, *many* wings.

All Starling had to do was whistle a few notes, and his name-sake birds answer his magic call. No matter how far, they always listen; they honor him as one of their own and recognize his call as if it was spoken word. And now hundreds of dark plumed passerine filter into the West Woods as a swooping murmuration. The masses dive and soar, curling around each other to create an ebb and flow of loose yet complex shapes. It would feel like witnessing a production of fine art, even to an untrained eye. Enhancing this, the birds' glossy feathers shine in the low light, casting them all in a metallic sheen that shifts from shades of violet to sapphire and pine. As they blot out the slices of delayed sky above, the white speckles cast over every inch of their bodies look like twinkling stars. The starlings glisten, and the ill-timed poet in me awakens. I want to write, to equate them to a glimpse of impossible lunisolar dusk, reflected inside a rain puddle glazed with a silken layer of iridescent oil. But a dumb little haiku will satiate my mind, for now at least.

IN THE AIRGLOW LIGHT,
  Wings weave stories in the sky—
  Forming stardust threads.

ITCH SCRATCHED, I witness how, in tandem, the starlings break formation to flood the surrounding trees and find their assigned places, taking up a roost scattered along the gnarled, sugar-strung limbs. The birds sit with us in relative quiet then. Only the occasional rustle of wings or click of their tiny, clawed toes clacking along the branches taints the silence. Starling summoned a whole battalion of these beautiful, albeit aggressive, songbirds, and they are fervid. With ebony eyes deeper than the slick rocks from the bottom of the storybook

River Styx, they watch him. The éclair-sized creatures hang on Starling's every breath, just waiting for his signal. He glances at Kestrel and me before pushing a soft progression of notes through his teeth, sending goosebumps rippling along my skin.

The three of us watch as the songbirds absorb the meaning of this whistle, tilting their little feathery heads in understanding. The melody is pretty, peaceful even. Which is not something I'd usually say when talking about Starling, but he's only ever on pitch when he's using his gift. It's a rare, graceful tune, and it makes me wish I understood what the birds are hearing him sing in their language. Even more so when the starlings move in a sudden flurry, each falling from their perch and forming once more. The star-peppered birds soar upward from the trees in perfect unity, flying farther and farther into the sky as if their destination was the sliver between the converging sun and moon.

Then, all at once, there's a shift, like the pull of a sail in a crack of wind. The starlings' wings tuck into their slight bodies, and they tip sideways, beaks pointing toward the earth before plummeting. I'm breathless and digging my nails into the branch beneath me by the time the birds extend their tilting wings in secession. The starlings create a churning, wind-sweeping funnel aiming for Baba Roga's aromatic, black-and-white-banded chimney.

They fulfill the plan I laid out for my brothers as they launch themselves into the witch's home like a flash flood storming an ant hill. Inside, the flock should be ambushing any foe, creating a seamless unforeseen attack that gives me and my brothers the upper hand while keeping us safe. We wait until the last of the chromatic tail feathers disappear into the candy cottage before we prepare for whoever comes out the front door armed with witchcraft or scissor-like weapons. Kestrel pulls his legs up and crouches on our branch, his weight even and center of gravity strong. He's the first of us to arm himself by taking the gold-strung bow from his shoulder and nocking an arrow.

Starling and I exchange a glance at this.

Then, Starling pulls one of two axes from his back as he stands, one hand grasping the branch above him for balance. Starling can only afford to throw one blade in a well-timed, and well-aimed, shot. Because at least if he misses and we need to switch to a backup plan, he'll still have one axe left to defend himself. Quantity of blades is becoming a problem for me too, since I couldn't recover every throwing knife I've spent on our journey thus far. So, for now, I collect two of my six remaining knives in one hand, leaving the other empty and available. Just in case.

The blip of time we wait with eyes fixated on the door feels like eons. It drags on and on, and after the half-minute mark, antsy twinges make my burning palms clammy. We're nearing forty-five seconds when Starling shifts his foot placement. None of us are necessarily expecting anyone to leave the house in a panic. It would be evident to anyone, bogeyman or not, that an entire fleet of coordinated starlings sweeping through the chimney isn't an act designed by nature. And we know from our meeting in the orchard that Allison Gross's poisoned control hasn't stopped Uncle Grim from being aware of who he is or what's happening around him. So, he would know that the birds are his nephew's doing. That's why it was safer to picture him exiting the house ready for confrontation, if it's him we're waiting for. This is why we took higher ground, to make our move from above, something a little more unpredictable.

But this nothingness is unsettling.

More than a tense minute goes by, and there's no sign of the hag, our uncle, or Starling's birds. Perhaps it's taking them a while to find them because Baba Roga's home is like her sister's? Maybe the inside is coated in her craft, making it larger than it appears? Or the starlings all got stuck somehow, maybe in a huge candy-floss web meant to trap us? I can't begin to fathom how so many of the deft creatures could go inside and not one makes their way out. Unless some way, somehow, there isn't a single bird left to attempt an escape?

My grip on my knives grows slippery.

I flag both of my brothers' attention and put my free hand out with my fingers together and palm facing down. With raised brows, I flip my hand over, asking Starling and Kestrel a single-worded question.

"Dead?"

Kestrel winces, craning his head to peer up at Starling, who gnaws at the inside corner of his lower lip. He's told us before that when he uses his gift, he can't physically feel the passerines' presence out in the world until they answer the call of his changeling gift. His tie to his namesake birds is only perceptible while he whistles, but after his song, he's unaware of their location or their state. I can only imagine that yawning emptiness, where the connection has fizzled out, feels twice as anxiety-inducing as he wonders if he's sent all those poor things to the gallows. The only thing Starling could do to see if there's any feathered souls left is to whistle again. Although, the birds' absence could be a risk or a trap, something that could reveal our hiding spot to our uncle or the witch puppeting him. Especially if they are sitting tight and waiting for us to come out of hiding first.

I'm about to put my knives away, to sign my proposal for a brand-new plan, when I'm startled by movement coming up from behind the house. I'm ill-prepared for just how quick and disorienting the explosion is.

Swan: Murmurations and Mutations

*T*he shadowy shapes rising from the marbled roof's backside, obscuring the strangely dim and monstrous tree, aren't Uncle Grim's wings. It's my brother's birds pouring out from some unknown exit, twirling together in one dark mass. Though just as quick as the murmuration appears, it splits apart and disperses into individual bodies. It would be impossible to count all the starlings, but watching the scattered stream take to the airglow sky and fly away, I'm almost confident that none were harmed inside the house. Still, as the last straggler slips past the top of the branches, my muscles tighten in anticipation.

Waiting.

Waiting.

Waiting.

Nothing follows the songbirds.

To be safe, my brothers and I stall for two more minutes, my thighs locked around the tree limb, cramping. The arm Kestrel holds out, ready to pull his bowstring back, is shaking. Starling stashes his axe along his back with a frown as he stares down at the candy cottage.

The West Woods are calm.

After a moment of hesitation, Kestrel eases his posture to un-nock his arrow and stuff it back in its quiver. The curving elder tree weapon hangs loose in his grip. "Was that it?" he whispers aloud.

"I think so," Starling murmurs.

Kestrel swings the bow over his head, strapping the glittering string across his chest. "What do we do now?"

Holstering my knives, I reposition myself, legs hanging freely and sore. Starling is looking at me for answers, and I'm a bit taken aback by this. Under any other circumstance, he would usually try to take control of this sort of situation, using his abrasive personality to sound superior. But now his face is open with what appears to be a modem of, dare I say, respect? He's used Mom's command about me being in charge against me every chance he's gotten. But not now?

I clear my throat. "There's nothing left to do but go inside. The eclipse is almost here, maybe only a few hours away. We can't make Time hold on for too much longer."

"Are we storming the house then?" Kestrel asks, fingers pressing down on his fists to pop his knuckles.

"No." I shake my head. "Even though the starlings left unperturbed, we still don't know what we're walking into. We need to enter quietly and on guard." Kestrel continues to push at his finger joints, so I squeeze his shoulder in hopes of calming his nerves. "Think of it like Phouka hunting. It won't be much different than sneaking through the forest outside the glade."

Starling gives me a firm nod and turns to start his descent. Kestrel sighs and drops from his crouch to swing one leg over the branch and lower himself until he hangs by his hands. His toes rest on the next branch below, allowing him to climb down quickly. I find myself watching him and Starling for a second. If I squint and try to forget why we've climbed a sticky, skeletal tree in the West Woods, I can almost imagine the three of us as children again. The memory of past adventures in the glade, and the knowledge of the ones that will never be, simultaneously make my heart swell and break. It even makes my eyes burn almost as bad as my hands. So much so that I rub at my lashes with the heels of my palms, and then shake out the hot sprinkling sensation in my fingers before following Kestrel and Starling to the sugared ground.

"I'd bet you an axe I could guess one of Baba Roga's favorite colors," Starling mumbles once we leave the safety of the trees.

I fight back a snort as my eyes trail from the alternating black, white, and red gumdrops to the same gothic palette of the witchcraft-preserved cottage. The only other hue constructing the small home peeks through the biscuit walls. It's clear to see, the closer we get, that it's made from the same cinnamon, ginger, nutmeg, and clove-laced dough used to make Christmastide ginger men. Also known as gingerbread men in the far-off, lost places we learned about in the Great Library. But the witch's home has none of the charm, nor cheer, of any cozy winter festivity. It's much more befitting of the spooky stories, the tales of woe, told late on Hallowtide nights around a lantern with sneaky midnight soul cake snacks. Although, I can understand why children are so often lured, and never seen again once they embark on Baba Roga's path. The desserts and candies, despite their dark colors, are still appealing. My mouth is almost watering at the sight of her abode, but I know that's because my stomach is empty. If a child was lost long enough, it's no wonder they'd approach the treasure trove of confections for a nibble, no matter how terrifying the Woods themselves might be. To them, the cottage would be like an abundant oasis in the driest desert, not a carnivorous trap—not the home of The Nightmare Weaver.

The noise our boots produce on the sanding sugar path set my teeth on edge, sparkling grains popping and grinding together as soon as the treads hit the surface. It's worse than the crunch of compressed snow, which gives me the sensation of a mouth full of cotton. Surely, if it weren't for Starling's birds going in the gingerbread house first, walking the path alone would've been enough to announce our arrival. Especially since Kestrel is always louder and less graceful than Starling or I, but I'll admit his grating steps are quieter now than during the hunting trip when Robin disappeared. If it weren't for the sugar's broken glass-like texture, I'd say he sounds less like the trolls and more like Dad right after he wakes up, or Crow when he thinks he's being sneaky and trying to scare one of us.

Those comparisons alone have me suppressing laughter and tears, fueling a new burst of motivated urgency. Passing my brothers, I take the lead, marching up to the striped, candy cane pillared porch. I notice that crushed bits of the minty sweets are inlaid into the creaking steps like holiday bark. At the same time, I note the piped femurs hidden amongst all the icing whorls decorating the doorframe. The irony is not lost on me, not when the knob of the door looks like a slice of velvet roll, and strips of licorice along the windowsills and their planters curl into skulls. Inside the boxes grow claret-rimmed flowers that I can only assume are Baba Roga's precious, sugar plum hellebore flowers. They are cruel, poisonous beauties, and the hidden horrors baked into all the details of this house only add to it. Seeing it up close is enough to give me a stomachache.

Behind me, my brothers ascend the porch stairs. One pair of boots seems to miss a step, judging by the loud *thunk*. It's followed by the heavier *thud* of this same foot coming back down, landing harder to catch itself. I sigh, Kestrel's name already coming out of my mouth before I've turned around. But it's not my clumsy brother that tripped. It's Starling. He's hunched over with one foot on the landing and the other a stair down, clutching onto the spiral banister as he hangs his head. Kestrel puts a hand on our brother's back, bending to see the side of his face.

"Are you all right, man?" he asks.

"I'm fine," Starling puffs. When he straightens, I get a good look at him. His russet skin has adopted a dramatic pallor, and his lips are the same color, nearly disappearing into his sweat-slick features.

I shake my head. "You're not fine. What's the last thing you ate?"

Starling shrugs, the slight action making him sway. "A half a piece of hardtack and some acorns."

Kestrel clamps onto his arm to steady him. "That was well before Uncle Grim showed up in the orchard. You need something to eat." He reaches out toward me. "Swan, hand me something from your bag."

Our pale brother tries to shrug Kestrel off, but the dizzied movement looks more like a tiny twitch than any real effort. "I said I'm fine."

"Yeah, you're fine, and my heart is just coursing with magic," I mutter. My natural reaction is to pat my cloak for my inner pocket, but I don't hear the signature crinkle of the waxen bag that was in there earlier. Turning out the front flap of the embroidered navy wool, I find the pocket empty. I forgot I'd finished the rest of the medicinal candied sunflower clusters after the ordeal with our uncle. I needed their salt to kick the rest of the bloodroot fog that was darkening my mind. Changing course, I reach to take off a knapsack strap from my shoulder. Then, I remember that the food I split for Starling and Kestrel to share earlier was the last of our supply.

Panic lines my guts with acid. If the sugars in Starling's blood are dropping, and we don't fix it soon, he'll either puke, pass out, or both. Worse yet, according to Robin and Lark's Healer training, if his sugar gets low enough, Starling could become comatose and die. We almost found that out the hard way once, and I can't have a repeat of that. That's why we all usually keep and replenish a small stock of candy on our persons every day. But after days of travel, we have nothing left.

But what if...

Turning in a half circle, I search for the easiest part of the house to break, something that will give my brother the largest and quickest dose of sugar he needs. Anything too close to the hellebore makes me nervous. Looking at Starling silhouetted by the scalloped trim hanging from the porch gable reminds me of the roof. Sweeping past him, I sit on the flat expanse of the railing and get one knee under me, pulling myself up enough until I find what I'm looking for. Once a rounded chunk of perfect pound cake comes away in my hand, I jump down and stand in front of Starling, who now slumps against a peppermint pillar. He looks worse for wear, and though he gazes at the cake I hold with disdain, I know he's desperate enough to eat it.

Starling reaches with a trembling hand, but I suddenly snatch it away.

Kestrel blinks at me. "Uh? Swan?"

From the outside, nothing appears to be wrong with the dense cake. The veins of chocolate and vanilla swirling together look identical to the ones Mom creates when she puts two different batters into a pan and drags a knife through them to create the same flowing pattern.

"Swan?" Kestrel prompts again.

If this were any other pound cake, it would be made with a pound each of sugar, flour, butter, and eggs. I'd say the moisture and crumb structure are identical, too, but I can't tell what its ingredients are just by staring at it.

"Care to share some of that with Starling?" A strained chuckle rises from Kestrel. My mind is churning too fast, weighing too many options for me to answer. "He's struggling here, Swan."

Starling releases a long breath through his nose. "Figures she'd be the one to kill me."

A distant part of me wonders if Starling still believes I could be the changeling from the prophecy, the one who's supposed to *"join the dark for the light to prevail,"* but I don't stop thinking long enough to feel a sting. Not as my ill brother presses shaking fingers into his stomach. He's nauseous and things are going to get very bad for him very soon if I don't do something quick. But when both his disease and this piece of the hag's roof could kill him, it's about choosing the least of the two evils. And I know which direction I'm leaning. Baba Roga's house is seemingly kept fresh and intact by witchcraft, but that doesn't necessarily mean that the house itself is infused with petals of poison. And I suppose there is only one way to find out...

With little thought for my own safety, I lift the cake to my lips and take a bite.

"Good grief, woman," Kestrel gasps. "What are you doing?"

Well.

I would never tell my mother this, and I will take this thought to my grave, but it's the lightest, most delicious pillowy pound cake I've ever had. My taste buds are bursting with buttery notes of caramelized vanilla beans and soft, velvety salted chocolate. There is no burning toxic tinge, or any sour hint of earthy mold. Though, to be sure, I wait after swallowing. Clicking my tongue against the roof of my mouth and smacking my lips, I search for a trace of corruption. If hellebore was baked into the cake, it would probably hit my system quick, but truth be told, I don't know much about poisons. And the person who does is judging me with a wrinkled brow. When our eyes meet, that weak expression slips away and is replaced with one of realization.

"You're an idiot," Starling states.

I nod. "I love you too." Taking one of his damp, trembling hands in mine, I flip the sizable remaining piece of roof into his grasp. "Now that we know it's not poisoned, get some of that in your stomach before you fall on your face. Robin and Lark would be mortified if I let you break your nose; we all know Hazel would use you as an extra-long lesson and they'd be the ones to fix it. And you also know Robin gets squeamish with Healing family." Brushing the cake crumbs from my skin, I scan the rest of the candy cottage's decorative elements for small portable pieces, just in case Starling needs another boost later.

I'm considering breaking a sugar-paned window when Kestrel finally catches on and squawks, "If I don't do it myself, Mom and Dad are going to kill you when they find out how reckless you just were."

"How would they find out?" I hum, narrowing in on the meringues bordering the iced latticework around the front door. "I suppose the same way they would know about every dumb thing you did to protect Starling and me leading up to this, huh?" When Kestrel doesn't respond, I glance over my shoulder. He's crossing his arms over his barrel chest. Starling has scarfed down the cake already, now resting his head against the pillar with his eyes closed. At least he's regained some color.

"Touché," my brother grumbles before joining me in my task as I wiggle the tip of my knife beneath the airy kisses, trying to pry them from the doorframe without cracking their shells.

By the time our hands are full, and we're satisfied with the pickings, Starling is steady on his feet again. I recognize the taut corners of his seafoam eyes, from past low blood sugar scares, enough to know that he's dealing with a headache now. Starling is probably fatigued too, more than any of us were before, which doesn't bode well considering what we might find inside the house. Still, we must keep moving, and he knows that. Taking the pilfered sweets from us, Starling loads all but one into his trouser pockets. He tucks the piece he saved into his cheek and makes a quiet sound of disgust in the back of his throat. "*Ugh*, peppermint. Why?" he mutters to himself as he joins us at the giant, burgundy wafer-like biscuit door.

I'm curious if the crisp, layered door is sandwiched with a filling like the ones in the villages. Throughout the year, the yellow-shuttered bakery across from Hazel's Apothecary buys

Robin's changeling gift-grown strawberries. The shipments get delivered by Fern and his messenger brothers, and sometimes the gnomes are sent back to the glade with samplings made from the fruits of my sister's magic labor. One of which is thin wafer sheets stacked and slathered with a creamy strawberry-based hazelnut praline filling. But the bakery only sells my favorite ones with interchanging swipes of milk jam and cinnamon-spiced plum butter at the height of autumn. I'm craving their taste of familiarity and safety terribly right now. But I will have to satisfy my irrelevant curiosity by finally getting to Robin, Crow, and Dad, who hopefully wait safe and sound on the other side of this confectionary door.

My brothers are at my back with hands on their weapons as I slowly open the entryway to Baba Roga's home. Standing still at the threshold, the only thing that greets us is chasmal darkness; I can't even see into the house. The air is stagnant and pressurized, like feeling the closeness of someone or something without touching them, just at a larger scale. It's strange, too strange.

I blindly unclasp my side bag, its leather walls falling open, unveiling the watery light of The Moon's enchanted object. But the candle's shimmering, periwinkle-lavender hue does little to expose what lies in the dark. I can only see about six inches of flooring past the doorway and that's it, none of the walls, or the ceiling, just blackness.

How big is this place?

Pivoting, I gift the candle to the steadiest brother behind me. Considering Kestrel's clumsy track record, that's Starling, even though his hands continue tremoring like tall grass in the wind as his blood and sugar get reacclimatized. And despite what we learned from his birds, I'm still nervous about Uncle Grim's and Allison Gross's whereabouts. So, I sign to my brothers instead of speaking now that the front door is open. "*I think Baba Roga's using the same kind of witchcraft on her house that Baba Yaga did. It's* massive inside; even with the candle, I can't see a single thing. Not even the floor."

"*Light a match*," Kestrel signs in reply. And when Starling and I stare at him like he's the most insane faerie to walk this forest, he continues with fluid, fast movements, "*Not for the candle. I meant, light a match to toss inside the house. At least that way, we'll see the floor and any traps.*"

It's hard to understand Starling when he first signs "*fire*" with one hand, considering it takes two, and he's holding the candle with his injured one. But using the context clues of his raised brows and expectant expression, Kestrel catches on to Starling's question.

"*If the floor starts to catch, I'm sure we can run in and stomp it out quickly. It's not a big deal,*" Kestrel assures him with an easy shrug. He makes it seem like such an easy decision to use one of our limited resources.

"*Are you guys okay with wasting one of The Moon's matches on this? We can only light the candle with magic, and once they're gone, they're gone,*" I remind them, ministrations slow and precise to ensure there isn't a misinterpretation anywhere along the way.

They both bob their heads, yes.

So be it.

Swiveling to face the doorway again, I retrieve the engraved box from the custom compartment The Sun crafted for the matches in the side bag. Starling holds the candle over my shoulder at head height for light as I fish out a twisted silver igniter. The matchsticks themselves are metal, almost braided with stardust and slivers of moonbeams. Each has an ornament at the end to hold on to, a starburst, a crescent moon, and a curvy-tailed sun. I choose the sun on the far left and swipe the head of the match against the striking pad on the bottom of the ornamental box. It flares to life with a hiss and brilliant glow of silver fire. A burst of heat kisses my burning fingertips, and instead of a smoke and powder scent, a constellation of otherworldly—yet soft—floral herbs wafts into my sinuses as I toss the magical match away from me into Baba Roga's house. Instead of landing on the floor, the match travels down...and down, and down...and down, down, down, until I can no longer see its pinprick of light.

The Moon's candle moves past my head, hovering above a shell of a hag's home as Starling stands on his tiptoes to catch sight of the falling match over my shoulder. Kestrel must lean into him to do the same. I don't know if he trips or misjudges how much weight he puts onto Starling's back, but the boys are too much for me to support. I have to curl my toes and grind my heels in my boots as I clutch onto the doorjamb, shoving backward to compensate for their weight. Starling grunts, and the candle teeters in his hold, the side of the metal pan catching on the bandage tied around his hand, pulling it taut into his wound. I see his finger looped in the chamberstick handle loosen the same moment that Kestrel does. In an effort to catch it, Kestrel bumps Starling, and it's more than enough to knock me loose from the threshold and send me forward with pinwheeling arms. The starry, Blessed object flies past me and careens into the massive bottomless hole as I fall along with it.

Grim: Vulture

I could enter the glade through the tree barrier and take the shears from where I stored them in the back band of my trousers, but she tells me to wait. So I do, obediently at her side, watching as the occupants scramble, preparing for our arrival beneath the strange, frozen sky. Little do they know, we're here. But we let them prepare. I dutifully told her the prophecy so they know that it's not time to move until the impending manufactured eclipse has come to pass. We lurk in the shadows outside the barrier and enjoy their panic as the menagerie of faeries are ushered onto the salted path that runs through the forest to the Healer's elder tree protected territory. We let them go, staying unseen.

How kind of you, really.

Why hunt mice when you can wait for a whole herd of deer?

You're no better than a bogey at this point. It would surprise me if we could still cross the perimeter right now.

And?

And Rose would be disappointed that you let yourself get this far. That you didn't find some way to come back to her sooner.

I don't want to go back to her. She controlled me.

Rose controlled you? Rose set you free! She gave you a life and a body and told you to run, but you chose to stay because you love her.

I don't love her; I love—

Don't you dare say that hag's name...

My body revolts against me, and a wave of dizziness causes me to release a long, steadying breath that sounds like a sigh.

"Be patient, trinket," she snaps, and it's beguiling. "We have weakened them and thrown them into disarray, but we still need to see who is remaining and who arrives to know what we are destroying tonight."

"Do you see any Numina?" she asks, grinding the end of her staff into the ground.

Peering back through the trees, the only forms that mill about, salting one of the old houses, are those of the Elder Mother, one of her changeling daughters, and the Healer. But there is no sign of the Healer's ancient husband or any of his counterparts. "No, ma'am," I confirm.

Traitor.

"There will be at least one," I say with the utmost confidence. "The eldest three are most likely sequestered at Wyrd Mountain working their magic to delay time and create an eclipse on this full moon."

Renegade.

"The concoction I've been gradually slipping to Fate and Fortune sickened them. But they weren't put over the edge until you gifted me that new strain of the Brume to mix in," I continue. "They're useless, and knowing this family, they brought them somewhere protected like Wyrd or the Infirmary."

Vulture.

"Death will be here for you," she says.

I nod.

Vulture. Vulture. VULTURE.

Stop it.

*That's what you are. Circling your family, ready to hurt them like your father hurt your mother. Ready to tear them to shreds like **you** did your father.*

Enough.

You are your father's son.

She grabs my face, talons pushing my cheeks until my dry, bloodied lips pout. "Too bad because she can't have you." The garden of her bloodroot breath roils into my face as she shoves up onto her bare toes and leans into me. "The reign of the witches is nigh and you will stay with me at my feet for the ages." She squeezes my face harder, and I am in awe. "Well, at least until I get tired of you. But for now, you're mine, trinket."

Then, she shoves me away, and I stumble back farther into the forest where an army of Phouka hide, also waiting for her call.

Swan: Of Spiders and Foxes

*B*ottomless may have been dramatic.

The hole is less of a hole and more of a tunnel. Maybe not even a tunnel, but something akin to a tube or slide, a system you'd imagine a terrifyingly large mole making deep in the pits of Purgatory. My screams would've fit right in had I not bitten my own tongue as I flailed my arms, looking for anything to grab before my feet completely left the entryway. Lucky for me, and *very* unlucky for Starling, I managed to snag the hem of his cloak before it was ripped from my fingers. It served a purpose though, not necessarily the one I wanted, but a purpose all the same. My momentum yanked Starling down after me, who must've, in turn, latched on to Kestrel, dropping my brothers into the belly of Baba Roga's true home right along with me.

Now, we lie in a jumbled heap, like a trio of overturned beetles. Kestrel's right ankle is pressed against my left cheek, and Starling's left knee is tucked into my right armpit. The bottom of my left boot must be resting against his chin while my right is pinned beneath Starling's draping spine. I'm unsure how he became sideways, but sliding down the packed dirt tunnel, headfirst, landed me next to The Moon's candle. If I didn't know any better, I would think that someone carried the pillar of magic-made wax to this spot and placed it with ginger hands right where it sits. But I do know better; The Sun was right, the candle did not suffer the breakable fate of its ordinary equivalent, and I am *oh* so grateful. I'm just not sure who to thank after this is over. The Moon, for making such a sturdy gift? Or Auntie Poppy for the luck that must've rubbed off on us over the years?

I'd have considered this for a moment longer if Starling's groan of pain as he rolls off me didn't morph into the beginnings of a screech. Being less than an arm's length away, Kestrel flops his over and slaps a hand over Starling's mouth. This smothers the shrill girlish sound, leaving the echoing remnants to peter off into the underground dwelling at a pitch I'm sure only a dog could hear. Not that Starling cares about who or what might be down here to hear it. No, he's too busy scrambling back into Kestrel and away from the pence-sized spider that skitters past us.

Once he deems Starling no longer a hazard, Kestrel removes his hand and shoves Starling off his lap. The latter quickly springs to his feet and turns in a tight circle, checking the surrounding area as he swipes at his clothes to dislodge any other possible arachnid that's latched on for a ride. Kestrel stands with a quiet grunt before pulling me up beside him and waving to flag Starling's gaze. But it's clear that Starling will continue working himself into a tizzy rather than accept that no other eight-legged creature inhabits his space or clothing. So, Kestrel uses the side of his boot to spray Starling's shins with dirt.

As soon as his seafoam eyes flick up, Kestrel uses the descriptive name sign that was officially bestowed upon Starling when Crow was four. All of us were terrified when Crow got sick that winter, especially after what the first illness he and I caught years prior did to his hearing and my extremities. But it was Starling who took Crow's newest bout of sickness the hardest. He refused to sleep in his own room the whole week, so Dad built Starling a nest of quilts and pillows at the foot of Crow's bed. We'd find an eleven-year-old Starling with his chin propped up in his hands on the edge of the mattress, having fallen asleep that way as he supervised Crow's fevered slumber. It wasn't too long after Crow's recovery that brushing his chin with a flat hand twice meant the name *"Starling"* instead of the word *"sweet."*

The panicked expression on my spider-deterred-brother's face abates at the use of the name sign, and his focus locks on Kestrel.

He shakes his head at Starling. *"For Fate's sake. It was just a tiny spider, calm down."* He then gestures to our surroundings before his fluid hands speak for him once more. *"Besides, we've got bigger problems."*

Kestrel's not wrong.

The dwelling we've spilled into is expansive. Its packed earthen walls are punctured by circular tunnels with rough, seven-foot openings, and its uneven, rooted ceiling is at least ten to twelve feet tall. The space is lit by melon-sized orbs, similar to the rosewood hue of Lark's favorite "cure all" poultice that reeks of rotting watermelon baking in the sun. These spheres of floating witchcraft cast just enough light for me to see that the space continues, and a farm of spiderweb-tangled sacs visibly taper off into the distance. I adopt Starling's horror as I stare at the drooping, suspended giants. The massive cocoons are shaped like water droplets, wrapped in layer after layer of what looks like more sticky, candy floss webs. From here, standing within the hazy radius of The Moon's candle at our feet, I can count twenty of them. Knowing there's more sacs ahead, trailing into the dark, makes my insides wriggle. I don't even want to know what's growing inside them. And Fortune willing, if we wade through this eerie lair quietly enough, we won't rouse anything on the verge of hatching.

Making a shallow analysis, I already know it would take too much time—more time than we have—to stick together while searching every inch of the false cottage's underbelly. Maybe it's stupid to separate, and perhaps that's precisely what a hag would want us to do, but our family is supposed to be somewhere in this Timeforsaken place, and the silence taking up residence doesn't bode well. So, I focus on the fact that witches are known for indulging in games instead of goalless murder. Although, what is it that Allison and/or Uncle Grim could be playing at now? Because they're either in the shadows playing hide-and-seek—which doesn't seem likely—or they're playing tag and not down here at all, which feels more likely. There is only one way to find out, and that means splitting up.

"*Let's do this fast,*" I sign. "*Kestrel, you go down that left tunnel, and Starling, you go right. I'll sweep from here back.*" I reiterate this by pointing to each of our assigned places. "*If you run into trouble, whistle the family signal once and get out of there. If you find Robin, Crow, or Dad, whistle it twice, and we'll come running. Got it?*"

Starling and Kestrel each sign their agreement with bobbing fists. Looking between them, the stress and nerves are palpable in their upturned brows and tight faces. We are so close to the end. Our family is within reach. And I pray that if—no, when—we find them, they can reach for us in return.

"*Both of you, stay vigilant, and be careful.*" My hands shake with my parting words to my brothers.

Occupying myself with a knife, I give Kestrel and Starling what I hope appears to be a reassuring, close-lipped grin. It feels unsteady on my mouth, but Kestrel doesn't notice; he's arming himself and dutifully supporting me by following my instructions. He disappears into the tunnel on my left without a second, doubting glance. Starling, though, he studies me. There's a weed metastasizing the longer we stand beneath the collection of webbed cocoons. It's slithered its way into my mind. It's snaking toward my attic desk drawer, where I've tucked a small scroll into the back. Its thorns have wheedled their way in, and it's unraveling the parchment, catching on the edges that I've mentally worried at time and time again. I hate that I've even created the list staining the imaginary scroll, but I'm a writer and thorough to a fault. Under Starling's scrutiny, the list is pouring onto the floor and deeper into my thoughts. The place where everything I've pushed aside when they threatened the effectiveness of Robin's sunflower medicines lives. But the scroll takes up all that space and it's boldly marked with concerns about the present and nearing future and then what-ifs that, logically, I know are improbable and cause me nothing but unwarranted mental anguish.

However, afflictions of the mind, like depression and anxiety, don't care about logic. And as I stare back at Starling, I'm pulled face-first into that list to memorize every line. Every worry. Everything from the fate and health of our missing family and the ones back home. To the battle we're approaching, and the end of the prophecy. From what will happen after this confusing event, to what will come of the Stygian Brume and the witch that created it after this suspicious "joining" and "prevailing of light."

It's too much to think about right now. I want to pull myself from this traitorous scroll, and jump from my attic window to warmth and freedom.

Starling's face softens, his head tilting with curious concern, and the motion only makes the thorny weeds choke me tighter, sending me further into my untimely spiral.

Will this darkness lording over us ever end?

Will our family ever honestly know peace?

If so, would I ever find my place in a world without use for someone whose passion lies only in the glade? Whose main job is being a Phouka hunter, an abomination that should cease to exist at some point?

What will I do when someday soon my siblings won't need me watching over them, and our parents want us to find our own paths and journeys?

What if I don't want my life to be full of exciting travel to new places and thrilling adventures exploring unseen things? What if my heart is lying to me, and I don't actually want a calm and cozy life, with poetry fulfilling my nights and a job with an inherited title rather than inherited magic fulfilling my days either?

Would Mom even want or be able to pass the title of Elder Mother on, and if she did, what if this disappoints Dad and Auntie Rose?

How could I do that to them when all they've ever wanted for us kids are the best and most exciting things, for us to reach our full potential? How could I be that selfish?

Does that mean when this age of darkness is done, the last witch's identity is found, and her reign of sickness and terror is over, I must depart from the trees I love so much?

Could I find a home away from home?

What would my life's purpose even be?

Where could I possibly end up?

Who will I become then?

Who am I now?

Am I enough?

What's wrong?

Hello?

"*Hello?*" Starling signs again.

All of a sudden, the list that consumes me is rolled back up and crammed into the recesses of my mental desk drawer, that snaps shut behind it. With a deep breath of musty, unceremonious air, I'm dumped outside my attic door and locked out. Starling's latched on to every trace of weakness that bloomed over me. He saw the fear weigh heavy like a spring storm, watering those blossoms with a preemptive pang of existential sadness. Surely, he witnessed the crown of it grow through my skull to weave through my hair like a set of Auntie Poppy's flower-ridden antlers.

I don't know whether to be embarrassed or ashamed of what he may or may not have seen. Though I suppose it doesn't matter, not now anyway. Not when all those unfounded fears are one grain of sand inside an hourglass, ticking down each second I waste on finding our family and getting them back home.

Presumably, feeling this push for time too, Starling bends to retrieve The Moon's candle with shaking fingers, though the tremor is milder now. *Is the remaining shakiness from sugar, spiders, anxiety, concern, or a cursed mix of all four?* Either way, Starling's shoving the dim, star-dusted light at me, and threading the pointer finger of my free hand through the handle. I don't process the movement. My digit wraps onto the curve, and just like that, the glowing pillar is in my possession.

"*Are you okay?*" Starling asks.

All I can do is blink.

This extra care from my typically cold brother lends me an unexpected seed of brightness, the kind Kestrel usually gives me. I haven't felt this particular warmth in years, a flash of uniquely *Starling*, all wrapped up in my favorite things. It's like dimpled smiles and sunflowers, red yarned pinkie promises and rain. And it's exactly how I remembered it being. The childlike nostalgia of being Starling's best friend swells. While that grows, the wiser older sister in me anchors it with fond resignation. It's time to put my best foot forward and convince my brother that I'm fine despite what spiral he might've seen. But I've never been good at lying. Starling knows this, so I just jerk my chin up and nod to the right, encouraging him to go on his way.

He squints at this non-answer until I shoo at him. Then, Starling pulls both axes from his back and advances on his assigned tunnel, and thankfully, he does so without looking back. I wait until I can no longer see him before letting out a shuddering, silent sigh. Then I bounce on my toes, trying to rid myself of the numbness crawling through them while also preparing myself for the task ahead. There is no telling what we could find in this den of dark dangers. A gale of residual dread rushes through me, coating my bones with the coldest trepidation I've ever had the displeasure of experiencing. Still, I force myself forward.

The combination of the watered-down, cool candlelight, and musty, blush witchcraft that illuminates my path makes odd shapes ricochet off the rounded dirt walls. They clamber along the ground, stretching over the suspended sacs like a colony of creepy-crawlies. I cringe just looking at them, and I hold my knife with a defensive grip as I stalk in and out of the reddish light, hastening my blue-purple auraed steps the farther I go. Occasionally, I stop and check behind me, listening for signs of anything following in my shadow. I'm wary, keeping my eyes on the darker pockets closest to the walls, looking for garnet eyes glaring through the holes of a manacle-like mask. The Moon's candle is my only company as I search for tracks in the dirt, or some clue as to where my dad and siblings are. But I'm coming up empty. Was I onto something with my earlier guess about witch-driven games? If so, this is the most messed up version of hide-and-seek I've ever played. And I'm not enjoying it, not one bit.

It kind of feels like a consolation prize when I reach the limits of the underground den to find what looks like a dais. There's only one platform and no stairs, but it's raised and wide, creating a half circle that frames a throne made of roots. The knotted wooden tendrils descend from the ceiling, entwined with stray autumn leaves caught up in spun sugar webs. The candy floss connects the throne to everything, trailing off into fading, splaying strings that run throughout the room, creating a network out of the different cocoons. But what bothers me the most is the strand attached to one of the throne's twisted arms, because it goes from the wood down to the dais top like a pin in a map. This lifeless strand drapes across the platform where its frayed ends point to an old, decrepit, three-legged spinning wheel. It's so different than the one that occupies Wyrd Mountain's temple, which has been lovingly tended to for multiple millennia, minus the years The Numina were in The Between. I've sat at Auntie Poppy's feet countless times growing up, watching her spin golden threads of luck and chance on that masterpiece of lacquered cherrywood. But this spinning wheel has not been cared for. It's cracked along the frame, and layers of paint and sealant are chipping off the surface to reveal gray, rotting wood underneath.

The witch's mocking mimicry is a sight for sore eyes, and a nightmare for an overactive imagination like mine. Especially with the tunnel openings on either side of the dais looking like the maws of twin beasts, and the roots dangling from them add to this visual by creating the illusion of snarling teeth. Even more so when Kestrel emerges from the left side with a sweeping arrowhead leading him like a compass. This imagery reminds me of how I almost lost him to the Gooseberry Wife.

I jump forward to pull my brother from the tunnel, but somehow, despite the small, ethereal beacon in my grasp, he hasn't heard or seen me yet. Kestrel's arm jerks back, his arrow aimed at the hollow of my throat as my breath hitches. My hands go up, candle above my head, the knife looped over my index finger swaying like a pendulum in front of my palm. Kestrel's silver eyes become bleary, and his chest heaves in panic. A boot scraping behind me worsens this and he swings his aim to the tunnel entrance on the right side of the dais. Craning my neck, I see Starling standing at its entrance, holding his axes crossed in front of his torso in an attempt to block everything vital.

"It's us," he hisses.

Kestrel lets down his draw with jerky movements and points the arrow at the ground, gasping. "I'm sorry," he gulps. "I'm sorry, I'm sorry, I'm sorry." Kestrel repeats this panting mantra, wiping at his streaming eyes and dampening forehead with his burgundy sleeve.

Starling gawks at Kestrel like he's grown two heads. With how unhurried Starling's entry was, I'm guessing his search has come up empty as well. I'm not ready for what that might mean, which is why, for the moment, I focus solely on Kestrel.

"Hey, it's fine," I whisper as I step forward, holstering my knife to grab his wet, woolen arm. "Are you okay? Did you find something?" My voice is hushed and soft, and I'm afraid my brother will shatter if I speak louder.

"No," he sniffs, erratic gaze darting from the weapon in his hands to Starling, me, and back. "I—I just—I just—"

I've never seen this rush of emotion from him before.

Kestrel has always been even-keeled and levelheaded, tempering himself, taking a breath when he needs to. But this wildness and unmeasured emotion is highly unusual. This must have been tamped down for a long time to erupt from him like a shaken, pressurized glass bottle. Starling doesn't see this though. He clicks his tongue, arms dropping to his sides. "You almost impaled us, you idiot. What's your problem? You start using your gift again, and suddenly you're all arrow happy, ready to strike us all down," Starling tuts. "I guess this is what we get for you holding it back for so long."

Kestrel's eyes scrunch closed, shoulders rapidly rising and falling.

Starling opens his mouth to say something, but I hold my hand up, effectively shutting him down.

Kestrel inflates his lungs with much-needed air, then blows it out through his lips in a long exhale before taking in an equally long drag. And as he repeats this process, Kestrel re-centers and regulates himself to the point that when his lids flutter open, his gaze lands on Starling and he says four calm but loaded words. "It's because of you."

Something steely glazes Starling, and as he gathers his defenses around him, his eyes become harder. "Come again?" They're almost a shade colder when his head tilts in a way that promises nothing good nor kind will come from him next.

Taking his arrow in hand, Kestrel slides it back inside its quiver. "I stopped using my gift because of you." He starts his explanation with a death grip on his bow. "It was that day in the garden with Swan's snails and your birds that did it for me."

I stay silent, wholly confused, studying the stark difference in my brothers' body language. Kestrel is drained, his posture soft with relief, but his vulnerable hands are still tight on his weapon. Starling is on edge and ready to fight with his words, yet his hands are lax, axe heads hanging in his loose hold.

Kestrel continues, strapping the bow over his shoulder. "I heard Swan screaming and threw rocks from afar when I saw the starlings, but my aim was never at the birds. I didn't want to hit them; I just wanted to scare them away. You wouldn't call them off, even after I got to the garden, and Swan was devastated." Kestrel's chest hitches, and my heart aches. "You laughed at how hard she cried for you to stop."

"I know." Starling squints. His face is raw with something that, despite his tone, mirrors an emotion much heavier than regret. "That's how one of those rocks you threw split my chin open, which made me lose control of the birds. And that's when they actually ripped the snails apart instead of just tossing them around. Your clumsy accident still succeeded though; they flew off not long after." Starling sounds relieved by that outcome, but there's a twinge of resentment in his following words. "Yet I was the only one who got in trouble that day."

"That's not true." Kestrel shakes his head. "Mom and Dad were fair; they grounded me from leaving the glade. I couldn't go to the Mountain, Apothecary, villages, Library, or literally anywhere for weeks. But you didn't realize it because you were too busy blaming Swan. Instead, you should've been mad at me, because...it wasn't an accident that the rock hit you." With a sigh, Kestrel runs his hands over his scalp. "I didn't want to admit it at first, but...I. Can't. Miss. In that moment, watching that melee of snails and birds, my anger festered deep in my heart, and it wanted to hurt you. My gift listened to that feeling, and the rock missed the birds as I subconsciously intended. And it hit you like I secretly wished." My brother's hands slip down the sides of his face to hang heavy at his sides. "As soon as I saw the blood on your face, and watched it soak your shirt, I was petrified. I was so disgusted with myself that I became afraid of my own heart. Since then, I haven't trusted my gift, knowing that it could be possessed by the smallest microaggression." Kestrel's laugh is halfhearted. "How could I know that I wouldn't hurt—or Moon forbid— *kill* someone I love? It felt like my heart betrayed me, betrayed what was right and wrong. I couldn't risk that happening again."

Starling's mouth opens and closes; silence fills the den.

"I'm sorry, man. I really am. The Gooseberry Wife made me realize that I can't run away from my heart forever, especially now." Kestrel wraps loose fingers around the bowstring crossing his chest. "I can't expect to fight a war unarmed and win, not when doing so would only result in hurting our family. Which is what I'm always trying to avoid."

"To be honest with you," Starling starts, and my pulse races. "I haven't spared a single thought about that rock in a long time.

I forgave you seasons ago." He shrugs nonchalantly. "I trust you with my life."

"Unfortunately, I do, too," Kestrel chuckles, cuffing our brother on the shoulder. "I'll always be watching you and that little book of yours, though."

"Speaking of..." I trail off, after a spot of color catches my attention. Raising The Moon's unlit candle above me, I make a multilayered discovery.

A claret bloom is trapped behind the outer layer around a nearby sac. I'm sure if the flower weren't compressed behind fluffy silk, it would still appear as full as its counterparts in the window boxes on Baba Roga's porch. But this blossom is laden with white, powdery mildew and black mold. The other sacs amongst the roots hanging from the earthen ceiling, sprout the same sugar plum hellebore flowers too. It was hard to see them before, all swaddled in webs, and with Baba Roga's orbs casting a widespread sickly warm hue. You need to be standing directly beneath a sac to see the moldering poisonous flowers. And the harder I look, the more I find. Hidden inside the milky, candy webs are also small white-headed daisy-esque flowers. It seems like both species of poison are equally mixed and rotting in each cocoon.

"Starling, I think you'd better have a look at this." I point.

He stashes his weapons in their holsters before standing beside me, head tipping to follow my finger. Recognition further lifts his face and he digs deep into his pockets, rooting past candy to pull out his journal. Starling speeds through it, thumb dragging along the edge of the pages to flip them faster. When he stops, he holds the book aloft, putting his sketch closer to the flowers.

Kestrel joins our examination, a *"huh"* rolling from his throat when he sees the match. "Oh yeah, bloodroot," he says. "Guess your final chart was right about Allison Gross."

Starling turns on our younger brother. "How do you know? You were sleeping when that last conversation was held."

A full, pearl-toothed grin saunters its way across Kestrel's lips. "Was I?"

I would've lost a lot of money had I bet on whether or not Kestrel was sleeping as we whispered beside him and the wood-wose. His snores had sounded real. Apparently, Kestrel is a talented actor. Had he done it so Starling and I could have a moment to communicate or—dare I say—*bond*? Based on his cheekiness, he had. I'm thankful for it, but Starling looks bitter about being duped. He snaps his journal closed, lips curling inward as his nostrils flare. He looks like he's ready to whack Kestrel upside the head with the slim leather book. I intervene by saying what's been fermenting in my gut. "Something doesn't feel right about this. The witches, the Brume and Phouka, the tree being empty. We followed the sister's web, and all we got was…these." I motion to the giant spider sacs.

The blackened prophecy staining Auntie Posy's skin can't be wrong. But this atrium, and apparently Kestrel's and Starling's searches through their assigned tunnel corridors, unveiled nothing. This whole haunt is empty save for me and my brothers, and Baba Roga's creepy spider sacs. I suppose each of them are big enough to count as a body—big enough to be a person—

Oh. Oh no.

"We need to cut the sacs open, now!" I draw three of my six remaining throwing knives.

"Wha—" I shove a thin handle into Kestrel's hand before he can finish.

Starling is already reaching for the second knife. "You don't think—" he starts.

"Yes, yes." My body is shaking as I stare at the numerous people-sized cocoons. "Robin, Crow, and Dad, they're *inside* the sacs."

"But there's so many of them." Kestrel gapes. "How do we know what's in the others?"

The answer is simple, we don't. For all we know, Baba Roga and Allison Gross created a new breed of witches and they're incubating inside these nightmare-inducing spider baby sacs. The possibilities are endless, and terrifying. Though, it's nothing compared to the other unknown horrors. Has our family been cocooned the whole time? Can they breathe? The only way to find out is to start cutting.

Without answering Kestrel, I approach the nearest sac and slice the bottom with a shallow, careful cut. At first, nothing happens. My heartbeat thunders in my ears along with my brothers' breaths behind me. Then, a wisp slips through the opening. It's like the smoke of a single extinguished flame, soft and trailing, tapering out before it reaches the ground. But nothing else happens. My cut was too shallow. I didn't want to nick whatever lay inside, but now I have no choice. I slice the gauzy chrysalis once more.

This second pass does the trick.

A misty, ebony fall spills from the opening. The shadows pouring from the witch-born bundle churn around the dirt, contorting into clouds of confusion as it tries to take on different sizes and shapes. Nothing sticks. I catch sight of a hoof and horn at one point, then a paw the next. When the mass of black does form a shape that looks vaguely like a pair of wings, there's a glow of yellow eyes. They appear bleary, dazed from forced sleep, and fevered with the starting drops of encroaching poison. Even though the creature's body is discombobulated, its gaze is full of waking intelligence. And a breath later, the black mass sweeps through the underground lair. I swear I hear a whispered, *"Thank you,"* coasting along the draft that the freed Pooka left behind.

"Should we assume the rest of these are also Pooka? Or should we be prepared to unleash some Phouka?" Kestrel asks.

"Judging by the busted sacs we saw earlier," Starling muses, "I say we prepare for the worst."

I nod. "Just avoid the mostly spotted and darker ones. I don't know that releasing those would do anyone any good."

Kestrel switches his knife to his other hand to wipe his palm on his trousers. "But what if Dad, Robin, and Crow are in those?"

Rivulets of prickling pain shoot up from my toes and into my fingers. "If it comes down to that..." I hesitate. "We'll deal with it then. For now, get going." Punctuating my words, I cut through the next sac.

Part of me feels guilty about how much work we're making for Auntie Rose after tonight, because each of these unchained messengers will need to be tracked down again. Since Uncle Grim obviously found them and brought them here once before, I'm sure they'll be able to listen for their whispers in the shadows and locate them again. The Pooka won't look kindly upon the Shadow Prince who brought them here, but perhaps they'll forgive Uncle Grim when he comes to offer them reformation and healing at Death's side? That is, if we can find our family, and release them from the grotty metamorphosis that awaits inside these cocoons of contagion first.

One after another, my brothers and I liberate the Pookas. The old prophets stream from their prisons, cascading onto the earthen floor, where they get their bearings before fleeing. Soon, the atrium is filled with a low rolling fog of haze and shadows. Very fitting for Hallowtide, I would say. The faeries stir around our ankles as they try to recall the animal shapes they used to transfigure into. With each slash and flood of smoggy ink and sulfur eyes, my heart sinks. This is indeed the worst game of hide-and-seek ever known to faerie and mankind. And to add to my growing misery, I realize the sacs soaking up splotches of dark magic like pools of sickening mold are starting to look more likely. I don't want to find someone we love dead or dying inside. That, or find them half trans-formed, dripping red-eyed monsters much like the Phouka. Imagining my father and siblings in such a state makes icy sweat bead along my temples, and a chill of rippling goosebumps rises on my exposed neck. My muscles are wound tight and surging with so much angst I can't contain my shakiness. And when I cut into a newer candy-enrobed, moldy flower-studded sac, expecting another Pooka to billow out, I let out a piercing scream. It's not smoke that slumps from the clean laceration... it's a five-fingered, flesh-and-blood hand.

Swan: Together

*W*holly unprepared for the sight of a hand dangling above me, I jolt, summoning my brothers with a shriek. Starling acts first. He pulls on the hand, ripping the bottom of the sac open. My own hand falls over my mouth when a small, limp body drops into Starling's awaiting arms. When he kneels, a banner of wavy sable hair fans atop the dirt. The impact of my knees hitting the ground is bruising, and the way my teeth click together is grating. Fear grips me by the throat. *Robin.*

Our sister's face is still.

Her rosebud lips are parted, paler than any pink petal I've seen her gift grow. And her eyes are closed, long lashes kissing the tops of her ivory cheeks. Remnant strings of sugary cobwebs create a veil over Robin, dusting her in white from her crown to her boots.

She looks peaceful…slumbering…*dead.*

Kestrel appears at Starling's back, a wobbly hand reaching to fist the wool covering his shoulder. "She's not—" he croaks. "She isn't—" Kestrel can't finish his thought, but it's clear that we're all thinking the same thing.

Webs and wilted, moldy flowers cling to the fibers of Robin's cloak, creating the illusion of clouds amongst a rust-colored sky. The stitched namesake birds, sewn by our father with bright threads, are in flight. They soar over tiny fields of trillium and meadowsweet blooms where nests cradling blue eggs rest. Starling pulls Robin closer and the crackling sound of wax parchment peeks from her inner pockets. The twigs of my heart crumple like that hidden bag and I fold, trembling as I set down the candle and cradle Robin's pale cheeks. My lips press against her temple, and my tears pour over her skin, an incantation of apologies pooling from the seams of my mouth, into the hollow of her bone.

I almost miss the soft, sleepy groan when I heave a raucous sniffle, making me choke on my own phlegm. I'd know that sound anywhere, I've heard it daily, for years. Every morning, when I rouse Robin awake, she makes the same noise, stretching like a kitten dozing in a patch of sunlight. A devastating kind of hope whirls through me. With my face only inches away from Robin's, I search for the telltale wrinkle in her nose, the one that forms mere moments before she opens her eyes.

"What time is it?" Robin mumbles.

Starling barks a laugh, twisting to avoid knocking my head into Robin's, and whipping our sister up until she's sitting. Her startled confusion as he pulls her into a hug makes me laugh through the tears sluicing down my cheekbones. Robin still hasn't registered much by the time Starling pulls back, smoothing her mussed hair and clawing the rest of Baba Roga's webs from her tresses.

"You scared us half to death," he says to her, shaking his head. "You're never allowed to leave the glade again. Better yet, you're not allowed to leave the house. Ever."

Robin blinks, her silver stare leaping. "What's going on? Where are we?" Her head swivels as she absorbs the haunting, candy-floss-filled den. "The last thing I remember is being out hunting. I was climbing down from a tree, and then Uncle Grim

—" Robin's small voice sputters as her memory catches up to her.

Kestrel's touch to the space between her shoulder blades as she searches the curving earthen shadows for our poison-possessed uncle, makes her jump. "Robin, where's Crow and Dad?" he asks.

Robin's face scrunches. "They're here too?"

Her answer is enough.

Kestrel gives Robin a weak smile before lightly cuffing her under her chin with a crooked finger. His relief is palpable, but it's not quite time to celebrate yet, not until we find our brother and Dad. Our search must continue. So, as Kestrel and Starling walk past us to cut into the remaining sacs, I help Robin to her feet.

"Uncle Grim has been taken over by witchcraft," I say, brushing off my sister's clothes. "He was forced to grab Crow, but accidentally brought Dad along for the ride."

With a wary gaze, Robin nods. "He didn't seem like himself when he showed up in the forest. It didn't really sink in until he grabbed my arm, and then it was too late for me to yell."

My chest tightens, thinking about the fear and sense of betrayal that Robin must have endured in that moment. I don't know what to say, or how to begin comforting her. Instead, I help Robin stand, and check her over for physical wounds, any real tangible hurt that I can tend to. But before I can confirm that she is unscathed, my little sister wraps her skinny arms around my torso. Like muscle memory, I hug her back, spine curving and head turning to rest atop hers.

"Thank you for coming to find me," Robin murmurs.

"Always," I say, the undertone of a promise steeping my words as I hold her tighter. "I would swim through a sea of nettles, all the way across the world, if it meant bringing you back home safe and sound." Before I entirely lift my head to look down at her, I brush a peck along the part of her hair.

"Even if it means I must deal with your eggy morning breath every day."

Robin jabs her fingertips into my ribs, making me bend away to protect my most ticklish spot. By the time I've separated myself from her, there's another set of scuffling feet bounding toward us. The pace is quick, and the fall of the steps light in weight. I don't have to squint through the new swirling haze of black Pooka mist to know who they belong to.

The second Crow launches himself at me, I scoop him up, twirling on my heel just to hear his hushed giggle. I can't help but hold onto the dip between his shoulders and neck as I take him in, almost as if reassuring myself that my youngest brother is here, alive. Feeling Crow beneath my fingers is nearly enough, but moving my hands upward to cup his small face is the confirmation I need. His pale tawny skin is tepid, though his cheeks are slowly warming beneath my fingertips, meaning his heart is beating and his blood is pumping. Crow's sugary, web-covered palm is sticky when he lays his hand over mine with a beaming grin. He excitedly pulls my grasp away and hugs our sister before signing, "*Swan, you found Robin!*"

Seeing his name signs for us makes me weep again. Robin's is a modified version of the word "*blue*," Crow's middle finger crossing over his index for the letter *R* before twisting his hand outward left and right. Crow created the unique sign for Robin after one of the many times she presented him with a bowl of fruits and vegetables that she'd grown as a snack with her then newly minted gift. But back then, the fresh foods were always robin egg blue, from strawberries and melons to carrots and corn. Thus, her name sign was born.

Crow took longer to find one he felt fit me.

It was stormy the day he found it. Loving the rain was something we both had in common. As a feverish baby, before he became hard of hearing, the rain soothed his pained wails when Lark wasn't awake to sing to him. Although, after Crow could no longer hear the water streaming from the sky, he could still smell an oncoming storm and would be ready to play in the puddles. If a storm was particularly nasty, he could feel the vibrations from thunder against the windows. Crow and I have often curled up together on the window seat inside the house, bundled up in one of Grandma Aspen's old quilts. We'd sit there, drawing through the condensation from our breaths on the glass, tracing the rivulets that raced on the outside surface. Sometimes, Mom would bring us steaming mugs of spiced cranberry and orange hot white chocolate. Those occasions our busybody siblings would join us for the sweet treat.

But enjoying the rain became a uniquely *us* ritual, me and Crow. And this earned me my own version of the sign for rain; Crow's hands were still palms down, and fingers spread as he bent his wrists up and down, starting at head height. But his movements were much softer when he signed my name, graceful. Crow's fingers weren't ridged when they splayed open. Rather, they were light where he concentrated the bending of his wrists from head to shoulders like fluid wings. It transformed the usually harsh sign into something much more beautiful, and *oh*, how grateful I am to see it again.

"Our brothers helped you, too," I simultaneously say aloud and sign to Crow.

He glances up then, looking around Baba Roga's den with his head cocked as if listening to faraway wind chimes, a sound that only his unique pointed ears can hear. Crow's eyes have a metallic glaze as his tawny fingers twitch, spelling something so quickly that even I can't catch it. Picking up The Moon's candle from the floor, I realize that Crow's changeling gift has picked up on something lost and forgotten.

With a slight forward shift to his upper body, as if his elder twig heart is pulling him, Crow begins to walk. And it's in the direction I originally came from. He must be sensing our father, right? But we're backtracking, and Starling, Kestrel, and I already checked; the tunnels are empty, and the remaining sacs are in the opposite direction. So where is Crow going? Nonetheless, I would never doubt him or his gift, so Robin and I follow, watching his small fingers flutter at his sides in a repetitive pattern. Crow is subconsciously spelling one word. The letter *C* is recognizable by the self-explanatory shape of his hand and *M* when he folds his thumb into his fist.

The three of us are back where our brothers and I were first spat out from the earthen tunnel slide when I figure out there's seven letters in total. As Crow spins in a slow, surveying circle, I identify an *H*. I'm so distracted trying to decipher his finger spelling that I miss the thick, sticky web he inspects. It stretches from the opening of the tunnel, into the wall's shadowy curved corners.

Crow stops his spelling and turns to me, that magic, mystifying quality from his gift still lingering in his young silver gaze. "*You lost something; it's important,*" he signs, and he doesn't express this like a question with raised brows. He emotes it like a matter of fact with flat features. Then, Crow points to the wall.

Robin, ever the brave one, goes right up to the sugary floss and speaks with both her mouth and her hands. "There's something caught inside."

"Huh." I lean forward and, true enough. When Starling, Kestrel, and I entered Baba Roga's abode and made our unexpected descent into the dark, we disrupted some of the webs from where they were attached. But enough of the strands stayed intact so that whatever we lost slipped between the wicked candy fluff and the wall, causing the network of webs to become a sagging pouch. "I have no idea—"

Before I can say much else, Robin's fingers dart into the web, breaking it apart and fishing out the mysterious lost item. What she unravels disappears into her fist before her hand plunges back into the web. Then, she's also pulling out a metal box the length of my thumb, shaking the straggling strings from its ornate corners, its contents rattling inside. She turns the two-inch silver container over in her hands and pushes its compartment out to reveal the interior.

"Matches."

I gasp, patting my side bag with my free hand to search for the magic-born matches the Moon created to light her Blessed candle. Setting the candle back onto the floor, I free both of my hands to speak to my brother. *"Crow! You perfect, beautiful, sweet, tiny, gifted genius. I love you so much I could cry."* I'm unable to hold back the shock and exuberance with my gestures. How did I not realize I lost the matches? I was holding them when Starling and Kestrel knocked into me. After the fall, and all the excitement of spiders and finding the Blessed candle in perfect condition, the existence of the matches we used to test the floor for traps never even occurred to me. Maybe on the way down our brains were magically replaced by stale, half-eaten pieces of licorice, because that negligence is ridiculous.

"I helped, right? I did a good job?" Crow asks before wiping his hands on his cloak over Dad's embroidery as a comfort gesture.

"Buddy, you did more than a great job." I kneel to his height with a chuckle, looking down at the gossamer glow between us. *"The Moon gave me a very special gift to help us win against the witches, and without those matches"*—I nod in Robin's direction where she produces the spent, sun-symbolled match that she found in the web first, and puts it back inside the matchbox with the others before closing the compartment—*"we wouldn't be able to use it."*

Robin tugs on Crow's sleeve and hands him the silver matchbox his changeling gift recovered. *"Sounds like you might've just saved us,"* she adds.

Crow beams at this. His smile is so big that I swear I can see his molars with the candle's under-lighting. His pride in himself floods my chest with warmth; I can already see how bright his future will be. Crow wants nothing more than to help people, and he's been dying to go out into the world to do so. I need to ensure that he reaches that potential by securing the world's fate first.

I herd my siblings back the way we came, letting Crow pocket the matches with the job of keeping them safe, while Robin carries the candle. And once I regain Crow's attention, I sign while I talk. "We're going to get you guys home to Mom and Lark. We just need to find Dad first."

"I think your brothers already have that covered." Dad's timbre echoes in my ears as it skates along the dirt-packed walls.

It seems like the tree roots above us tremble at the rich sound. Or perhaps that's me. Tears spring to my eyes when my father and brothers emerge from the dissipating messenger faerie mist. There's something about seeing a parent after trials and tribulations, no matter how big or small, that opens the floodgates. I've tried so hard to keep it together and be strong.

It's difficult, but I point forward and alert Crow to Dad's presence and take the candle from Robin, allowing my youngest siblings to reunite with Dad first. I'm barely holding it together when it's finally my turn, and I step into his arms. His cinnamon scent, and the tickle of his locked hair, consume my senses, the familiarity filling me with a pang of safety. Even in the belly of a witch's home.

A thick laugh bubbles from my throat. The droplets of happiness from this reunion shower some of my previous worries, washing them away like a mop to a dusty attic floor. My siblings and Dad are here, and they're alive. But they have no idea what happened since Dad first heard the prophecy, as he and Crow were taken only moments later. Not to mention, Robin doesn't have the faintest clue of anything past the forest, including the state our aunts are in.

"Uncle Grim has been ensorcelled with poison and is

secretly under a witch's control. He was forced to take you guys," I murmur into my father's collarbone. "He's responsible for Auntie Poppy's blindness and Auntie Posy's fever."

Robin, who interprets our conversation for Crow, pauses her movements, looking at me in confusion. Dad is nodding, no doubt already having figured out this information for himself.

"They're safe," Starling jumps in before I can elaborate for Robin's sake. He places a hand of reassurance on Dad's shoulder when I pick up my head. "Time will have taken them to Wyrd days ago with The Moon and Sun."

Dad's silver eyes widen as they flicker over us older kids. "Days?"

I untangle myself, and we all stand in a loose circle as my brothers and I try to quickly recount as much pertinent information as possible. With Crow watching and Robin signing, the three of us come to an unspoken agreement to skip over everything involving the Rye Mother and Gooseberry Wife. Instead, we repeat the prophecy and what we've done to unravel it thus far. We include what Time and the two eldest Numina have done to aid our journey in slowing the progression of the eclipse. As well as what Lark, Hazel, and our mother are doing to get the faeries to safety while they prepare our home for what's to come.

"Witches? In the glade?" Robin squeaks.

Dad pulls her closer to his side, rubbing warmth and comfort back into her arm. But I can see the worry in his pressed lips. Even the emerald green shimmer under his skin has taken on an unhealthy lime beneath the orbs of witchcraft above us. It flashes along his cheekbones as he turns to Crow, who tugs at the cream wool over his elbow.

"*I had a nightmare when I was up there,*" Crow signs, pointing his chin toward the spider-esque sacs. "*I saw Uncle Grim walking outside Mom's trees. The witches were with him too, but—*" Crow frowns, scratching at the twists along his scalp. He's hesitant

275

when his fingers move once more. *"But there were three witches with him."*

An expression like a dawning sunrise raises Robin's sable brows. "I think I had that dream, too. And the sun and moon were just a teensy-weensy bit apart in the sky. They were practically already touching."

A resounding *humph* puffs from Dad. "So did I. I could've sworn before I was put to sleep, I heard another woman's voice, someone other than Baba Roga or Allison Gross."

Starling and I share a look.

We'd been right about who the second witch was when we made the bloodroot connection from Starling's notebook, but hearing Dad confirm it brings little comfort, especially the involvement of the last remaining hag. Starling noted a Cornflower Wraith, but that doesn't really make sense, considering cornflowers aren't poisonous; on the contrary, the blue flowers are edible. Mom uses her homemade cornflower sugar to add a floral note and blue tone to some desserts. Even Healers use the petals, leaves, and seeds in teas and topical treatments at the Apothecary. Could someone even weaponize a medicinal flowering herb? Would such a Wraith, who is supposed to be responsible for the start of the Stygian Brume, be strong enough to have created it? Does that moniker actually exist?

Or did my brother hear this folklore name blow in on a breeze with some travelers, and it's nothing more than someone's home-grown scary story? Like when Starling read aloud The Noon Witch, and Nanny Rutt suggested that she was a fable because Nanny—once a prominent witch herself—had never heard of her. She hasn't exactly steered us wrong. So, surely this third witch is somewhere in Starling's book. Someone that was accidentally ruled out? Though names don't matter much right now. What does matter is that another powerful witch is advancing on this dark playing board, working with Baba Roga and Allison Gross, moving unnoticed for a long time. It can't be a coincidence that my siblings and father all dreamed the same thing. Which means that a worse evil has made its way toward our home and precious family, a home that's preparing to open its doors. And our family is none the wiser.

We need to get home. Fast.

Kestrel is already a step ahead of me as he lifts his bow from his shoulder. He poises his crooked, calloused index finger on the golden string from Fortune's spinning wheel and plucks it.

Once. Twice. Three times.

The enchanted string shivers, stretching taut between the elder wood limbs. But after it settles, there's nothing. The six of us stand in silence, only the sound of our breathing to occupy the space. Panic alights my skin with crackles of nervous energy, and the burning in my fingers flares. It's never taken Auntie Rose this long to answer our call, and I can't help imagining all sorts of terrible scenarios—

My aunt appears in all her glory.

Unlike the last time Kestrel summoned Death, she does not arrive in her usual burst of lustrous light. And there is no snowdrop and midnight-scented air accompanied by a masculine peat and pine. The crown of gloom that typically flares above her head like dancing flames is lifeless, flipped, and lying over her brow in the shape of a sharp multi-edged circlet. Even her clothing is different, her pooling dress of starry ink has been replaced with armor. A gorget hugs her throat while the mantles that cap her shoulders flare out into pauldrons, reminding me of bat wings. Bracers shroud her Phouka-inked forearms and padded shins, and there's a tasset belt draping over her hips and thighs under a corseted breastplate that enrobes her chest and torso. The leather pieces are dark and foreboding, like a sea of oil and nightmares. Their swirling depths are studded with silver rivets and lined with thick scales. Even though she hasn't worn it in years, I find that the only familiar staple in her new matching ensemble is the black patch covering her one-stone eye.

After Death surveys us and our surroundings, her rigid posture crumples and she tenderly touches Robin's and Crow's cheeks, kissing their foreheads and ruffling their hair before throwing her arms around her half-brother's neck. Dad returns Auntie Rose's hug, the leather that shields her body audibly squeaking with the force of his embrace. When she pulls away, something pretending to be wry and youthful chisels its way onto her lips.

"You seem like you've aged years," Auntie Rose says, black nail pointing at my father's beard. "It looks like you've gained some more silver hairs, too."

Dad ignores her attempt at diffusing the grief and tension soaking us all to the bone. "What are you wearing?" he asks, tone not unkind, but scrutinizing.

Death sniffs a hollow laugh. "This old thing?" She glances down at the armor, hand hovering above the empty sheath on her hip.

I swear my heart sinks between my kidneys.

The beach glass braided into the ropes of Dad's hair clinks as he shakes his head at her. "Primrose—"

At the argumentative tone of Dad's voice, and the use of her full name, Auntie Rose abandons her sarcastic charade. Hardship fortifies her deceptively young, ageless face with an immovable, stony resolve as she crosses her arms. "There's a battle coming to the glade, and I need to protect myself."

"Yes." Dad mirrors her posture. "By going to the Mountain where you'll be safe."

"No, Rush."

My father's fingertips turn green and melt back into his deep skin tone as his hands repeatedly squeeze and release his opposite biceps. "You're risking everyone." His first three fingers are a light sage now. "And everything," he entreats.

"I—" Auntie Rose squirms under the implication of how quick she could unravel everything we know and love if she became like Macha, the Fortune before Auntie Poppy. "I can't just sit back," she breathes. "I refuse."

"Primrose." The way Dad says her full name again is twice as damning.

Death prickles at this, although there is a tinge of desperation in her voice now. "I understand that it's selfish, and that I'm putting the future in peril; I am painfully aware, and I hate myself for it," she grits out, shoulders raising as she pulls her crossed arms tighter against her sternum. "But if Grim is beyond repair, it needs to be me," she continues, her tone almost begging. "You have to see that."

My father's teeth stay locked together.

And when he says nothing, Auntie Rose becomes sharp. "You can't tell me that you wouldn't do the same if the roles were reversed, if Sparrow were in Grim's position. She is your beginning, and if it came down to it, she would be your end. Just as you would be hers." Death spares my siblings and me a glance before she digs into our father further. "I know that Grim and I have an unconventional relationship, but you would never let the woman you love face that without you." Her silver eye flits between his matching stare. "So don't make us."

It's clear by his tight face that Dad understands, but doesn't like the fact that my aunt's statement is so accurate. Or he doesn't like how much the truth puts so many lives in danger. Still, he can't refute it. None of us can, not for any member of this family. But when it comes to the typical romantic love between someone like my parents or Hazel and Icarus, and the special agamic love between Death and her Reaper...well, bonds that true would let the world burn if required.

Dad exhales like he carries the weight of the world on his back. "We'll need to create a plan, something that guarantees your safety. Your well-being is more than imperative. But we also must make sure no one else gets hurt in the process."

Auntie Rose gives a fervent bob of her head, a silent thank you shattering the last of her walls as her arms fall to her armored sides. "Of course. First, let's get you all home," she says, meeting Robin's and Crow's wide, onlooking stares. There's a phantom smile haunting her lips when she focuses back on her half-brother. "Then, we can have a brief homecoming and consult that brilliant wife of yours." Dad laughs, and Auntie Rose scans our faces until she lands on me. Her eye drops to my abdomen, to my empty belt, the last spot she saw her shears. She does a quick sweep of my body, checking the six empty sheaths on my leg, and around my candle-less side bag. Then she lingers on the straps of my knapsack clinging to my shoulders.

How am I supposed to tell her what happened at the orchard?

If worse comes to worst, will she be able to do her divine job without her shears?

A small onslaught of questions scale my attic ceiling, similar to an imp climbing the barn rafters. But there's no time to gently coax them down and out the window. Instead, they're burned away like a spat of flames from tiny-fanged mouths when my aunt's search ends on my teeth whittling away at my chapped lower lip. She has her answer. The shears are gone.

"We'll figure this out, together," she promises to everyone, but Death looks directly at me as the words leave her relaxed mouth.

My stomach clenches as I stow away the Blessed candle for safe travel. I wish it was from the emotional thought of "*togetherness*," of a united family unit, or a successful conclusion to the worst days of our lives, but it's not. As the seven of us join hands, creating a chain that connects me, my siblings, and our father to Auntie Rose's power, it's the unknown that puts my guts in an iron fist. More specifically, the things staining that scroll in my attic. The feeling that *"together"* might not be as many people as we think. After all, there are the ebony words etched into Fate's fevered skin that—against all hope and benefit of any doubt—say one of us will destroy any foolproof plan we think we might be creating. They haunt me as we're consumed by the Numina's magic. Soon, all the changelings of the glade will be back in one place again. And soon, one of us could raze that *"togetherness"* to the ground.

For a child of the changeling must join the dark for the light to prevail.

Swan: Returning to the Nest

*R*eturning to the glade, amongst the familiar safety of our gourd-filled garden, should be comforting. Keyword *should*. But my home looks different beneath the partially frozen and sinister, airglow sky. If I were to close one eye and put my hand in the air, I don't think I could even fit my pinkie nail between the remaining hair that separates the sun and moon. The eclipse that the eldest Numina promised us is almost upon us. We were told to finish our fight before it ended, but we're not ready yet.

Not even a breeze stirs the towering sunflowers lined like soldiers to our right. The only hint of noise nearby is coming from the perimeter, behind the vine-covered trellises at our backs. It's a writhing kind of sound, weaving somewhere outside Mom's trees. After years of hunting in the forest, I know exactly what's making it. And I'm afraid that if I look past the sugar snap peas, between the crossed slats of wood they crawl over, I might see unnatural sets of red eyes peering back at me. A lot more than I'm used to. But I don't want to imagine how many Phouka are stirring, circling the perimeter like buzzards.

Our steps down the paved path towards our house hold the only other signs of life, the faeries who occupy the glade having been evacuated to Hazel's cottage for safety like Auntie Rose planned. The eerie glowing grins of the pumpkin lanterns lining the stone seem like mocking omens. My skin vibrates as I count the pools of candlelight we briskly step in and out of, trying to ignore what such a sign could mean. Thankfully, I don't wonder for long because Lark appears, barreling toward us. She doesn't hesitate to throw herself forward, burying Crow in her arms before pulling Robin into her as well. Then she's propelling into Dad, wrapping herself around him before quickly diving at me. The breath is knocked from my lungs as Lark departs with equal speed to hug Kestrel and Starling. When I finally catch sight of her face, there are dark smudges beneath her puffy turquoise eyes. Stray locks of hair poke from her mussed double chestnut braids, and a halo of baby hairs splay from the edges around her temples and forehead.

She must be exhausted.

It doesn't compare to the harrowed fatigue on the faces of the two women blazing down the path. Hazel is toting what looks like a bulging sack that's been haphazardly made from spare bedding, and it's easily almost as big as her, if not wider. Mom is hot on the Healer's trail. When he sees her, Dad is on the move, meeting his wife partway. He's stooping, his hands on either side of her ivory face as he kisses her, holding Mom back from flinging herself from her wheelchair and into his embrace. The cry that she seals into his lips as she claws at the neck of his cloak, soothes my wooden heart. My eyes burn with welling tears at the solace they find in one another. And now, with their foreheads pressed together, their love and devotion becomes poetry:

WHEN TWO PEOPLE, *who are destined for each other, are connected by an invisible red thread, the thread will never stretch, tangle, or break— regardless of the time, place, or circumstances. It's binding.*

Whispered words exchanged only inches away, bind this love.

Words melted into each other's lungs to become a part of their very beings, bind this love.

Childhood spit handshakes and teenage death rattles, bind this love.

Cinnamon and berry kisses, bind this love.

True love and happily ever after, bind this love.

Thread red and curling, bind this love.

DAD TUCKS the stray hairs that slip from the bun behind Mom's ears, and it's like he was never gone. The only thing that shatters this illusion is how Robin and Crow approach them, tears in their silver eyes. Mom breaks away from Dad to hug them close to her scarred chest. She peppers their still web-dusted heads with kisses. It's only when Robin joyfully notes the charm bracelet that Mom's been wearing, that my own tears finally spill.

"You did well, Swan," Hazel says, grasping my elbow with soft fingers as she drops her heavy bundle with an audible *thud*.

I jolt. The tension from being on guard, running, and hiding for days has yet to leave my body. And being back in the glade doesn't mean I can relax, not one bit. How I would love to find even an ounce of alleviation in my godmother's gentle touch. Especially as she presses her other hand to her sternum in a sincere gesture and rubs at my bicep with a tired, yet proud, gap-toothed smile on her divinely youthful face. But the fact that she's wearing a round wooden shield strapped to her back and an ensemble not unlike what Auntie Rose wears, makes me even more wary. She's also prepared for battle, though her armor is old and worn, and not made by any of the Numina. The set seems more like a relic or an heirloom.

The warm, chestnut-toned leather is worn lighter from years of use, and there are visible stitches along the thick bodice and leg greaves where repairs have been made from past battles. The pauldrons broadening her shoulders are scratched by many weapons past, marring the braided, intertwining knot design of an ancient tree. There's even a small split in one of the arm bracers that resembles a raven's wing. It's about an inch long and runs down the outside of her forearm; it must've never gotten repaired. Although, a multitude of aged brass buckles, that hold the armor snugly to her stockier frame, all seem to be intact. Are there more pieces to make it a full suit? Pieces that didn't fit Hazel correctly? The leg greaves almost go to her knees rather than just spanning her shins, and there's nothing to cover her thighs and hips. My godmother has strapped on her Healer's belt to cap off the long bodice where it would go beneath a tasset set. This armor must have belonged to someone much taller, someone more willowy in build, but who?

"I knew you would bring them back." Hazel's belief in my leadership restores something in me.

I hold this warm, proud seedling close as she moves past me to greet Kestrel, then Starling, who still clings to Lark. I might've been surprised by his display of affection a few days ago, but after everything we've seen and done, that was an old me and an old Starling. The way he held Robin when we first found her in Baba Roga's den showed me just how many layers he's shed now. It shines all the more when the sound of Mom's wheels against the stone path draws closer. When Starling approaches her, he looks like a little boy seeking comfort after a bad dream, more so when he squats, dropping back onto his heels so he's closer to her height before giving her a proper hug around the middle.

Kestrel is soon behind him, waiting, and when it's his turn, he's murmuring his relieved hello into the bones above her heart. Our mother smooths her pale hands on the burgundy material stretched over his frame, tinted fingertips bumping along the larger embroidered yellow crocus and sunflower designs lining his shoulder blades. One might think this was a normal movement, but I can tell Mom's reassuring herself, feeling for proof that her children have flocked back to the nest.

When it's my turn to be received, her jade gaze is soft. "All my little birds are home at last." Her arms stretch open with palms up. "Come here, swanling."

"Hi, Mom." I fall into her, melting until my face is pressed into the side of her neck. My bangs are pushed down into my eyes, forcing me to close them, but I don't care. I can absorb everything that is both Elder Mother and purely Mom this way. I'm enveloped in complete maternal love, soaking in her warmth and identifiable, honeyed elderberry and sticky bun scent. If I could stay here in this moment, capturing it in its own special jar for my attic shelf, I would. But a disturbing whistle from the trees beyond the perimeter douses its tenderness with a chill, washing away the moment, and tearing me from her arms like a riptide.

"Was that—" I start.

"That was the family signal." Robin blanches.

Turning in a half circle, I search Crow out, making sure he knows we heard something. But he's already looking in the right direction. He probably even sensed the whistle was coming before it happened. I meet Kestrel and Starling's wide stares. We heard this baleful version of our safety call before, and that was right before our uncle tried to kidnap me—right before I stabbed him in the shoulder with Death's shears. Is the Shadow Prince waiting for us, shears clutched in his bloodroot-stained hands?

There's only one way to find out.

"Grim and the witches have made themselves known," Hazel murmurs. "It's time for the prophecy to see itself out." The Healer blinks, snapping herself out of her daze as she returns to the giant, makeshift sack she dropped. "All right, everyone, dig through these pieces and suit up." The bedsheet unfurls into the grass, and piled on top of the white cotton fabric is a bunch of miscellaneous armor pieces. It's a curious collection.

Crow is kneeling above the pile, hands moving but not actually saying anything. It's almost like he's overwhelmed? No, his gift is overwhelmed. *"These things—they were forgotten for a long, long, long time, weren't they, Hazel?"*

The Healer answers by knocking her fist against the air as if there were an invisible door.

"They were some of my family's spares, stored at the Mountain, pieces that had been saved of my mother's shieldmates. Icarus found them." She drums her fingers on the armor she wears. *"This was my mother's; she wore it in the Corvus Clan Wars when she fought alongside Morrigan, Nemain, and Macha. They all fought valiantly, but my mother said their deaths on the battlefield not only stopped the war, but made them three of The Numina."*

Hazel stoops to retrieve a cuirass from the pile. "I believe this belonged to Nemain. For you, Sparrow." She offers the ornate leather piece to my mom, who straps it over her head and around her midsection. Then, the immortal Healer points to a set of blonde leather arm bracers dyed almost a rosy gold, and branded with an intricate, ancient northern design. "My mother said those were Macha's, and she always swore up and down that they were lucky." My godmother's duo-toned eyes find me across the way. "Swan, Fortune would've wanted you to wear these."

The thought of wearing the Numina's armor feels like an intimidating honor, but honestly, having something that belonged to the woman who became the embodiment of luck sounds nice, too. I retrieve the well-crafted armor pieces from the sheet, and Kestrel helps me lace them onto my forearms.

Hazel assigns everyone else arm bracers. A chest plate and shield goes to my father, a second shield and pair of gauntlets and greaves to Starling, and a single pauldron to Kestrel. My brothers get padded vests under their cloaks while I get a waist guard over mine, one that almost looks like a leather corset below my bust, though it's reinforced. And once everything is decided, my godmother gestures to the rest of the meager pickings. "If there's anything else you want to try on, go ahead, but those were the pieces I knew would fit each of you."

All three of my younger siblings move for the battle armor, but our mom bends in her wheelchair, waving her arms to get Crow's attention. Once silver meets green, she speaks aloud to my sisters and signs to my brother at the same time. "Whoa, wait, you three. You will not set foot on the grass outside Grandma Aspen's old house. Do you understand me?" My siblings groan.

"Children, listen to your mother," Dad affirms, fortifying his wife's authority with crossed arms and thick, raised brows.

Mom's close-lipped smile of gratitude is delicate before she continues. "You are not ready for what is outside those trees. I know you want to help us, but the best thing you can do is to stay safe." Mom looks at Lark. "Hazel put a perimeter around the house; you're in charge of keeping your siblings inside. You've been here helping me, sweetheart. You understand how important this is."

Lark dips her dimpled chin. "Yes, Mom."

"Robin, listen to your sister, please." Our mother looks at the youngest and most headstrong of her daughters.

Robin's thin, bird-like shoulders droop, sending the bracelet now back upon her wrist jingling. "Yes, Mom."

"*Crow, you look after your sisters. You're the man of the house,*" she signs with a wink.

My brother's answering giggle sounds like a sweet, high-pitched bell. "*Yes, Mom.*"

"Off you go," Auntie Rose gently shoos my siblings. "Listen to your parents and be safe; lock both doors and double-check all the windows. I love you little doves."

Amidst the last round of hugs, kisses, and goodbyes, Robin

rewards me with two spare doses of sunflower clusters from her cloak pocket. One I put in my pocket for later, one I eat now as I watch my younger siblings flee down the path to the fortified house with the knapsacks from my and Starling's backs in tow. Knowing Hazel, she probably dumped a whole larder's worth of salt both inside and outside the house to keep the kids safe. No bogey could get through any entry point, even if something happened to the main circle around the structure's exterior. No way.

"Now, for you three..." Mom starts with a sigh. And all I can think is, *Uh-oh.* "I want you inside that house, too—"

"What? No way!" Starling interjects, cutting her off before she can sequester us to the kids' table. "We are not sitting inside there all nice and cozy while you four risk your lives. Not happening."

Kestrel agrees with our brother by aggressively pointing at him. "Yeah! You couldn't keep us in there if you tried."

"We want to help, Mom." I try a gentler approach to getting our point across. "I might not have a gift to contribute to the fight, but I know for a fact we're stronger together as a family. Besides." I shrug. "Seven against four seems like much better odds to me."

Hazel hums. "I don't have magic either, Swan. You and I are tough and worthy of being here. Nothing—and I mean nothing" —the faintest scrunch wrinkles her forehead—"could make us sit something like this out."

I'm giving my godmother a firm, appreciative nod when Mom continues. "I was going to say, but I know that you three would never go inside Grandma Aspen's house unless you were knocked unconscious."

Auntie Rose sticks up her opalescent index finger. "That can be arranged."

Dad reaches out and pushes her hand down. "No, it cannot."

Mom fondly shakes her head at the half-siblings but quickly

forges on. "Just please promise me that you will be careful and keep your wits about you. Witches are tricksters and liars, they love nothing more than playing games. And often their tricks sound like they'll benefit you, give you exactly what you need, but in reality, they will destroy you or someone you love."

"Your aunt will be targeted. Her protection is a priority, but if you get injured, get back to the house. Okay?" Dad tacks onto the list of small asks.

My brothers and I share a look. For the first time in a long time, I speak to Starling with just my eyes, and somehow, my attic feels lighter. Like the shelves have been dusted, the rug's been beat, and window thrown wide open.

We're just going to agree to appease them, right?

Of course.

We can't leave them on that battlefield at any point.

No matter what.

No matter what.

"We promise," Kestrel says, crossing his fingers behind his back for our benefit.

Before we can echo his hollow sentiment, Uncle Grim's whistle sounds once more.

We follow the airy sound, past Grandma Aspen's old home, off the paved path, and into the empty grass field. A disquieted symphony of our footsteps fills the silence, and the unsynchronized crunching feels unnaturally loud. Enough that it makes a consistent whirring in my ears as we approach the ring of impenetrable elder trees that separates us from the bogeyman outside. The closer we get, the noise from the Phouka weaving through the forest limbs, sounds more and more like a sea of dead reeds in a windstorm. When we're about forty-five feet from the perimeter, the sounds hush, leaving only a whisper of their stirring. Their sudden quietness stops our progression, leaving my family to squint into the far-off shadows bending from the trees. There's no sign of the witches, nor Uncle Grim.

"Can anyone see anything?" Kestrel mumbles from my right.

"No, but I can smell them. The scent of rotting flowers and bitter poison is hard to miss." Dad turns his head to question his half-sister. "Rose, do you think you could see anything with your tiger's eye?"

Death's ebony brows furrow as she ponders this, giving him a small shrug before answering, "It's worth a shot." Then, the armored Numina peels the eyepatch from her scintillating skin to reveal the tiger's eye stone that replaced the one that Baba Roga's sister stole all those years ago. As she moves her head, scanning the tree line, the golden amber ribbons inside the black stone glint. There's a gasp to her first words when she speaks. "It's Grim. The witches don't have threads to see, but his...so many of them are saturated with chains of black. I can physically see the hold they have on him." Perhaps subconsciously, Auntie Rose takes a step forward.

Hazel pulls her back, making my aunt stumble. She looks down at the Healer when she abruptly stops, nearly tripping again. Death's pearl-like eyelids peel back, showing more of her stone and silver orbs, almost a mirror to my godmother's, who stares back at her, surveying with the same wide eyes. Hazel looks at Auntie Rose with something like sternness, a steel set clamping her lips tight together, bleeding the color from them. On the other hand, my aunt looks at my godmother with an expression I can't quite put my finger on. Is it shock? Or dread? There's also a flicker of what could either be eagerness or perhaps confusion there, too. None of which have a place here and now.

"Rose?" Mom asks now.

My aunt clears her throat. "Hazel, you don't look well. Should you go back to the house?"

Did Death see signs of the Brume on Hazel?

"I want to see what hags saunter through the perimeter and hear what grand spiel they'll inevitably have prepared." When no one reacts to the smirk she wears, the immortal Healer gives up her sarcastic mask and responds truthfully. "I'll admit, I don't feel the greatest right now, but I saw the creation of witches firsthand, and I will see their end, too. It's my duty at this point, dear, especially as a Healer."

"You don't think even that's too risky?" Auntie Rose presses again.

"I can hold my own," Hazel pushes back.

"Uh, I don't mean to interrupt whatever is happening here," Kestrel says, "but I'm pretty sure the sun and moon are minutes to touching."

Kestrel's right, the eclipse is on our doorstep and ready to knock. We need to follow the eldest Numina's instructions before it crosses the threshold. Mom knows this too. The soft lavender glow of magic warming beneath her clenched hands is evident. The Elder Mother is ready to unbar our home, and she lets her trees know this by raising her purple-glazed palms outward. When her fingers flare open and then curl in one after the other, her wrists twisting in, she bids the trees to come to life, and they listen. The gray-barked giants shake and shudder until one of them bends in our direction, almost as if bowing to Mom. Then, like a paladin to its queen, the tree concedes to her wordless inquiry to break the line of safety, creaking and popping as the earth around it crumples. Long gnarled roots twist from the ground, rising from where they've been embedded for the last decade. The roots stretch skyward, groaning as clots of disrupted dirt rain down from its limbs, reminding me of a creature surfacing from a deep slumber, shaking off dregs of sleep.

Thick roots curve back toward the ground, creating clawed feet, like those of an old chair, before the trembling elder tree pushes itself up. Once the base of the trunk has removed itself from the dirt, the last of the tendrils tying it to the earth hang free. The new, shorter growth sways, the elder tree crackling as it walks forward and to the side, creating an opening in the perimeter. And when it finds its new temporary spot, the tree drops itself with a great *thud*, rooted legs splaying out over the dry grass. An aftershock sends a jitter beneath my feet.

To save the world, the protective circle around our home has been broken, opening the glade to the wicked world outside, essentially a door letting in a bitter draft. A welcome sign for the witches and their poisoned shadows beyond it.

Swan: The Witches

*T*he women who creep past the overturned dirt are everything I was a taught a witch would be. They're hauntingly beautiful, yet sickly creatures, corrupted and too thin, wholly eaten by their own witchcraft. They're comprised of sharp edges and bones, and these attributes highlight their even sharper smiles and higher cheekbones. The hags don't stroll in arm-in-arm by any means. But it is a united front, which is strange, because working together goes against their very nature.

Desperate times call for desperate measures it seems.

The tallest witch, the one carrying a striped staff of gnarled wood, can be none other than Baba Roga; she matches the color scheme of her candy house perfectly. Her blackened lips stand out, even from far away, followed by her skin, which is the same hue as the orbs of witchcraft that lit up her underground den. It's not pink, but an anemic red. Baba Roga's hair falls to her hips, and though the majority of its color matches her lips, the black licorice hued mass is streaked with shades reminiscent of candy apple red and marshmallow white. The backlight from the impending eclipse almost makes the strands glow, contrasting with the deep, gingerbread brown tunic-dress that hangs from her frame. But it's the short, hooked horn that protrudes from the middle of her forehead that really catches the light. From this distance, it appears no longer than a child's hand, but I can tell its thin, pointed end is sharper than any of my blades.

Allison Gross doesn't have a bone growing from her forehead, but she does carry something shaped like a horn. It looks like it would belong to a ram, although the bony curl is as green as spring grass. It swings at her side, brushing against the hem of the embroidered mantle she wears, a sleeveless, scarlet garment adorned with fringe and golden flowers, something that feels out of place. Perhaps stolen? She looks like a kid who's raided their parents' closet to play dress-up. But despite this silly image, there's nothing funny about the witch. Not the bloodroot dripping from her dirty-blonde hair, or the blood-like sap that's stained her rancid lemongrass skin. Even her needle-toothed smile is outlined in slick garnet, and the reflections that bounce off it make my stomach turn.

It's the silhouette that emerges behind the two women that makes my insides do a violent flip though. The towering wings of roiling shadows that sprout from his back rise high above them. They create an even more menacing background than the Phouka still waiting outside the trees like obedient, twisted guard dogs. But Uncle Grim is not really one of the Phouka. Nor is he Pooka turned Death's ghostly Reaper, not anymore, at least. Now, with his dragon-esque wings and smoky half-mask hiding everything but his lower face and gore-red eyes, he's a dangerous lindwyrm monster on a witch's short leash. And it's so tight around his neck that when Allison Gross snaps her talon-tipped fingers and points to the ground beside her, he obeys and moves to stand at her side.

I hear Auntie Rose's breath hitch at the sight.

The Hallowtide air is still as the three poison-dark figures stand together. But we're seven strong just forty-five feet opposite them, and we *are* more powerful as a family. However, that doesn't stop me from remembering some of Mom's journals shelved in the library. The ones she and Dad wrote together, recounting their adventure twenty years ago. Their words, describing the horrors that Black Annis committed the day she massacred so many faeries in the glade, were vivid. Luckily, the haven's current faeries aren't here, so we can avoid that awful parallel. Still, a sense of foreboding pervades.

Especially when a foretokened, dirty mist rolls in behind the hags and my uncle. It swirls around their ankles to cover the dead autumn grass, seeping out toward us like a churning high tide come inland. When it closes the distance and stops inches from the toes of our boots, the mist becomes a thickened dust, like a cloud kicked up in a cornfield. But this is no ordinary dust and dirt. Sitting back on my heels to get a closer look, a wet, rotting scent of decay claims my senses. It's reminiscent of the stem rot, or powdery mildew, that forms on decomposing flowers if they sit in a vase of water too long. The same kind of molds that crawl inside the Stygian Brume... Through the foul must trickling into my sinuses, I spot motes of blue-tinted witchcraft floating in the suspended, earthen mixture, like tiny, moldering fireflies.

Mom is bent at the waist in her wheelchair, squinting down at the dust, too. She stares up at Dad, a glaze over her features, one that pinches the corners of her haunted jade eyes. "This blue," she whispers. "I haven't seen a hag this color since—"

Dad nods. "Black Annis."

"That wretch is dead, Sparrow. We killed her ourselves, exploded her to shreds with my elder dagger, and replaced her with a nice flowering tree," Hazel murmurs with a shake of her head, long tawny braid rasping up against her leather bodice. "Not even the darkest evil could survive that."

I stand, tired knees popping. "All witches had their own poison plant of choice, thus a unique color of witchcraft. But there's only so many colors in nature, so there had to be another one with blue magic at some point, right?"

Auntie Rose is still fixated on Uncle Grim and his flared wings, but she answers without taking her eyes away. "Madgy Figgy had this light seaside blue because she used beach aster. And I remember shortly after I became Death, Grim came back to Wyrd covered in grayish, navy blue particles from iris petals after taking care of Peg Powler."

Starling fumbles with his gauntlets, setting his shield down, resting it against his legs to take his journal from his trouser pocket. He flips through the pages, the edges catching on metal and cloth bandage until he finds his chart, the one that identifies witches with corresponding plants, as well as some unassigned poison options. "Didn't you used to say Black Annis's witchcraft was kinda like a sapphire shade?"

"I thought it was cerulean?" Kestrel pipes up, leaning past me to look at our parents. "Or a lighter-azure."

Dad guides Starling's arm down, nudging him to put the book away and pick up his shield with a sense of urgency. "I know you're trying to reassure us, and I love you kids for it, but that's not helping right now."

Auntie Rose finally looks away from her familiar to inspect the dust we've been discussing. "It's extremely close, but it's not her. Black Annis is very, *very* dead. I went back to her cave, looking for Grim at one point. I guess I was looking for closure, too. The elder tree is still rooted in place, the metal links of her rusty belt are still hanging from that branch."

"You never said anything." Mom gapes.

"It wasn't the right time." Death brushes her off, though not unkindly. "Now isn't really the time either; we have company."

My aunt's words have a much deeper meaning. Baba Roga and Allison Gross aren't the ones behind all the illness and degradation over the last five years. The line they've created with Uncle Grim breaks apart as he steps to the side to create an entryway. On edge, with fists clenched and teeth gritted, my family and I watch as a fourth figure emerges from the cloak of shadows and past the marred border of trees. A woman saunters into the glade, a wall of dust following close behind, pausing at her heels once she stands a couple feet ahead of the other witches. A sure sign of dominance and hierarchy. Curls of dust leave the wall like wayward tentacles to reach forward for the woman, affectionately brushing against her. One curl pets the crown of what looks to be half-dead, moldy flowers in her bright ginger hair. A second curl glides along the outside of a bare blue arm while another ruffles the blackened hem of her white sundress. Her eyes are solid black, and they're staring right at us.

"She looks just like her," Dad says under his breath.

"*Oh.*" Hazel gasps. This seems like a strange response until I realize that wasn't a response to Dad at all. It's a widemouthed, horrorstruck realization of her own. "Oh *no.* No, no, no, no—"

"Hazel?"

The Healer wavers on her feet, one shaky hand pressed to her stomach and another to her pale lips. It looks like she's going to be sick. Mom tries to steady her, and in turn, Hazel clutches onto the handle of Mom's wheelchair like someone desperate not to drown in the depths of their past. "This can't be happening," she almost pleads, duo-toned eyes boring into my mother's as Hazel loses hold of the poise I've always known her to possess.

"What in Fate's name is happening?" Starling says. "Who is that hag?"

"It's Quince," Hazel mumbles. But we all hear her clearly.

"The original witch?" my brother confirms.

Hazel bobs her head slowly, appearing numb with shock. "She was my best friend first. But—but after she killed Fortune,

I killed her, and at the same time Quince killed *me*. When they were stuck in The Between, The Numina brought me back to be the Elder Mother, but I had no idea they brought her back too..."

It's always our family, isn't it?

As if she heard my thought, Death speaks. "Looking back at the tapestries of life in the Observatory at Wyrd, I remember seeing in Nemain's weaving that the first witch's influence had already spread then: other witches were already in the making, and The Numina couldn't have stopped it from The Between. They had to wait for all of us to follow our destinies. All they could do to set them in motion was to keep the balance." My aunt places her patch back over her tiger's eye. "My best guess, for the sake of balance, is that they couldn't have put you and your good-natured, elemental magic back without putting your opposite pairing back as well."

"Everything that's happened thus far has happened for a reason," Mom states, seemingly bolstering us—as well as herself —as she sits straighter in her chair.

And only moments after the last syllable leaves her lips, Quince stalks forward.

Quicker than a blink, the seven of us each draw a weapon. From salt-annealed throwing knives to a twelve-inch blade, arrows, axes, an elder wood dagger, glowing magic, and a pair of ancient, enchanted shears...except we don't have that last weapon.

"Primrose! Are you unarmed?" Dad hisses at his half-sister.

But my aunt quickly and quietly shuts him down as their leader advances. "Grim has my shears. I will do my best to get them back, but I don't want to fight him."

"Yep." Kestrel pops his lips. "We are all going to die."

Starling and I each smack either side of his chest with the back of our hands, though Starling's gauntlet hits harder.

Baba Roga, Allison Gross, and Uncle Grim have stayed put,

but Quince still walks. Her empty, talon-tipped hands are up in the air with her palms facing us, and it feels like a false gesture of peace. She crosses the field through the fallen leaves, five feet, ten feet, fifteen, twenty, before Dad yells for her to stop with a commanding voice. She halts, her grin sharp. The dust swirls around her calves before it lazily glides along her unnaturally gradient-stained dress, where it settles around her bare feet in a suspended, undulating cloud. Between the gaps, I watch the dry, brittle grass beneath her blacken and decay until the ground appears scorched. Similar to the dark edges of the plants, creating the ring resting on the crown of her head.

There's a replica of Auntie Posy's beloved Latin Floriography book sitting inside my attic on a mahogany bookshelf. It only takes a blink for me to disappear inside and read it so I can recall all three of my aunts' lessons on the Language of Flowers and identify what I'm staring at. The village whisperings were true; The Cornflower Wraith is real, and the flowers atop her head represent good fortune, purity, and hope. But that's not the only plant that decorates her hair. The festering weeds choking the cornflower mean quite the opposite. Blue thistle is a plant of intrusion, pain, pride, and aggression. I was always taught that they should be taken as a sign of suffering. And suffering these plants are. From where I stand, I can see the clear evidence of stem rot and powdery mildew spotting them. Their dank scent wafts from Quince's head in waves.

"Well, well," the first witch purrs. "Looks like the family is all back together." Her vast, onyx eyes survey us, lingering on the middle of our line. A hum curls from the blackened center of her indigo lips. "Almost." She turns her head toward my godmother and aunt, and with the movement, I catch a glimpse of the side of her cheek where an ebb and flow of Stygian-hued veins pulse under her skin. "It seems that you're missing quite a few of The Numina. Are the old cowards hiding away in their precious Mountain creating this miracle?" Quince gestures with a flippant hand toward the airglow sky, a trail of hazy mist weaving through her abnormally long fingers.

"You—" Hazel breathes, still unable to fully grasp the sight of the friend she lost to witchcraft and death so long ago. "All of this was you. The Phouka, the Brume—"

"I had a smidge of help." Quince shrugs, obviously proud of her years-long plan of destructive collaboration. "I needed more witches on my side to take on some of the heavy lifting if we wanted to preserve our kind, because *someone*"—she whips her head toward Death with a snarl, dropping her saccharine expression—"had the bright idea to bring back The Numina and become the catalyst of our extinction. My influence could've spread much farther if it wasn't for my dearest Hazel, and her husband, putting a six-century-long wrinkle in my plans, and a giant hole in my memory."

My godmother points a shaky, condemning finger at Quince. "You murdered my Ellery, my little brother, just to become the first witch."

"Typically, I'm called The Cornflower Wraith or Lady Midday." Quince taps her chin with a pointed smirk. "Even The Noon Witch in some regions, but The First Witch has a nice ring to it."

Hazel shakes her head, bypassing Quince's passive mirth. "You tried to kill my husband and my friends. Icarus and I didn't deserve to be torn apart. Macha didn't deserve to die, the world didn't deserve to live without Fortune, and without The Numina around. I had to put an end to your terror." The Healer's voice cracks. "I didn't have a choice."

The First Witch deadpans, "You stabbed me through the back, Hazel."

"When friend became foe, I didn't have a choice," Hazel repeats, and it's tinted with a plea for understanding.

"To be fair," Quince starts with a conceding tone, "I did get you back. Your blood warmed me as we died together. Like sisters." She spits the last word as all faked consideration disappears. "I would've been back sooner to claw out your neck again if The Numina hadn't taken most of my memories before they brought me back to life. I didn't remember who I used to be or where I came from until Christmastide ten years ago. I spent the next couple of those just trying to find you."

Hiding behind the singsong tune of Quince's words, the barest whistle from Starling on my left slips by unnoticed. The witch continues none the wiser.

"I found out you were the Elder Mother first, only to track down the wrong one." The First Witch looks at Mom and waggles her fingers in a taunting wave before turning back to Hazel. "But this family led me to you and your little shop. Once I learned how close-knit you were, I knew I needed a bigger plan, something to weaken you all, and pull your attention in different directions. I just had to make the rest of the world more vulnerable first. More...*susceptible* to my goal."

Another whistle, no louder than an exhale, slides from between Starling's lips. Kestrel shifts his weight, pressing his boots into the ground harder than necessary, covering up any trace of the harbingering warble.

And Quince speaks right over it, lost in her own inciting monologue. "What did Icarus's father used to say, two birds with one stone creates grand wings?"

"Don't speak of Daedalus." An old, achy pain edges Hazel's voice, but there's also something else. A flush of this goading, a prodding current to her tone that she uses with Lark and Robin when she wants them to work through a problem at the Apothecary. Hazel is fishing, trying to keep Quince talking while Starling summons his birds.

Quince's voice becomes high-pitched and mocking. "*Oh, but the great Daedalus. The greatest inventor and Healer of our times!*" She spits into the grass with disdain and a thick film of ichor stains the yellow blades. "Well, I could've been even greater if The Numina had just Blessed me. So much of this could've been avoided had they listened and made magic more accessible. Now they've left me no choice but to send them back to The Between again so I can ring in the next age of magic."

Another minuscule tune falls from my brother.

Mom picks up on Hazel's tactic now, buying us more time as the first of Starling's star-speckled passerine friends arrive. "Let me try to understand this, you're bitter that you weren't chosen to have power you have no business wielding? And you've come into *my* territory to kill *my* children in cold blood so that you can share your evil like an infectious disease?" Mom shakes her head with a disheartened droop to her features. "Are you really foolish enough to think you're doing this world some sort of kindness?"

"You're one to talk," Quince growls, beady black eyes narrowing. "You gained your title by killing my first daughter." Her gaze drops to the scars from Black Annis's claws poking from the collar of Mom's emerald cloak, and the witch simpers like it's some sort of consolation prize. "Although, I heard she left her mark on you."

"But my wife is still alive, and your daughter isn't." Dad joins in the distraction, birds now quietly hopping along the trees behind the hags and Uncle Grim. "Unless you want to join her in Purgatory tonight, this is your chance to turn around and return to the dark corner whence you came. Maybe you'll buy yourself some time before The Sun and Moon inevitably find you."

"Run? And be hunted like a frail deer?" Quince cackles. "Oh no, no, sweet hybrid, I am no fawn. I am a wolf, and you are all mere chicks that've wandered from the coop."

Songbirds perch on the bare elder tree branches like green and purple-dappled onyx leaves, waiting for a signal from Starling. I'm not sure what his message is, but maybe he can make them into a murmuration of sharp-beaked weapons. Either way, they're on our side.

"Ah, but you're scared of us, enough to try to split us up beforehand," Death finally speaks up, chin tilted to look down her nose at the blue-skinned woman. "You know that united, you don't stand a chance."

"Did you forget I have one of your own, little flower? Your Reaper is no longer a part of your garden, he has joined me and my flesh." The First Witch smiles wide, exposing needle teeth dripping with malice and torment. "After all, a quince is a pome fruit."

That was a part of the prophecy that we didn't understand. Had we known what a pome fruit was, or Auntie Posy was in a frame of mind for us to ask, we would've known that Quince was behind this from the start. Perhaps, someway, somehow, we might've had the upper hand. Though I suppose not with her in Uncle Grim's ear; she's no doubt known everything every step of the way.

Auntie Rose is boiling with rage, hands balled and jaw working as her silver eye heats into molten steel. "I'm going to drag you to Purgatory, and you will burn for what you've done."

The First Witch gleefully laughs. "How? You are your own biggest liability." Quince holds her hands up. "Wait, don't tell me. I'm going to rip out Hazel's throat first, and then I'd like to see you try killing me. Because I've killed one of The Numina before….I can do it again." With a wicked grin, Quince flicks her fingers. The wall of dust and blue-tinted mist waiting inside the trees surges forward and floods the field with a strong gust. It joins the pool at our toes and slams into us. All I can do is bend my knees and lean into it as I'm shoved backward, sliding over the ground like gritty ice. The sound of my younger siblings pounding on the windows inside the safety of Grandma Aspen's old house is a war drum behind us.

When I turn to look back at them, I catch a glimpse of

Kestrel being pushed off to the side, too many feet away from me, and Starling being separated in the opposite direction from him. Auntie Rose is propelled from my side while Mom and Dad are sucked diagonally way ahead. In seconds we are all engulfed and rendered blind to our surroundings. The First Witch has broken our line and sealed us inside the glade with enemies we cannot see.

Swan: The Eclipse

*D*ust hangs in the air like fog, not thick enough to choke, but enough that if I put my arm out, I can't see past my fingers. And as the scent of rot and mold assaults my nose, a flurry of far-off muffled noise makes the fine hairs on the nape of my neck stand on end. Burbling shrieks and garbled, keening cries slither into my ears. The whispered hisses and wet grunts tell me that the Phouka are pouring in through the broken perimeter. But nothing charges me yet, not the deformed, sickly bogeys, nor Quince. And somewhere out there, my family is stumbling around while the witches prowl. I'm a lone duckling sitting in a dirty pond of alligators.

I need to move.

With numb hands and burning feet, I step forward into the muzzy gray. I hold my left arm up, bent in front of me in a defensive position, clenching the handle of my knife so that the blade runs parallel to the side of my arm. My right wrist is propped up on the back of my bracer, thumb looped in the handle of my second knife that juts from my fist outward. Creeping on, I keep myself blocked as vague shadows of twisted black masses race by me. Streaks of cold air tainted with the stench of rusted blood and decay ruffle the curls along my forehead. Outside the clicking bubbles coming from the Phouka that undoubtedly circle me, the glade is otherwise quiet. Quince's witchcraft has padded the fetid air and seemingly thrown all sound. Trying to identify where my family might be is too much of a distraction, though, before I can sense it, something bumps into me. Hard.

Whirling around, I meet the thing pressing into me with equal force and shove my left arm up against the resistance, my knife shaking only centimeters from skin. My salt-annealed blade is nearly against Auntie Rose's neck. Quickly, I disarm myself, and we steady each other by the biceps, exchanging silent puffs of gasping breaths. We wait to see if anyone or anything heard our collision. When we come to the wordless mutual conclusion that we haven't become a beacon of noise, we sign.

"Are you okay?" my aunt asks.

I bob a closed fist to answer yes.

"We need to get eyes on Hazel and *protect her."*

Obviously, protecting my family is my priority, but my aunt's insistence on Hazel specifically, and the emphasis she puts into her signs and expression, is strange. *"Of course, but the witches will be coming for you. If they get their claws on the only Numina out here, this is all over."*

"Swan, Hazel is pregnant. And I don't think Time knows, or she wouldn't be in the glade."

My gut swoops like a gull plummeting into the sea. But I don't resurface victorious with a fish. No. This new information has me mentally tumbling. The times I've recently seen Hazel appear ill and touching her stomach make much more sense now. She's not sick with the Brume, or sensitive to the terrible information that keeps getting disclosed to her, she's with child. And she's on a literal battlefield about to fight for our lives... against her ex-best friend turned hag, at that. A larger sense of impending doom rises inside me, finally carrying me out of choppy waters enough that I can raise my tingling hands to respond to Auntie Rose.

Although, the sound of Robin's voice slicing through the thick dusty mist throws me off course. "Mom?" she shouts, worry making her muffled exclamation wobble twice as much. Another quieter voice that sounds suspiciously like Lark trying to silence our younger sister soon follows.

My siblings' voices have the effect of a struck match dropped into oil. The field bursts into action, engulfed by pounding feet and animalistic growls. Even the Hallowtide sky is set on fire, though not by my sister's actions. Another piece of the prophecy has come to pass. The celestial lights above are now converged, and the sun is hidden by the moon, silhouetting it with a ring of flaming red. It casts the glade in a stellar, warm hue that visually lessens some of the dust's thickness. Still, it's not enough to be purifying to any bogey. But at least I can see outlines and movement now.

One of my brothers yells in the distance, or maybe it's my father? I'm caught on the ruby-ringed eclipse reflected in Auntie Rose's gaze, on how her eye flits over my shoulder before it widens. Her pale fingers dig into the wool over my arms, and she tries to pull me sideways, but it's too late. A great weight plows into my back, and I'm airborne. I'm thrown many feet away, landing face-first with a *thud*. The wind is knocked out of me on impact, and my shoulder zings with pain. Spitting grass and my own hair from my mouth, I flip onto my back, gasping. Just in time too. A Phouka that might've once resembled a small, emaciated bear descends on me, two sets of teeth bared, dislocated jaws aiming for my jugular. A set of front paws box in my head, and the second spindly set pins my shoulders down. I can't move my arms to reach for a knife, and its gaping maw is drawing closer to my face, a waft of smoke and decomposition trickling from its abundance of disgusting teeth. Turning my head from the black wisps, another Phouka darts in the direction Auntie Rose and I had stood. But I can't see her silhouette. Maybe I was thrown farther than I thought? It doesn't matter; I don't dare call out for fear of distracting Death and getting her hurt, so I fight back silently.

The Phouka burbles a growl in my ear, and I thrash against its inky form. It presses into me harder, damp paws grinding my shoulder bones together as it shifts to get a better hold. I feel the stance of its back legs widen. With this, I have enough wiggle room to bend my leg and get it up under the infected creature's belly. My knee is almost against my chest when I plant my boot square in the middle of the bear's sunken sternum and shove with all my strength. The Phouka rears up from the blow and falls from me. The disregulated weight of its small, mutated body parts works in my favor, giving me enough time to scramble to my feet and pull a knife from my leg sheath. Then I center myself, ready for the faerie's next attack. Which comes with the swinging of two left front paws, each tipped with smoky razors and drips of decay leaking from its rough pads. I dodge, swiping at the Phouka with my own blade. It morphs into a horrifically choreographed dance.

But, for my part, the dance is slow, less like a Phouka hunter and more like a drained, moody teenager. I keep looking for an opening, some offensive tactic, but I don't find one. Instead, the bear made-of-skin-and-too-many-bones gets closer with each attack. Maybe I'm exhausted from the journey? Or maybe the last line of the prophecy, the one I've been trying to push under the rug of my attic, is weighing me down in mind, body, and spirit? Maybe it's a little bit of both. Either way, I'll need a good dose of luck, or a miracle, to make it through this battle. Macha, in The After, must be watching over of me, because one of the Phouka's claws narrowly misses the side of my neck, scraping against the back of my left bracer on the way.

A shower of salt rains down on me and the bear, fizzling against the beast's patchy hide. The Phouka roars in pain, the grains burning through the festering witchcraft that's transformed its body. This distraction is the perfect opportunity for me to launch forward and bury my knife into one of its paws, pinning it to the ground. Like the fox I hunted with Kestrel days earlier, it shrinks into itself, becoming a ball of wriggling smoke, stuck beneath the tip of my purified blade. I can only hope no one trips over the weapon that holds the faerie captive. It's unfortunate that I must leave a knife behind though, because I only have five left.

My shoulder is throbbing as I wade farther into the battlefield, in the direction I first saw the witches, to find the source of the flying salt. A sachet sails ahead of me. It appears loosely tied, with spare thread, as it leaves an arching trail of salt, dispersing plumes of Quince's magic wherever it spreads. When it lands, the sachet explodes, and the mist further dissipates. Stopping in the freshly cleared area, I find a square of pink and yellow floral fabric, a pattern I recognize from an old quilt Grandma Aspen made for Lark. Which means the fabric came from one place only.

As more cloth bags arc overhead, I run back toward Grandma Aspen's house. There's salt on my lips as I pant, sprinting past sizzling Phouka that try to flee. The shrill caws of Starling's birds fighting off winged Phouka pierce the air at my back; I push myself harder. When I near the salt-circled house, I see Lark with a burlap bag from the larder, filling the fabric scraps in a pile at her feet. She twists the plump package until it resembles a large onion, and Robin loops thread around the extra fabric at the top like a poultice, temporarily enclosing its contents. Robin hands the bundle to Crow, who tucks it in the leather projectile pocket of the slingshot Uncle Grim got him for his birthday. Crow pulls back the cord and shoots the salt into the field as far as his little arms can manage, and it flies.

I'm within shouting distance when I look back towards Robin and find her already staring at me. She raises her hand in greeting, and I raise mine in return, slowing to catch my breath so I can reprimand the little geniuses for leaving the safety of the house. Then, Robin's sable brows furrow, and a complicated expression claims her face. The section of ground at my feet shakes until it cracks, and the next thing I know, a spike shoots from the earth. Tripping backward, I almost land on my butt to avoid being impaled by the brambles that rise up, sharp and unruly. A wall forms in front of me, cutting me off from my siblings, and for a moment, with a battle-clouded mind, I wonder if Robin is the changeling the prophecy spoke of. If maybe Starling's theory wasn't correct, and the meaning was much more sinister. If I hadn't moved, that spike would've killed me...but Robin would *never* hurt family—

Parts of the new wall curl toward me.

Robin would never hurt me.

The brambles grow closer.

Robin would never hurt me.

It looks like they're aiming for my chest.

Robin would never hurt me.

They curve over my head.

Robin would never hurt me.

A Phouka, shaped like a vulture, plummets from the eclipsed sky, diving at me with the longest talons I've ever seen. And my sister's weaponized plant meets it halfway, skewering the faerie I didn't see coming.

Robin would never hurt me.

I step from her thorny shield and around the makeshift wall. My harrowed, saucer-eyed siblings stare at the Phouka. The beast weakly flaps its five and a half wings as it saws with a razor beak at the gnarled plant protruding through its moldy feathers and out its side. And past the bramble wall, outside my siblings' widened perimeter, another red-eyed, moose-like Phouka approaches through the dust. But it retreats just as fast when Crow nails it with a salt sachet. I exhale. It seems my littlest siblings are safe, and very capable of keeping themselves that way. Mom and Dad will forgive them later, after they revoke their dessert privileges for a while.

"Swan, catch!"

Swiveling toward Lark's call, I see her poised, salt pouch from the Healer's belt around her waist ready for an underhand throw. Opening my hand, I wait for her to toss it across the short distance between us. It's full and heavy, much heavier than the pillar of wax strapped into my side bag, but I loop it onto the belt, knowing the sack will be emptied, fast. Thinking of The Moon's candle reminds me of Crow's job well done. And after he fires another sachet, I wave my arms above my head to get his attention, shoulder complaining in protest. Once I have his focus, I sign, "Hello, Bank of Crow. You did amazing keeping those matches safe for me, but I think it's time to withdraw."

Crow beams at me, bright enough to rival the luminaries above us. I'm glad such a silly phrase, harkening back to days of playing pretend, brings that child-like wonder to my brother's face again. A ten-year-old does not belong on the battlefield, and being his sunshine, the way Kestrel is mine, is the least I can do right now. I can hear his giggles when he slips the matchbox from his charcoal cloak pocket and loads it into his slingshot. He arcs it to me softly, and I'm able to catch it, tucking it back in its compartment beside the candle. Before I twist away to forge a path back into the fray, I form a specific sign for my siblings. My thumb, index, and pinkie stand tall while my middle and ring fingers are bent down at the first knuckle, telling them I love them. Then I'm off, throwing fistfuls of salt from Lark's pouch to clear a broad trail through the dirty mist.

Soon, a familiar, displeased grunt bellows, and I follow the deep cadence. The closer I get, the clearer the dark silhouette becomes. Starling swipes at a Phouka with his axe, but the moment I pelt the unrecognizable malformed faerie with salt, it's off and running, snorting and snarling toward the opening Mom made in the glade. *Good riddance.*

"Thanks," Starling huffs, wiping the sweat from his peaked brow with the inside of his bicep.

"You look like you could use some more sugar," I respond, so unused to his gratitude that I miss the opportunity to say, "You're welcome."

Starling just nods, handing his shield for me to hold before reaching into his pocket with gauntlet-clumsy fingers to fish out a piece of Baba Roga's candy house. As he pops a meringue into his mouth, a salt sachet flies by. I point at it. "You see that? The kids filled those with salt and cleared out most of the witchcraft around the house. But they can't launch those much farther than this. Do you think your birds can help spread the salt so we can see everyone?"

Once again, Starling only nods. He quickly crushes the hollow sweet between his teeth and swallows before wetting his lips. His whistle of instruction to his murmuration of namesake birds is melodic, a beautiful light song that promises goodness to come.

I point ahead. "I will keep clearing out this way, but we must find Auntie Rose and Hazel. They're our highest priority."

Starling cocks his head. "Hazel?"

"She's pregnant," I say as I rub at my sore shoulder, then palm a knife. We've been standing here too long; a Phouka is circling. "If you find Kestrel, Mom, or Dad first, make sure they know so she has some backup." Starling's promise is at my back as I take off. I know he'll tell them. We can't waste any more time. My godfather warned us to finish this fight before the end of the eclipse. And I know he, The Sun, and The Moon are trying their best to slow it down, but right now, it doesn't feel like enough. We need to move faster.

Overhead the starlings begin to carry the parcels of salt by the string, allowing them to unravel, the white grains falling like sand in an hourglass. The birds fly in formations, going in opposite directions, crossing back and forth to cover every inch they can. While the mist doesn't entirely disappear, it dwindles from a slight haze, to thin, foggy sheets of dust that reach no higher than my ankles. A bulk of the Phouka have dissipated, but a fair share still try their luck at navigating any earth that isn't salted.

Beyond them are the women orchestrating the chaos.

Baba Roga and Allison Gross prowl toward my parents now. Dad has no weapon in hand, but he and Mom hold firm. Mom's eyes are bright, her vibrant, lavender power clashing with the light from the eclipse overhead. She calls to one of the trees and a limb snakes toward Dad, shifting shapes above his outstretched hand. Moments later, my father holds a sword hewn from the elder trees. He uses it as Baba Roga spins spider-like webs of witchcraft, trying to wrangle his legs while Mom faces Allison Gross. The hag blows her curled green horn, the glow of her lemongrass witchcraft forming some sort of signal.

I wince away from the burst of light that explodes from them when they clash, and I catch sight of Quince standing in the center of the field, watching the chaos with a feline grin. Hazel is cutting her way down toward her though, her long knife swinging at every Phouka who dares to cross her path. Starling fights his way to Hazel, but there's an overwhelming number of monsters surging in his direction, hindering his progress. Kestrel, who fires arrow after arrow, seems torn between helping our brother and moving for Auntie Rose, who's come to meet Uncle Grim. No Phouka dares interfere with that divine pair; they have a wide and uninterrupted berth. Death and her familiar circle each other, and though neither has attacked, the battle has well and truly begun.

Grim: Hope

"Grim, please," Death begs, right foot crossing behind her left, stepping back in this circling dance of ours. Her shadow moves to the same nonexistent music as the Phouka trapped inside it riot. "Please come back to me."

Primrose! Primrose, I'm here!

No, you're not.

"This is getting a little silly, don't you think?" I ask, advancing on her, following the rounded shape we're burning into the grass with our feet.

"Just talk to me, Grim." Death puts her empty hands in front of her body in peace. "How are they controlling you? What can we do to release you?"

She's unarmed. For Timesake, why is she unarmed?

Because she's a fool.

Or because she doesn't want to hurt us...

"Come now," I tut with a teasing chuckle. "Did you really think I would answer any of those questions?"

Death's hands turn toward the eclipse with a shrug. "There's nothing wrong with a little hope. Do you still have hope, Grim?" Her silver eye is searching, trying to peer behind the mask that was lovingly locked onto my face to give me my new identity and help me start my new life with her.

A snort spills from my lindwyrm snout. "Hope?"

"Yes, Grim. Hope. Is there a part of you in there somewhere that still hoped we would find each other again, Grim?" the Numina asks, but she has said my old name twice in that statement, and it's out of place. As a matter of fact, she's been saying my old name in every response and question so far.

I narrow my eyes, seeing the garnet glow bounce off the edges of the mask's eyeholes. "Why do you keep saying that name?"

"I'm trying to remind you of who you are!" Death shouts.

Clever.

It's annoying. That's not who I am anymore, I'm her trinket.

This woman will retrieve us from the witch's clutches one way or the other, and you will just have to accept that.

Never.

You'll be grateful later.

"I know who I am!" I yell back, but my feet slow.

Do you, Grim?

Death stops moving, and soon we're standing only feet apart. "Do you, Grim? Because the monster I see right now is not the man I know, and I want *my* Reaper back."

Reaching to the back band of my trousers, I grasp her blood-stained shears in my fist. "We can't all have everything we want in life." With a grunt, I lunge forward, arm swinging from behind before curling into the air and coming down. Death anticipates this and sidesteps the hit, tasset belt swaying against her thighs. I pivot on the front of my right foot and turn my hand before stabbing outward, ignoring the pain in my wounded arm. Again, the Numina escapes, twisting until she stands on my other side.

"What is it you want then?" she asks, panting.

A growl of frustration rips from me as I bare my teeth. "I want you to stay still!"

Swing.

Miss.

Swing.

Miss.

I can't catch her. She's too light on her feet, wasting no energy fighting back or defending herself. It's an infuriating match between cat and mouse. My wings unfold, poisoned shadows searing through my back as they flare behind me. The time for games is over.

The armor-swathed Numina shakes her head. "Grim, this isn't you."

Well wouldn't you know.

Shut up.

"So I've been told." I prowl forward.

Death falters, confusion knitting her black eyebrows, wrinkling the skin around the sharp circlet covering her forehead. "By whom?"

Me! Despite what my current actions are saying, I swear I'm still in here, Primrose.

Before she can recover from her puzzlement, I aim for the small space between her gorget and breastplate, where I see a slice of pale, vulnerable skin. Death blinks, and her hand shoots out, her closed fist connecting with my face and throwing me off course. The shears harmlessly ding off her mantle.

"Sun on a scone, I'm so sorry," Death apologizes, tented hands rising to her lips in surprise at her own actions. "It was a reflex, I swear."

Only Primrose would apologize to the enemy for a punch to the mouth.

The voice in my head laughs as I blink repeatedly, dazed. There are multi-colored pinpricks in my vision, and when I glance up, I see her. "Rose?"

"Grim?" She gasps, pulling the eyepatch from her left socket to let it hang around her neck.

For a moment, I take in her stone eye and all her armored glory. Then, I survey the battlefield and the dwindling beasts that either lie dying in burning piles of salt and ash, or sit trapped as spheres of smoke by annealed weapons. Rush is trying to protect his half-sister by pushing back her advances toward us, and Sparrow does the same with her. Meanwhile, Swan fights her way toward her mother as she prepares her horn to bombard the Elder Mother by summoning a group of Phouka away from their primary goal. Which is hindering anyone from getting to Hazel, like the two changeling brothers.

"Grim, look at me."

I hear the plea, but I can't tear myself from the cataclysmic sight of Hazel and her finally meeting blows. One with a foot-long blade and the other a sickle hewn from witchcraft. A cold, tangible evil rolls off the blue-skinned witch in billowing waves, and the misty air seems to bend around her as she creates a deadly grasshook from only her own dark magic and the dust it's formed. The way the old friends fight is a practiced dance and not one of circles; it rings of the past. The women are familiar with each other's steps, with their strength and movement. Granted, they have done this dance before, but it ended badly, for both of them.

"This isn't the world we've been trying to make. Old friends shouldn't fight because of things like senseless evil and jealousy, death and destruction." There's a hesitant touch on my arm and the color of my gaze solidifies. "Husbands and wives shouldn't have to be pitted against each other, either."

When I turn, there's a slight glimmer of hope in Death's face. It wavers when I flex my jaw from side to side and touch my fingers to the corners of my mouth. The tips come back tinted with blood and I click my tongue. "It's not very nice to hit. It hurts, you know." And that hope dies when I advance on Death with shears in hand once more.

Please kill me.

Swan: Darkness

By the time I decide if I should help Mom or Dad, I make it halfway to my mother and Allison Gross, with one fistful of salt left. The witch has blown her horn for a second time, and there's a small hoard of Phouka bounding towards them. Mom raises her dominant hand and fires off a blast of purple energy tapped straight from the elder trees. Allison Gross bends away from it and the power bypasses the witch, slipping back into a tree far behind her. It absorbs the magic light radiating from the tips of its branches, through the trunk, and into the ground, back to whence it came.

My feet are pounding against the charged earth, burning with the harsh contact. I can feel Mom's magic in my heart, like calling to like. That desperate part of me that wished for my gift for years, especially in a time of need, stirs. But I know the yearning for that is over, which is why I push myself until my lungs contract, my ribs pinch, and my shoulder aches. I'm not as quick as the beasts I race against though. I'm no match for the twisted animals and their too many, lanky limbs. Their hooves and paws thunder over the grass, covering more distance than my legs could ever dream of. No matter how fast I sprint, or how far I try to throw my remaining salt, the Phouka still reach our shared destination first.

One moment, a wide circle of the Stygian-black bogeys hurl themselves upward, and the next, they are diving on top of my mother in a sticky, decaying pile. As they crawl over one another, they tangle together like a massive heap of compost, each trying to get a piece of their prey.

There's no sign of the Elder Mother's figure, or her wheelchair beneath them.

Past the glowing garnet hue from the plethora of eyes, only a dim lavender-tinted light peeks through the living, writhing shadows and their sharp teeth. I don't think much when I palm a knife and let it fly, but it doesn't sink into vaporous faerie flesh. It slices across the back of Allison Gross's hand, making her drop her horn. The witch sneers at me and my approach, though she's not deterred, lifting the horn from the tangle of her mantle's gold fringe and poising the bony, green curl before her mouth once more. Vengeful emotions emerge from the darkest corners of my mental attic, like the creepy-crawlies of Starling's worst nightmares. They scuttle down the pins and needles, biting at my hands like fire ants, consuming my extremities as they dip to my thigh once more. This time, I put a little more thought into my next throw.

My knife sinks into the yellow-green lemongrass flesh of a gleeful throat vibrating with laughter. Allison Gross's cackling is cut short as her lengthy brown nails feel the smoking blade. When she touches the hilt, she hisses in pain and pulls her hand away, stunned. Still, the hag does not fall. Instead, her face melts into aggravation, enhanced by a blood-soaked, lip curling, nose-scrunching snarl. Her skin around my salted knife is bubbling, scorched skin flaking across her chest as she's purified from the inside out. The hag's hands become claws, and her mouth widens into a gorge of needles as she shrieks. She's even louder when one of Kestrel's arrows sinks into the soft spot right below my knife.

Allison Gross persists, howling as she stalks toward me. "You sniveling little wretch! I will be your undoing," she grates out around the weapons puncturing her throat. "I will kill every last one of you, starting with your moth—"

The witch's words are stopped short by the large, curved blade that slices through her. Her red, slick mouth is still frozen on her last letters when her head drops to the ground, soon followed by her crumpling, thin body and Starling's axe.

May you burn in Purgatory for all of eternity, witch.

To my dismay, the Phouka do not stop slithering in their pile upon the death of Allison Gross. When I glance around, my father is locked into battle with Baba Roga, visibly tiring with each swing of his elder tree sword, but still holding his own against the gingerbread witch. And Uncle Grim still lunges at Auntie Rose with her shears clutched in his fist, though she quickly sidesteps him. It's clear she's trying to speak him out of his poison-induced control, yet that won't work until Dad takes care of Baba Roga. But first, I need to save my mother with only three knives and no salt. My attic is spinning like a plate on a stick when that peek of lavender light shining through the Phouka grows brighter. And brighter. And brighter, and brighter still.

I shield my eyes with my arms.

The glade explodes with lavender light, more than the trees probably had to offer, and the Phouka are expelled. The sound of their bodies landing is sickening, and the ones that can still stand immediately flee in broken droves. They whiz past me, heading for the open barrier, the scent of rotting leaves and smoke in their wake. Through the inky flurry, I find my mother slumped in her wheelchair, smeared with blackened sludge. She's bent over her knees, scratched hands locked over the top of her mussed head. Blood leaks from her knuckles into her now unbound sable waves, tinting the gray strands woven throughout. The back of Mom's cloak is dotted with holes, some deep enough that they've gone through the sweater she wears beneath, right to her skin. I can't tell if the dark splotches staining the fabrics are from the Phouka, or if it's also saturated with her blood.

I should move, but I can't. Knowing the answer might kill me.

Kestrel is already passing me though, kneeling in front of our mom before I can exhale. The body of Allison Gross lies close to them. The tar that's oozing from her isn't like anything I've seen before; it's not blood, the Brume, nor Phouka poisoned decay. It's something different, unworldly. Like a seed of darkness itself. It wriggles through the grass until it finds the tip of my boot, engulfing my foot to start its journey up my leg. Even though the darkness is slow as pitch-black molasses, seeping through the material of my trousers, I can't move. It's cold, but in the most thirst-quenching way. And as it sinks into my skin and enters my blood, I know it's evil itself. I don't mean it's just bad; it's the very fabric that witchcraft is made from. This substance that's crawled from Allison Gross is the material from which her kind was first cut, and the original source is across the glade fighting Hazel right now. It's almost like Quince planted three corrupt seeds, to start the beginning of the end, the first being inside herself. When they became the last of the other witches, she must've given the other seeds to Baba Roga and Allison Gross. But now I have one of them.

And I want them all.

The darkness is addicting. It heals me. My limbs no longer sting, but instead, relief floods my veins. For the first time in years, I cannot feel my nerve damage. I'm overwhelmed by clarity. Depression and anxiety flee. There is no trauma inherited and gained, nor duty or responsibility. The higher the darkness rises, now up to my knee, the more it filters into my mental attic, seeping through the crack under the door, spreading along the floor and soaking into the rug.

Through the make-believe window of my precious, dissociative spot, Kestrel lifts Mom's head. She groans, and Starling yells for her, darting toward us, through the now Phouka-less field. Starling's running past Auntie Rose and Uncle Grim, away from Hazel and Quince's faraway battle and toward Dad and Baba Roga. He needs to pass the fighting pair to get to Mom. Hearing his son's cry for his mother breaks our father's concentration, and Dad's scruffy face crinkles with concern, first for his wife's well-being and then his son's. Baba Roga uses this moment of fragility to find a new target, one that will bring Dad to his knees.

With a vicious smile, the witch turns her attention on Starling. "Oh, there's the little birdie I could smell," she says, pointed, pixie-like nose tilted to the air. "You have pieces of my house inside your pockets, how naughty." Baba Roga's gray tongue pokes out to lick her ebony lips. "If we were still in the West Woods, I'd throw you underground and fatten you up for a gingersnap stew." The hag points her striped wooden staff at my brother, and webs of her rosewood-tinted craft lash out in his direction.

"Starling, stay back," Dad shouts, slashing at the witchcraft with his sword while protecting his body with the shield. The long blade deflects the witchcraft as if it were a solid metal weapon.

Starling skitters, desperate to reach Mom, but he can't get to her without being in Baba Roga's line of fire. And fire she does. Again and again, one after the other, she throws her craft, but Dad fights her back valiantly. He meets each tendril, his elder sword cleaving through them all with a clean *snick*. That is until the witch whips her single-horned head, sending two waves of her power at once. Dad catches one shot with his sword, and the other his arm. The glowing witchcraft wraps around his lower bicep and tightens, pulling taut and cutting off his circulation until he yells through gritted teeth. My father drops his shield in pain, falling to one knee, unable to stand and unable to let the blade in his hand go. Just when I think Dad can't take it any longer, there is another *snick*.

Followed by a *thud*.

Then, an agonized bellow.

And my father's amputated arm is lying in the grass, still holding the elder tree sword.

He crumples to his side, clutching onto the bleeding stump where his elbow used to be. His cream cloak is soaked in red. My mother screams for her husband, and my brothers cry for their father.

I convulse, snapping out of the impairing darkness. My extremities are on fire, and my shoulder is so sore, there's even a bleak heaviness in my mind again. My siblings' screams are panicked, and I've never been more thankful for hearing such a terrifying thing because it wakes me even more. Slipping my fingers in my cloak, I retrieve Robin's last dose of medicine, hoping to clear my mind enough to figure out what I need to do.

Though the darkness now tugs at my thigh, I walk straight toward Baba Roga with empty hands.

Her gray tongue darts out to taste the air. "What a scrumptious little button you are," the old, beautiful candy witch chirps. Her staff pokes out before her, almost beckoning me. Or perhaps prodding for my boots? Baba Roga's solid, butterscotch syrup eyes have a slight milky film-like quality, like a batch that's gone bad. They're searching, similar to Auntie Poppy—

The witch is blind!

I try to slip the matchbox and The Moon's candle from my side bag as quietly as I can manage. Freeing the matches from the compartment is easy, but the crescent hook to unlatch the candle from the leather walls gets stuck. Baba Roga hears when

MCKENZIE CATRON

it releases. Her staff points to me with deft accuracy, and I have less than a second to duck and roll closer to the hag before she sends a bout of nasty witchcraft at my face. I'm at arm's length now, as I get a knee up under me and I put the Blessed object on the ground between us. The soft, celestial periwinkle glow illuminates the bottom of Baba Roga's skinny face with hues that contrast the harsh garnet eclipse behind her head. It's a dramatic, haunted effect, one I'll surely write about later. But right now, before the witch realizes where I am and what's about to happen, I swipe the match against the box's strike pad.

Nothing happens.

As my siblings try to save my father bleeding out at my back, I strike it again. But the only thing the match produces is a loud scraping noise, which clues Baba Roga in to my location. Glancing down at my prickling fingers, the curvy-tailed sun ornament at the base of the silver match glints. This was the one I lit inside her house; Robin had put the spent match back inside the ornate box, and I forgot to take it out. I grab the unused starburst match just as Baba Roga's bony hand clamps onto the front of my throat. The match head scrapes against the rough strip and ignites when the witch lifts me to my feet with an eerie strength. I choke and sputter, clutching the tiny, flaming stick as the earth disappears beneath my toes.

"Tricksy girl," Baba Roga snarls, reaching for my other hand, the one that holds the engraved matchbox. She wrestles it from me, and once it's in her possession, she holds it up between her fingers so I can watch the witchcraft-induced, mold-like rust corrode the magic-born metal. Then, forming a fist, she crushes the matchbox and the crescent moon ornamented match still inside as if it were little more than a flake of silver leaf. The ash-like remnants fall from between her knuckles like sand.

"No," I gurgle, losing feeling in my darkness-infected limbs. Kicking my legs doesn't help me breathe or make the hag release me. If anything, she relishes the struggle. Even more so

326

when the match singes my fingertips and I drop it to claw at her choking hand as dots dance along my narrowing vision.

It feels like another miracle from Macha when a familiar melodic whistle rings out.

A murmuration forms a color-shifting cloud above and Starling's birds swarm us, circling like a windstorm before diving to peck at Baba Roga's arm. With a screech, she releases me. And when I fall, the sole of my boot smothers the fading starburst match. I swoop forward to snatch The Moon's candle out from under the witch's foot while she stomps around, allowing me to stow it away as she swings her staff at the birds plucking her face. Baba Roga loses hold of the striped wood, though, and must swipe at the songbirds with her talons instead. This does little; the starlings tear at her relentlessly. The birds only stop when Dad's fallen sword glows purple, rooting itself back into the earth as it twists into a thick limb that arches from the ground. Just in time for the hag to sense the sharp tip of the transformed limb coming right at her. The Elder Mother gives Baba Roga a befitting death, one of retribution for her gravely injured husband, but also for her sister-in-law. The elder tree spike skewers the witch's eye as her wicked sister had once done to my Auntie Rose. Although, Mom's makeshift weapon goes in *much* deeper and *much* farther than Baba Yaga's nail did. Deep enough that Baba Roga is left dead on her feet, literally.

Her death releases the remaining Phouka crawling along the edges outside the glade. More importantly, it releases Uncle Grim who falls to his knees across the field. The sound of small boots over crisp grass draws my gaze as my three younger siblings run toward Dad, holding the sheet Hazel had carried the armor in. Kestrel moves from Mom to try to intercept them, but he only catches Crow. Robin and Lark kneel beside our father, assessing the damage. Dad keens in pain, and Mom, with tears pouring violently down her cheeks, slides from her wheelchair to cushion her husband's head on her legs.

"Hold on, Rush." She pushes the thick ropes of his hair away from his face and kisses his forehead, murmuring words of comfort into his peaked, mostly green skin. "You're going to be all right, my love. Stay with me, okay?"

During this, Starling stares at our father's lifeless arm on the ground; something like blameworthiness and horror drips from his face, along with his tears. Kestrel reassures Crow, signing in an attempt to keep him distracted from the gruesomeness around us. All the while, my little sisters move in practiced tandem, working as Healers rather than terrified young daughters. Robin staunches Dad's blood by ripping the sheet apart and tying a length of fabric tightly above his severed arm. Lark digs through her Healer's belt, beginning a tender song, something quiet and gentle sung beneath her breath that she infuses with her changeling gift. Even though she's focused on finding her supply of Hazel's clotting powder in her belt, she has Dad in her heart, and her gift's magic is influencing him alone. It's a song to calm him and dull his pain, but the look Lark gives Mom when she finds the bottle and uncorks it, is telling. Her gift can only do so much. Mom holds on to Dad tightly as Lark shakes the powder over the witchcraft's neat cut. Dad's body arches and he cries out in guttural pain.

This haunting, soul-shattering sound wakes something inside me. The darkness has stopped spreading up my leg, halted right below the last salted knives strapped to my thigh. If it weren't for the purifying metal, the evil would've overtaken me. I would've willingly succumbed to the darkness...

I would've joined the dark.

This is what the prophecy meant by *"a child of the changeling must join the dark."* Starling was right—the changeling would be me—but not for the reasons he thought. A snake of darkness oozes from Baba Roga and off the end of the elder tree limb poking through the back of her head. It drops to the grass and slithers toward my father's prone form.

No. I can't allow that.

I made an unexpected descent into the dark when I fell into Baba Roga's house, but when I plunge into darkness this time, it's of my own volition.

With leadened feet, I walk nearer to my family, the weight of the pure wickedness encapsulating my leg, making it hard to move now. But I don't feel any heaviness inside anymore. This is my destiny. This outcome would always be my fate. I was made the way I was for a reason, and I was given this life because I am strong enough to live it. So, I prop open the door and window to my attic, walking away from the once comforting, dissociative spot. And as I do this, I release myself from the gifted version of me I always thought I needed to be.

I don't need her to be strong or to be worth something.

I don't need her to love or be loved.

I don't need her to be capable of great things.

It's taken me such a long time, but now, I know and truly do love who I am, poetic soul, stormy mind, magicless heart, and all. But perhaps my true gift is the love that I have for my family? Because it's no longer the self-ingrained sense of duty from being the eldest child, the repeated patterns of family trauma, or the wish to be free from the illness in my mind that drives me forward. When I lean down, scooping up the darkness that crawled from Baba Roga, it's because I have felt the beauty of both emotion and its absence. I understand what a privilege it is to have felt the ups and downs of life. To have learned that there are no flowers without rain, no calm without a storm.

And there is a storm inside me when the next pool of evil enters my system. I can feel its iciness in my bones; the cold burns like tongues of flame licking their way up my skin. There's a thunder beating in my heart, and it takes everything in me not to let the rain loose through my eyes. I blink repeatedly to clear the moisture, and when I do, I meet my littlest brother's wet stare. He's the only one who sees me in this moment, the only one who saw my exchange with Baba Roga's corpse. Crow's the only one who sees me trudge toward the other side of the field with the inky darkness of witchcraft running up my hand and over my torn bracer like a glove. Crow is the only one who sees that I am lost.

Swan: The Black Swan

*M*y body is trembling.

The eclipse begins diverging when I hit the halfway mark to my destination. The witchcraft has visually spread to my shoulder, though internally, it's everywhere. My nerves are consumed with a new kind of frozen numbness, feeling as if I've plunged into the glade's stream during Christmastide. It takes all my concentration to keep my legs moving; I so badly want to collapse.

Not unlike the way Auntie Rose and Uncle Grim sit in the grass, catching their breath as I come upon their resting spot. Now that the witch's control over my uncle is gone, his giant wings have disappeared. I catch the tail end of his transformation back into his old self as the half mask of a lindwyrm's horned head dissolves away, revealing his colorless upper face again. Uncle Grim's eyes open, and his signature luminescent yellow eyes have finally returned. Auntie Rose is cupping his pale cheeks, almost reassuring herself that this moment is real. She leans in, pressing her wobbling lips to his forehead before whispering, "I knew you would come back to me."

Death's Reaper caresses her wrist. "I always will."

At the sound of my dragging footsteps, the pair peer up at me.

"Swan! What have you done?" Auntie Rose gasps, wide gaze roving over my dark, stained limbs. Her uncovered tiger's eye stone locks onto the left side of my chest. "I can't—I can't see your threads."

"She's fulfilling the prophecy." Uncle Grim climbs to his feet with a creaky, pained groan.

My aunt shakes her head, standing to advance on me, but I step back. "Chickadee, you don't know what you're doing."

"I do," I whisper. Clearing my throat, I repeat myself stronger this time. "I do. You can't help me now, but you can still help Dad. He's really hurt."

Somehow, Death's pearly skin blanches further. The blood drains from her face when she spots her half-brother lying on the ground with his wife and children around him like a vigil. My aunt appears more like her seventeen-year-old self than ever, scared and vulnerable.

"Go." I jerk my head back toward our family. "Keep everyone away. I'll finish this; it was always going to be me."

Auntie Rose reaches for my unsullied arm, but Uncle Grim tugs on her leather-padded elbow, drawing her away. When I meet his weary, solemn sunflower gaze, I know that he understands. He knows that I've found my path, and there's no time for me to explain how I got here, or where I plan to go. I just don't think he knows that, when I drag my body onward, I haven't made an arrangement to return. The darkness has already reached my chest, and its bitterness renders me breathless. It's an icy plunge into corruption, but it certainly woke my mind. Evocative of bruised mint on my tongue, the temptation of witchery thrumming through my veins is refreshing in a curious way. I can understand why the taste of power can become an irreversible, all-consuming enslavement...

Vibrating with energy now, I close the distance between me and my fate.

"Stop!" My yell shakes, but it's not from weakness. Not as the darkness coasts through my heart and over my armored sternum.

After Hazel's blackened, slashed shield deflects a blow from a small, churning sickle made of witchcraft and dust, Quince turns her beetle-black eyes to me. When she sees the evil seeds she planted slowly consuming me, her stained lips pull into a smile, revealing her sharpened teeth. "So, a bird has fallen from the nest."

Hazel shakes her head, panting and weakened with nicks dotting her skin. "What are you doing, Swan?"

Quince huffs a musical laugh to herself. "The Black Swan of the family. What a fitting name for such a beautiful trans-formation."

The First Witch's words remind me of all the times I've been set apart by Starling for not having a gift. It's an old wound of marred bone that's now fused. Quince doesn't need to know that, though. So, when I speak, I direct my words to my godmother. "Fate's prophecy did say, 'a child of the changeling would join the dark.' You all should have seen this coming."

"Isn't this wonderful? One of your own, willingly coming into my fold," Quince jeers, rubbing this betrayal in Hazel's face as if this matter was nothing more than a sibling rivalry. Some-thing as trivial as one of my siblings getting a larger slice of cake and bragging about it. How broken this woman must be to care so fiercely about such an old, pointless grudge—to ruin the world over it. "The power feels extraordinary, doesn't it?" she asks me.

"It feels like home," I say honestly. Being pain-free again, returning to the state of body from my feverless childhood before the age of seven, does remind me of home.

"Of course it does. With the craft in your veins, you have a place where your darkest wishes belong, a place where you're revered and respected," Quince says, playing to all my biggest years-old insecurities. "Folks listen to creatures like you and me, they notice our greatness. *I* noticed you before. You're the only bird here with clipped wings, right?"

I nod. Did Quince actually notice me, or did Uncle Grim tell her all these things? Does she actually see potential in me?

"Well not anymore. With this power, you can soar through the dark. You can be *free*."

For a moment, I look to my family. But then a talon hooks under my chin and pulls my focus back. "You're so much more than them. And I promise, someday, you can be more powerful than all of them combined." Quince smiles at me, the black veins under her skin pulsing with each beat of her decrepit heart.

I won't lie...I am curious about her promise of such lofty things. "How?"

"I am the first and the last witch, the most powerful of our kind. I've been strong enough to survive the centuries; I am more than strong enough to teach you how to fly and help me revive our kin." The First Witch holds a welcoming hand out to me. "We can rule them all and change this world forever."

Hazel laughs, bending over with her hands on her knees from the sheer force of it.

"What?" Quince's arm drops, snarling when the Healer continues mocking her, "What is so funny?"

My godmother straightens, small giggles escaping her lips as she wipes under her eyes with mirth. "You are not the first and the last witch because you are the most powerful or strongest of your putrid kind. You are the first and last witch because you are a coward. You hid away for all these years, used the other leeches to sicken this world for you. The only reason you crawled out from the dark was because you felt the pressure." Hazel lifts a brow with a knowing half-grin. "You knew The Numina would eventually find you, and making your move first was the only shot you had at escaping death."

The First Witch's features darken, her ears shifting back as the muscles around her ginger brows contract. "I will always outrun her; I will be her doom." The blue-skinned woman lifts her flowered head, and Purgatory reflects in her dark eyes. "Better yet, I will become her. I will be the only Death that my new world will ever know."

"I wasn't even speaking of Rose, I spoke of your extinction. But at least your bitterness is consistent." Hazel tuts. "A jealous, cold heart made you rise and become the hag that you are, Quince. Now your jealous, cold heart is what will make you fall."

"I have risen from the depths to claim my rightful power. Now I'll rise to meet my Black Swan's fall from grace, and you will watch as she becomes everything you hate." Quince turns to me and offers her hand once more. "Come to me, pet; come home and seize your power."

"Swan." Hazel says my name both as a plea and a warning.

"I'm sorry." It's the only thing I can manage.

It looks like Dad is going to be okay. He's wrapped in that old sheet now, and it's become part bandage, part sling as Kestrel and Starling work on helping him sit up. Robin continues to flutter around him, while Lark looks over Uncle Grim and Auntie Rosie as they join the group. Crow, of course, has found his way to Mom's side, ushering her back into her wheelchair from the ground. Hopefully I can do what needs to be done before they see me this way. Because I won't be relinquishing my life to Quince's dark cause. Although, that's what it feels like I'm doing when my shoulders drop, and I walk into The First Witch's arms, curling into her cold embrace like a lost duckling searching for any semblance of shelter. It takes everything in me to lift my hands from my witchcraft-encased thighs to embrace the hag in return.

"You should've stayed hidden in the dark," I whisper into her shoulder. "You might've lived."

The salt-annealed blade clutched in my fist finds its home between Quince's fourth and fifth left ribs. Her hiss in my ear sends chills down my curved back, but I hold on tight. The witch tries to pull away from my hug, but I clasp onto her with my dark, consumed arm, pulling her closer. When the knife shoves deeper into her heart, she gasps and thrashes. With tears welling in my eyes, I twist my wrist, and the blade follows, cleaving through muscle and tissue. I feel the drenching rime of the tar spilling from Quince's mouth trailing down my shoulder. It spreads over my skin and sinks into every knob of my spine, enshrouding my bones in an unholy frost so frigid that my limbs implode. I can't hold back the shivers wracking my body as my teeth clack together. The glinting darkness has swathed everything but my head, the hip holding my annealed knives, and The Moon's Blessed candle. Otherwise, I'm soaked in witchcraft that looks like crystal-studded ebony honey. The moment the last seed hits my joints, the weight of my transformation, and The First Witch's body, are just too much. When the darkness spreads up my neck and sinks into my face, I swear I hear a click inside my head, like the unlocking of a hidden door. My knees buckle, bringing the both of us down. But Hazel is there to take the brunt of her old friend's crumpling weight with hands under her armpits. My godmother releases Quince from me so I can collapse fully into the grass. Before my eyes close from the force of my progressively aggressive shivering, I see Hazel lay her down with rueful tears in her multi-colored eyes. She's once again mourning for the person her friend used to be.

Soon, my body reflects the warm tone from the dying eclipse above me, my temperature seemingly matching the red hue behind my eyelids. At first, I think it's from shaking and generating heat, my body creating movement to survive this cold. But

I realize I am growing hot now, fevered to the point that my cloak feels stuffy. Even though I wiggle out of the wool, the heat worsens, and it feels like my skin might burst at the seams. Sweat plasters my bangs to my forehead and seeps into my closed eyes, though the sting of it is nothing compared to the fire that engulfs my hands and feet once more. My nerve damage returns at full force and I moan in pain, eyelids peeling back to squint at the sky. But it's steam that I open my watering eyes to, trails drifting above me into the nippy autumn air. Steam that's coming from me. My sweat and tears are evaporating instantly from the heat I expel.

"Swan, are you okay?" Hazel's hand touches mine for the briefest moment, but the quick contact is enough for her to pull away with a sharp gasp. "You scalded me." She clutches her fingers to her chest, lightly blowing on them. Bewildered, my godmother stares at me, rose-petal lips pursed, gaze wary.

My chest is blazing.

It's a blistering kind of torment, one of flames and devastation, the kind of pain that lives inside a wildfire. It's suffocating, and my chest quickly grows tight, constricting my heart and setting it ablaze like my prickling limbs. The pain continues to bloom in intensity, but a golden charmed glow now shines through the knitted cables of my sweater. I know what this is. I've seen this gentle light illuminate from my siblings before, wished it would shine through the woven elder tree twigs creating my own heart for far too long. But I never knew that finally gaining my changeling gift would be so agonizing.

Swan: Cleansing

S *wan?*
    There's thunder rumbling low in my ears.
Swan? Are you okay?
I can feel a crackling in the air, the buzzing charge before a storm.
Can you hear us?
My skin crawls with electric pinpricks of energy.
Something is wrong with her!
The fine hairs over my body stand, and the curls around my face lift as if floating in water.
What's happening?
Bolts of lightning race across my vision, and I know I'm not just seeing them in the sky.
Swan?
Another clap of thunder echoes in my ears and reverberates down to my toes. The heat of the next lightning strike exploding in my brain lingers at my fingertips. Sitting up to look at my numb hands, I find that the whorls of my fingerprints are alight, glowing like hot embers. The building storm corresponds with the zings of pain that run along my palms,

and it's like I'm seeing the physical evidence of my years-long affliction for the very first time, both in my hands and in my eyes.

"Swan?" It isn't until Kestrel crouches before me that I can pull myself from the squall of pain.

"Be careful, Kestrel," our godmother murmurs.

The ground sizzles under my hands as I push myself up to clamber to my feet and stagger away. I've left black scorch marks on the dry grass and burnt the fallen leaves beneath me to ash. Kestrel steps right on top of them, holding out an easing hand as if I were a startled foal. Balling my hands into fists, I shake my head at both him and Hazel when she follows my brother's lead. "Stay back!" The rest of my family is also approaching. Starling is supporting our ashen-faced father's weight, while Lark walks on Dad's opposite side, tightening the ties of the makeshift dressings. Robin follows close behind, still holding tight to what's left of their Healer's tools and fabric scraps, her small knuckles white. Crow is clenching Mom's hand, nearly bumping against her spokes, and Auntie Rose and Uncle Grim are arm in arm. All pairs seeming to support each other in different ways.

"I said stay back," I yell, a roll of thunder pealing beneath my words. My eyelids are searing, and judging by the flash, followed by how my family halts in their tracks, I can only assume they saw the lightning in my gaze. Their fear makes me cry out, "I don't want to hurt you."

Mom gently untangles herself from Crow and wheels herself closer, but she can see that she's reached my boundary. "It's okay, sweetheart. You're not going to hurt us. Just tell us what's happening."

"Please," I beg. "It's my gift, I don't know what it'll do to you. I don't know what it's doing to me." My gift is eating away at the darkness from my fingerprints outwards, somehow dissolving it. But it also feels like it's dissolving my body. "I thought I could take this on; I wasn't trying to become a witch. I swear. Please believe me." My eyes slip to Starling, remembering over the last few days, during our journey when he accused me of secretly siding with Baba Roga and Allison Gross. "Please," I entreat again.

"We believe you, chickadee," Auntie Rose croaks.

"You're okay, dear," Hazel laments.

Varying agreements echo from everyone else.

"The prophecy said a child of the changeling must join the dark for the light to prevail." I stare at Starling, hoping that he'll understand my desperate logic. "I don't think the good side is the light. I think it's literal. I had to let my body collect the witchcraft to trigger my gift, which is light. Or lightning, I don't know—" I shake my head to clear my thoughts, though it ends in me shaking out my hands and shifting my feet, trying to find any sort of relief from this extraordinary pain that's bringing me to smoking tears. "But it *burns*."

Starling's eyes go far away as he mulls on this. "Lightning is hotter than the sun…"

"Which is purifying to witches." Kestrel snaps like he's just solved the greatest riddle.

A small murmur comes from behind Dad. "But it's hurting her," Robin says, tears cascading down her flushed cheeks.

"Her gift is killing her," Hazel corrects.

Uncle Grim's yellow eyes peer at his companion. "What if Swan were to use The Moon's candle?"

"It *might* be enough to destroy the witchcraft and stop"— Auntie Rose gestures with a shaky hand—"this."

Keyword *might*.

It would be worth a shot if it weren't for the fact that Baba Roga destroyed the matchbox. "I can't," I groan. "The Moon said the wick may only be lit once with something born of magic, and the last match she gave me was destroyed in the battle."

"She didn't say the candle had to be lit by the matches specifically." Starling sharpens then. "Changelings are born of troll magic."

"It's your time of need, honey," Dad's wounded voice rings out.

His words open the floodgates, lightning arcs through my body, lighting up my veins in violent, stormy flashes. Head thrown back in pain, I see that the eclipse is minutes from ending; it's time to finish this. Unhooking the flap sealing the Blessed candle in its bag, my gift burns through me, slowly eating away at the dark as I continue to heat up. However, my gift alone isn't enough to kill it all, not before I die and the darkness escapes out into the world to find its next host, at least. While I'm still alive, the last trace of witchcraft is being cleansed from the earth, but my heart is quickly becoming kindling. My gift is killing me quicker than I can purify the seeds of evil. The twigs in my chest are popping and crackling like I'm sitting in front of a campfire, and my lungs are squeezing despite the feeling of fullness expanding them. The sensation worsens, and a puff of smoke billows from my mouth when I cough. There's ash on my tongue. It flakes from my lips and falls to the pan of The Moon's candle now that I cradle it in my glowing hands.

My family is terrified, whether *of* me or *for* me, I can't decipher. Both scenarios crumble my heart further. Still, I can't help searching for reassurance from my parents. Or perhaps permission? Love and grief mingle in their gazes. My mother gnawing at her trembling lips, trying to keep her composure; memories of my childhood pour out her eyes as she looks at me. I can see them dripping down her chin, and if this is what seeing your life flash before your eyes as you die means, it's beautiful. But it's my father who gives me what I need the most. Through the deep sadness creasing his wan face, there's pride for me. Though his acceptance and encouragement is what I cherish most. Dad nods, and I know he's telling me it's okay, no matter the outcome. It's okay to use this magic and shine. It's okay to utilize The Moon's blessing. It's okay to be the end of this prophecy. It's okay to let go.

So I do. Because I would burn myself down to the ground for my family to feel the warmth of safety and serenity.

Pinching the curled fern-like wick between my fiery fingers, I ignite the superlunary candle. An explosion of magic flares, casting an orb of luminescence around me. A galaxy of stars, like tiny suns dance over my skin as thunder sings in my ears. And a celestial song rings through my being, a righteous hymn of unmaking that harmonizes through every part of me as my gift approaches its crescendo. It feels like holy fire and hailstone, suffering, and relief as both the candle and my tempest rid the witchcraft from my body, and this earth, eternally. In a beautiful and terrifying, lyrical way, it's burning me from the inside out with a cleansing stormy flame. This elegiac ending was my destiny. I was made to save my family, to better this world, and its future. My whole life has been an epic prelude. The finale of good versus evil. A decades-long fated histrionic with an arc better than any poem I could ever write. A Numina parable.

I see the transformation into a wickedless world all the way through, refusing to stop the wave of magic feeding The Moon's candle until the rest of the darkness is melted away. The bolts searing through me make white symmetrical marks on my skin, just like the ones that usually break through thunderclouds. My heart catches fire, its shape visibly glows through my chest like hot coals. Only when there is no trace of the bitter cold left in my veins, and my family screams, do I stop. Crumpling in on myself, I collapse to the earth once more, resting, knowing that I've killed the witches once and for all. My sputtering chest heaves, and with each attempt to pull air into my damaged lungs, my heart decrepitates. I'm choking when my mother appears at my head, sliding from her wheelchair to cradle me, similar to how she held my father. Even when my lightning-scarred skin scalds her, she just pulls her sweater sleeves over her hands like mittens and holds me closer. I can hardly hear her sobbing over my insides snapping.

Dad, equally bloodless and bloody as he is, kneels at my side, his only hand brushing the singed hairs away from my face. "Rose," he calls out to his half-sister, his voice thick with tears. "Tell me she's okay."

Death and her Reaper both loom over me, pale faces wet and full of sorrow. "Her threads are charred," my aunt whispers.

Looking as far to my left as I can, I see my siblings. Crow is signing to our Healer-in-training sisters and godmother. "You and Hazel can help her, right?" When Robin wails harder at this, knowing nothing can be done for me, Crow turns to Kestrel and Starling. "Auntie Rose and Uncle Grim won't take her, right? She's not going to The After, she's staying home...right?"

"I—I don't know," Kestrel replies, his usual fluid movements now disordered.

"Swan?" Starling calls out.

"Yeah?" I cough. I haven't heard my real name from his lips in such a long time.

"I'm sorry for everything." My brother tentatively moves closer, as if he was afraid to hurt me with his presence. "I don't know why I did all the things I did, and I know that's not enough. But please forgive me," he breathes, kneeling with his littlest finger held out to me.

His words and gesture make me want to cry, but there's no moisture left in my body and I can't move a muscle. All I can do is twitch my pinkie and gasp, "I already did, you nib."

Starling sniffles a laugh, reaching out with ginger hands to wrap our pinkies together for me. "I love you."

"I love you too, Starling."

"Please," he says. Knowing that he's pleading for me not to go is the thing that brings a single tear to my otherwise parched eyes. And seeing my little brother again, Kestrel's and my best friend, heals something in me. He's back to stay and he'll be there for Kestrel, and that means everything to me.

Sometimes, it's a hardship that brings distant siblings back together; sometimes, it's personal growth, or even a celebration. Starling's and my reconciliation, as brief as it might be, is a little bit of each in many ways. I'm just grateful to have experienced it in my last moments; not everyone gets to have this kind of reunion with family or friends. And this knowledge makes my last full exhale sweet with peace and closure.

"Hazel?" Kestrel shouts for our godmother. Her lips press together, and my brother balls his hands into fists at his sides before sinking them deep into his pants pockets.

Mom sniffles, reddened gaze staring up at the former Elder Mother. "You fixed my heart once upon a time. Black Annis cleaved through it, and you and the trolls repaired the broken pieces. Can't you tell me how to do that?" she asks Hazel, despair trickling along with the tears that fall from her lashes.

The pregnant Healer tugs at her braid. "The twigs of Swan's heart aren't just broken, Sparrow. Repairing yours was much different; the damage wasn't as extensive, this is ruination. It would take much too long for the kind of healing that Swan needs for her regrowth." Hazel runs her fingers down the bridge of her nose as she thinks, then winces when she touches a nick from her fight with The First Witch. "The laws of magic and balance won't allow you to reconstruct her heart quick enough, or Icarus to slow time for that, even if he was in the right condition to do so. He told me what he, The Sun, and The Moon would be doing when he brought me from the Apothecary to the glade. After slowing time and creating the eclipse, The Numina will have been completely drained. That's why they aren't even here right now, they can't travel without recouping for a while." Hazel's voice cracks. "Swan would have to do the healing work naturally, but in this state, her body wouldn't survive that sort of timeline. I don't even know that she'll make it to sunrise."

"How long would the repair take?" Dad asks, throat audibly thick.

"I suppose it depends." Hazel rounds my prone form to inspect the lightning branch scars on my exposed skin. "After, say, a wildfire or lightning strike, a tree's recovery depends on the severity of internal and/or external injuries and the environment it's rooted in. It would take a lot of nurturing, years or even a decade of care, supports, pruning, and watering in good soil."

Mom stares up at the Healer, resolute. "Then we'll care for her."

"Sparrow, your daughter is not a tree," Hazel sighs, though you can hear how badly she wishes this were true.

My mother poses an impossible question. "But if she was?"

An involuntary laugh slips from my godmother. "I'm sorry?"

"If she were a tree, would she make it?" Mom presses again.

Hazel's dual-colored gaze searches the Elder Mother's face, trying to judge how sane and probable this idea is. She must find something to run with though, because she concedes with tears in her eyes. "There's a chance."

"If, in time, even trees can heal, then it's good enough for me." There's the barest hint of doubt in my mother's tone, but it's overtaken by belief as she continues. "This family is known for defying death and achieving the impossible. You did it once. I did it; Poppy did it. Swan will do it too." Her words are coated with the softest, most gentle lie, a reassuring untruth meant for herself more than anyone.

But despite the odds, Mom still coaxes the crumbling wood in my chest to grow.

It's torture when the charred, gold-glazed tendrils first

pierce through my lightning-scarred skin, though the sensation of my heart growing outside of my body far outweighs the pain. The popping twigs become creaking branches that appear dusted in the trolls' signature charm. Most are fissuring and snapping as they attempt to move and grow, sliding upward from my chest. The branches reach and expand until they become boughs easily twice the size of any other elder tree surrounding the glade. The dimly glowing boughs groan as they stretch high and wide, mirroring the same symmetrical pattern of the missing pigment marring my body. Then, much like the tree that Mom summoned to open the barrier earlier this evening, the craggy limbs bow down toward me. The soot- and magic-stained wood arching from my chest, slither beneath my frame. Some pieces of my heart poke back into the earth to burrow inside the dirt, while others scoop me up like a creaky cradle.

Gingerly, the pieces supporting my body lift me skyward, into the early morning sky. Golden spheres, the size of fireflies, float to meet the stars of the new month. They drift lazy, yet graceful, as the boughs twist until I'm upright. My toes are inches from touching the grass as the new tree formed from the husk of my slowing heart grows thicker, forming like a rib cage to surround my body. The bark is closing around me as a final long, relieving breath seeps from my lips. Before my eyelids slip closed, I manage a true smile for my family. Their hopeful half-smiles mirror my own, and their tear-streaked faces and tired eyes filled with love. It cocoons my body like a well-worn, treasured quilt, one that tucks me into a long, tranquil sleep where I'm encased inside the trunk of the burnt, lightning-scarred elder tree that was once my changeling heart.

As the Swan Song plays the threads materialize
    Ten pinkies wrapped in red

Trailing, winding, stretching, looping,
Connecting to the roots of an elder tree
Stripped of pigment and life
A tapis strung between slumbering limbs
The tale of family, love, and loss,
And the birds that brought deliverance from the dark

Grim: Epilogue

*T*he seasons have cycled many times.

There's a heart pulsing throughout the glade; the land is full of life. The spring garden is brimming with flowers and fruit. There's more folk than ever in the glade, but the newcomers do not call this place home. They pass through and pay their respects, bringing gifts of gratitude to the Elder Mother and her family, laying them at the base of what they call The Empress Elder Tree, Vanquisher of Darkness, the reason for their freedom. People can see it standing proud in the center of the glade from miles away, drawing them in like a beacon.

Humans and faeries alike are free to travel, having no fear of the outside world now that no bogeymen exist to crawl through the shadows. Even the Stygian Brume has dissipated after The First Witch's death. Its incurable mold and mildew-like proper-ties weakened, and The Sun was able to save most of the Infir-mary's infected patients with his purifying light, though not all damage could be reversed. The Healers worked diligently to treat the survivors' other symptoms and soon, the back room of Hazel's *Herbal Apothecary & Infirmary—Home of the Healers— Makers of Tonics, Tinctures, and Salves*, was empty.

The Blessed medicine workers frequented the glade for the

first two years, trying to find ways to treat the charred tree and quicken its recovery. It couldn't be rushed, however, and the eldest changeling child, swaddled inside the lightning-patterned bark remained, caught between life and death. Despite this, Swan made her presence known. She's been in the deliberate storms that roll in at the strangest times of year, and the brilliant lights that flash through the sky in shapes that nature alone could not form. It's brought much comfort to the family.

While the glade is no longer a haven, in terms of a place to be protected from great evil, it is still a beautiful, vast home to faeries, and the Elder Mother still watches over it. Sparrow cares for the land and the faerie folk who originally called it home, just as she did before, but now it's without the worry of keeping monsters out. It's given her more time to spend with her family and do what she loves. Like reading in front of the fire in her mother Aspen's old house, and filling the family library's shelves with her own handwritten tomes. She's even bound their journals to add them to the gilded collection. And she started compiling Swan's poetry scraps from around their house and from different journals into a book to hopefully be published in the villages. Sparrow's also been writing and baking new recipes with the dreams of opening her own little storefront for visitors inside the glade. In the same entrepreneurial vein, Robin has declared, with new curvy-tailed sun and starburst ornament additions to her charm bracelet, that she wants to open a floristry shop next door. Her idea was to sell a menagerie of "out of season" blossoms all year round. It was a swift shift from wanting to be a Healer, but the adults of the family believe the change is from the horrors of treating her own father on that battlefield.

Lark, on the other hand, dove deeper into medicine. After saving her father's life, The Sun and Moon Blessed her at only fifteen, the youngest Healer in history. Ever since, she's been gladly working shifts at the Apothecary and doing her own studies in the glade, trying her hardest to figure out how to help her older sister. Lark has also been doing treatments at home with Rush, exercise therapies to ensure he uses the remainder of his arm properly and keeps his strength up. Because of her, Rush has made a full recovery and coped well with his new way of life. At first, it was hard for the half-goblin man to learn how to do daily tasks with one arm. Every now and again, he forgets that he doesn't have two, especially when he goes to kiss Sparrow and move the hair from her face now that she's cut it to her jaw again. Or when Hazel and Icarus's son sees his beloved godfather and trips with his chubby, uncoordinated toddler legs and Rush goes to catch him. Though the man has found a new passion in beekeeping, it was maybe the hardest for him when he first realized he could no longer sew. Rush had always embroidered new cloaks for his children when they outgrew them. Crow had his growth spurt a couple years ago, and it crushed Rush not being able to hold a needle with his unsteady, singular hand.

That's when Starling asked his father to instruct him. They had daily verbal lessons, starting with simple things like buttons and quilts that were donated to the Infirmary. Starling would practice independently for hours, sitting at the base of Swan's tree with an embroidery hoop upon his lap. In his needle and thread endeavors, he ended up making felted ornaments and baubles for every season and holiday, and we now decorate Swan's branches with them to include her in the celebrations. But when Starling had mastered his new craft, he designed Crow's new cloak with his father. Later, under the family's watchful, teary eyes, he finally got down Swan's precious cloak from where it hung above the library mantel behind a pane of glass, and Starling mended the tear that was made by a fox-like Phouka while hunting years ago.

Kestrel hasn't strayed far from his brother; their bond has grown stronger than it was even when they were children. Back when Hazel's pregnancy was still furthering, he grew quite the attachment to his godmother, spending more time helping at the Apothecary, ensuring she wasn't overworking herself. He also pitched in at Wyrd Mountain in the temple and observatory once Poppy and Posy were on the mend. Even more so, when Poppy's eyesight never fully cleared to what it once was. My nephew has flitted around, seemingly unsure of his purpose or direction, like a sunflower without the sun. But he's expressed some interest in travel at sea, going to the ocean where the rain and storms are aplenty. Kestrel even considered an offer from Posy, extended to both him and Starling, to apprentice under scholars at the Great Library, which his older brother accepted. But it didn't feel right to Kestrel. So, for now, the young changeling man continues to help Rose and me, although not by hunting Phouka, as there are none left to hunt, but by finding the few Pooka remaining. Without the dark blight of witchcraft, the Phouka had been reverting. It was a slow, painful process, and by the time we tracked most of them down, the unchained messengers were ready to be released into The After. That was especially the case for those Rose sealed and imprisoned into her skin and shadow. They wanted peace and rest after she pulled them from the black bands on her arm, and Rose gave it to them.

And now, the golden prophecies are flowing across Posy's skin again, and the world's fate appears bright once more. There's even a simple prophecy that I believe might be about Crow, that is, if my hunch about the lanky teenager being a Chime Child is correct. When he's not causing mischief, doing chores, or helping with shop construction in the glade, Crow's at Swan's tree. He's either walking around it in circles, trailing his fingers on the marred trunk, sitting in some of the lower branches, or swinging from them. As he does so, he's usually signing, speaking to Swan in our family's hand language about his day and what's going on in his life, what annoyed him, and what excited him. I don't know for sure if the possible Chime Child can see the ghostly form of his sister sitting above him on a higher branch of her tree, dangling her legs and listening to him with a fond smile. But considering that Crow periodically looks up at that exact branch, I believe, at the very least, his changeling gift might sense Swan due to that lost, missing feeling from her absence that we all carry daily.

However, it doesn't take being a special child born at the midnight hour, nor a magic gift, to see the frail, first ever elderflower that blooms on that high branch this spring.

THE END

ACKNOWLEDGMENTS

To say my blood, sweat, and tears went into this book is an understatement.

A Child of the Changeling has so far been the longest book it has taken me to write, and the first book of mine that had to take a hiatus/publishing gap. This story was originally supposed to be published in October of 2024. But of course, my body had other plans. In March of 2024, just weeks before my deadline, I had only six chapters left when I had one of my worst neurological episodes to date. It started with the most gnarly migraine and ended with the right side of my face and body temporarily drooping and paralyzed. It was terrifying. Since then, I have noticed a physical change in my brain, which is evident in the way I speak and think. I'm not as sharp, and words are much harder to find and process. This, of course, affected my writing abilities, and I genuinely thought my career was over.

I tried many times to pick up this book and finish those last chapters throughout 2024. When I looked back at what I had written, it was like reading someone else's writing. I didn't feel capable of it anymore, because it certainly didn't come as naturally and quickly as it used to. And I know I'm harder on myself about it, that episode felt like it changed and weakened me for the worst, so I've been comparing my current self to my past self. It frustrated me to no end that I was able to write and edit A Daughter of the Trolls in a month and wrote what was supposed to be its sequel and A Goblin of the Glade in the same year. But what killed me more was the thought of quitting. With how I was raised and encouraged to be, and as someone on the spectrum, I couldn't leave something unfinished. The scenes I didn't get to write haunted me daily. So, around November 2024, I secretly picked up the A Child of the Changeling manuscript once more and sought to complete it. I didn't even tell my publisher, Micheline, that I was writing again until I had about a chapter or two left. I wanted to make sure I could do it first, even if sometimes I felt like I was just replicating who I used to be as a writer.

But I did it. And I am proud that I got to finish Swan's story the way I had wanted to for years now.

This story was chock-full of representation, and a lot of it was Own Voices. From Swan's nerve damage, disassociation, and depression to Starling's hypoglycemia. I definitely infused a little bit of my ADHD into Kestrel too. But I knew I also wanted to try including some other representation that I haven't necessarily experienced through other characters as well like Kestrel's colorblindness. Not to mention, Crow being hard of hearing, something I knew I wanted to write about since drafting Goblin. (Fun fact: I homeschooled myself and graduated very early. And instead of learning Spanish or French, I took ASL courses! When I was sixteen, I managed a vintage soda/candy shop that was right next to a movie theater, so whenever there were accessible movies playing with subtitles, I would get a lot of customers in that candy shop that were hard of hearing and/or deaf. I'll never forget how happy it made people see someone working who could sign.)

I also knew for this story that I wanted to focus a little less on a romance/unconventional romance subplot and hone in more on familial love like I had in previous Numina Parable books. We got to see Sparrow's love for her mom in Daughter, and the triplet's sisterly love in Goblin. But the reality of family and siblings isn't always so picture-perfect, and I wanted to show another side of a tough, but loving bond.

I grew up with a half-sister fourteen years older than me who I only became closer with in my early teen years. One sister ten years older than me that only I became closer with in my preteen years. And a sister nine years older than me that I only became closer with in my late teen years closer to adulthood. These last two sisters have always been the best of friends considering they are only eighteen months apart. But I have always had such a different relationship with each of them. There was even a time when I didn't speak to one of them for a year. Although we didn't always get along, and even now there are times we don't, I still love my sisters. I did in the hard times and the good. And I think that is a truer reflection of family and sibling relationships, and I used Swan's sibling relationships with Kestrel and Starling to show this other side.

So, I want to thank my sisters for loving me and supporting my career even though we've terrorized each other. You guys have made beautiful families, and I am so excited for the kids to be able to read the books Aunt Kenzie wrote.

Of course, thank you to my parents for always being my biggest fans and the first to read my manuscripts. Your pride in me has made me believe that I still have that same old piece of myself that can write like I used to.

Thank you to my husband for letting me be dramatic and cry about not being able to pull through and finish the goals I've set out to accomplish. Your encouragement and belief in me made me want to prove you right. So, I guess you've earned a loving 'I told you so.'

Thank you to my service dog, Grimm, for being my ever-present shadow keeping me company, and staying by my side as I write, even at this very moment as I type this. I can smell your Frito paws from here.

Thank you to everyone who has worked on this book with me, editing and proofreading. A Child of the Changeling wouldn't be what it is without you. But most of all, thank you to

Micheline. You've shown me how to grow as an author and making you more and more proud with each book is something I cherish. Thank you for making my dreams come true by putting my story into people's hands and helping me spread all the disability, mental health, and chronic illness representation. You are the best book mom I could've asked for.

And last but not least, a huge thank you to my readers for sticking with me, even after a year hiatus. I'm so glad you could see the end of this epic story with me. It means the world to have your support, and it is so fulfilling whenever I hear how much you've resonated with my writing and characters. Folks like you are the reason I wanted to become an author. I can't wait for you to see what new world I've created next!

ABOUT THE AUTHOR

McKenzie is a wheelchair-bound, autistic, twenty-one-time award-winning YA fantasy author of the "Numina Parable" series, co-author of "A Traveler's Guide to The Lucky Gryphon: Recipes & Regalings," and children's book writer specializing in Own Voices stories featuring disability, chronic illness, neuro-divergence, mental health, and service dog representation.

She's a new Michigan resident who lives with her husband and her service dog, Grimm. McKenzie is also a full-time creative makeup artist and alternative model fighting against disability stigmas one creation at a time. When she's not spending her anxious days writing novels or taking photos in her studio, you can find her over on Instagram sharing her art.

instagram.com/mckenziecatron

www.ingramcontent.com/pod-product-compliance
Lightning Source LLC
Chambersburg PA
CBHW051944240626
47153CB00005B/1618